Leaf Season

By Dee Thompson

Cover photo by Linda Harris

MAIN CHARACTERS

Cavanaugh family:

Tom Cavanaugh and Barbara Donnelly Cavanaugh
      Son: Luke
      Daughter: Sally*
      Son: Sam

Jamison family:

William Jamison and Catherine Fellows Jamison
      Son: Wendell Jamison and Amy
        daughter Nora
        son Wyatt
      Son: Hugh Jamison [no spouse or children]

*Sally Cavanaugh spouse Steve Odalshalski [divorced]
      Daughter Miranda

** Wyatt Jamison spouse Sharon
      Son: Thad

Marcus Jamison marries Josephine Adams Jamison, and fathers Jack Jamison [1866-1927] and two girls who die in infancy.

Jack marries Mary Hughes and fathers William Jamison [1890-1975] and Michael Jamison [1891-1927].

William marries Elizabeth Fellows and fathers Wendell Jamison and Hugh Jamison.

To my mother, Elva Hasty Thompson, who taught me to love the mountains and to always have faith.

CHAPTER 1

Saturday June 4, 1975 2:53 p.m.

Thirteen year old Sally Cavanaugh sprawls on the front step of the porch of her house on Honeysuckle Road, sucking on a cherry blow pop, idly twisting a bit of her dirty blonde hair around her index finger. Her complexion is pure Celtic, with a few freckles, blue eyes, and a snub nose. It is a soft, warm day, the sky clear of clouds, with low humidity and a temperature of only 80 degrees -- a cool day for June, in Georgia.

Sally lives in a house constructed in 1897, a white clapboard 2 story with a wraparound porch and 10 foot tall ceilings inside. The crown moldings, carved corbels, heart pine floors – all their beauty is lost on Sally, who only knows she lives in an old house that's hard to air condition and they have no garage, just an old carriage house her father uses to store odds and ends.

The small white wooden house next door was built decades before Sally's house. It's a farmhouse that looks incongruous beside its more architecturally grand neighbors. Acres of land behind it and adjacent to it are dotted with bigger, newer homes, where there were once crops.

Beyond the houses, surrounding them like a blue barricade, are the majestic Blue Ridge Mountains. The valley protects the tiny town of Crossroads, which sits in its center, adjacent to the railroad tracks. In 1855 the rail line had been routed through the valley to connect

Asheville in the north with Atlanta in the middle part of
the state.

As cars pull up to the modest next door neighbor's
house and people get out and walk inside, Sally watches,
curious. Some of the well-dressed people exiting the cars
carry dishes. Most of the women wear black or navy
dresses. The men are in dark suits.

Sally wears her standard outfit -- denim cutoffs and
an old white tee shirt that belonged to her oldest brother
Luke, who foolishly left some clothes behind when he
joined the Marines. As soon as he had gotten into the car
with their Dad to go to basic training, his younger siblings
had raced to his room and divvied up what he had left.

After finding the Blow Pop in the kitchen, Sally has
been observing the folks next door for half an hour.
Crossroads can only claim 2,450 inhabitants, including all
of Bell County. Some of the cars next door are from
outside Bell County, making them interesting to her.

As Sally sucks on her Blow Pop and watches, a
white station wagon pulls up with a DeKalb County license
plate. Sally knows it's a family from Atlanta. Atlanta is a
huge place, two hours' drive south, and it fascinates Sally.

A skinny, nondescript girl of about 19 in a navy blue
dress gets out of the white DeKalb County station wagon,
then a boy climbs out. He looks about 15 years old, and he
is tall and long-limbed. With blonde hair and wire-rimmed
glasses, he looks a little like John Denver, Sally's favorite
singer. He is dressed for church in a white shirt, khaki
pants, and a blue blazer. *Boy he is CUTE*, Sally thinks,

watching as he awkwardly trudges up to the little house, up the stairs to the tiny porch, and goes inside.

He looks familiar but Sally has never seen him before. There is no logic to that, yet there it is.

Sally's mother Barbara pushes open the screen door and joins Sally out on the porch. She shades her eyes with her hand and peers next door. "Oh look, that must be the crowd coming back after the funeral for old Mr. William Jamison, God rest his soul." She crosses herself and shakes her head, but her brown bouffant hair does not move, shellacked into place with White Rain. Barbara pulls off the apron she wears atop her pale blue cotton house dress.

"Why didn't we go to the funeral, Mama?" Sally asks. "You and Mr. Jamison used to talk sometimes. He and his wife are good neighbors."

"Well, they are Protestants. We don't go to Protestant churches for any reason. Mr. Jamison was a Lutheran, I think... I put a condolence card in the mailbox and took over some scalloped potatoes this morning. I think that's enough," Barbara replies, lighting a Virginia Slims menthol cigarette.

"Did you save any scalloped potatoes for us?" Sally asks, ever hopeful.

"Of course. Between you and your brother you all could eat a 10 pound bag of potatoes in one meal. Must be part of that bog Irish ancestry," Barbara chuckles.

Sally knows her mother has mixed feelings about marrying a plumber, since she had been homecoming queen at the high school. Sally doesn't know that her brother Luke was already on the way when Barbara graduated, so there was nothing to do but get married. When 9 lb. Luke was born six months later nobody was so impolite as to argue when the Cavanaughs said he had arrived early.

Barbara stares at the homely, nondescript house next door. "Well, look there at that shiny white station wagon from Atlanta. That must be his son Wendell and his family. I never met them. I hear they have plenty of money. My my…." Barbara says.

Sally knows her mother is impressed by money, although she would never admit it.

Tom Cavanaugh, Sally's father, makes a good living as a plumber in a small Southern town and Tom and Barbara are raising three children in a three bedroom, 2 bathroom house. There are so few Catholics in Crossroads, Georgia, that they have to drive thirty minutes over to Clayton to go to mass.

"Don't forget you need to bathe Barney," Barbara says as she turns to go back inside the house. Barney is their Bassett hound and the children bathe him in a baby pool on pretty days.

Sally hears the Jamison back door open and shut as she hops off the porch and races around to her own back yard, to stare across the grass to the house next door. *There he is! The cute blonde boy!*

He carries something. What is it? Oh, a book -- a heavy book, probably a textbook. He sits down at the rickety old picnic table on the back patio, opens the heavy book, and starts reading. The breeze ruffles his blonde hair and the sun shines down and lights it softly.

Sally decides he looks like a prince in a fairy tale, like he would leap up and mount his horse and gallop off any minute.

Sally ponders his handsomeness from the safety of the side yard, partially behind a magnolia tree. After chewing the last of the Blow Pop, she devises a plan. She can show off her baton twirling skills and get him to notice her. After all, the two back yards are adjacent and he would have to look up if he noticed a pretty girl twirling a baton, right?!

Sally runs inside, to her room, and puts on her one piece blue and white bathing suit, which is as close as she can get to a majorette costume. She quickly brushes her thick dirty blonde hair into a ponytail and applies blue eye shadow and red lipstick filched from her mother's room.

Hearing the TV on in the den, she knows her mother is glued to Days of Our Lives, so Sally slips out of the back door and observes the house next door from the back porch. The boy still sits at the picnic table, reading. He doesn't even look up when Sally appears in her bathing suit.

Sally strolls casually over to the driveway, which is the dividing line between the two properties, and starts twirling the shiny silver baton, practicing all the moves she knows. She arches her back. She smiles. She snaps the baton smartly. She desperately wants to try out for the majorette spot with the band next year in high school. The boy never looks up from his book, though.

Frustrated by his ignoring her, Sally decides to throw the baton high up in the air, and catch it behind her back. It's a daring move, but she has done it successfully before. She throws the baton high and catches it. She tries it again, and again it falls into her hand.

Time for the big move – higher than ever. Sally takes a deep breath. The moment she starts to throw the baton, her cat Ignatius comes up and twines himself around her legs, startling Sally so much the baton flies up, wildly out of kilter. It soars high into the air, up and up, and it starts downward over the picnic table.

Stunned with horror, Sally watches the end of the baton thwack the boy on the crown of his head. Her first thought about it is: Thank God the tip has a rubber end on it.

As if that horror weren't enough, her little brother Sam, 6 years old, runs out of the house at the moment just after the baton has left her hand, and he sees the baton hit the boy. There is a 2 second pause, then Sam's tiny pink mouth forms a perfect O and his eyebrows shoot up to his hairline. He grins and chants "You're in trouble! You're in trouble, trub-bull trub-bull trub-BULL!"

Sam's voice taunts Sally as she watches the Jamison boy rub his head and glare at Sally. Embarrassment overwhelms her. Sally feels her heart hammering, and her cheeks burning, but she cannot move. She cannot look away. She can only stare into his impossibly blue eyes, at his large hands and feet, at his gorgeous face, un-marred by acne.

Sam is still chanting "You're in trouble! You're in trouble, trub-bull trub-bull trub-BULL!"

"SAM! Shut up and go get my baton!" Sally hisses, turning to glare at him. "Hurry!"

Sam stops his chanting and shouts "No!"

The boy unfolds his long limbs from the picnic table, picks up the baton from the ground, and walks towards Sally, crossing the yard and driveway impossibly fast. In a flash, he stands in front of Sally and holds out the baton to her.

Now Sally is truly paralyzed with fear and embarrassment.

"I – I – I am SO sorry!" she stammers, taking the baton.

The boy examines her as though she is an exhibit in a museum. Sally is sorry she doesn't have bigger breasts, or glamorous hair and makeup. Her hair is called "dirty blonde" and she isn't actually allowed to wear makeup yet. She hates that she has short legs and a wide butt. Before she can think further on her many perceived flaws, the boy speaks.

"I'm fine, but you need to be more careful," he says. His voice is deep, a man's voice.

Mesmerized by his voice, Sally can only stare.

The boy stares back for a moment, but then turns and walks back to the picnic table, sits down and starts reading again.

Sam and Sally watch the boy for another few moments, then both turn and run back into the house. As soon as they are inside, Sally grabs Sam.

"Listen, don't tell Mom what happened."

"Why not?!" he demands. "Let go of my arm!"

"Because if you do, I'll sneak into your room, in the middle of the night, and pull your hair!" Sally hisses.

Sam hates anyone pulling his hair. "Okay," Sam says, reluctantly. "And you have to play checkers with me!"

"Okay, fine," Sally says, rolling her eyes. "First I'm going to change clothes, though."

As she passes the laundry room she can see out the window to the next door yard. The boy is looking up from his book, staring at the Cavanaugh house, thoughtfully.

I am in LOVE! Sally thinks.

Hugh Jamison, uncle to the blonde boy who got hit with the baton, stands in a back bedroom of the small house next door, exhausted. Big occasions like weddings and funerals always terrify Hugh. He much prefers his quiet apartment in Atlanta, near the Georgia Tech campus.

He has been a professor of History there for almost 8 years. He is a slight man with an acne-scarred face, rapidly going bald, and painfully shy.

Hugh opens the small white envelope that his mother has just handed him. He starts reading his father's awkward handwriting, spidery and lopsided on the page, as though a giant had just sprinkled letters down.

Hugh -

You remember the old trunk in the root cellar? You need to figure out how to open it, and see what's in there. Rumor has it, there's some kind of a treasure. Sounds like a fairy tale to me. I've never seen that old trunk opened.

I am too old and feeble to go up and down the old steps and I am pretty soon going to meet The Lord. You have always been a smart boy, and you love history, so I leave the solving of this mystery to you.

Love,

Dad

Hugh finishes the letter and frowns. Hugh only vaguely recalls the root cellar, but then he rarely went down there as a child. His parents pretty much ignored the dusty little space. *Dad must have been getting senile*, he thinks.

He resolves to ask his mother about the trunk, and puts the letter in the pocket of his blue sport coat. A laugh emanates from the other room, which is crowded with people. *Lord help me*, he thinks, wondering if there is anything worse than having to be nice to strangers.

Roberta Kingston, wife of the pastor of the First Lutheran Church peers speculatively around the small house filled with mourners. She wonders if her girdle could be removed and put in her purse without screams emanating from the small hall bathroom during the process. She hates the thing, but her mother would kill her if word got back to her that Roberta was seen in public with her fanny jiggling obscenely. Roberta reluctantly decides to stay in the living room, and tries to stand very still and not sweat.

Where could the root cellar be? She has a huge curiosity about the small house. However, she has quietly looked in every room and cannot find what she seeks.

Across the tiny living room, Roberta spots Wendell Jamison, tall and handsome, talking to someone, and feels a familiar ache in her chest. He probably doesn't even notice her artfully styled bouffant, or her black dress that flatters her plump figure, or her Tahiti Tingle Pink lipstick. *Why on earth that man would move to Atlanta when there were plenty of jobs and eligible girls right here in Crossroads, I will never know*, she thinks.

"Hi Roberta, how are you?" a voice trills from over her left shoulder. Roberta plasters a smile on her face and turns in the direction of the voice, switching instantly into her Minister's Wife persona.

CHAPTER 2

2012, April 9th

Wyatt Jamison turns into the parking lot of the Resurgens Bank, drives behind the building, and turns again to pull up to the drive up teller window. He lowers the window of his silver Toyota Highlander. The bank's metal drawer slides out and he puts the check and deposit slip in, then smiles at the teller, an older woman with glasses.

The years have been kind to Wyatt since the baton incident. He is now 52 years old, and although his blonde hair is thinning and mostly gray, and there are fine lines around his eyes, those eyes are still bright blue.

Wyatt owns a small but lucrative law practice, focusing primarily on personal injury plaintiff's work. He doesn't advertise, unlike some of the big flashy personal injury firms, but he usually makes about $200,000 a year, and that combined with his wife's income as an office manager for a cardiologist affords them a very nice house just off Briarcliff Road inside the Atlanta perimeter.

Wyatt has just written himself a check for $2,536,811.34 from his trust account. It is his fee from a settlement of a medical malpractice case he has been litigating for three years. His client, Ann Baker, a young stockbroker with two small children (her father was an old school friend of Wyatt's) died after going into the emergency room at Eastside Hospital and complaining of feeling weak. She had a slow and irregular heartbeat. It was a Friday night and there was a lot of activity. Ann was lying on a gurney in the hallway, ignored for thirty minutes while victims of a large automobile accident on Clairmont Road were treated. During that thirty minutes she closed her eyes and quietly died.

Depositions were taken. Motions were filed. Experts were retained. An expert was brought in who calculated that Ann's lifetime earnings would have been in excess of $7 million, based on her youth and income. They settled for $8.6 million, which included her family's emotional suffering. The hospital did not want the publicity of a trial.

Wyatt's share is $2,536,811.34, after he has paid himself back for the case expenses.

Wyatt's wife Sharon is very happy about the case settlement, but greatly annoyed that he won't discuss with her what they might do with the windfall.

"I'll still have to declare it as income and pay taxes," Wyatt says as he sips his one Scotch and soda and regards the steaks on the grill. The check has been safely in the bank for four hours.

"Well damn, what about a nice vacation, at least?" Sharon grouses. She lounges on a nearby chair wearing white cotton pants and a pale yellow tee shirt. At 49, Sharon is still lovely, with professionally colored long blonde hair, a trim size 4 figure, and carefully-maintained skin. She flips the pages of a Vogue magazine on her lap, then sets it aside and starts looking at her phone.

"Maybe Thad would go with us," Sharon says laconically. "We could take a cruise."

Wyatt shakes his head. "Doubt it. He prefers the company of his friends," Wyatt moves the steaks to a cooler part of the grill so as not to overcook them.

Thad, their only child, is a junior at Berry College majoring in Business.

"Oh my, look at this, Wyatt," Sharon said, standing up to show Wyatt a photo from Thad's Facebook page, on her phone. "Isn't that the girl he brought home for Easter weekend?"

Wyatt takes the phone, pulls his reading glasses out of his pocket and puts them on, and stares at the photo. Yes, it is definitely Daisy, with her long red hair, freckles, and tiny frog tattoo on her shoulder. She wears a halter top and has marigolds twined in her hair. She and Thad are snuggling in a hammock. Thad is shirtless and wearing only jeans. He is a good looking boy with his parents' fair coloring, even features, and blue eyes.

"Looks like her," Wyatt says, handing the phone back to Sharon.

"I don't know about that girl. She's not in a sorority. She is majoring in Women's Studies. What kind of job do you get with that degree?" Sharon asks skeptically.

"I am pretty sure she told me she wanted to raise goats and make goat milk products, somewhere out in the country," Wyatt replies. "She's got a good heart."

Sharon sighs and thinks about Wyatt's pronouncement. He is usually right in his assessments of people. "I hope she and Thad are just a fling, then. She'll probably be the type to forego underwear and breastfeed in public."

Wyatt spears the steaks and puts them on a plate. "Well, if it makes her happy, so be it. Thad isn't going to live in the country. You know that. So I doubt they will wind up married."

Sharon is still frowning. "What does she want with him, then?"

Wyatt chuckles. "Just because you went to the university to find a husband, that doesn't mean girls nowadays go to college for that reason." Sharon shoots him an annoyed look. "I went to college to learn about business, and it's a damn good thing I did because you don't have a head for it."

Wyatt smiles. She is right. For years, she managed his business, part-time, in addition to her duties at her own job. She has great business instincts, which is why his law firm never loses money, unlike many. Now he has a part-time office manager, but it took years to afford one, and find one Sharon liked.

Wyatt takes another sip of his drink and looks at the sky. "Looks like we might get a thunderstorm. Let's go inside and eat," he says.

"Fine," Sharon replies.

Wyatt turns off the gas grill and closes the cover. He knows the thunderstorm will drench everything on the patio in approximately 14 minutes.

Wyatt contemplates his future happily now that he has the money to retire early. He is tired of the 60 hour weeks. Tired of the clients always calling him. Tired of writing briefs. Tired of drama.

Maybe now that the house is paid off and I am finally debt-free, I can have a different life, he thinks.

CHAPTER THREE

Sally Cavanaugh, 49 years old now, lives in the same house she was raised in, but without her parents, who are both dead.

Sally still sometimes thinks about Wyatt Jamison, even though she has not seen him in years. She spent her teenaged summers with her paternal grandparents in Knoxville, working at their dairy, so missed Wyatt's visits to his grandmother.

Sally wonders if her childhood crush could have grown into something more if she had stayed in Atlanta after college, but that longing has become a constant ache, like the ache where a bone was once broken, that only hurts when it rains. She occasionally spies a tall blonde man in the distance and her heart skips a beat, but then it's over.

Her ex-husband, Steve, was a tall blonde man but she realized early in the marriage he would never replace her lost crush, Wyatt Jamison, a fact which probably led to her divorce years later, after the requisite "staying together for the child" time had passed.

Just before 7 p.m., Sally gets home from her job as head librarian at the Bell County Public Library and pulls her 10 year old blue Nissan Pathfinder into the carriage house that passes for a garage. She presses the remote and the garage door slides down.

Sally hefts the bags of groceries out of the car, and balances her purse, the bags, and two books, and walks across the grass to open the back door to her house. Her blonde hair is now carefully colored, and she dresses more for comfort than fashion, but she feels compelled to put on a little eye makeup and lipstick most mornings.

Blanche, her Bassett hound, runs to Sally and jumps up for a hug. After putting down her burdens, Sally smiles at her. "Yes, yes, I see you Sweetheart, Mama's home, it's okay," Sally says, rubbing the old dog's velvety head. She grabs Blanche's leash to take her outside.

Her ex-husband used to make fun of her for talking to animals, but it came naturally to Sally. Sally thinks of Blanche as her furry child.

Sally opens the back door so Blanche can go out and squat, and walks outside with her. "Be a good girl!" Sally trills. Blanche sniffs and walks around the back yard for a minute before finding the perfect pee spot.

Sally glances over to her left, to the 8 foot high brick wall surrounding the back yard of the Jamison house, and wonders why the wall exists. The wall was constructed years ago, after Mrs. Jamison had died and her son Hugh had come to live in the house.

Hugh Jamison had walled the entire back yard, and the only way in was through the house. Everyone in town had talked about it because the wall had seemed to go up in a matter of a few days, by masons unknown to anyone in the county – brought in from Atlanta, it was rumored.

Most people who wanted privacy erected a fence, not a brick wall. Hugh didn't even have a dog, or even a pool, so why the wall around the tiny home?! Everyone was puzzled. Hugh wasn't friends with anyone in town and rarely even chatted with anyone. He was known to be a painfully shy man, a real loner.

Hugh had grown up in Crossroads but moved to Atlanta as a young man, to teach history at one of the colleges, Sally had heard.

Hugh had returned to Crossroads in 2007 and moved into his parent's house after his 98 year old mother died. He decided to retire in Crossroads.

Wendell and Amy, Wyatt's parents, had been happy for Hugh to have the house. They rarely visited, and only exchanged cards at Christmas. Amy came from a large family in Atlanta, so holidays were always spent with her family, not the Jamison family in the little mountain town.

During the years after old Mr. Jamison died, the Cavanaugh children grew up and moved away.

Sally earned a degree in Library Science at the University of Georgia, then married Steve Odalshalski, a large animal veterinarian who worked on all the farm animals in Bell County. They lived on a farm outside of Crossroads for 14 years and raised their daughter, Miranda.

When Steve decided to move out to Wyoming, Sally was not surprised. He liked to vacation in the west. She thought about it, about their marriage which was like two comfortable roommates but nothing more. She couldn't imagine living in a town far from her friends, a town where the beach was a 2 day drive away and everyone spoke with flat accents.

After a boozy evening involving margaritas and tacos with her best friend Marybeth, Sally informed Steve that she would not be relocating to Wyoming. They divorced amicably.

Sally moved back in with her mother Barbara, at Barbara's request, and decided to just stay and live with Barbara rather than try to find an apartment. Crossroads had only one actual apartment complex, and it was rundown. Sally could live with her mother and her daughter could graduate high school in Crossroads, which she did.

When her mother died, Sally's siblings agreed she should stay in the house. She had nursed her mother through Alzheimers for three years.

Sally's daughter Miranda had inherited her mother's blonde prettiness but got her father's long legs and Slavic bone structure. She moved to Atlanta with a friend instead of going to college, then went to beauty school and became a hairdresser. She changed her named to Miranda Cavanaugh, and became a stylist at a very upscale salon in Buckhead before marrying a rich stockbroker. She liked living in the city and didn't come home to Crossroads much, which saddened Sally, but she was resigned to it.

Sally worked at the public library and researched a book about the history of Crossroads, Georgia. She loved history. Her manuscript was already 21 pages long, and grew at the rate of about 8 pages a year.

Sally reflects on how much she loves her lush green back yard with the mountains in sight all around, as she stands outside with Blanche that warm April night. Nothing gives her greater pleasure than planting her gardens every spring, and harvesting every summer.

Watching her gardenias, azaleas, and camellias bloom, turning her yard into a riot of color, also fills Sally with joy.

After wandering around the yard and sniffing everything, Blanche starts barking insistently. She pulls Sally over the driveway at the edge of the yard and stands and barks at the Jamison wall. Thinking it must be a squirrel or perhaps a rabbit distracting Blanche, Sally coaxes Blanche inside using the magic word "cookie" – meaning mini Milkbone, Blanche's favorite treat. Blanche inhales the Milkbones but still watches the door and whines softly as Sally reads.

As she prepares for bed at eleven p.m., moisturizing her face and setting her alarm, Sally has a nagging feeling that there is really something wrong next door at the Jamison house. Blanche is never that excited about anything, and her actions seemed to be saying to Sally *Go check it out Mom!*

Sally sighs and turns out the lamp. *I really wish I could speak dog language*, she thinks...

CHAPTER FOUR

The next morning, Sally gets up early and eats a piece of toast while she drinks her tea, as usual. She goes outside with Blanche for the dog's morning potty break. As Blanche squats, Sally notices a strange smell. She sniffs the air and closes her eyes, puzzled. She walks closer to the Jamison house. It's a cloying, putrid odor.

Sally is puzzled but goes on to work at the library, wondering if a dead animal got trapped in the next door back yard.

When Sally returns from work late that afternoon the smell is stronger, now spoiling her enjoyment of her zen-like back yard. As soon as Sally snaps on Blanche's leash and opens the back door, Blanche goes running out to the porch and down the steps to the back yard, pulling Sally behind her to the brick wall, and barks at it urgently.

Sally stands there and stares at the brick, wondering what to do. The smell is very strong, a nasty spoiled meat smell.

Sally finally pulls Blanche away from the wall and they go to walk, a loop around the quiet streets of old homes, which is Sally's way of unwinding after a long day of work. As she walks, Sally tries to focus on the beauty all around – the blooming azaleas and redbuds, the sounds of laughter from a patio, the faint piano music coming from one home where a child is practicing, the neighbors who have daffodils and tulips in their yards. Sally loves the architecture of the Victorian homes, most built in the late 19th century.

Sally wonders what to do about Blanche's fascination with the wall. Her friend Marybeth always says dogs are smarter than humans are, in ways we are not smart at all. They smell much better than humans, which is easy to see. They sense good and evil. They are loyal to the bone.

After Sally gets back to her house and goes inside, she kicks off her shoes and pours herself a glass of Chardonnay. She sautés some spinach in olive oil and throws a chicken breast in the skillet as well, liberally adding butter and garlic powder.

As she eats at the old oak table in the kitchen and listens to a Mozart CD, Sally finally has to admit that Blanche is trying to tell her there's something wrong at the Jamison house. With a heavy sigh, she puts her shoes back on and prepares to go check on her neighbor. Blanche sees her getting ready and whines. Sally reaches down to stroke her head. "You stay here, Sweetheart. I'll be right back," Sally comforts her.

As she shuts her back door, Sally winces at Blanche's sharp barks.

Sally quickly walks next door in the early evening gloom, and climbs the four steps to the small porch. Sally knocks on the front door. There's no response. She knocks again, and listens. Finally, she calls "Mr. Jamison? Are you all right? It's Sally Cavanaugh, from next door."

Jamison is always home and always cordial. The lack of response troubles Sally, especially considering his old car is parked in front of the house. Truly concerned now, Sally decides to call Mark Wisham, the Sheriff. It's not late. Only 7:30.

Since Crossroads is a small town, Mark doesn't have a lot to do. He hangs up from talking to Sally and grabs a breath mint, then re-tucks his shirt tail and smell checks his armpits. He leaves Dean, his deputy, in charge, and gets in his cruiser trying not to look excited.

As Mark drives through the streets of Crossroads, he wonders if any of the rumors about Hugh Jamison are true. Is he practicing black magic? Running a massage parlor? Growing and selling marijuana?

Mark parks in the driveway of the Cavanaugh house since there is no driveway to the Jamison house. There is an old Honda Accord in front of the house, which he assumes belongs to Hugh Jamison, a nondescript beige car.

Sally, sitting on her porch, walks over. Mark is aware that she is a bit more plump than she had been in high school, but she still has lovely skin and her blonde hair is carefully colored and cut in a flattering long bob. Sally always wears black pants and large colorful tops to conceal her extra pounds. She's still beautiful, Mark thinks with admiration.

Sheriff Mark Wisham has maintained a crush on Sally since high school. Unfortunately, she has never returned his feelings. He was polite when they were in tenth grade Biology class together, but he couldn't make small talk about anything but the weather.

Sally looks at him as she walks over to the cruiser. "Hey Mark, thanks for coming by. Blanche is still barking at whatever is causing that smell."

Blanche's insistent bark can easily be heard coming from the Cavanaugh house, a low sonorous woofing that basset hounds love to make.

"Well, dogs are generally pretty smart about things being wrong, and I can smell that stench, too, so let's see what's going on," Mark replies. They walk the short distance to the front door of the Jamison house.

After he knocks, Mark waits. As he surveys the neat expanse of yard in front of the house, Mark shudders, picturing himself sweating behind a push mower. He prefers apartments.

There is no answer.

Repeated knocking on the front door of the Jamison house brings no response. Mark suspects what the odor is, but says nothing to Sally.

Despite his bald head, tiny chin, and paunch, Mark wants to appear to be a competent, strong man. He finally decides he will bring down the door of the house, and to hell with getting a warrant.

"Stand back. Time to bust it down," he says to Sally. Before he can enact that plan, Sally reaches down and tries the handle on the front door and it turns easily, admitting them to the house. They both laugh, a little nervously, as they walk inside.

"Mr. Jamison? It's Sally Cavanaugh, your neighbor," she calls out.

Mark follows her into the foyer of the house, but he warns her not to touch anything. "It could be a crime scene."

"Okay," Sally says, thinking old Mr. Hugh is probably just hard of hearing.

As they creep through the house, Sally looks around curiously. She has never been inside the home. The house is an antebellum home, but it was clearly renovated in the late 1960's. All walls are beige. The furniture is from the Sears catalog, in Early American brown and orange splendor. The brown and green shag carpeting, wood paneling, and olive green kitchen appliances are so retro, Sally feels as though she is in a time capsule, as though she should be wearing a mini skirt and a beehive hairdo. The house is neat as a pin, though.

Sally calls out "Mr. Jamison?" a couple more times, but there is no response.

They move through the kitchen and family room of the little house and open the door that opens onto the back yard. The smell hits them both at the same time.

"Oh my GOD!" Sally gasps, taking a step back and putting her hand over her nose and mouth, feeling her gorge rising but ignoring it. She notices the old picnic table is still right outside the back door, on the small patio. She is vaguely aware that there are very few trees and just a few scraggly shrubs but what really draws her attention is the body.

"Just stay back!" Mark orders, moving towards the body. The wall is only about ten feet from the back door.

Hugh had obviously fallen next to the wall, and he lies on the ground. He has been dead a while. His body is surrounded by fluids and he looks like a giant meat balloon. Flies have been laying eggs in all of his orifices and the crawling maggots are everywhere.

Mark Wisham has only seen one other dead body in his entire law enforcement career, a 10 year old that had accidentally drowned in the pond just outside of town, and the child had been dead ten minutes when Mark saw him. He had looked like an angel.

Hugh Jamison has been dead at least two warm spring days, and he looks nothing like an angel. He looks like something from a horror movie.

Mark pokes at the body gingerly with his foot, trying to see what Hugh had been holding in his hand, possibly a flashlight. The crawling maggots and flies move also, of course. Some of the air escapes the body in a loud, liquid gurgling fart sound.

To his horror, Mark can't help but turn away from the body as he immediately and violently vomits, expelling the partially digested ham and cheese sandwich and coffee he had consumed for dinner.

Sally sees the start of the Mark's vomit and runs back into the house, to the bathroom in the hall, where she vomits neatly into the toilet.

I can't un-see that, she thinks. God help me.

CHAPTER 5

Three days earlier...

Oh dear, let's see, how did I get here? I was heading out to the back yard to work on my project, flashlight in hand – and the next thing I know I am lying on the ground and it feels like a bomb has exploded in my insides.

A massive wave of pain hit me, then mercifully it just stopped. Then it was like a curtain closed, a blackness of black, so deeply black it felt like outer space, but there was no pain. There was only peacefulness.

Now I am here but I do not see anything unusual in the yard... Wait. No. A body. Wait just a doggone minute, there I am, lying on the ground. Whoa.

Shocking. How can I be there and here?

I am floating. I am on level with the tops of the apple tree and the cedar tree, more than ten feet off the ground.

There's a bird's nest. There's a hot air balloon way off in the distance.

How did I get up here?

I must be dead.

I drift among the treetops for a while, adjusting to the new reality. Dead is not so bad. It's nothing to fear, actually. I am still here, just floating, not down there in my poor body, already starting to bloat and smell.

I drift up, over the house, and gaze down at the trees in my neighbor's yards. I have always been afraid to fly, never set foot on an airplane, but this is fine. This is glorious, in fact.

I gaze at the roofs of houses amid a grid of streets. I study the sky – it's like an overturned bowl of cerulean blue, scudded with clouds. I can even see where the earth curves. I marvel, as always, at the serene and majestic Blue Ridge Mountains surrounding my little hometown like friendly giants, guarding our valley.

I survey the houses and streets in my neighborhood, all the graceful homes mostly built in the 1870's. What a peaceful lovely place, with azaleas and camellias and gardenias everywhere, due to the recent rain. So lush and lovely.

I float over Crossroads, now, the little town of my birth.

It's laid out haphazardly. It got its name because the northern route to Asheville, Highway 25, crossed the east west old road, when that road didn't have a name, and since the Bell River is close by, the folks in 1832 thought it would make a fine place for a town. By the time the railroad came along it was thriving.

Just off Main Street there's an old building that was the first building ever constructed, the Hill House -- amazing it's still in use although now it's a bed and breakfast. I bet they don't even realize Davy Crockett once slept there. I bet they don't know Elizabeth Hill had lovely red hair and made the best chocolate cake ever.

There's the courthouse, the post office, the library, the First Lutheran Church, the First Baptist Church, the First Methodist church, the elementary school, and middle school. The Kroger and Winn Dixie are not far from each other, and there are various other small businesses set along the roads that meander out of town.

Oh my, look at the old pine tree near the school. That's where I grabbed a girl named Jeannine and kissed her when we were in third grade. I loved her freckles. She's now lying over there, two blocks down, in the cemetery, killed in a car accident five years ago.

Heading on downtown, there's the medical arts building, the old Mills office building, and the Mercantile Store that fellow bought and restored. Thank heaven we still have a thriving downtown.

Walmart hasn't leeched away everyone to the suburbs.

Floating on down Main Street, I see the diner, owned by my elementary school classmate Bob Smith, an excellent diner owner but a terrible student. I'm amazed he finished high school, he's so stupid. He can make great biscuits, though, so that's something. His cook Polly can make incredible fried chicken and her cherry pies are heavenly.

What's Bob doing?! Oh, I see. He's standing outside smoking a fat cigar and talking to Ed Wilson, our mayor. Those two need to stop smoking. It's not good for you.

Now I am floating above the Goodyear Tire place, the Quik Trip, and the hardware store.

I glance over to the mountains and notice a hawk climbing, like he's hell-bent on getting to the top of Warrior Mountain -- named after a Cherokee legend long before I came along. Some say it's a haunted place, and maybe it is, but from here it just looks like any other mountain.

Amazing how I cannot feel the heat or the humidity, but I marvel at a bright yellow butterfly right beside me, and the robins swooping by, looping like ribbons across the sky.

I have to wonder, what will happen to my house? To my trunk? Will Wyatt or his sister come live in the house? I cannot imagine that but who knows.

I reckon I will just have to stick around and see what happens.

CHAPTER 6

It's a clear spring day in middle Georgia, 84 degrees and low humidity, and the sun beats down on the lake waters.

Wyatt swats at a mosquito. He sits on an old weathered wooden dock at the lake home of his friend John Merriman, sipping a cold beer, listening to the Braves game. Without much interest in the fish, he watches a cork bob in the bluish gray water. He wears baggy old green gym shorts and an orange tank top – an outfit his wife thought he had taken to Goodwill years ago.

Wyatt has not caught anything. His fishing pole lies on the dock beside his canvas chair.

John sprawls in a canvas chair beside him, also drinking beer. John's grungy white tank top and old gray cotton gym shorts look worse than Wyatt's outfit. At 54, John is completely bald, and has a substantial belly. Also a lawyer, he handles divorce and family law, and he is as boisterous and outgoing as Wyatt is quiet and reserved.

John knows his friend very well. John knew settling the big case was going to change Wyatt's life, and they have talked about it over the past few days. The cabin at the lake is a cherished retreat for both men, who relish time away from wives and busy law practices.

John informed his wife two days prior that under no circumstances would he tolerate phone calls when he was at the Lake Oconee cabin. His wife Emily had rolled her eyes. "That's what you always say. I wouldn't dream of calling you during your sacred communing with the fish and beer drinking time." She shook her head and continued applying mascara.

That's not the point, thinks John. *The point is that my clients can't call me and bitch about their horrible wives and husbands.*

Wyatt feels the same. Wyatt would not tell his wife Sharon this, but sitting on a dock with his best friend, drinking beer and listening to the Braves game is his idea of heaven. He doesn't care if it's 95 degrees. He doesn't care if John periodically stands up and pees off the dock. Catching fish isn't even the point. The point is that Wyatt can relax at the cabin.

Sharon is at her sister's house on Isle of Palms for the week, but Wyatt had said he needed to work and begged off that vacation. Sharon thinks he is writing a brief at John's lake house. Taking vacations with his wife is no longer relaxing. As Wyatt told John, "All she wants to do is shop all morning and lie near the pool all afternoon, then make me go out to an expensive dinner every night."

Ever understanding, John had grunted sympathetically. "She should hang out more with Emily."

Wyatt's cell phone vibrates, nearly making him drop his beer. *Why didn't I listen to John and leave the damn phone in the house*, he wonders.

"Sonuvabitch," he swears softly, then pulls out his phone and stares at the screen. It's a call from the 706 area code. The only person Wyatt knows who has a 706 number is his uncle Hugh. He motions to John to turn down the volume on the radio.

"Hello?" Wyatt says, wondering why the phone works in the middle of nowhere middle Georgia, and wishing it didn't.

"Wyatt? Ben Walters, attorney in Crossroads, Georgia."

Wyatt frowns, trying to remember if he has ever crossed paths with a lawyer named Ben Walters. He cannot recall ever meeting him. However, from his voice it's clear that Ben Walters is far older, so like all southern gentlemen, Wyatt responds amiably.

"Yes Sir, Mr. Walters, how are you this afternoon?" Wyatt inquires.

"Just fine, just fine. Listen, you are the sole heir of Mr. Hugh Jamison, as I understand it. Mr. Jamison was your uncle?"

Wyatt cannot think how to respond. "Was my uncle? He's not still my uncle?" Wyatt stammers, feeling the effects of the beer and the hot sun, wishing he had eaten more for lunch than a bag of Doritos.

"Oh dear, well, I thought you would have heard. I'm so sorry, son. Mr. Hugh Jamison has passed away, just three days ago, in fact," Walters says gravely.

"I see," is all Wyatt can think to say. He has only been around his uncle Hugh a few times in his entire life, so he is not going to weep.

"What did he die of?" Wyatt asks.

"He was found in his yard, by a neighbor. The cause of death is unknown at this time."

Unknown? How bizarre, Wyatt thinks."Was he murdered?" Wyatt asks.

"There is no reason to think so. No signs of foul play. Nothing stolen from the home. He had his wallet with him," Walters says in a reassuring tone. He sees no reason to say that body had been decomposing in the hot sun for several days and made Mark Wisham projectile vomit.

"Okay, so... What do I need to do?" Wyatt asks, wishing his father was alive to handle the situation.

"Well, ah, Mr. Jamison came to me to prepare his will a few years back, and according to the will you are the sole surviving heir. Mr. Jamison never married and had no issue."

Wyatt gets a mental picture of Hugh, a small, quiet man. He was just there, sometimes at weddings and funerals, like a servant in a grand manor house, unobtrusive. Hugh was the opposite of his brother Wendell, Wyatt's father, who was tall and gregarious. Wendell had died three years previously, though, of an aortic aneurysm. Wyatt suddenly feels strongly that Hugh probably had an aortic aneurysm. It would explain the sudden death.

"Hmm. Well, I am not surprised, I guess, that I'm the sole heir. My sister Nora lives in Knoxville and likely wouldn't be interested. My mom passed in 1983 and my dad died three years ago. I'm afraid I really didn't know Uncle Hugh too well, unfortunately," Wyatt says, getting up and walking to the end of the dock. He takes off his flip flops, sits on the side and puts his lower legs into the cool water.

"I understand. Well, he left his house and everything he had to you."

Wyatt frowns. "Okay, so how quickly can we get probate done?"

"Things move pretty fast up here as long as there are no complications. I mailed a copy of the will to your office the other day. After you've had a chance to read it, can you just give me a call? I called your office and the girl said you were on vacation. Sorry to bother you, but I figured you'd want to know about the inheritance, plus there are some matters we need to discuss, like disposing of the body."

Wyatt sighs, thinking he wants to get the deal over with. "I'll get my assistant to scan the will and email me a PDF. I can come see you tomorrow, if you have time," Wyatt says.

Ben Walters cannot operate a copier and has no idea what a PDF is. He looks down at his paper calendar, which is completely blank for the next day, a Friday. "That's fine. Why don't you come on about 9 a.m. I can give you directions how to get here."

"No need. The address of your office is on the will package right? I'll just put it in the GPS," Wyatt says. "Thanks for calling. See you tomorrow."

He hangs up the phone and stares at the water for a moment, thinking.

John Merriman looks at his friend. "You okay?"

"Yeah, yeah, fine. Death in the family. I barely knew my uncle Hugh, but he died the other day. Neighbor found him."

"Dang buddy, I'm sorry to hear that, you need anything?" John asks, looking at Wyatt closely.

"Yeah, no biggie. I need to go see about the estate. Looks like I have to cut the vacation a bit short, I'm afraid," Wyatt says.

CHAPTER 7

Sally snuggles into the old blue sofa and rubs Blanche's tummy. Blanche is sound asleep, on her back, her four paws in the air, snoring softly.

She decided long ago that no dog is cuter than a Bassett Hound.

Sally wears sweat pants and an old tee shirt. She is tired. It's after 9 p.m., the second day after the body was found, and Sally is still processing the horror. The dinner dishes are done.

Sally has been reading a book but the characters are not holding her attention. She cannot get the sight of the body and the smell to quit her memory.

Sally takes her landline phone and dials the cell number of her best friend since third grade, Marybeth Durand. Marybeth is married to an orthopedic surgeon and lives in Dunwoody, just outside of Atlanta. The two friends talk several times a week.

Damn, I hope she is finally home, Sally thinks. Two weeks in Europe without a cell phone is just ridiculous. She has missed Marybeth terribly. The two friends share everything.

After three rings, Marybeth answers. "Buttface, damn, can't a girl have some peace?!"

Sally smiles, and puts her feet on the coffee table. "Stinky, how dare you accuse me of violating your peace!

You've been in Europe! Were you sitting on the potty?!" Sally laughs.

They have been calling each other Buttface and Stinky since they were freshmen in high school.

"Hell to the no, Buttface. That would be more fun. I was trying to unpack two weeks of Ed's dirty laundry and get it started. Ugh. What's new and improved in East Bumfuck?!" Marybeth asks, settling into her husband's leather recliner in the family room.

"Well it just so happens, a LOT is happening in Bumfuck Valley," Sally replies, taking another sip of white wine. "I found a dead body, the mysterious next door neighbor!"

"Good Lord, tell me," Marybeth commands, stopping her temporary examination of her toenails, all thoughts about the need for a pedicure forgotten.

"Well, the other day I noticed a weird, creepy smell, and Blanche was barking at the brick wall between our house and the old Jamison house. The next day the smell was worse. So I called Mark Wisham – "

Marybeth's barking laugh stalls Sally's story for a moment."Oh lawd, the Barney Fife of Crossroads. Go on. You know he's never gotten over you turning down his invitation to Senior Prom," Marybeth says smugly.

"Yeah whatever. That was eons ago. Anyway, I called him and he came by in his patrol car, and we went over there and the front door was open –"

"Does he have a big old pot belly now? Has he let himself go?" Marybeth interrupts. "They always accuse women of letting themselves go. I think that door should swing both ways." She opens up a decorative china box on the coffee table and takes out her toenail clippers and goes to work. She forgot to take clippers to Europe and her toes look like dragon claws.

Sally rolls her eyes. "A little belly, not too bad, but who cares? He still doesn't have a chin or a personality, although he's as sweet as can be. Anyway, he gets over here and so we went in that house – the door was not even locked -- and – oh my God that little house is creepy. It looks graceful and old outside but inside? Ugh. Looks like it was frozen in time in the 1970's. Ugly 1970's wallpaper. Ugly wood paneling. Shag carpeting. Avocado green and harvest gold everything, everywhere. Looks like a before photo on an HGTV show –"

"Right Stinky, I get the picture but NOW I want to hear about the body!" Marybeth says, carefully positioning the clippers over her left big toe.

"Okay. Just hang on to your panties. So we check out the rooms in the house, all six of them, and he's not there. So we go in the back yard and see old Mr. Hugh, on the ground next to the wall, and he has been dead a while. SO GROSS. He is covered in flies and maggots and stinks to high heaven! I will never forget that sight as long as I live! Mark started to vomit and I ran inside and vomited."

"Shit fire and save the matches!" is Marybeth's response, the same one she has given to all Sally's startling news items over the years. It was a redneck expression but

Marybeth could say it to Sally without fear of being chastised.

"Oh Lawd," Sally sighs.

"What killed him?!" Marybeth says as the grabs her next toe.

Sally shudders and takes another sip of wine, wishing she had poured more into the glass, and trying to erase the memory of the sight of the body. "Nobody knows. They took the body to the hospital in Clayton for an autopsy but I don't know if it's been done yet. I think a family member may need to sign off on it."

"Hmm.. Did you not hear anything from over there before he died? A scream maybe?" Marybeth frowns, finishing her toenails and wishing she could go ahead and get a glass of wine.

"Nope. I almost never hear anything from over there, though. It was like he wasn't actually there, you know? No radio or music noises. No car noises. No discussions outside," Sally says.

"That's so weird."

"Yep." Sally pictures a grownup Wyatt Jamison there at the house, living there, right next door to her. She had looked at his photo on his firm website once.

"I wonder what's going to happen to that house, now the old guy is dead?" Marybeth says, walking into the kitchen for a glass of wine. She looks down at the empty plate on the kitchen floor, and sees that her Shih-Tzu, Lulu, is standing quietly by the back door wagging her tail.

"I cannot imagine anyone buying it. Maybe it will just get torn down. It would be a bitch to get that huge wall down," Sally says.

Lulu whines softly.

"Let's talk some more tomorrow. I need to go take the furbaby to walk. She was not happy while we were gone, and didn't do well for the house sitter. I just fixed her some scrambled eggs and I think she needs to go potty," Marybeth says, scooping up Lulu and kissing her furry head.

"Okay, but I want a call tomorrow. I'll be home and done with dinner by 8."

"Yep, gotcha. Later Gater."

Sally hangs up and rubs Blanche's furry head, thinking. Who would inherit the house? Could Wyatt inherit? It might be time to go on a diet...

CHAPTER 8

The next morning at 8:52, Crossroads is awake and bustling. Businessmen are in their offices working. Housewives are on their second or third cup of coffee. The birds are chirping merrily in the trees. Daffodils, up a while in front of many homes, are already starting to wilt. Wyatt drives through the outskirts of the little town and finds the only McDonalds, and hopes he can get an apple pie or a breakfast sandwich.

Andrea Hawkins sits on the curb outside the same McDonalds, contemplating the parking lot and wondering if she should get something to eat. Andrea, age 17, has lank, long brown hair that looks as though it was chopped off with a weed wacker, and wears torn jeans and a tank top under a black tee shirt. She has a pierced eyebrow and wears a gold ring in it. A small gold stud adorns her left nostril. Her eyes are ringed with black.

Andrea left her home in the small North Georgia town of Ringgold four days ago and hitchhiked south with a trucker who tried to feel her boobs. Andrea pulled a box cutter on him and threatened to cut his balls off and he backed off. It wasn't the first time she had had to defend herself. She got away from him at a truck stop.

At 5'2 and 100 lbs. Andrea looks like a waif but she is fast and tough. Growing up in a trailer with a mother who was a truck stop waitress and a father who left when she was a baby, Andrea hasn't had too many breaks in her short life. She hopes to get to Atlanta, though, and sell some of the marijuana her friend Derek grew in his basement, and maybe find a job as a waitress or something. Derek had given her the weed as a going-away present.

The ride she found last night with a farmer got her east to Crossroads instead of south to Atlanta. Asleep in the back of his pickup truck, Andrea had not realized the geography mistake.

Andrea didn't really care. Anywhere was better than Ringgold. She had to get out of her mom's trailer before her mom's boyfriend Jimmy did anything else to her. As Andrea told her friend Derek, Jimmy was trying to get in her pants all the time but fortunately he drank a lot and couldn't get it up much, and Andrea stayed gone, hanging out with friends who smoked weed and occasionally took pills.

After looking around Crossroads a bit, Andrea has a feeling she might be in a lucky place, although she cannot explain why. It looks like a sweet little mountain town, and she hasn't seen any homeless people or drug dealers or trailers yet.

Wyatt Jamison parks his silver Toyota Highlander outside the McDonalds and goes inside to use the bathroom. Andrea notes he doesn't lock his car and he has a license plate that says DeKalb County, which she thinks might be part of Atlanta. As soon as he is inside, she walks over and casually opens the car's hatchback, throws in her backpack, climbs inside, and pulls the old beach towel over herself before closing the door. She can curl into a ball and hide in surprisingly small spaces, a skill which has served her well in her 17 years.

Wyatt comes back out a few minutes later, sipping a cup of coffee and eating an apple pie. He has been up since 6, driving from Lake Oconee to Crossroads for his meeting with Ben Walters.

Wyatt has earbuds in his ears and he is listening to the Rolling Stones. He is tired. He doesn't notice that Andrea is in the back of his car as he pulls out and heads to downtown Crossroads. *The town has hardly changed a bit since I was last here*, he marvels. There are a couple of antiques places downtown, and some trees planted at intervals along the sidewalk, but it's still a sleepy little place.

Everywhere he looks, though, the Blue Ridge mountains surround Crossroads, giving the little town an almost fairytale feel.

He parks right outside the 4 story red brick office building next to City Hall, and gets out, looking up at the building and wondering what offices rent for there.

Andrea stays put, and dozes off.

Two hours later, Wyatt and Ben Walters stand outside Hugh Jamison's house, talking. Wyatt holds the house keys. Ben Walters is a tall man with gray hair and a tan that comes from playing a lot of golf.

"Ronny down at the Chevron said he would buy Hugh's car for a fair price, $2,500. That okay with you?" Walters asks Wyatt.

"Yeah, absolutely. You have the keys?" Wyatt asks, looking at the car.

"No, but they are on the kitchen counter. Just take a look through it and get out anything personal, is my recommendation. Drop the keys off with Ronny on your way out of town. Big guy, older. He'll get the car and give me a check. I trust him," Walters says laconically.

"Great. Thanks for taking care of that," Wyatt replies, his gaze falling on the grass which has gotten too tall.

"I've got to be heading on. Nice to meet you, Wyatt," Walters says, shaking Wyatt's hand.

After he shakes Wyatt's hand, Ben Walters gets into his Lincoln Navigator and heads back to town.

Wyatt stands outside his car and surveys the small white clapboard house with its neat shrubs, small front porch and rocking chair near the front door. It looks just like he remembers it from his grandfather's funeral. It doesn't look like a crime scene. *That brick wall around the back yard sure does look weird though*, he muses. Eight feet high, he estimates.

He walks towards the front door, whistling an old Creedence Clearwater Revival song, "Run Through the Jungle," a personal favorite.

As soon as Andrea sees Wyatt enter the home she grabs her backpack and scampers up to the back seat and lets herself out of the driver's side door, very cautiously, staying out of sight of anyone walking down the street.

She climbs out of the car, crouches beside it, and listens. The front of the house is quiet. She hears what sounds like the front door of the house opening, and Wyatt whistling. Closing the car door softly, she scurries over to the front door and slips into the house. Just inside the door is a coat closet and she hides in there, her heart pounding.

Maybe I have finally found a safe place, she thinks.

CHAPTER 9

Sally is getting ready for work, unaware a long-held dream is about to come true.

A distant movement draws her attention to her bedroom window and she looks out that Friday morning, startled to see Wyatt standing there. Her heart starts hammering as soon as she sees his face. *It's the boy from all those years ago, grown up, looking just like the photo on his website,* she thinks -- except instead of a suit he's wearing khaki pants and a blue Polo shirt, looking like he just stepped out of a magazine.

Oh my God, she thinks. *He is finally here.*

Sally is fully dressed for work, but she sits down hard on the bed, her head filled with old thoughts, old longings, and she wonders if she can finally get some closure.

She closes her eyes and lets the memories come -- all those times she gazed next door, hoping to see him again, hoping he would visit his grandmother, and then his uncle. He never did, at least not when she lived next door. She told herself, *he lived too far away. Let it GO.*

Sally thinks of the time when she was 21 and at the University of Georgia. She had driven to Atlanta on a Saturday and gone to Lenox Mall to look at wedding dresses. Her college boyfriend had proposed marriage and she had been tempted to turn him down flat, but she couldn't think why. He was handsome and nice and solid. Not terribly interesting, except for his love of the Allman

Brothers and his passionate devotion to college basketball, specifically Duke, his undergrad alma mater.

Sally looked at a few wedding dresses, but couldn't work up much enthusiasm. She left Macy's and wandered around Lenox Mall, wondering what to do, despairing. Finally, after a few frantic prayers, she had her answer.

Sally stopped in front of a bookstore and was looking at titles, and something made her turn and look at the couple walking towards her.

Wyatt walked beside a beautiful girl and they were laughing and talking. The girl wore jeans and a green LaCoste shirt with a white sweater. A gold add-a-bead necklace sparkled, and her grin showed off very white, even teeth. She looked like a model in Seventeen magazine. She looked up at Wyatt adoringly. Wyatt, wearing jeans and a purple Polo shirt, smiled down at her, not noticing Sally standing ten feet away, staring.

They looked like they belonged on the cover of a college catalog.

Sally noticed the engagement ring on the girl's finger.

After they walked by her, Sally stood there numbly for a few minutes, then walked quickly to the ladies' room and looked at herself in the mirror.

Sally stared at her forlorn face, not seeing the lovely young woman, but the awkward 13 year old in bad makeup and a bathing suit. As usual, she gave herself a pep talk, unconsciously channeling what her mother would say to her. *You saw that guy years ago, for a few minutes, and then you pined after him like a nitwit, for years, always wondering. Well now you know. He's part of the Buckhead crowd, the Atlanta elite, probably doesn't even have to work to get through school. You're the child of a plumber. Marry the veterinarian, little girl. It's a step UP.*

Sally finally walked dejectedly out to the parking lot and started her old beat up VW Rabbit, and sat there for a few minutes, pondering whether she should stay in Atlanta and get a job or just marry Steve. Finally, she sighed and put the car in gear. To HELL with a crush. Steve is nice and he loves her and why not marry a veterinarian? Sally found a 7-11 and bought three Hershey's candy bars and ate them on the way over to her friend Marybeth's parents' house.

Once there, Marybeth fixed her a lime daiquiri and they sat on the shaded back patio, chatting about nothing. Marybeth finally frowned and said pointedly "What the HELL happened to you, Stinky?! You look like shit."

Sally sipped her drink and then poured out her tale of woe, crying. Marybeth hugged her and urged her to marry Steve Odalshalski. "Wyatt made his choice, honey. Don't waste your life pining after a guy who's taken. Just let Wyatt go and marry the blonde. He's a hunk!"

Sally sniffled and wiped her nose and eyes. "He is gorgeous. I'm not sure why he is with me."

"Good godalmighty girl YOU are gorgeous too! You and Dr. Hunkalicious are gonna make gorgeous babies!"

The two old friends laughed, and started planning Sally's wedding.

Years later, Sally's mind is roiling as she gets in her car to go to work. She throws her purse and lunch bag on the seat and gets into the driver's seat and starts the engine. She turns to back out of the carriage house she uses as a garage. She hits the garage door control, but slams on the brakes and puts the car in park when she sees Wyatt Jamison come striding out the front door and into the front yard next door. He looks towards her house.

Wyatt looks fit and tanned and his nails are manicured. Sally's heart starts racing.

I need to go on to work. I'm going to be late, she thinks.

She sees Wyatt has seen her. An excuse to go talk to Wyatt has popped into her head.

Since he is looking in her direction Sally can't check her face in the mirror so she just takes a big breath and gets out of the car and walks over. *Why didn't I wear something more flattering?* she thinks. *Why didn't I put on some lipstick?!* She is wearing her standard black stretchy pants and a white button down shirt over a black cotton tank top. Her blue eyes are her best feature. She turns them to Wyatt.

"Hey there. Sally Cavanaugh. I am so sorry about your uncle," she says, sticking out her hand. Her heart has slowed. She is taking deep breaths and practicing a relaxation technique – breathe in through the nose, out through the mouth.

"Thanks. Nice to see you again," Wyatt says, shaking her hand with a white toothy smile. "I'm really glad you're not holding a baton this time."

"You remember that?!" Sally says, shock in her voice. Her heart starts beating wildly.

"Well yeah, of course," Wyatt replies. "You have really really blue eyes. Hard to forget those."

There is an awkward silence as Sally digests this fact: *he remembers me from all those years ago..*

"Wow. You have a great memory. So are you going to move up here and live in Crossroads?" Sally asks, hating that her voice has risen – it always goes up in pitch when she is nervous. As soon as the words are out of her mouth she thinks *what a bizarre thing to say! He's a rich lawyer from Atlanta, why on earth would be move here?!*

Wyatt looks thoughtful for a moment. "You know, it hadn't occurred to me, but that's a thought. It's a nice little town. Very scenic. Is there anywhere around here to do any fishing?"

Being a librarian in a small town has its perks, Sally thinks. "Why sure. I'm the town librarian and I've lived here most of my life so I happen to know the answer to that, even though I don't fish. Lake Rabun is about thirty minutes away. There's also a small pond called Benton's pond that's just outside of town."

"You are the go-to person for teaching me about Crossroads obviously," Wyatt says. "Where is the pond, can you give me directions? I might drive over there and I doubt there's an address for the pond I can put in my GPS."

Sally smiles, thinking *only an Atlantan would say that. Everyone here knows where Benton's Pond is.* "You follow the old Asheville Road, and you'll turn left on Mill Road and go a short ways and there it is. My ex-husband used to like to go up there. He would usually catch some nice bream, and sometimes a bluegill. It's a small pond but it's fed by streams coming out of the mountains. It was a mill pond at one time, though the mill is long gone."

"Cool. I'll check that out. Thanks." Wyatt looks at Sally and thinks *she's still really pretty, and those blue eyes are amazing. Her heart is filled with kindness and generosity, and she is highly intelligent. Maybe I should move up here where I can see her every day.*

"Well, I have to get to work. Nice seeing you again," Sally says. She smiles awkwardly, then reluctantly turns to get in the car.

"Hey, um, where is the library? I don't recall seeing it when I drove in," Wyatt asks, taking a step towards her.

"It's on Applebee Branch Road, 2781 if you want to put it in the GPS," Sally says, grinning.

"Thanks."

Wyatt watches her drive off and wishes he could have thought of something else to say. He senses more than one presence in the house but thinks *I bet there are spirits there, that's all*. He believes firmly in spirits, having sensed them often in his life.

Andrea, meanwhile, has crept out of the closet and she watches out the window of the house as Wyatt and Sally chat. Andrea gazes out through a tiny space parted in the long orange drapes. Wyatt and Sally are smiling and friendly with each other. She wonders if they are old friends.

As soon as Andrea had heard the front door open and close again and Wyatt's whistle sound had moved out the door, she had run for the bathroom, then crept around the house. Now, fascinated, she watches Wyatt stand in the yard, car keys in hand.

After Wyatt drives away, Andrea experiences a moment of regret. That was her ride to Atlanta.

Then she realizes that since Wyatt lives there and not in Crossroads, he will likely be gone for days. *No need to get all uptight, I can hang here,* she thinks.

Andrea checks out all the rooms, noting the old rolltop desk in the corner of the largest bedroom. It's stuffed with papers, and there are heavy old books piled haphazardly around it – the only messy spot in the otherwise neat house. The volumes all appear to be dusty old history books.

She finally settles in the kitchen, where she is delighted to open cabinet doors and discover plenty of food. The laminate countertop and cheap cabinetry and linoleum floor are spotlessly clean, and the neatness and order appeal to Andrea, accustomed to a dirty trailer.

Andrea opens a closet door, thinking, *it's just a closet*. It's not. She gazes at the sight of pantry shelves stocked with food, her eyes wide with wonder. She has never seen so much food at one time, outside of a grocery store. There are cans of Campbell's soup, tuna fish, Chef Boyardee spaghetti, pinto beans, green beans, blackeyed peas, potatoes, Ritz crackers, tomatoes, mandarin orange sections, crushed pineapple, jars of Classico spaghetti sauce. There are boxes of pasta, unopened.

There is a package of Oreos, Andrea's favorite cookie.

Andrea walks back into the kitchen and grabs the package of Oreos and opens it, then with her mouth full of cookie, opens the brown refrigerator.

Here again, all is neat, clean and orderly. There are two dozen eggs, packages of cheese, hot dogs, ketchup and mustard, a half gallon of milk, a half gallon of orange juice, and two plastic containers with lids, probably holding leftovers. She shuts the door and opens the freezer. The ice maker is full of ice, and the shelves are stacked neatly with frozen Stouffer's entrees, frozen vegetables, and three half gallons of ice cream. Andrea takes the Mayfield vanilla ice cream out and opens it. Untouched. WOW.

I think it will be awesome to just stay here for a while, she thinks. *The electricity is working. I bet the guest room bed has clean sheets on it. I can take a hot shower and wash my hair. I can get high and nobody will bother me.*

Andrea doesn't believe in God but she says a quick thank you to "whoever is in charge" for providing her with a place to rest for a while, until she can figure out how to get to Atlanta.

Andrea doesn't see across the street that a curtain has been pulled back, and a face is staring at the small house.

She has no idea of the malevolent energy emanating from the neighbor's house.

Andrea's grandmother always said "Don't be tendin' to other people's business. Go on about yours."

She was right.

CHAPTER 10

Benton's pond is about double the size of an Olympic-sized swimming pool, and surrounded by towering pine trees, with the mountains seemingly just a breath away, as the pond sits towards the edge of the valley. Like faithful sentinels of the past, the ruins of the old mill and old wheel linger beside the pond. No traffic noises disturb the air. Birds swoop in and out of the trees. The beauty captivates Wyatt.

There are no boat ramps, no marinas, and no cabins. The silence at the pond is true silence, tranquil and blessed.

Wyatt stands on the pond's shore and gazes at the water, captivated by the beauty of the place. He knows that fish teem beneath the surface in the cold mountain water. He decides he prefers the pond to Lake Oconee, where John has his cabin.

In the 1930's the Tennessee Valley Authority flooded a lot of farms in Tennessee and Alabama, to create man-made lakes. Wyatt found those lakes beautiful but spooky. Lake Oconee, in middle Georgia, was created when Wallace Dam was built in 1979. Wyatt loves fishing but sometimes he finds it disturbing to know there were farms and graveyards flooded to create the lake. He senses restless spirits around the lake.

Wyatt has an ability that he never discusses, the ability to sense there are things unknown that he needs to know, underneath. It helps him as a lawyer, of course, but as a child he understood early that it was as much a curse as a blessing.

His first vivid memory was being four years old and knowing there was a birthday cake for him, hidden in a cupboard in the kitchen. His mother had bought the cake and stuck M&M's in the icing as decorations. Wyatt had dragged a chair over to the counter, then climbed up and opened the high cupboard door, and quietly and methodically picked off every M&M from the cake, and eaten them.

An hour later, when his mother discovered the cake, the screaming had awoken him from a sugary nap. Amy Jamison had never seen her son climbing in the kitchen because she didn't like to cook and spent as little time in there as possible, but at 11 the night before when she had finished decorating Wyatt's cake and put it in the cupboard she had known he was sound asleep in his bed. There it had stayed and he could not have known it was there. Amy didn't believe in ghosts or psychic abilities and was utterly freaked out by The Cake Incident.

Wyatt had sensed that, and never caused his mother to freak out again, although as time went on his abilities grew sharper.

At age twelve, Wyatt had known that Billy Jones had been cheating on his math test with the answers stolen from the teacher's desk. Billy had stuck the stolen test in his book casually, and Wyatt had been able to tell Mrs. Williams about it and she caught Billy. He was suspended from school for three days and never knew who had turned him in.

Even if Wyatt had told him the truth, Billy wouldn't have believed it.

At age fifteen, Wyatt had known there was a package of condoms in his twenty year old sister Nora's purse and asked her if she was going to have sex with Jim, her college boyfriend. They were in Nora's room talking. Wyatt was both fascinated and repelled to think of his sister having sex with someone, but also a bit afraid of her response, so he just blurted out the question.

Nora was a junior at the University of Georgia and not pretty, but not ugly either. She was athletic and intelligent, with long brown hair and long limbs, despite being only 5'5. Her brown eyes narrowed as she regarded her tall, gawky little brother.

Nora looked at Wyatt knowing his secret, recalling the birthday cake incident, and decided it was time to confront Wyatt. She had put the condoms in her purse less than an hour before and just walked in the room with her purse. There was no way he could have seen the package. Wyatt had followed her in the room, asking her about her weekend plans because he wanted her to teach him to drive.

Her first reaction was to yell at him, but Nora checked that instantly. "You know when things are hidden, what they are, right?" she had asked her brother, watching his face for a reaction.

Wyatt felt himself blushing, the curse of all true blondes. "Yeah, sometimes," he mumbled, wishing he was anywhere else. Wyatt and Nora had always been cordial but not close, because of the almost 5 year age gap.

"Well, let's figure out what would be the best career for you, because that's quite a gift," she had said evenly. They talked for two hours, and their relationship shifted to a real friendship.

Part of the gift was that Wyatt could sense when someone was honest or not, sense their true character – unless it was someone close to him. Then his abilities were unreliable.

That conversation with Nora changed Wyatt's life. He decided to become a lawyer because he knew his gift would give him an edge. He also thought attorneys were heroes for representing people who needed help.

After high school, Wyatt decided to go to Emory in Atlanta not just because his father was a professor there, but because he wanted to stay in town, sensing his mother would be diagnosed with breast cancer his sophomore year, and his father would want him to be close by during that ordeal.

Two years after his mother died, Wyatt decided to marry Sharon because she was unaware of the gift and he was quite sure she didn't want to know about it. She was beautiful, but more importantly she was as simple and direct and honest a girl as he had ever met, without deep wells of thought, not easily read by anyone, and he prized those qualities as much as her beauty. Just before Sharon he had dated a girl who almost figured out his ability, which made him very uncomfortable.

The ability could be a curse -- not just in knowing when there was a lump in his mother's breast but in other ways.

Wyatt's ability wasn't always reliable.

When Wyatt had seen Sally years after their first encounter he sensed that she was filled with love and light in a way Sharon wasn't, and he knew she was passionate and funny and brilliant at History. He knew it like he knew his own name. Her kindness and beauty shone out of her.

He had never been unfaithful to Sharon. He had always had contempt for people who committed adultery. Suddenly, however, he could sense that Sally would be a joy to live with, a true companion. He hadn't realized that he might be happier with someone else until the possibility was right in front of him. It made him very uncomfortable but it was also exciting -- something he would not admit to anyone.

Wyatt picks up a small rock and tosses it in the pond, watching the spreading ripples. *One small gesture*, he thinks, *can cause lots of ripples.*

CHAPTER 11

More than a week after Hugh's death, Wyatt and Sharon arrive in Crossroads on Friday evening, at 6:45. Traffic getting out of Atlanta had been brutal and stretched the normally 2 hour trip to nearly 3 hours.

Sharon only reluctantly agreed to the trip. She has only been to the house once during their marriage and cannot recall anything about it except that it was small. To Wyatt's amazement, she packs 4 boxes of stuff. She also insists on bringing 400 thread count Egyptian cotton sheets, linen kitchen towels, a lounge chair so she can work on her tan, a large rolling cooler, and two romance novels.

"Come on in and let me show you how nice the house looks," Wyatt says, noting Sharon's look of disappointment as they pull into the driveway and Sharon surveys the small house. "Hugh kept it very clean, and everything is in good shape."

"All right but is there electricity? Is there water?" Sharon asks skeptically. She had played Candy Crush on her phone in the car, and said barely two words to her husband during the entire trip.

"I kept all the utilities turned on, so yes, we'll be fine," Wyatt says, pulling out his keys.

Wyatt watches Sharon get out of the car and stretch her legs, and sees the neat, small older homes in the neighborhood through her eyes – fixer uppers, all of them, she thinks. None of the homes have 5,235 square feet like the home Sharon shares with Wyatt in the Atlanta suburbs.

As they enter the house, Wyatt has the sensation that someone is watching them. He assumes it's a spirit.

Sharon lets out a loud gasp, and Wyatt turns to see her standing in the front doorway, staring at the small living room in horror.

"My God. I had forgotten about this décor. It's like a before photo on one of those shows where they fix up crappy old houses. I feel like I'm in a lost episode of The Brady Bunch," Sharon says, distress mixed with horror in her voice.

"Sharon —"

"I thought surely Hugh would have renovated!"

Exasperated, Wyatt snaps at her. "Oh good grief, it's just an old house. Uncle Hugh didn't care about the décor!"

Sharon wheels around and glares at him. "This is NOT my idea of a vacation home!"

"It looks great, for its time. Look at the TV trays! We can eat dinner in the living room and watch Jeopardy on the TV!" Wyatt says half jokingly.

Sharon stares at the hulking behemoth of a TV, opposite the green tufted sofa.

"When you said we now have a weekend place in the mountains, this is not what I pictured."

"Yeah, but c'mon. You've been here before," Wyatt reminds her.

"Not recently! I pictured something like that beautiful old Victorian next door. Most of the houses on this street are like that, not like this little crackerbox. Your grandmother was like a prisoner of the 1970's Sears catalog! We'll have to gut this and start all over," Sharon says, half to herself, as they pass through the living room and into the tiny paneled den, then the kitchen with its wallpaper of cheerful red and yellow flowers and red formica table with metal chairs.

Wyatt shakes his head in disappointment but Sharon doesn't see it.

"Come out to the back yard. You can see the mountains. Oh, and hey -- look at the nice private yard," he says weakly as they step out the sliding glass door and survey the small yard.

Sharon looks at the lush but weedy lawn and a few scraggly shrubs, and the high brick wall, puzzled.

"Why did your uncle build that wall?"

Wyatt shrugs. "I don't know. I asked the lawyer that and he said nobody in town knew why. Hugh kept to himself."

"Well, we can get a landscaper in here and put in a pool, I guess," Sharon says. "Is that where they found the body?!" she says in a voice filled with disgust, gazing at flattened grass next to the wall.

Wyatt looks at the spot next to the wall. Fortunately, the flies and maggots are gone.

"Yeah, I'll get out here tomorrow and mow, if I can find a mower."

"Well, please get the cooler out of the car so we can have some dinner. I'm so glad I stopped by Whole Foods before we left town. I doubt there's a decent place to buy organic produce anywhere in this town," Sharon says brusquely, heading back to the house.

Wyatt goes back out to the car, thinking *it was a mistake to bring her here. She cannot imagine a place where cell phone service is spotty, there is no Whole Foods, and her social calendar isn't always full.* He wishes he had invited John to spend the weekend.

As he hefts the heavy cooler out of the car, then grabs the handle to roll it in the house, he looks up and thinks he sees one of the bedroom curtains move.

The feeling is more than a feeling, now. Wyatt knows there is somebody else in the house. He senses it's a benign presence, not a threatening one. The house has been locked up, though, since he was last here, and there are no signs of a break-in. It must be a spirit, he thinks. Got to be.

Wyatt realized years before that his abilities included the ability to detect spirits, and he assumes that's what is occupying the house, a benevolent spirit. That doesn't bother him. He has learned over the years to ignore a lot of the input his brain receives, because otherwise he couldn't get anything done.

Input into his brain was a problem when he was a kid. When Wyatt was a freshman in college he called Nora long distance and told her about the problem. He knew his English professor had a dirty magazine in his briefcase. He had seen that one of his fraternity brothers had a bottle of his father's best brandy under his bed. He knew there was a nest of spiders under his booth at the IHOP and had to leave quickly. Nora had laughed when he told her about all of it.

"You are just going to have to think of something else, and ignore most of that stuff," Nora had advised. "Think about songs – I will send you one of those new tape players, a Walkman, and you can listen to tapes. Maybe that will help."

It did help. He listened to music or hummed or whistled much of the time, except when he was in court or with clients. It helped direct his thoughts away from all the information.

A few minutes later, Sally pulls in the driveway of her house. She had stayed late at the library, catching up on ordering new books.

As Sally turned the corner and steered the Accord down the street in the gloom she noticed the lights burning in the Jamison house.

Now she stares at the silver Highlander sitting in front of the Jamison house. *I'm pretty sure that's Wyatt Jamison's car*, Sally thinks.

As Sally pulls her key out of the ignition, she hears Blanche barking and quickly unfastens her seatbelt and grabs her purse and sweater.

Next door, while Sharon puts the food on the kitchen counter, Wyatt wanders around, whistling "You Are My Sunshine."

The entire house is less than 1,800 square feet, so it doesn't take long. He checks the bedrooms, the closets, and the back patio thoroughly, in 5 minutes.

Wyatt switches to humming "Time After Time" as he notes the old desk covered with papers and books in the biggest bedroom and figures it's where his uncle worked on history papers. There are men's clothes in the small closet.

In the smallest bedroom, containing only two twin beds and a dresser, the only thing he sees which doesn't seem to belong is a set of earbuds lying on one of the beds. His son Thad leaves earbuds everywhere.

It seems odd that Hugh, a man in his 70's, would have earbuds. Then again, since he had only seen Hugh a few times in his life, Wyatt couldn't presume to know Hugh's habits. Wyatt whistles Bohemian Rhapsody as he ponders whether or not to keep the bedroom furniture or turn it into an office.

"Wyatt, come on to dinner," Sharon calls. "And stop with the whistling. It's too loud in this house." He walks back to the kitchen, where the small formica table is set for dinner. He pulls out one of the aluminum chairs.

"I forgot about eating in the kitchen like this," Wyatt says, sitting down at the table. "I grew up eating in the kitchen."

"Well, if we're going to stay here I will have to hire a contractor to completely gut this kitchen. It's hideous. This whole kitchen and den area should be open concept," Sharon says, tucking into her shrimp salad.

"Why would it have to be open concept?" Wyatt asks.

"Then we can have a big island with stools around it so we can eat there."

"Did you get any bread?" Wyatt asks.

"No, neither one of us need the carbs."

Wyatt sighs. He never argues with his wife, because his parents used to argue a lot and he vowed he wouldn't have a marriage like that. He takes a bite of shrimp salad and chews. No mayo. It tastes weird. He swallows some water from a tall glass by his plate. Sharon is always trying to make him drink more water.

"Did you bring any beer?"

"There's a bottle of wine on the counter."

"No beer?"

"No. You could have brought some."

"The deal was, you were supposed to get what we needed all ready to put in the car so we could get out of town quickly."

"I did exactly what you asked," Sharon says, peeling a banana. "You don't need beer. You're getting a beer gut."

"Is there any dessert?"

"No junk food. I brought six bananas. They're great for you. Potassium."

They both chew in silence for a few minutes.

"I've had a long day," Wyatt says finally, wiping his mouth with a napkin. He pushes his chair back from the table. "I'm going to bed."

"I haven't made up any of the beds yet."

"I don't care. I'm going to read a while and then sleep in one of the smaller bedrooms, likely one where the sheets are not Egyptian cotton. I like roughing it. Good night."

Sharon shrugs, not caring about the hostility in Wyatt's voice, and gets up to throw away the paper plates. Wyatt often sleeps in a separate room, especially when he brings home work.

Wyatt grabs his overnight bag and goes into the room with two single twin beds. He opens the closet again, sees nothing but old clothes, and closes it. He senses there is more to the closet, something hidden, but he decides to just call it a day, as he hums Our House.

After he strips down to his boxers, he brushes his teeth in the bathroom across the hall, admiring the bare walls, plain white shower curtain, and small toilet. Simple furnishings appeal to him. Sharon likes sinks shaped like big bowls, granite counters, and shower curtains that look like drapes in a bordello.

Wyatt reads for a while, lying on his belly with the book propped. He hears Sharon in the den watching TV and ponders telling her to turn it down, but that might cause an argument, so he decides to just try and go to sleep.

Andrea hides just below the room where Wyatt is reading. She had seen Wyatt and Sharon pull up in the car and it had given her time to throw her clothes under the bed and get out of sight. She wishes she had her earbuds, though.

In her explorations in the house she had found that the closet in the smallest bedroom was more than a closet. Andrea had opened the closet door and been fascinated to see very old 1970's women's clothes hung there. The polyester dresses were like costumes for a play about aliens, she decided. As she reached down to pick up some sandals, Andrea had stumbled over a pair of white vinyl boots and fallen against the side wall of the closet and felt it give way. She had seen the movie of The Lion The Witch and The Wardrobe, so she thought in a childish way that the closet might be like the wardrobe and offer a portal into a magical world, but it was not the case.

However, there was a hidden door.

At the side of the closet she found that the wall was hinged, like a door, but it wasn't obvious. Instead of a doorknob there was an old piece of rope. She pulled the rope. Nothing happened. She poked the wall and it swung outward.

Andrea looked into the space, but it was dark and in the weak light she simply saw a narrow, rickety wooden staircase dropping into the darkness. She fetched a flashlight from a drawer in the kitchen, and shone it down into the blackness. Narrow wooden stairs led to a small cellar of some kind. After she propped open the hinged door with a coat hanger, Andrea gripped a flashlight in her mouth and descended the stairs, and found a pull cord. She pulled it and a lightbulb lit up.

The cellar was very small, about 8 by 10 feet, with shelves on two sides. A few dusty jars sat atop the shelves. A small cot was folded up next to one wall. Beside the other wall, she saw a huge old trunk. The wooden trunk was dusty and ancient, and it had a rounded lid that Andrea couldn't open. She tried hard, pushing and pulling, and even tried to pick the lock, but nothing worked. The trunk also didn't move, no matter how hard she pushed.

Andrea had decided that somewhere in the house there was a key to the trunk. She had tried picking the lock with a knife, a paper clip, and tweezers, but nothing worked. They always made it look easy in the movies. It wasn't easy. In the coming days, Andrea then began a meticulous search of the house. In between eating, watching television, and occasionally venturing into the back yard, she searched every piece of furniture, every drawer, every closet, even the two bathrooms. No key.

During her microscopic examination of every inch of the house Andrea poked around the old desk and found a number of old history books. A large, very old Atlas of the United States, weighing about ten pounds, contained within its pages five twenty dollar bills. Andrea had seriously considered using the money to buy a bus ticket to Atlanta, but she wanted to know what was in the trunk, and since she seemed relatively safe and had enough to eat, continuing the search seemed like a good idea.

Now, with Wyatt and Sharon in the house, Andrea wonders if she made a good choice. She feels it best to stay in the tiny airless cellar for the moment. Thankful for the small cot, she had put a blanket and a bottle of water down there in case of just such an emergency. Andrea knows she will have to pee after a while, but decides to ignore that. Thank goodness there's an old Coleman lantern in the space, so she can use it instead of the old light bulb, which has burned out.

Andrea pulls out a worn Stephen King paperback book she found in the house, and burrows into her blanket to read. She loves to read and has an insatiable curiosity about the world, a fact her mother has never understood. Huddled in the cot, Andrea wonders if her life is about to change and decides it probably is, a premonition that both scares and pleases her.

CHAPTER 12

The next morning, Sharon awakens at 9:14 and grabs her phone, which is beside the bed on a charger. Only two bars of service, after charging all night. Wow. She checks messages and tries to text her friend Missy, again. SERVICE NOT AVAILABLE flashes on the screen.

What kind of backwater is this place? she wonders.

She uses the small master bathroom, then checks the smaller bedroom where Wyatt slept last night. He's gone. His bed is made neatly. He always rises before she does, so she is not surprised that he is out.

She wanders into the kitchen and finds a note scrawled on the back of the Whole Foods receipt – *Went for a walk. Back later. – W*

Sharon eats a piece of whole grain toast and drinks a cup of coffee, then wanders out to the back patio, feeling a chill in the air. *Ugly backyard, but we can fix that,* she thinks. *Mountains. Always cooler up here. So much for laying out and working on the tan.*

She decides to watch TV for a while.

Wyatt stifles a belch and looks at the table in front of him. *What a breakfast.* Fried eggs, grits, country ham, and toast.

Bob's Place is the breakfast bomb, he decides, as he softly hums "Rambling Man." All around him, people are eating and he doesn't want to think about them or know their thoughts.

Wyatt's mother didn't like Crossroads, so they had only visited a few times during Wyatt's childhood, and then his grandmother had had a stroke and been put in a nursing home, and they never visited after that.

He has no memory of Bob's Place as a child.

He doesn't mind the large portrait of John Wayne on the wall, or the sound system that plays Waylon Jennings, Merle Haggard, and other country greats.

Wyatt had awakened at 6:30, as always, and decided to walk into town, only a mile away. Unlike many places, Crossroads is a bustling place early on a Saturday morning. As he walked past the houses he marveled at the abundance of trees and flowers, with birds and butterflies swooping around in the sunshine.

What a nice little town, he thought. Very little traffic. Folks were out walking their dogs, and he saw only two joggers. Everyone smiled and nodded as they passed him.

Bob's Place is on Main Street but at the end of the road, almost out of town. The building is set back on its own, clearly a diner and a convenience store, with a sign out front that says LIVE BAIT and Breakfast Special $5. It has a gravel parking lot, a bare bones interior with lots of fluorescent lighting, vinyl booths, and formica tables filled with families. The store and restaurant are on opposite sides of the building.

Wyatt chose a 2 person table. The menu is limited but grits are included with every entrée except the "diet plate" – a bowl of Cornflakes and "seasonal fresh fruit."

Sharon would eat the diet plate, and complain, he thinks, after he gives his order to a short chubby waitress with a very retro bouffant hairdo.

From "Ramblin' Man" the jukebox switches to "Hello Walls," then goes through three Waylon Jennings songs. After Wyatt pays his check and leaves a big tip because his waitress Delilah called him Honey, he heads over to the store side.

He's gazing at fishing lures, humming softly, when the door to the café opens and an older woman walks in, pivots sharply, and looks at him as though he is a recalcitrant child.

She is at least seventy, he surmises, a short lady with a squat, compact body like a mini sumo wrestler, black curly hair shot through with gray, cut in a pixie style, and bright blue eyes. She is wearing black knit pants and a man's blue button down shirt.

"Come on over here. I want to talk to you," she says to Wyatt, nodding at an empty table.

Wyatt has never seen her before in his life, that he can recall. He looks around, but clearly she addressed her command to him.

She marches over to a table and sits down, back ramrod straight, and looks sternly at Wyatt.

He goes over to the table and pulls out the chair and sits opposite her.

"I'm sorry, do I know you?" he asks, confused. The waitress is pouring coffee for the woman and automatically pours Wyatt a cup, too.

"You are Wyatt Jamison," she says sternly, as though lecturing a stubborn child. She pronounces his name as "white" instead of two syllable why-uht.

The waitress walks over, pen poised over her order pad. "Morning."

The older lady touches the waitress's arm and says in a softer voice, "Tell Polly to scramble me an egg and bring me some grits without butter, too," she commands, then her voice softens. "Oh, and you're looking real trim there Delilah. Good job with the weight loss!"

"Thanks Roberta," the waitress says shyly before she walks back over to the counter. "Your food will be ready in a jif."

Roberta turns her attention back to Wyatt.

"I'm Roberta Kingston. Your daddy Wendell Jamison and I went to school together, right here in Crossroads, long time ago," Roberta says, forcing herself to sound casual, but not smiling at Wyatt. "I'm sorry about Hugh."

"Thanks."

"When is the service?"

"Um, service?" Wyatt asks.

"When is the funeral?" Roberta says, sipping her coffee.

"Oh. Um... I hadn't really thought to have one," Wyatt says, noting the instant look of shock and disapproval on Roberta's face. Her hazel eyes drill into his face.

"My husband George is the minister over at First Lutheran, where your people have always worshipped. Hugh was a quiet soul, reclusive even, but he was from here and he should be buried here, with a proper Christian service."

Wyatt sips his coffee and ponders this for a moment. "His body was cremated. It's what his will directed."

"Well that's fine. The ashes can be interred," Roberta says. She pulls a card out of her pocket and hands it to Wyatt. "That's got all the information on it about how to contact George, or you can just walk over to the church sometime. Go out the door here, turn left, walk 4 blocks over and go right on Sycamore."

He accepts the small white card and reads it dutifully.

"If you don't mind me asking, what will you do with the house?" Roberta asks, trying to sound casual.

"I beg your pardon?" Wyatt says, startled.

Roberta sighs and leans closer. "The house where Hugh lived?"

Wyatt sits back and sips his coffee. "I don't know. I may keep it for a weekend place."

"It has how many bedrooms?" Roberta asks.

"Um, three. Yeah, three."

"I was in that house once, when your grandfather died. They had kept it real nice, as I recall," Roberta says. "Nice place, and a good location. Good neighborhood. Settled," she continues.

"Yeah, it appears to be well-maintained," Wyatt offers.

"It's just the one story, right?" Roberta asks, sipping more coffee.

"Well, yeah, everything is on one floor," Wyatt responds. "The décor would need a bit of updating, according to my wife," he finishes lamely.

Robert stares at him, mouth pursed in disapproval.

Wyatt can read her, but he's not sure if he's going by facial expression or using his ability. She has an unusual interest in the house.

There is an awkward silence. *She has a very low opinion of people who are just tourists or weekenders,* Wyatt thinks. *So I can read her a little bit, but not well,* he reflects.

Roberta finally shakes her head mournfully. "I liked Hugh. Such a sweet man. Never said an unkind word to anyone."

They sit in silence for a moment.

Wyatt clears his throat. "Well, I'm just here for the weekend, I'm afraid. Uh, I really hadn't planned on having a service but I will, since you think it's the thing to do..."

"Well, Wyatt, this is a small town. You have a service when someone dies. Folks need closure. I was there when your granddaddy died. We even drove down to Atlanta and went to your dad's service, although you likely didn't see me and George. Respects must be paid."

Wyatt cannot think of a reply to that.

The waitress puts a plate down in front of Roberta, who bows her head for a brief silent prayer and then heavily salts and peppers her food, and then starts eating, pushing the grits and egg onto the fork with a piece of toast.

Wyatt recalls a voicemail from the funeral home asking about the disposition of the ashes, but he hasn't returned the call. *She's right, though. I need to go ahead and plan the funeral, get it over with, get it done*, he thinks.

"I will give George a call this week," he says, pocketing the card. "Thanks for reminding me," he says with a smile, getting up. "I need to get back to the house, check on my wife."

There is an awkward silence.

Roberta fixes Wyatt with a pointed look. "What was the cause of Hugh's death? Nobody seems to know."

Wyatt is silent for a moment. Roberta waits patiently.

Wyatt swallows hard. "I was told it was likely an aneurysm. No signs of foul play," Wyatt says. *That's the real reason she wanted to talk to me. She is powerfully curious. There's a hidden agenda. It's not just Hugh either,* he realizes, startled. *It has something to do with the house. Hmm.*

"All right then," Roberta says, washing down a bite of grits with her coffee. "And don't buy anything here. Stuff is too pricey. Drive ten miles up the road to the super Walmart. It's worth the drive."

"Thanks for the tip, M'am." Wyatt nods at her, and heads out the door.

Roberta watches him walk out and wishes she was 40 years younger and not married. *My my my what a fine looking man...*

She shakes her head and reminds herself not to lust after men, then looks towards the kitchen.

"DELILAH! Get me a fried egg sandwich and a cup of coffee to go, for George. He's not eating enough.

Bob, a huge man wearing an apron, comes out from behind the counter, wiping his hands.

"I already made the sandwich," he says, handing her a paper bag. "So that's the Jamison boy?"

"Yep, that's him. Favors his daddy," Roberta says, putting some dollar bills on the table.

"Seems like a nice fella," Bob says.

"Pure Atlanta," she says, shaking her head. "I had to remind him to have a funeral for Hugh."

"Think he knows what his uncle was doing all those years?"

Roberta fixes him with a withering stare, and Delilah, who has walked over to listen, flinches. Roberta's eyes have narrowed and her voice has lowered, signs she is powerfully annoyed.

"I don't think Wyatt has a clue about anything. He's a fool not to move up here, though, since he has a free house."

"And leave Atlanta?" Delilah asks.

Roberta glares at her. "We have natural beauty, a slower pace of life, and the super Walmart just up the road. Doesn't get any better than that."

Bob stifles a chuckle and just nods.

Wyatt looks at his wife, who is dozing on the brown plaid sofa wearing only a tee shirt and panties. At one time that sight would have stirred him, but now it doesn't. He walks back into the kitchen and drinks a cup of coffee and stares out at the yard.

When did she become a stranger? He wonders. *How did we get here? Not talking? Not wanting to share a bed?*

He recalled the Sharon from college, a cute Tri Delt with a great smile, athletic and outgoing. He was in law school at UGA and she was a junior. He had been amazed that she agreed to go out with him. He was usually awkward with women. However, she made him feel at ease. They both came from good upper middle class families, both wanted the same things out of life, both liked good food and going to concerts.

Over the years, though, Sharon had become absorbed by her job as the office manager for a cardiology practice, raising their son, her book club, her church activities at the largest Presbyterian church in Atlanta. She was always busy.

Wyatt worked all the time, too, always taking work home. He liked being a lawyer, liked helping people. He disliked writing briefs but he always had a law clerk to do that for him.

After listening to Sharon's faint snores, Wyatt decides to take his fishing pole and just spend the day fishing.

Three hours later, Sharon is fully dressed and exploring the house. She has eaten a small salad for lunch, then watched some TV, dismayed by the ancient set and its small screen, and the few cable channels available.

Sharon walks into the small bedroom where her husband had slept the night before and shudders at the shag carpeting, the polyester green bedspreads, the cheap laminate bedside table. She opens the closet door and gasps at the hanging clothes from the early 1970's.

Look at all this vintage stuff, she thinks. *I wonder what this stuff would bring at a consignment shop?*

As she pulls out and examines the clothes she feels disappointed. The items are K-Mart clothes, all double knit polyester, not designer clothes.

As Sharon critically examines a polyester blouse with a huge collar, she hears something beneath her feet. *What the hell?*

Sharon doesn't notice the door in the closet. The scratching comes again. She gasps, then backs up a step or two and looks down at the floor. The scratching sound happens again, this time louder.

OH MY GOD RATS! she thinks, dropping the clothes hangar and running out of the room.

CHAPTER 13

If this is heaven it is totally unlike what I was taught in Sunday school. However, I do not think it is the end, for me. I think there is some reason I am still here, floating around earth, and not reunited with my parents, grandparents, my brother, or any others. What is it, though?

Don't get me wrong though -- I am not alone. I now accept that ghosts and echoes exist everywhere. The world is a far richer tapestry than I ever knew when I was alive.

I will be drifting along, lighter than spider's web, and sense other spirits, sometimes crowded alongside me, thickly as clustered grapes. I know others are there but we do not connect – sort of like life, at least how I lived my solitary life.

I realize now that the purpose of my life was not to be ordinary, to marry and have children, to work as a typical contributor to society. No, my purpose was to have a direct and profound influence on my nephew, on Sally Cavanaugh, on Andrea Hawkins, and most importantly on my hometown of Crossroads.

My purpose is to uncover the past.

I often visit the site of my parents' old home on Honeysuckle Road, where I died.

I drift down the main road amazed by the houses and stores that have sprung up since I was a boy. The older houses run east, the newer houses to the west, built after my parents sold the farmland to a developer.

I turn down the lane and come to the curve in the road where our house is, and the magnolia tree is once again in the back yard, and the old oak tree with the swing. The barn is long gone.

As I hover beside the old magnolia tree I realize that a shimmering of light is happening, like a crack in the fabric of time, and suddenly the overcast day has turned to sunny, the brick wall has gone, and our little house stands there once again as it was during the farming days, the fields stretching out beside and behind the house.

The echoes of the past are all around me, and now I see them.

The scene is so beautiful, and so serene, I want to cry.

It has always been a small house, just a main room, kitchen and three bedrooms. The bathroom was put in just before the war, the second bath just during the 1970's renovation. The bare wooden boards in my vision now are weathered but not painted. The porch is swept clean. Two rocking chairs on the porch are filled,

one with my mother, and the other with a lady I
think was a neighbor in the 1940's, Mrs. Wright.

Mother, no older than thirty, still lovely,
wears a housedress and an apron, her blonde hair
twisted into a knot on top of her head. She has a
pile of string beans in her lap and a pot beside
her. She methodically takes each bean and snips
off the ends with a small knife, pulling the strings
off the hulls, breaking each bean in half before
tossing it in the pot. The pot sits on the old table
beside her, and next to it is a volume of poetry
by Walt Whitman, a favorite author of hers.

Wendell is a ten year old. I am seven. I can
see us in the yard, playing marbles.

Mrs. Wright asks, "Why does your husband
keep farming? I know he's been offered a lot for
the land?"

Mother smiles. "Mildred, this house has
stood for decades, since before the War Between
the States. Jamisons have farmed this land for
generations," Mother says evenly.

"I bet Will could make a lot more money at
the sawmill, more than he makes as a farmer out
here," Mrs. Wright says. She is the type of
woman who likes to tell people what they ought
to do. I remember her well.

"Well, now that the old Harvey textile mill has shut down, all those folks are working at the sawmill. I doubt they need anyone else," Mother opines, snapping a bean and placing it in the pot.

After rocking for a minute, Mildred tries again."Well, y'all could open a restaurant near the train station."

"A restaurant? Why would we do that? Where would we get the money?" Mother snorts derisively.

"Your family —" Mildred starts, but mother's hostile glare shuts her down. Mother's family disowned her when she married Daddy. We have never met any of them. Everyone in town gossips about Mother being from a rich family but she never talks about her family. It's as though they don't exist.

Mildred takes another tack. "The railroad comes right through and people will always like to stop and get off and eat, before they go on to Asheville," Mildred says primly. "Crossroads will prosper, as always."

She was right. Crossroads did prosper, but mainly as a farming community and a small tourist destination. The sawmill shut down in the 1960's.

Another shimmer, and the scene is gone. The magnolia disappears (struck by lightning and killed in 1962) and the modern house replaces the old farmhouse.

I drift back down the street towards town but I find myself in another crack in time's fabric when I realize the roads have turned to dirt and many of the houses are gone, replaced by scrub pines and underbrush.

Crossroads is a small town today but back then it literally was a crossroads, where two roads intersected, and then of course there was the train depot.

The small, rude houses I see now are made mostly of weathered boards, with bare dirt instead of lawns, but as I get closer to town there are some more respectable looking houses.

A thin white woman in a long dress and a bonnet walks down the street, a basket over her arm, a small boy holding onto her skirt. She glances fearfully back and I see what she sees, a wagon pulled by two large horses rumbling down the bare city street. There's a man driving the team who looks like quite a rough character. In the wagon are wooden boxes, although it's hard to tell because a canvas tarp is stretched across it all.

This looks to be quite interesting, I think, as I keep up with the wagon, watching as it makes a couple of turns. I must have drifted back more than a hundred years!

I drift along overhead, marveling at the lack of electricity poles and the sight of outhouses behind the houses, and I watch the wagon. Finally, the driver pulls up at a small clapboard house on Honeysuckle Road – my house! There's no porch yet, and no grass, just dirt, but the magnolia is there, as a sapling, and it's definitely our family house.

The rough man jumps off the wagon and heads into the house. I follow along.

The house is quite different inside, of course. Walls and floors are bare, and there is little furniture.

"We got to get a secure place for our loot, Marcus. We can't keep it in the wagon," the rough man driving says.

Marcus, a tall thin man, spits a stream of tobacco juice towards a spittoon and misses. He paces nervously.

"See, Joe, this whole area could go back to the rebs. Can't take a chance on that. These are mountain folk. They don't take kindly to strangers."

"What about the widow lady?" Joe says, glancing back towards what looks like one of the bedrooms. I can see the edge of a bed through the half open door.

"She's about half crazy, I reckon, since both her boys were killed at Shiloh. I'm thinking I'll marry her, just so the property will be mine, nice and legal. She's got a root cellar, she says, and I reckon we can put most of this down there," Marcus says decisively.

"How in hell is that a good plan? What if she looks in the cellar?" Joe demands.

Marcus spits another stream of tobacco. "She won't go down there. Told me she never goes down there nohow, since she got trapped down there one day last year for about 6 hours before a neighbor heard her. She don't like closed in spaces. I'll fix it so even if she does go down there she won't see nothing" he says.

The two men grin at each other.

"You sure you want to marry her?"

"Hell yeah, she ain't bad lookin' and all her menfolk are dead."

I study Marcus. He has dirty blonde hair and bright blue eyes, and a tall rangy build. He must have married her. He must be the father of my grandfather, Jack Jamison.

The widow appears in the doorway, a lovely woman, but petite, thin and pale, about 35 years old. I realize as I study her face that she is my great grandmother, Josephine Adams Jamison. Marcus must be Marcus Jamison, her second husband. I have always been fascinated by genealogy.

Suddenly I find myself in a vortex, with a great WHOOSH, and I am back outside, high above the trees, drifting through time but not in any particular time. My mind is reeling with what I've just witnessed.

It confirms what I suspected for years.

I feel a deep sense of shame at being descended from a Union soldier who was a thief, but also great excitement. Marcus and Josephine had a son named Jack, my grandfather, and his son William was my father. Jack and William were farmers. How my mother got two university professors as sons -- well, unlike most mountain women, she had been to college and she always encouraged us to read, and make good grades in school. She was our guiding force.

But what happened to the treasure? I spent years looking for it, not knowing if it was real, but now I know it actually was real!

CHAPTER 14

Andrea, crouched by the window in the smallest bedroom, watches as Sharon throws her suitcase and a box of other items into the car, and gets in the driver's seat.

Wyatt stands beside the car, furious, his hands on his hips. He says evenly. "For God's sake why are you freaking out? You heard a rat. What's the big deal?"

Sharon puts her head out of the car window. "I WILL NOT STAY IN THAT CREEPY LITTLE HOUSE ONE MORE NIGHT WITH THE GODDAMN RATS! YOU EITHER GET IN THIS CAR RIGHT NOW AND COME BACK TO ATLANTA WITH ME OR YOU CAN TAKE THE BUS HOME!"

For a long moment, Wyatt just stares at his wife. "You are really overreacting."

Go on and get in the car and leave! thinks Andrea. She is accustomed to family drama but she has never seen someone as calm as Wyatt.

Sharon glares at Wyatt, throws the car into reverse, and backs down the driveway.

Wyatt pulls out his cell phone and punches in numbers as he walks back towards the house in the late afternoon gloom.

Andrea dashes for the bathroom, afraid her bladder will burst. She comes out to peer out the window and sees that Wyatt is still standing in the yard, his cell phone at his ear.

The phone doesn't work, and Andrea watches Wyatt shove it back into his pocket with obvious disgust.

Then she sees the neighbor lady come out of her house. Neighbor lady and Wyatt talk and he goes into her house.

Well, thank God, finally, thinks Andrea. *I need something to eat.* She heads into the kitchen for a snack.

Sally studies Wyatt while he sits at her kitchen table, but she tries not to be obvious about it. It feels surreal to have him in her home, sitting at the table where she has eaten thousands of meals.

For a man whose wife has just had a screaming hissy fit and taken their only car, Wyatt is remarkably calm. When he walked in the house Blanche had run up to him and stood up on her hind legs for a hug, and he had knelt down and spent a few minutes petting her and talking to her, which melted Sally's heart. He had started whistling "Hound Dog," the Elvis classic, and Blanche had wagged her tail enthusiastically.

Now Wyatt and Sally sit opposite each other at the scarred old oak table that has been in Sally's family for a hundred years.

"I've never seen Sharon that freaked out. Wow," Wyatt remarks, sipping his beer.

"Is she deathly afraid of rats?" Sally asks. She is drinking a glass of Chardonnay.

"No, I don't think so. Maybe? I don't know. She takes care of pest control at our house. I know nothing about it."

"What do you do for a living?" Sally asks, although she knows the answer.

"I'm an attorney. I work a lot of hours," Wyatt says, feeling vaguely uncomfortable. Sally's large blue eyes are mesmerizing.

"I was married to a doctor. I know about long hours," Sally replies with a smile.

Sally didn't really mind her husband working a lot of hours, though. She was quite happy to be on her own with her books and her daughter, Wyatt thinks. Wyatt is intrigued by that, and resolves to Google Sally's husband sometime and see what he looks like.

"What was your married name?" he asks.

"Odalshalski. It was a nightmare to spell and to tell people on the phone. Most people called Steve Dr. O," Sally explains with a chuckle.

"Now I have to figure out how to get back to Atlanta. I have work to do tomorrow," Wyatt says, sipping his tea and wishing he could stay in Sally's kitchen forever.

"You can catch the bus back tomorrow. I know there's a 2:00 one that leaves from Clayton and gets you back to Atlanta sometime late in the afternoon. I can give you a ride to Clayton. It's only 20 minutes."

"Thanks," Wyatt says. "I'll be happy to reimburse you for gas."

"No need, but thanks," Sally says, sipping her wine.

"Say, when I was in the house it seemed like there was someone else there. You think there might be squatters?" Wyatt asks. He doesn't really think that but he is struggling to make conversation.

Sally's eyebrows shoot up to her hairline. Squatters or vagrants in Crossroads are unknown.

"I don't think so. I've not seen anything amiss over there since Hugh died," she explains.

"Hmm. Probably just my imagination," Wyatt says.

"Are you hungry?" Sally asks, hardly daring to hope he might agree to eat dinner with her.

"Yeah, a bit. Is there any place to eat around here to eat, besides Bob's?" Wyatt asks.

"Well, there are six other places in town. The café near the train depot, which is good but always crowded on Saturday night. There's an S&S Cafeteria about 5 miles up the road, almost to the Walmart. The Citgo sells fried chicken although you wouldn't want to eat it. Kentucky Fried Chicken is near the Walmart. There's a Hardee's out on the highway, and Ike's Fish Camp."

"Fish camp?!" Wyatt asks, eyes twinkling.

"Oh yes. I know it sounds pretty... primitive, but it's really good. Lots of us go there on Saturday nights. For nine ninety-five you get fried catfish, hush puppies, coleslaw, corn on the cob, pinto beans, and apple or cherry cobbler. All you can eat."

Wyatt smiles, thinking how much his wife would not enjoy eating at Ike's. "Well let's go to Ike's, then. Sounds like a great place. Do they have beer?"

Sally chuckles. "No, they don't have a liquor license. Everyone takes their own, though."

Later that night, Sally curls up in her favorite armchair with a glass of wine and calls Marybeth to tell her all about the evening.

"He drank a lot of beer and ate a lot of catfish and we talked pretty much the entire evening."

"Get out! Did you eat anything, Stinky?" Marybeth says in a scolding tone.

"Well, yes. Yes I did, MOMMY DEAREST. I am not 22. I was not going to pick at a salad. I had two plates full, as a matter of fact, and then we split a dessert, peach cobbler. I am almost 50 years old. I have cellulite and wrinkles. Either he likes me as I am, or he doesn't."

There is a pause. Marybeth senses she has hit a nerve.

"Well, okay," Marybeth says, laughing. "I am just happy you are dating."

"He's married. I wouldn't call it a date, Buttface."

"Oh come ON. He wouldn't have asked you to dinner just for the food. He wants to get in your pants."

"Good Godalmighty I HATE that expression!" Sally harrumphs.

"I call them like I see them," Marybeth says smugly, nibbling on an Oreo. She doesn't usually use that type of expression but she knew it would irritate Sally.

"Look, you dated Ed and married him when you were, what, 22?"

"Yeah, so?" Marybeth says, cuddling Lulu on her lap.

"Well it's different when you aren't a kid any more. My purse wasn't stocked with breath mints or condoms. I didn't worry about my hair. It's just different."

"I was really just teasing you. Married – to me -- means unavailable," Marybeth says carefully.

Sally sighs.

"Yes, yes YES! He is married. That woman is one cold bitch, too. Are you channeling the spirit of my mother by any chance?"

"Oh come ON. You know there's no future with a married man, no matter what age he is."

"I know. I won't be sleeping with him, if that's what you're wondering. There's nothing wrong with two neighbor friends having dinner though. Nothing improper happened."

"Okay, but remember, you live in Northern Bumfuck. It will probably be all over town tomorrow that he was seen having dinner with you. Just get ready for it."

Sally frowns and picks at the cuticle on her index finger. Marybeth was right. Roberta Kingston, the old gossip, had seen them. It would be all over town. So be it.

"I don't care. They already gossip about me so what difference does it make?! I had a really fun evening – the first one of those in a long time. Hang on. I've got another call. Call you back." Sally disconnects the call with Marybeth and accepts a call from a 404 area code number.

Wyatt's voice fills her with disappointment. "Hey, Sally, listen, I talked to a friend and he's going to drive up here in the morning and pick me up, so don't worry about getting me to the bus, ok? Appreciate the offer, though."

"Sure, sure. I understand."

"Well, maybe next time I come up we can go eat catfish again. That sure was a fantastic meal. Don't know when I've enjoyed anything that much," Wyatt says, noting the disappointment in her voice.

"Yep, well, there's no fancy food around here but next time I will cook something for you. I like to cook. Have a safe trip," Sally says, trying to sound cheerful and breezy.

"Take care, Sally."

When the call ends, Sally just sits there, musing about Wyatt and their magical evening together. He had talked about some of his more interesting cases. She had talked about her love of history. As Sally has done all her life, she says to herself *Don't get excited. That was fun but he's a married man and so that was just a friendly dinner. Let it go, Cavanaugh.*

She looks at Blanche, asleep on the sofa beside her. "You are my one true love, furbaby."

Blanche snores softly, not even waking when Sally kisses her head and says goodnight.

Roberta is enjoying the fine soft night, as she sits in her bathrobe and slippers, sipping on her tea. She pushes the old porch swing by pushing the floor with her feet, pondering the sight of Wyatt with Sally Odalshalski earlier that evening at Ike's.

Sally had looked absurd, giggling and looking into Wyatt's face like he was the Lord God Almighty, like there was nobody else in the world. Roberta had nearly choked on her catfish filet as soon as she had caught sight of the two of them.

Scandalous and shameful – both of them.

They had been laughing and talking like a couple in love. The very air around them was electric. It was disgraceful. *Wyatt needs to remember those wedding vows*, Roberta thinks. *God sees all*, she adds.

Maybe he's going to get a divorce and marry that hussy. She ponders that for a moment, and stops swinging.

Roberta remembers her mama's teachings very well. *Jews are skinflints. Avoid them. Evangelicals are crazy. Never trust a Roman Catholic. They don't care about anything but their own kind. Steer clear of those folks. You can trust a Baptist, Methodist, Presbyterian – all good, solid Protestants. Not a Catholic. Not Episcopalians either – they are as bad as Catholics.*

Obviously Sally wasn't to be trusted. She should be ashamed of herself, out with a married man like that.

Roberta had heard that Dr. Odalshalski was a Roman Catholic but she was sure it wasn't true. She had never heard of him driving to mass, to the Catholic church in Clayton. He was a fine man. Such a gentleman. So compassionate.

Maybe they will have to sell that house, then. I will buy that place and find that treasure, she muses. She stops swinging when she hears the phone ring inside her house.

That will be Mavis, Roberta thinks. *Boy do I have a lot to tell her.*

Mavis lives across the street from Sally Odalshalski. Roberta never called her by her maiden name, Cavanaugh, even though Sally had changed it back after the divorce.

Wyatt Jamison should be ashamed of himself.

As Roberta heads back inside her house, to the phone, the thought occurs to her that Wyatt really needs to get divorced and sell his house in Crossroads.

CHAPTER 15

It's just after 9 the next day, Sunday morning, May 12. It's an overcast day and fog hangs over the mountains, creating a lovely effect, ghostly, but Wyatt doesn't even notice the beauty of the mountains. He's too intent on getting back to Atlanta.

Wyatt puts his bag in the back of his friend John's red Porsche Cayenne and shoves the house keys in his pocket.

Wyatt has wet hair from the shower, and he's wearing jeans and a white Polo shirt.

"Thanks for driving all the way up here to get me. I just need to get home," Wyatt says, getting in and buckling his seatbelt. "I didn't sleep much last night."

"Anything for you, buddy," John says casually. He has rarely ever seen Wyatt so unkempt and agitated. There are two cups of coffee in the car, and a selection of CDs in the player, including Creedence, Supertramp, Tom Petty, and the Rolling Stones.

"Thanks for bringing some decent coffee," Wyatt says, taking a sip. "I can't make anything but instant and it's crap."

"Sure," John says casually, wondering if Wyatt's marriage is over.

Fifteen minutes pass in silence, as John backs the car out and drives through town on the way to the interstate.

John wonders why Wyatt isn't whistling or humming, as usual.

Finally Wyatt sighs. "I just don't understand what happened yesterday with Sharon."

"Y'all had a fight. No big deal. Shitty of her to take the car, but it happens," John says casually.

"Not to us. We never fight. It's bizarre," Wyatt says thoughtfully.

There is silence for a few minutes.

"It's a pretty drive getting up here. Beautiful area, and a nice little town. The house is good, too," John says, having gone inside and looked around when he had arrived. "It may look retro but so what. It's obviously well cared for."

"Yeah, it's a sweet little house. Not big, not fancy, but solid. It was built before the Civil War, and it's been in my family ever since. Sharon hated it. Said she heard rats. You believe that?"

John shook his head. "I've heard everything. Sorry to get you up so early. Hate meeting clients on a Sunday afternoon but sometimes it can't be avoided."

"It's fine," Wyatt says. "Let's put on some tunes."

One hour and 40 minutes later, they have listened to a lot of music, discussed the Braves pitching lineup, the NASDAQ, and who put out the best album in 1982. The big Porsche SUV turns into the driveway of Wyatt's house in Atlanta. The elegant two story contemporary home with its manicured lawn appears serene in the late morning light.

John puts the car in park.

"Home again," Wyatt says distractedly, wondering what he will find and hoping it won't be too bad. He idly wonders when the lawn service will cut the lawn again, as it looks scraggly.

"Hey, I need to use the bathroom, okay?" John says, getting out.

"Sure," Wyatt answers, trying to ignore the feeling of dread in the pit of his stomach as he gets his bag out of the back of the car.

Both Jamison cars are in the garage, but there is a car parked in front of the house he doesn't recognize, a white BMW.

Wyatt and John go in the house through the garage. John heads off to the guest bath on the first floor, and Wyatt goes into the foyer, and cocks his head to listen. He hears a faint noise he can't identify.

After taking a deep breath, he climbs the graceful curving stairway to the second floor and turns right, walking to the end of the hall and the master bedroom. Seeing that the bedroom door is half open, he pauses a few feet away. He hears a slapping sound, and labored breathing, then Sharon's voice, low and guttural.

"HARDER!"

Wyatt very quietly steps close enough to see around the door, and he looks towards the king-sized bed. It's normally covered with a lot of pillows but at the moment it's a tangled mess, and there are clothes on the floor. Wyatt hears house music on the stereo.

None of that captures his attention for long, though. His wife is on the bed on all fours, naked, a large heavyset white man behind her, holding her hair while he roughly rams her.

"Oh baby!" the man grunts. Wyatt grimaces at the sight of the man's large and flabby white buttocks.

Wyatt steps into the doorway and just stands there, watching them for a moment, transfixed with disgust and horror.

Sharon and her lover both collapse on the bed panting.

Wyatt feels the morning coffee roiling in his stomach and tries to ignore how he feels about this sordid scene.

Sharon reaches for a glass of water on the bedside table and glances towards the doorway. She sees Wyatt and screams, and grabs the sheet to cover herself. The man, startled, turns and looks at Wyatt, fear in his eyes, as he scrambles to grab his clothes.

"Hello, Henry," Wyatt says, recognizing the man as Dr. Henry Wallace, a doctor in his wife's office.

"Huh – uh -- hi, Wyatt," Henry stutters. "Thought you were in the mountains."

"Obviously."

Sharon jumps out of bed and grabs a blue silk bathrobe. "Did you enjoy the peep show?!" she snarls, trying to sound tough as she ties the belt of her robe.

John has come upstairs now and he stands beside Wyatt. "I heard a scream. Is everything –" John starts to say, but at the sight of Sharon and Henry he stops.

There is an awkward pause as everyone stares at everyone else.

"Never thought I'd see you cheating on my friend, Sharon. What a shitty thing to do," John says with mock sadness.

"Shut up John. You know nothing," Sharon snaps. She turns to looks at Wyatt. "So now you know."

Wyatt just stares at her in disgust, then says quietly. "How long has this been going on?"

"Henry and I have been together for three years," she says defiantly. "We're in love."

Wyatt shakes his head. "I'm leaving then. You obviously don't want to be married."

Sharon's face contorts into a grimace. "Who gives a shit! You are NEVER HERE!" Sharon bellows, furious at how

Wyatt calmly heads into the walk-in closet, takes a suitcase off the shelf, and begins throwing his clothes into it.

"John, I think there are a couple of empty boxes in the garage. Would you go grab those for me?" Wyatt says evenly.

"Sure thing, buddy."

Wyatt stands in the garage of his house fifteen minutes later, happy that his golf clubs and most of his fishing gear fit in his car and John's car. He had emptied his dresser contents, taken his clothes from the closet, and grabbed a few mementoes out of the family room.

As Wyatt stares at the garage, which holds nothing now except Sharon's car and a few plastic storage boxes of old clothes and knickknacks, Wyatt thinks back to his parents' garage. There was an old fridge always stocked with cold beer and often styrofoam cups of long pink nightcrawlers for fishing. His father had a workbench where he did woodworking, and there were tools, a lawn mower, baseball equipment, water skis, an old radio for listening to the ballgames – so much stuff. Wendell Jamison had made his garage his haven, where he worked on projects, and whenever he had anything important to say to Wyatt they sat out there in folding chairs. It was Wendell's escape from his wife, and the clutter reflected a busy man who loved to work with his hands, despite also being an academic at a prestigious college.

Wyatt's garage is sterile and spotless. Wyatt shakes his head as he takes a last look.

My life is so clean and safe, and empty, he thinks.

John has offered the use of his guest room until Wyatt can find his own place. Wyatt starts walking out of the garage, and hears the door into the house open and close.

Sharon comes out to stands in the driveway, still in her robe. "So you're really just retreating, you pussy?!"

"Yep. There's no reason to stay," Wyatt says evenly, turning to face her. "I never thought you, of all people, would do something like this." He walks towards his car.

"What did you expect? Thirty years and you would rather WORK or PLAY GOLF or go FISHING than spend time with me."

Wyatt stops at the door of his car and looks at her, amazed that she can be so accusatory.

"You were committing adultery. I did nothing wrong except work hard."

"You were a COLD BASTARD!" Sharon hisses.

Wyatt stares at her and wonders how he could have ever loved her. Quietly, he says, "If you wanted out, you should have come and talked to me, not screwed your boss behind my back. You'll be hearing from my lawyer." Wyatt gets in the car and slams the door, something he never does. He smiles at Sharon, then rolls down his car window and sticks his head out to call loudly.

"You're naked under that robe and the way the sun is shining, the neighbors are seeing everything! Bye!"

Wyatt enjoys the look of horror on Sharon's face as he backs out of the driveway.

Half an hour later, Wyatt and John are standing on the back patio of John's house, having unloaded the car and put Wyatt's things in the guest room.

John looks closely at his friend as he hands him a glass of bourbon. "What was that you yelled at Sharon right before you left? I heard you two screaming two blocks away."

Wyatt grins. "I hollered and said you're naked under that robe and the way the sun is shining, the neighbors are seeing everything!"

John laughs.

"I'm glad you said that. You were amazingly calm, my friend. Proud of you."

Wyatt takes a long sip of the bourbon. He doesn't like bourbon. He just feels like he should drink it.

"I was putting up a front. I've known for a long time things weren't right between us, but I had no idea about Henry."

"Don't feel bad. Spouses often don't pick up on it when there's cheating," John lies. Spouses usually know when there's cheating, he thinks. He doesn't want Wyatt to feel worse, though.

Wyatt knows John is lying but he ignores it.

"I got a feeling last night she was hiding something... BUT GODDAMN HER! CHEATING LITTLE BITCH!!"

John's eyebrows shoot up. He has never seen Wyatt get really angry. He is known for being cool and calm at all times, something his clients value.

Wyatt hands John his drink, which slops over the edge, and he grabs a rake that is leaning against the house. He walks over to the manicured lawn. He makes a guttural sound in the back of his throat and starts beating the rake on the ground.

John just shakes his head. In all his years of handling divorces, he has seen everything. He's glad Wyatt didn't lose it in front of Sharon.

Finally, Wyatt stops and looks at John, breathing heavily. "My parents used to have screaming fights all the time, real knock-down-drag-outs and man, I hated hearing them go at each other. I vowed I would never do that. Ever. And I didn't."

"Nothing wrong with trying to have a peaceful home."

Wyatt drops into a chair and puts his face in his hands. "I should have been home more, though. I should have gone along with all the silly crap she likes to do, the meals out, the museums, the vacations. It just felt like I spent so much time working, when I had time to myself I wanted to do what I wanted to do, you know?"

John shakes his head as he settles into the other lounge chair. "I do know. It's not easy. You don't want to let down your clients. You don't want to not make payroll. You get caught up in the gamesmanship, too, in wanting to win. You always operate in crisis mode. At home you just want to be left alone."

The two men sit in silence for a while, staring at the lawn and the fire pit.

"Yeah, but I was a blind fool. Shit," Wyatt says. John has rarely ever heard him curse.

John clears his throat and looks at Wyatt. "We've never really talked about it, but I know you... know things a lot of times. You knew about the missing records in the Parker case. You knew that witness in the Washington case was lying. So how did you not know about Sharon's affair?"

Wyatt looks at the fire pit, frowning as he rakes his hands through his hair. "My... intuitions aren't infallible. With people I am really close to they don't work at all, sometimes. Sharon has always been completely closed off to me, somehow, and maybe that's what attracted me to her, the mystery of her. Most women are easy for me to read. Not her."

"So that's why you decided to go into private practice instead of working for the FBI?" John said with a faint smile.

"Something like that."

"Wyatt, I am your best friend, and I have to tell you, Sharon is extremely smart and she never backs down from a fight. That's just a fact. You need to be very careful until the dust settles on this divorce," John says, then takes a deep swig of his drink.

The two men sit down on patio chairs and sit in silence for a full five minutes. Wyatt's mind is racing. He closes his eyes and takes deep breaths. Finally, he opens them.

"I never thought I would hear myself saying this, but how quickly can you get me out of the marriage?" Wyatt asks. He is thinking about his evening with Sally, and how different she is from Sharon.

John sighs heavily. He always hates this question. "It all depends on how much arguing y'all do about who gets what. I find in cases like yours, it's usually good to bring in an accountant to get a clear picture of the financial situation. My guy Terry Kellerman can do an audit. That can take some time."

"Okay, but are we talking months or years?" Wyatt persists, trying not to sound whiny.

"I don't know," is John's honest answer.

The two men sit in silence, hearing only the sounds of the neighborhood; the drone of a lawn mower, a faint chatter from next door, a car going down the street, the sound of crickets.

Wyatt shifts in his seat and looks at John.

"There is a bright spot. I met a woman in the mountains. Her house is next door to my uncle's house. She's beautiful, and funny, and we ate dinner together last night."

John stares at Wyatt. "In all the years I've known you, I've never heard you say anything like that, buddy."

"Well, I'm being honest here. I really like her. Her name is Sally. I met her long ago, when we were kids. Funny story – she was about 13 and I was 15. My grandfather had died and I was up there for the funeral, sitting in the backyard of the house, studying for a Chemistry final, and Sally started twirling a baton and accidentally lost her balance and it flew over and bonked me in the head," Wyatt recounted, chuckling at the memory.

"No shit?"

"No shit. We had a good laugh about it last night. I think all those years ago she developed an adolescent crush on me, but I didn't know it. I sense it's something she held onto for a long time, though, which is sort of flattering. What she saw in gawky 15 year old nerdy me, I'll never know."

"Hmmm," John says lamely, not sure how to respond.

Wyatt looks at his friend intently. "I need to see her again. She's completely the opposite of Sharon. I can read her, but I like what I sense. I feel really relaxed with Sally, like I'm in the right place. I guess getting older means I value clarity over mystery."

John frowns. "OK, as your friend, I'll say GO for it. Your marriage is over."

"Thanks. And you know –"

John holds up his hand. "HOWEVER, as your attorney, though, I have to caution you. Be very careful. Sharon will give you hell about this woman if she gets wind of it. Right now you have an advantage. You caught her cheating, and she doesn't like that."

The two men sit in silence for a long minute. Wyatt looks thoughtful.

"I know you're trying to look out for me. I need to go back up there, though, and plan my uncle's funeral, and figure out what to do about the house. Funny thing is, I was really thinking just yesterday what a great place it would be to retire to – small town in the mountains, house is paid for, get out of the rat race of Atlanta."

"Go for it, buddy. You settled the big case, so maybe you can live modestly, kick back more. Do more fishing. Just do it. Just be careful, though."

Wyatt smiles. *This day may not be a total nightmare after all*, he thinks.

CHAPTER 16

The following Tuesday morning, Marybeth calls her friend Sally, knowing she doesn't go in to work until noon. Sally doesn't pick up. Marybeth tries again 30 minutes later. The old wall phone in the kitchen rings and rings. Sally has a cell phone but rarely uses it because of the poor reception in the mountains.

Pick UP, Sally! Marybeth thinks, picturing the liver-colored old phone in the kitchen with the twenty foot cord.

Finally, Sally answers the kitchen phone. "Only you would call me at 8:45 in the morning, Buttface. Who the fuck is dead?"

"Language! Have you had your coffee, Stinky?!" Marybeth demands.

"Drinking it now. Just walked Blanche, all over the place. We're both exhausted. Blanche said she wants a cup of coffee."

Marybeth laughs.

Sally pops a piece of whole wheat bread in the toaster, then sits down at the kitchen table and flips through yesterday's mail. "Talk to me."

"Look, I know you think here in Atlanta nobody knows anybody's business but girl, the medical community is a different story. Ed heard that Wyatt has moved out of his house because he caught his wife cheating with one of the doctors she works for!"

"Good GODALMIGHTY! Why didn't you call me sooner?!" Sally hollers, nearly spitting out her coffee.

"Good LORD. Chill. I didn't find out until 8:30 this morning when Ed was eating his cereal and he just casually mentioned it. Looks like old Wyatt will be on the market again SOON. His best friend is a high-powered divorce lawyer named John something or other."

Sally remembers Wyatt the way he looked the other night, and wonders how it would feel for him to kiss her. She stands up and checks her toast.

"You know any juicy details?" she demands, winding the cord around her hand while she paces the kitchen.

"No, just that Wyatt caught them literally screwing in the bed, doggy style, which is really gross," Marybeth says, rubbing Lulu's tummy and sipping her tea.

"That is gross. However, Wyatt is such a sweet guy, he may take her back," Sally remarks reluctantly, pouring a cup of Special K cereal in a bowl.

"Let's hope not. Rumor has it she has been screwing her boss for a while," Marybeth says as she eyes the dirty dishes in the kitchen sink.

"Well, they were up here Saturday night and even in my house with the door shut I heard her screaming at him, in the yard. I got the feeling there was something weird going on. She took the car and left. You don't just leave your husband in the mountains, two hours from home, because you think you heard a rat in the house."

"Maybe your dinner the other day was the start of something," Marybeth says brightly, remembering Sally's excited email, sent right after the date.

Sally pours the milk on her cereal and gets a spoon out of the drawer. "Maybe. But I've been divorced and so I know this: even under the best of circumstances, when you are going through a divorce, you are not fit to date anyone. Plus, the lawyers always advise against it."

Marybeth ponders that. "You can at least give him an understanding shoulder to cry on. That's something."

"Yep, it is, but he doesn't strike me as the type of guy who will be crying. He's really calm and quiet."

"Well that's good. He's the opposite of you, Stinky."

"Ha! I am as cool as a cucumber. I gotta get ready for work. Thanks for calling me, Buttface."

"Love ya. Mean it."

"You too."

Sally hangs up the phone and sits at her kitchen table with the spoon in her hand for a minute, picturing Wyatt, then sighs, as she hears the toaster ding indicating her toast is ready.

Her mother Barbara's voice is in her head, as always. *"You got divorced, going against everything the church teaches, and now you're going after a married man. A Protestant man. Have you lost your mind? What are you doing?"*

Sally shakes her head and eyes the dirty dishes in the sink, and thinks of her usual remedy for unsolvable problems: staying busy.

CHAPTER 17

I watched that wife of my nephew act like a witch and realized something: she is evil. She is not a normal person. Her soul is as black as coal. That must be why Wyatt cannot read her.

I decide to pay her a little visit. Amazing how fast I can get there. The rooftops and treetops are so easy to navigate now.

It's late at night and she is awake and watching television. I swoop in through the window that shows light.

Her lover snores beside her. A gross man, corpulent and repulsive. What a wastrel.

Sharon looks old, without any makeup on. You can see the web of lines around her eyes, and her thin lips. Her roots are showing some grey, too.

I have never loathed anyone so much. (Obviously, ghosts are not always filled with angelic thoughts.)

I decide to have some fun.

I concentrate on the power of the television, and the picture starts to falter, and becomes distorted. With a pop, it goes out.

Good.

Sharon looks annoyed, and keeps jabbing at the remote with her blood-red talon fingernails.

I go over to the bed and sit beside her. She shivers.

There is a photo of her and Wyatt on their wedding day in a silver frame, atop the dresser that had been Wyatt's, so I decide to topple it. I focus on it with all my energy, and it tumbles over and lands on the carpet but doesn't break.

Sharon looks startled. Her eyes grow huge. She looks around.

I head over to the curtains and they blow outward, hard, as though a storm has blown through – but the windows are closed.

Now she looks terrified.

Good.

I walk over and wrap my cold arms around her, and she shivers uncontrollably. I concentrate my energy to bounce down hard on the bed and she feels the mattress give way.

With a shriek, she jumps up and runs into the bathroom and slams the door.

I sit on the bed laughing.

This ghost thing can be fun.

CHAPTER 18

Andrea likes poking around the back yard of the little house because she keeps finding interesting things. The fact that the high brick wall completely shields her from view is a blessing. Andrea can get fresh air and not worry about being detected.

The yard is a curious place.

For instance, there are numerous places where holes have been dug, then the dirt filled in again. Andrea ponders this and decides the old man that lived in the house before was probably thinking the key to the old trunk had been buried somewhere in the yard.

While in the yard, over time, she finds an old bottle that looks like it contained liquor, plus what looks like an old pot handle, a wooden clothespin grimed with dirt, and what appear to be the bones of a dead animal.

Andrea realizes after making her third discovery that she needs to be organized about her search. After finding a legal pad on the old rolltop desk, she sits outside one afternoon and meticulously draws a map of the backyard. She carefully draws grid lines, marking the grid with x's, to indicate the location of everywhere she has found something, and what it is.

Andrea also looks through all the old papers and books on and around the old rolltop desk in the biggest bedroom. Lots of stuff about history, bills for the house, a few business letters but no computer, and nothing personal. She thinks that is weird, a history professor without a computer.

Then again, anyone over thirty is a mystery to her.

Andrea spends most of her days sleeping, and most nights awake and watching TV. After the second week the entire stash of pot is gone.

Andrea doesn't care. For the first time in her life she isn't stressed about school, or worried wondering if her mother will be bringing home a new creepy boyfriend that might try something with her. There is literally no stress in the little house on Honeysuckle Road, except keeping out of sight and eating the food carefully, so it will last.

The second week, she starts reading the history books the old man had left in the house. They are not all that interesting except one, an archaeology textbook. That one is fascinating.

On a warm Saturday in May, two weeks after the screaming rat incident, Andrea awakens at 5:36 p.m. There is a tall man standing over the bed looking at her. He has light brown hair and wears jeans and a white Polo shirt.

It's the guy who came in that weekend a while back, she thinks. He looks confused, but not mean.

Shit, had a good thing going and now it's done, she thinks. *SHIT SHIT SHIT.*

Wyatt regards the sleepy teenager in the single bed. "What are you doing here?" He can't get a sense about her, at first. She obviously wants to look tough, but she doesn't.

Andrea sighs, and rubs her nose, which is threatening to drip. "I needed a place to stay, so I decided to crash here for a while. Nobody was living here. I didn't hurt anything. Just ate some food, which nobody was eating anyway. I'll go."

She throws off the faded green polyester bedspread and stands up, fully dressed in shorts and a ragged tee shirt with a sweatshirt over it.

"Wait a minute. How did you get in?" Wyatt asks.

Andrea debates about whether to lie. "You came here a few weeks ago and I slipped in when you opened the door," Andrea grumbles. "Please don't call the cops. I'm leaving."

She takes her backpack out from under the other single bed and starts filling it with her few possessions.

Wyatt sits on the edge of the other bed, acutely aware of how small and skinny she is, how forlorn and lost, despite the badass haircut and pierced nose. "Hold on a minute. Let's talk."

Andrea stops what she is doing and regards him warily. "About what?"

"What's your name?"

"Lady Gaga," Andrea replies flippantly.

"Try again."

"Why do you care?" Andrea says, annoyed.

"You're in my house. I would like to know. So what is your name?" Wyatt says calmly.

"Andrea Hawkins."

"Thank you. Were you here when my wife was here recently? Did you hear her screaming?" Wyatt asks, watching her face closely.

Andrea tries not to smile. "Yeah."

"It was you she heard, wasn't it? She thought you were a rat," he says, smiling.

Andrea chuckles. "Yeah. I don't know why she jumped to that conclusion. I don't think she liked it here. I think she just wanted to leave."

Wyatt nods, thinking *she is pretty astute for a kid. I was thinking she was a ghost.* "Why do you think that?"

She doesn't answer, but cuts her eyes to the closet.

"This has something to do with that closet, right?" Wyatt says.

Andrea still doesn't answer, but stares at the green shag carpet on the floor.

Wyatt gets up and opens the door and pushes aside the old clothes. He sees, at the side, the small open door, which he pushes open. He steps into the closet then turns around and looks at Andrea. "There's a hidden cellar down there?"

Andrea shrugs. "Yeah. Nothing interesting down there, though. Just junk."

Wyatt knows she is lying.

He peers down, regarding the old wooden stairs leading down to darkness.

"How do you see down there?"

Andrea sighs and gets up. She pushes past Wyatt and heads quickly down the stairs, holding a small flashlight, then lights the Coleman lantern in the small space. The lightbulb hanging on a chain had burned out. Wyatt peers down and surveys the room, and sees the old trunk. It looks massive, rusted and dusty, but sturdy enough.

"What's in there?"

Andrea lifts the lantern higher, showing him the trunk. "I don't know. It's locked."

Wyatt tries to open it. The ornate old-fashioned lid doesn't budge.

Wyatt realizes the trunk is a mystery Andrea wants to solve. *You've been searching for the key, hoping it contains a treasure*, Wyatt realizes, sighing. "Okay. Come on up and let's talk about it."

Half an hour later they sit at the kitchen table, finishing up two chicken club sub sandwiches Wyatt brought with him.

Andrea has relayed everything she can about the trunk, her search for the key, and how she has evaded being found. It took all of three minutes.

"You are how old?" Wyatt asks, gazing at her with his best lawyer interrogation face.

"Eighteen," Andrea lies. Wyatt knows she is lying.

"Try again."

She just stares at the floor.

"I'm a trial lawyer. I know when someone is lying. If you and I are going to be friends, to trust each other, you need to tell me the truth."

"Why would we be friends?"

"Well, as a friend, I wouldn't have you arrested for trespassing," Wyatt says evenly.

Andrea ponders this for a moment, wrapping a piece of hair around her finger. Finally, she blows her nose on a paper Subway napkin and looks at him defiantly.

"I'm seventeen, ok?"

There is a silence, while Wyatt thinks.

"Where are you from?" Wyatt asks.

"Ringgold," Andrea answers in a bored voice.

"Don't you think your mother is worried about you?" Wyatt asks.

Andrea shrugs. "I doubt it. She works a lot, or parties with her boyfriend. She doesn't care what I do."

Wyatt senses this is true, unfortunately.

"When you left Ringgold what was your plan?"

"I was going to go to Atlanta. I have friends there," Andrea says.

A partial lie, Wyatt thinks, but decides not to press.

Andrea's clothes are clean but threadbare. She hunches over in a posture of wariness, looking up at him. She wears two shirts, even though it's warm outside, and her arms are crossed over her chest. *This kid has been abused, but she had nowhere to go. That's why she has stayed here,* he thinks.

Andrea is clearly smart, and he doesn't want to just kick her out of the house but he isn't sure what to do.

A knock sounds at the door. Before he can blink, Andrea has grabbed her backpack and gotten into the utility closet off the kitchen and closed the door.

Shaking his head, Wyatt goes to the front door. It's Sally. She wears a blue cotton dress and white sandals, and blonde highlights gleam in her hair in the setting sun.

"Hey there. Saw your car and thought I'd walk over and say Hi," Sally says with a smile.

She knows about the divorce, Wyatt thinks.

"Good to see you again," Wyatt replies, smiling.

Sally hands him a dish wrapped in foil. "Just made a coffee cake. Thought you'd like some."

"I would, very much. I love cake," Wyatt answers with a smile. He quickly makes a decision. "Hang on just a second, I'll be right back."

Two minutes later, Wyatt, Sally and Andrea are sitting at the kitchen table eating warm coffee cake.

Wyatt had introduced Andrea and Sally, hoping Sally would not be shocked. If she was, she hid it well.

"I've never eaten anything this good," Andrea says with her mouth full of warm cake, cinnamon, and pecans.

Wyatt and Sally exchange glances.

"Where did you grow up, Andrea?" Sally asks with kindness in her voice. "You can finish chewing before you answer."

Wyatt tries not to chuckle.

Andrea chews and swallows. "My mama and me live in a trailer in Ringgold, you know, up near the border with Tennessee. She works at the truck stop off I-75."

"And your father?" Sally asks.

Andrea shrugs. "Never knew him."

"OK. How long have you been in this house?"

Andrea tenses, really wary now. "A few weeks. Not long. Didn't bother anything. I'll be leaving now."

"Where will you go?" Wyatt interrupts.

"Atlanta?" Andrea said softly, her tough manner betrayed by the obvious fear in the way she said the word. Atlanta was a huge city, a scary place to a child who had never been out of the small towns of North Georgia.

"Well, why don't you let us talk for a few minutes, okay? Head on out to the back yard while Sally and I chat," Wyatt says, smiling.

Andrea hesitates, but Sally's blue eyes are warm, not cold and hard, and with a belly full of cake, Andrea reluctantly nods and walks out the slider to the yard, where she sits on the bench of the old picnic table.

Sally sits back and sighs. "OK, well, that's quite something. She's not stupid, just a bit lost. She might really complicate your life, though, if your wife finds out she's here. What are you going to do?"

Wyatt wipes cake crumbs off his mouth and looks at Andrea's hunched back. "Well, obviously I can't let her stay here. She's a minor. I'm going through a divorce. No good would come of it. I was wondering, though, if you would consider being her foster mom?"

Sally's eyebrows shoot up. "What? Why would I do that?" she blurts out.

"We talked a bit before you got here. She has nowhere else to go. Didn't you tell me when we had dinner that you had considered fostering a child?"

"Well yes, years ago I did, but I wasn't thinking about a teenager."

"I'm a pretty good judge of folks. I think she's basically a good kid," Wyatt says evenly. "I've been a lawyer a long time."

Sally ponders the thought of a teenage girl in the house again, and the possible drama, but then decides this waif will be very different from her daughter. "How old is she?"

"I don't know. Seventeen, I think. That's what she said."

"Why not just take her back to a relative's house, or turn her over to Child Protective Services?"

Wyatt ponders this for a moment. "I hate to see her get lost in the system. She's a smart kid, and she needs help. Besides, I have a feeling she can be a big help in discovering whatever it was Hugh was looking for, what caused him to build a wall around that yard. She showed me a trunk a little while ago, in an old cellar I didn't know was here."

Sally thinks for a moment. "Maybe she could be an emancipated minor. A friend of my daughter's did that. Why don't we go over to my house and Google that, see if she would like to pursue that?"

"Sounds like a plan."

Two hours later, they are at the kitchen table in Sally's house, laptop in front of Wyatt, and they have agreed the best plan is to simply keep Andrea out of sight until her 18th birthday, only weeks away. In the meantime, she will stay with Sally, and do some housekeeping.

Sally had defrosted a pan of lasagna earlier in the day, and after it heats, they all have some. Wyatt has never had homemade lasagna. "Wow," is all he can say, between blissful mouthfuls.

Wyatt is pleased about the plans regarding Andrea, but cautions Andrea about being careful, staying out of sight until her birthday.

Andrea agrees. "I want to see what's in the trunk, don't you?" she says to Wyatt, trying not to sound eager.

Sally remembers Wyatt had mentioned that. "Me too. I am dying of curiosity."

Wyatt looks at Andrea, unwilling to tell her there is nothing interesting in the trunk. Sally looks at Wyatt and senses he doesn't think much of the trunk.

"The trunk may not be that interesting, you know," Sally says, looking at Andrea. "I have given this some thought," Sally says. "I think what Hugh was doing was trying to see if there was a tunnel under the yard where perhaps something was buried. You noticed all the bare patches of dirt out there?"

Andrea nods eagerly. "Yes, I noticed. There's also a pick and a shovel layin' in some tall weeds. I've done some digging out there, but didn't find much of anything."

Wyatt frowns. "Why would Hugh dig up the yard looking for treasure? Did he not know about the trunk? He was eccentric but not crazy."

"Maybe he thought there was a tunnel leading into the old cellar, and it came out someplace in the yard, at one time?" Andrea offered.

Sally clears her throat. She loves to discuss local history. "Years ago there was a rumor that two Civil War soldiers hid a treasure somewhere around here, gold and valuables stolen from farms and plantations when Sherman came through."

Andrea's face is blank as she asks "Sherman who?"

Wyatt and Sally exchange a look. Wyatt says "General William Tecumseh Sherman, a general in the Union Army during the Civil War. He came through Georgia and his men looted farms and homes, stealing valuables and killing livestock. He was a terrible man."

Andrea gets a funny look on her face. "I went through some of the papers on the desk. There is a note in there that says something about a treasure. Want me to go get it?"

Wyatt, startled, looks at Sally, who shrugs. "Sure. Just come on back asap," Wyatt says. As soon as she has left he looks at Sally. "Are you serious?"

Sally frowns at his skeptical tone. "Well, yes. It's an old rumor. I've had time to think about it. Hugh came into the library one day right after he moved back here, and asked me for books on Sherman, and he spent a lot of time reading about Sherman. Then another time, he asked me if I knew anything about a legend of two of Sherman's soldiers coming to live here in town, hiding out. Well, I didn't know anything about it, but I asked Mama, and she knew of it through my grandmother. The old rumor was that two of Sherman's soldiers came here, buried a treasure somewhere, stuff they had stolen from plantations. Then they became town residents. Nobody could prove it, though. Strangers were coming in and out all the time, since the trains came through, and the town was literally a crossroads, hence the name."

Andrea came back in the door, then, and hands Wyatt the yellowed piece of paper. He reads aloud:

Hugh -

You remember the old trunk in the root cellar? You need to figure out how to open it, and see what's in there. Rumor has it, theres some kind of a treasure. Sounds like a fairy tale to me. I've never seen that old trunk opened.

I am too old and feeble to go up and down the old steps and I am pretty soon going to meet The Lord. You have always been a smart boy, and you love history, so I leave the solving of this mystery to you.

Love,

Dad

There is a silence for a moment as Wyatt and Sally ponder the letter. Sally motions for Wyatt to hand it to her and he does. She takes out her reading glasses from her pocket and reads the note carefully.

Andrea rubs Blanche's belly. Blanche already adores her.

"Well, it sounds like you just need someone to pick the lock so you can see what's in there," Sally says evenly. "Hang on."

She gets up and goes back to her room, appearing a few minutes later with a wire coat hanger and a bobby pin.

Wyatt and Andrea both stare blankly at her.

"Y'all don't know the tricks?! My mama always could pick a lock with one of these," Sally says grinning. "Come on."

"I already tried picking that lock, but knock yourself out," Andrea mumbles.

They all go next door, after getting another Coleman lantern from Sally's carriage house.

Wyatt and Sally carefully descend the stairs. The three stare at the old trunk in awe. It is a rough wooden trunk, not fine, but encircled with steel bands. The lock looks easy to pick. Sally kneels in front of the trunk and works at it with the bobby pin. Nothing. She then takes the wire coat hanger, untwists it, and tries that. Still nothing. Andrea tries both. Nothing.

Wyatt ponders breaking the old lock.

They decide against it. Wyatt isn't sure he has the strength to break it, nor does he have any tools.

Finally, they all ascend the stairs and go back in the living room of Wyatt's house.

"I'm sorry, Wyatt. I thought for sure I could pick that lock," Sally says.

"No big deal," Wyatt replies, stretching. "Listen, I need to get some sleep. The memorial service for my uncle is tomorrow at 1:30, at the church."

"Want some company at the service?" Sally asks. *Oh my God I just invited myself to a funeral! What the hell is wrong with me!* she thinks.

"Sure. I don't know who will be there. He was such a hermit. Still, it's the thing to do," Wyatt says.

"He was a nice man, your uncle," Sally says. "Very quiet, but really nice. Always polite and sweet when we spoke." She can hear her mother's voice in her head saying *we don't go to Protestant funerals. Hush, Mama, she thinks.*

"Thanks. I will come over and get you about 1 o'clock, okay?"

"Why don't you come over at 11:30 and I will fix us some brunch?" Sally asks, mentally reviewing the contents of her pantry.

"Sounds like a plan."

As soon as they get back to Sally's house, Sally and Andrea walk into the family room and Andrea looks around. Her eyes search the table tops and corners. She looks in the kitchen, too. Sally watches her, half amused. Finally, Andrea asks shyly, "Where is your TV?"

Sally smiles. "I don't have one. I prefer to read, or be on the computer, or listen to music."

Andrea's face registers shock. "Really?!"

"Really. Let's head upstairs. "

"OK."

As soon as they get upstairs, Sally says "Look, I'm tired, and I bet you've had a long day, too. You're in the pink bedroom right there on the right. It was my daughter's room. She left some books you might like. I put clean towels in the hall bathroom. That's my room, just down the hall. You can holler if you need anything, okay?"

Andrea nods. "I am pretty tired."

"I understand. Good night," Sally says.

"Night," Andrea says, and watches Sally walk down the hall. "Sally?" Andrea calls, running over to Sally, who turns to face her.

"Um… I just wanted to say thank you for letting me stay here. It's really nice of you. I promise, I will be a big help."

Sally smiles. "You're a good girl, honey, that's obvious. I'm glad to have you here. Good night."

"Night," Andrea says, almost wanting to hug Sally. She decides against it and turns and heads back to the bedroom.

A few minutes later Blanche lumbers into the room, tail wagging. Andrea rubs her head.

Andrea pushes the door open to the daughter's bedroom and goes in, her eyes wide. Andrea has never seen white furniture, pink drapes, a frilly pink and white bedspread, and a pale pink area rug. *The room looks like something out of a magazine.*

Andrea decides to search the pink and white bedroom, just in case its former occupant left a small TV. She didn't. There is a small white bookshelf and lots of titles, novels a young girl might like.

I think I will like it here, she thinks sleepily, as she peels off her pants and sweatshirt, and gingerly gets into the bed.

She has no idea she is being watched.

I love to enter rooms and look at sleeping people. They look so angelic. Andrea sleeps the deep sleep of a child, Blanche on the bed beside her.

I look around the room, approving the girlish loveliness.

Sometimes I regret not marrying and having children, but my work was all-consuming. Also, the shyness was crippling, and to be honest, most women didn't find me attractive, so it was easier to concentrate on work.

I am so happy Andrea is being cared for properly. She needs that.

I drift into Sally's room and see her standing in front of her closet, frowning at her clothes. I wish I could reassure her and tell her she is still a lovely woman, despite a little extra weight. She looks younger than her years, unlike some older women who are stick-thin and stringy.

Sally regards her clothes, pushing aside coat hangers and frowning.

Finally, Sally closes the closet door and sits down in a well-worn flowered chintz chair by the window, after taking a rosary out of her jewelry box. She fingers the beads and her lips move in silent prayer.

How fascinating. She doesn't go to mass any more, but she still believes. Beautiful.

CHAPTER 19

Early Sunday morning, Sally awakens and allows herself for a moment to relax. She lounges in her bed for a minute, listening to the crickets, feeling the stirring of the world, watching her windows, as the black night turns to ashy gray, then watery early sunlight.

As she watches, she thinks about the amazing events of the past few weeks. Here she is, nearly fifty years old, and she is feeling excited about a man. It has been such a long time since she has cared about anything but slogging through daily life.

First, the divorce had turned her from a part-time librarian and full-time wife and mom -- the kind that attended every PTA meeting and hauled her daughter to piano lessons and soccer practice and made gourmet dinners -- to a different person. She had thought the divorce would be liberating, but it wasn't, really. She no longer had to do all the heavy lifting of trying to keep the marriage going, but she became a woman who worried constantly.

Financially, she was fine. Her mother's failing memory, however, made life tricky.

Barbara Cavanaugh's Alzheimers came on quickly. She had always been an avid crossword puzzle solver, an avid reader, and a crochet enthusiast, but the disease took all that away. One day Sally found her sitting outside a neighbor's house, dazed, not knowing her own house was 4 doors down.

Once a robust eater and enthusiastic cook, Barbara became a thin little woman who couldn't remember how to boil an egg, and ate with her hands. Sally had hated seeing it, but she felt like she could handle her mother and still work part-time, until she couldn't, one day.

Trying to handle her mother, plus work, plus shuttle Miranda back and forth to piano lessons and cheerleading practice and church youth group – it was exhausting. There were not enough hours in the day.

Finally, after Barbara wandered away from the house and was found walking down the street wearing only a bra and panties, it was time to admit defeat.

For the next year, Sally visited her mother every day in the nursing home, and make sure she was cared for properly. That was a 25 minute drive each way. Some days her daughter would go, but Miranda had graduated by then and moved to Atlanta. She preferred to stay in Atlanta and "party" – a verb Sally hated.

Sally's periods stopped, then started back again, which was weird. Weeks of heavy menstrual-type bleeding, and a scary diagnosis of stage 1 uterine cancer for Sally resulted in a hysterectomy. While she was recuperating, Barbara died.

The past 5 years since then had been so difficult that sometimes Sally had wondered if the hollowness she felt as she slogged through each day would ever get better, if she would ever feel normal again. Calls with Marybeth had helped. Seeing her daughter married and happy had helped.

However, until Wyatt Jamison had reappeared in Crossroads, Sally had not felt whole again.

Now there were things to look forward to, like the funeral. *That is so weird*, she thought, as she got up and headed to the bathroom. I am looking forward to my neighbor's funeral.

After Sally takes a quick shower, she throws on jeans and a tee shirt, and goes downstairs. After starting the coffee, she quickly straightens and dusts the family room. Then she dusts off the table on the screened-in back porch. She sets out orange juice, and tomato juice, then gets out the eggs and bread. She wipes out her cast iron skillet and starts the bacon in it.

A short time later, Sally sits at her table on the back porch and looks at Andrea and Wyatt, and her heart sings.

"Let's say a blessing," Sally says with a smile.

Andrea looks pleased.

Sally takes Wyatt's hand and Andrea's hand. She bows her head and says "Heavenly father, thank you for this food which we are about to receive, and for all your many blessings, especially the gift of friendship. Amen."

"That's nice," Wyatt says, smiling.

"I know most people don't pray before meals any more but I like it," Sally replies.

"I like it too," Andrea says. "My grandmother used to always pray before meals."

Sally serves Wyatt and Andrea French toast with bacon, orange juice, and poached eggs.

Andrea has never had French toast, and after she eats 4 pieces of it with butter and syrup, Sally shows her how to make herself 2 more pieces. Andrea has never cooked and she takes great delight in it.

They eat on the screened-in back porch, at a white wicker table with a glass top.

Dressed in jeans and a tee shirt, his hair still wet from a shower, Wyatt feels a wave of contentment as he surveys the porch, with its wicker furniture, ferns in hanging pots, and gardening clogs by the door. It looks homey. They listen to Bach playing softly while they eat.

Andrea has never heard classical music and she wonders when people might start singing.

After Wyatt admires the lush green back yard, with its many blooming trees and shrubs, they talk about the trees in the back yard. Sally points out the three graceful magnolias, and she directs Andrea as they carefully pick a blossom and float it in a bowl for the center of the table, while Wyatt looks on and rubs Blanche's belly.

A little while later, the sky overhead is a beautiful medium blue, with just a few wispy clouds, and Wyatt hates to leave the pleasant brunch and go to the memorial, but after the dishes are washed and the kitchen straight, and Andrea is settled into a hammock, reading a book, it is time. He goes back to his house, and meets Sally in the driveway fifteen minutes later.

Sally's dazzling smile after she emerges from her house -- wearing a navy blue dress and pearls, her hair in a chignon, wearing fresh lipstick -- makes Wyatt want to escort her all over town.

He wears a dark charcoal gray suit, white shirt, and subdued blue tie.

When they are walking over to Wyatt's car, Andrea comes running out to the driveway, looking more like a waif than an angry teen. She hugs both Wyatt and Sally.

"I'm sorry about your uncle. I can tell from his house he was a good guy," she says awkwardly.

"Thanks, Andrea. We will be back soon," Wyatt replies.

He and Sally get in Sally's car and head to the service.

As they pull up outside the tiny church, Sally can hear her mother's disapproving voice, scolding her for going to a Protestant church with a married man. *Oh hush, Mama*, Sally says inwardly.

The service is less than twenty minutes long, and besides Wyatt and Sally there are only four people in the tiny sanctuary. There is a plain wooden cross in the front, but no statuary and no depictions of Mary, or of Jesus on the cross, which Sally finds odd – but then again, she has only been in a Protestant church a few times before, at the weddings of Marybeth and her daughters.

Several ladies are sitting on the front row, to the left of Wyatt and Sally. Wyatt recognizes Roberta, the pastor's wife, wearing black pants and a black tunic. There are two elderly ladies with Mamie Eisenhower hairdos wearing black dresses, and an elderly Hispanic

man wearing dark slacks and a white shirt buttoned to his neck. He looks very uncomfortable. Wyatt knows he is the janitor of the church.

The prayers are said, and they sing a weak rendition of Amazing Grace to a recording. The homily is brief because the pastor had only met Hugh once, at the diner, and there just isn't much to say.

After the service, the pastor leaves the altar and goes through a small door. Sally wonders where he went.

Wyatt and Sally greet the two elderly ladies, who explain that they went to school with Hugh. Wyatt knows they come to all the funerals because they have nothing else to do, but he thanks them warmly.

"Hugh was a fine man," says the taller lady.

"A fine man, and so smart," the other lady says, nodding. "We don't care about that wall. It was his house and he could do what he wanted."

Wyatt inwardly chuckles. "Thanks so much." He knows she wants him to tell her what Hugh was doing. He takes Sally's arm and they start to leave, but then Roberta corners them in the back of the church.

Sally inwardly groans.

Roberta reminds Sally of an elderly ninja, in her black stretchy pants and severe black tunic, and black flats. Her reading glasses are atop her head, and she doesn't carry a purse. She stares at Sally, then turns to Wyatt, and he sees she is holding a paper.

"George said to tell you he's sorry he can't come and speak. He just got a call to go to the hospital and see about one of our church members who is dying."

"It's quite all right —" Wyatt starts to say, but Roberta cuts him off.

"You get the ashes yet?" she asks Wyatt.

"Uh, well, no, I need to go pick them up. I just haven't gotten over there yet," he replies, careful to maintain a neutral tone.

"If you will sign this," she says, showing him a paper, "I can go get the ashes, and go ahead and inter them. We have the plaque ready."

"Thanks for your kind offer," he says with a smile, the big one with teeth he reserves for the courtroom, usually. He doesn't know why Roberta is radiating hostility towards Sally but he wants to deflect it. He takes the paper and pen and quickly sits down, putting the paper atop a hymnal so he can scrawl his name. He hands the paper and pen back to Roberta.

"So what are you going to do with your uncle's house?" Roberta asks pointedly.

"I really haven't made a decision," Wyatt answers evenly.

There is an awkward pause.

Roberta looks pointedly at Sally. "When have you heard from Steve?"

Sally returns her laser-like glare with a gentle smile. "Not in about 5 years. I hear he's doing well."

Roberta frowns. She loved Dr. Steve Odalshalski, as did most everyone in town. "What about your daughter? Doesn't she see him?"

Sally tries to keep her voice neutral. Her mother would have gracefully sidestepped such personal questions but Sally knows Roberta is a huge gossip and thinks she has the right to say anything to anyone.

Sally straightens herself up to her full 5'6 [in two inch heels] and looks down at Roberta.

"Steve hasn't been back here to see Miranda in years. She has seen him only a few times since she finished high school, including her wedding."

"I haven't seen Miranda at the Fall Festival in a while," Roberta says.

"Miranda is really busy with her life in Atlanta. She doesn't get home too often," Sally replies. *She thinks I'm a hopelessly dull person and she blames me for the divorce, so we are NOT EXACTLY CLOSE you old biddy.*

Small towns always pass judgment in a divorce of someone prominent. Sally is acutely aware that her ex husband had the reputation of being a saint, and she was viewed as cold and heartless for not following him out west. Her distant relationship with her daughter is seen as further proof of her coldness. Since Sally is the town librarian she has learned to ignore the gossip, but few people are as blatantly rude about it as Roberta.

Roberta just glares at Sally, which is noticed by Wyatt. He decides it's time to go.

"Well, thanks again for the service. It was very nice," Wyatt says, taking Sally's elbow to steer her out. "I'll send you a check to cover Hugh's internment."

Back in the car, Sally almost laughs. "I know why she hates me, but what did you ever say to her to piss her off like that?"

Wyatt shakes his head. "I have no idea. I can't imagine why my house is such a big deal." He actually wonders if Roberta wants the treasure she thinks is in the house.

Wyatt takes Sally home and heads back to Atlanta a few minutes later, because he has a brief due the next day.

As he drives back he ponders the sensation in his gut that tells him he has just left home and is headed back to a circus, where he doesn't want to perform any more.

CHAPTER 20

Wyatt doesn't realize the fallout from his peaceful Sunday until a few days later, back in Atlanta. It's a sunny Wednesday morning and Wyatt is in his office, reading through his mail, a cup of coffee cooling by his side. He sets aside a demand letter from another attorney, and a few routine letters.

Under the pile he finds a large envelope from a law firm he doesn't recognize. He grabs the letter opener and opens it. A letter, several pleadings, and some 8x10 photos tumble out on his desk.

He looks at the photos first. They look like they were taken with a telephoto lens. One shows him with Andrea in the driveway of Sally's house. Andrea is hugging him. The other one shows him just before he left later that afternoon, standing and talking to Sally, again in the driveway.

SHIT SHIT SHIT he thinks, wondering how the photographer was undetectable to him.

He is very uncomfortable just from seeing the photos, and that turns to rage when he reads the letter from Sharon's attorney, Bryan Stein.

Dear Wyatt and John,

I am representing Mrs. Sharon Jamison in the divorce. I have enclosed a copy of my Notice of Appearance.

As you can see by the enclosed photos, it's clear that Sharon is not the only one who has had relationships outside of the marriage. I have it on good authority the affair with Sally Cavanaugh has been going on for months. The relationship with the underage girl is even more troubling, and may be of interest to the Crossroads police department.

I have enclosed a Proposed Settlement Order so the divorce can be settled quickly and amicably. Sharon will receive the house, all the furnishings, and all of the marital assets including the $2,536,811.34 in settlement of the Baker case, in lieu of alimony. Wyatt will retain the house in Crossroads, Georgia, left to him by his uncle Hugh Jamison, and his personal effects.

Wyatt doesn't finish the remainder of the letter, but throws it on the desk and buries his face in his hands.

John Merriman, whose office is just two blocks from Wyatt's comes strolling into Wyatt's office a few minutes later. His tie is askew, and he is sipping coffee from a large Dunkin Donuts cup. Merriman is pale and worried about his friend, after reading his copy of the letter.

"Now Wyatt, I read the letter from that a-hole and I have a plan. This guy Stein swings a big dick in the family law community but he can be beat, buddy. They want to play dirty, we can too. We can get phone records of Sharon and Henry, and prove the affair has been going on for years. We can get photos –"

Wyatt just glares at his friend. "She will expect that. I don't want to sink that low."

John leans over to speak slowly into Wyatt's red face, "Look, I know she once did your books but she does NOT deserve ALL that settlement money! What a cunt!"

"She is, I agree, but I simply want OUT -- without a big slugfest."

Puzzled and angry, John tries not to glare at his friend.

"Look, Wyatt, as your attorney I have to give you options, and we need to discuss strategy –"

"I do not want to fight with her." Wyatt says, his voice low but menacing, almost a growl.

John looks at his friend. "She cannot take your entire fee from the Baker case. That's extortion."

"Yes, yes it is. However, if Child Protective Services gets hold of Andrea they will send her back to her mother in Ringgold, and the mother's creepo boyfriend will keep molesting her. I told you about that situation. It's tricky."

John Merriman sits heavily in the chair opposite Wyatt's desk. "You have an uncanny ability to see things that are hidden. I don't know how you do it. Why didn't you know about the photographer?"

Wyatt shakes his head, slowly. "I don't know. My abilities are not infallible. That's why I am a lawyer, not a professional psychic."

"OK, fair enough. But JESUS! Sharon has no right to take your entire commission on the Baker case. That's not right and you know it. How would she know the exact amount, anyway? You show her the check?"

"I don't know. Probably. I was really excited about it. She put those digits on there to antagonize me. Didn't work."

Wyatt turns to stare out the huge window at the Atlanta skyline. "See if you can get her to back off that number. Offer half, but that's all for now," Wyatt says evenly.

"Okay."

Wyatt turns around with a heavy sigh and once again buries his face in his hands. John claps him awkwardly on the back.

"I know you're upset. Let's give it 24 hours and then talk some more about how to settle the divorce."

Wyatt lifts his head and shrugs. "You can wait 24 hours. I am going to go ahead and start closing the practice and planning my move to the mountains. I don't want to be here anymore."

"I understand that, but I think you need to stay away from Crossroads until the dust is settled on the divorce – for the sake of Andrea, Sally, your son. Why don't you go up to Knoxville and see Nora and Ed for a while?"

Wyatt nods. "That's a good plan, but I need to make sure my cases get wrapped up, or refer them out to other attorneys. I don't have that many clients but it will take some time, and I've got one going to trial in 5 weeks."

"Let's talk about everything tonight at dinner. I'll take you out to The Fish Market, my treat," John says trying to lighten the mood.

"Okay," Wyatt says. "Later."

Wyatt is at John's house changing clothes after work that day when his cell phone rings. He looks at it and grimaces. It's his son, Thad.

"Hey there, Son, how are you?" Wyatt says with false bonhomie.

"I am fine, Dad, but I just got off the phone with Mother and she was crying and saying y'all are getting divorced! What the fuck!"

Wyatt sits down on the bed, dreading the conversation.

"Your mother and I are divorcing, yes. I was going to drive up to school and tell you this weekend, in person."

"Look, I never thought you had the greatest marriage but SHIT DAD," Thad says, his voice heavy with sarcasm and hurt.

"We still love you very much," Wyatt says heavily.

"Really?! Mom said you instigated the divorce --
that she didn't want to split up. Are you having an affair?"

"No!"

"Well, Mom thinks since you settled that case you
might be looking for someone younger."

Wyatt ponders the situation for a moment. He
doesn't want to add salt to a wound but he needs his son
to understand the truth.

"I found out your mother is having an affair with
one of the doctors in her practice, Henry Wallace. I can't
stay with your mom. I'm sorry. We haven't been happy for
a long time, so it's for the best."

There is a dead silence on the other end of the line.

"I cannot believe you would say something like that
about Mom. That's just gross, Dad. She told me about
Henry a while back. She said they are friends but she has
never cheated on you."

"Of course that's what she said," Wyatt says
quietly. "Look, once trust is gone, there is no marriage, so
it might as well end."

"So you think she's screwing him?! FUCK! Has the
whole world gone crazy?!" Thad was shouting now. "I
DON'T WANT ANY PART OF THIS!"

The call ended with Thad disconnecting.

Wyatt sits there looking at the phone. He thinks
about Thad as a little boy, blonde hair, blue eyes, looking

like an angel, mischievous as an imp, smart, opinionated, funny.

So many emotions are just roiling in his head. Pity for Thad. Disgust with Sharon. Anger. Regret that he hadn't seen it coming. Longing to get the divorce done and over.

John knocks on the open door of the room. "Ready to go eat?"

"I just talked to Thad. He was pretty upset. Sharon told him a very skewed version of things. Before we go eat, how about we go to the driving range and hit a few?"

John looks at Wyatt's face and recognizes the shock and grief of divorce.

"Sure thing."

Two hours later, Wyatt has whacked more than 200 golf balls, and they wind up eating chili dogs, picked up from The Varsity, sitting by John's fire pit.

Wyatt wipes his mouth and looks at John. "Any luck getting her to be reasonable about the money?"

John looks pained. "No, she's out for blood, I'm afraid. I heard thru the grapevine that Henry has made some bad investments and he's paying alimony to two exes now, so they need your money if they want to live lavishly."

"Shit," Wyatt says quietly, pushing away his onion rings.

"This is not unusual. I hate it for you though, buddy."

Wyatt sits and stares at the pool for a minute.

"Nora and I talked the other day. She wants me to go in there and get Mother's set of Spode and the Oriental rug in the dining room. Also some silver julep tumblers and three paintings. She wants to actually come down and go through the house with me and get out everything that was in my family. Can we do that?"

John shakes his head. "Nope. Not until we get a Final Decree. You already got your personal effects, but let's not make waves."

Wyatt shakes his head.

"I feel like my whole life is just a big mess."

"It will get better. It just takes time," John says quietly.

CHAPTER 21

Wyatt calls Sally later that night and tells her about the situation with Sharon.

"Wow, what a nightmare," is all Sally can think to say. She takes a sip of Cabernet and rubs Blanche's tummy. Sally is wearing pajamas and is propped up in bed, Blanche beside her. Sally's landline phone extension is next to the bed.

"Yep. It's a mess," Wyatt agrees. Wyatt, too, is propped up in bed -- the guestroom bed at John's house. He takes a sip of beer and suddenly feels a spasm of longing, picturing Sally's mouth.

"How do you feel?" Sally asks, softly.

Wyatt is quiet for a moment. "I have lived a very calm, ordered life, and except for my mother's death everything has been predictable and fairly easy, even law school. But now... I feel like a giant meteor has just hit everything and it's all exploded and I'm... standing in a shitstorm with no umbrella, as my friend John would say," Wyatt said.

Sally is silent for a moment, then a giggle erupts from her. "Never thought I'd hear you use the word shitstorm," she says gently.

"It's John's word. I don't normally use it. I just feel down."

Their conversation has shifted, and she realizes that she recognizes how Wyatt feels.

"I know this feeling. Even though I instigated my divorce, and it was very civilized, I still felt like I couldn't cope, right at first. I moved back in with my mother. Then I was dealing with a 15 year old who missed her father terribly, and blamed me for the breakup, and dealing with my mom's early Alzheimers, and trying to re-establish a career. At times it was just so depressing, I just went through the motions... but then one day I realized that it was good, too."

That last word startles him. "What do you mean, good?" Wyatt asks.

"After the divorce was finalized, and I moved into this house, and I had my job at the library and my routine, one day I realized that I was okay. I was myself. I was just me, not an extension of my husband. I wasn't just Miranda's mother either, or Barbara's daughter. Took me some time to figure out what I liked, but I did. I started researching the history of the town, and planting my own herbs and vegetables, and I fixed up the back porch and screened it in. I redecorated my bedroom. I had time because I didn't have to get up at 3 a.m. and make breakfast for my husband when he came in from tending to a sick cow."

"Wasn't that stressful, though -- caregiving for your mom?" Wyatt asked.

"Yeah, but I got breaks. Miranda helped me with Mom. Some weekends my friend Marybeth and I would go out of town, just a girls' weekend, while my brother watched Mom and Miranda was at her friend's house. That helped."

"When did your mother die?" Wyatt asked.

"A few years ago. Mom actually died of a stroke, not the Alzheimers, and she went quickly, which was a blessing."

Wyatt sighed. "I am sorry. I wish I could just go away for a weekend. Do you like to sit on a dock and fish and drink beer?"

Sally laughed. "Nope to the fishing, but I would like to sit on a dock and read a book, though, or perhaps listen to music, or listen to the Braves game. I used to listen to the games with my dad."

Wyatt is speechless for a moment. This is a breakthrough - a woman willing to let him fish in peace. A woman who likes to listen to Braves games.

"What about shopping?" he asks.

"I'm not really all that interested in shopping. My mother was a shopper, not me. I'm more of a bookworm."

Wyatt is quiet for a moment, marveling at a woman who doesn't view shopping as a competitive sport, and who loves to read as much as he does.

"That baton twirling thing never worked out then, huh?!"

Sally chuckles. "I was never very good at it. Auditioned for the band majorette gig but didn't get it. Joined the French Club instead. That was fun, to me."

"D'accord, Mademoiselle. Un belle langue. I took three years of French, only because the girls in there were cute," Wyatt chuckles.

"Tres bien. Except I would be Madame, not Mademoiselle. So what's your immediate plan?" Sally asks.

"Well, my plan is to let John negotiate and get Sharon to be reasonable so I can keep some of my fee from the Baker case, close my practice here, and then move to Crossroads."

There is a pause, as Sally's heart leaps.

"How long do you think that will take?" Sally asks, trying to keep her voice calm.

"There's no telling. Closing down my practice will take some time. All my cases need to be either referred out to other lawyers or settled. I've got a case that's going to trial in five weeks, a special setting, so I have to keep that case. It's a personal injury involving a trucking company, but I think the jury will see things my way."

"Are you sure it's going to trial, it won't settle?" Sally asks, thinking she had read somewhere that most cases settle.

Wyatt chuckles, mirthlessly. "I am always willing to hear settlement proposals, but my client has to approve, and this client is bound and determined to get his day in court."

"Wow, what happened?"

Wyatt shifts around uncomfortably. "Truck driver was talking on a cell phone and plowed into the back of my guy. He had two broken legs, broken ribs, and more. "

"Yikes. What a mess."

"Yep. I specialize in fixing messes," Wyatt says with a smile.

There is a companionable silence.

"Hey, I have good news," Sally says, shifting in the bed so she can rub Blanche's silky ears.

"Great. I can use some good news."

"Well, two pieces of good news, actually. Andrea is studying for the GED, and she turns 18 on July 24th."

Wyatt sits and ponders this for a moment.

"I'm glad she's going to get her GED, but more glad about the turning 18. That will ease up some of the pressure on us, not having to worry about her being a runaway. Do you think she could go to community college? Is there one near there?"

"There's a two year school in Gainesville that's good. She needs to figure out what she wants to do first, though."

"True. Is it weird having a teenager in the house again?"

Sally chuckles. "It was at first, but now we're into a groove. She helps me tidy up and walk Blanche, and she is settling in. I am teaching her to cook. She is still a bit freaked out that I have no television."

Wyatt didn't realize that before. "You don't? Why not?"

"When my mother was alive she became kind of obsessed with it. She would sit in front of the TV for hours, like a zombie. It got on my nerves, especially because she was losing her hearing and it had to be super loud. After she died I just got mad one day and grabbed it and put it in a closet. My daughter took it back to Atlanta a few weeks later. I truly don't miss it."

Wyatt, not a big TV watcher himself, was amused. "How big was the TV?"

"Not that big. Why?"

"Well, TV sets are usually pretty heavy. I was picturing tiny little you wrestling a TV into the closet..."

Sally smiles in spite of herself. "Well, I was motivated. My daughter's boyfriend got it in the car, actually. I just cheered from the sidelines and offered him a drink afterwards."

Wyatt laughs.

Sally shifts on the bed to accommodate Blanche." When do you think you can come back to Crossroads, I mean just to visit?"

Wyatt stops laughing and sighs, then takes a sip of beer. "I wish I could come up there tomorrow, but I can't. John says I need to steer clear of you and Andrea, not give Sharon any more ammunition, especially since we don't know who took those photos. So... as soon as the divorce is final, I will be back. A few months, hopefully. Can you keep an eye on the house for me in the meantime?"

"Sure. You gave me a spare key, remember," Sally says, quietly. She is very disappointed she will not be able to see Wyatt any time soon. "Do you want me to keep trying to get that trunk open?"

"Nope. There's nothing in it."

"How do you know?" Sally asks, startled by the certainty in his voice.

Wyatt pauses, wondering how much to explain. "Well, I just don't think there is anything in there, or if there is, it's nothing like treasure – if there were, I think Dad or Hugh would have gotten it years ago. Best to let it be. If I am wrong, anything valuable I find, Sharon might try to get it in the divorce. Let's just postpone hunting for buried treasure while I get the divorce finalized, ok?"

"Okay, sure. I will tell Andrea. Hopefully she won't be too disappointed. She was convinced there was some kind of treasure. She has a vivid imagination."

"Yeah, well, I am really glad she is with you, and not on the streets."

Wyatt regrets drinking a beer with dinner because now he urgently has to pee. "Well, uh, it was great talking to you. Listen, I will call you periodically to see how everything is going, ok? Not from my cell, though, from landlines. Cell phone records can get subpoenaed in a divorce. Good thing John has a landline."

"Call anytime. After 8 at night is best, since my cell phone rarely works here in the mountains, but I'm always home by then." Sally says, trying to keep her voice neutral.

"Will do. Good night."

"Good night. Good luck with everything." *Did that sound wistful? I didn't want it to sound that way*, Sally thinks.

"Thanks," Wyatt says softly, picturing Sally and wishing he were there to take her in his arms.

CHAPTER 22

I am hovering over Honeysuckle Road, watching the clouds drifting by, which is a delightful pastime, and suddenly I see an old black Chevy Impala pull up to the small brick house across the street from my house. The car stops and Roberta Kingston steps out.

I remember Roberta from school. A fat, bossy little thing, always talking, always getting in trouble for talking, always up to something.

She had a crush on Wendell. I remember that. Wendell paid her no mind. He was too busy with the debating club and the football team.

Roberta grew up and married the Lutheran minister, guaranteeing I would never set foot in that church. Ironic that my memorial service was held there.

What is she up to now?

Mavis Johnson owns the little house. She is some relation of Roberta's. A cousin? An in law? I'm not sure. All I know is Mavis is another busybody and between the two of them..

Well, I better eavesdrop on that conversation.

I swoop in and there's Roberta, now sitting in the front room fanning her fat face and drinking iced tea. The big front window of Mavis' house is just across from Sally's driveway.

Well, look at all the cameras. Mavis and her husband used to own a photo shop in town and they would also take all the school photos. That's right, now I remember. I used to see them setting off with all the equipment to all the schools. There are big cameras, small ones, a veritable plethora of new and antique cameras, including one on a tripod, set up in front of that window.

"It's hotter than chicken fried hell," Mavis says.

"Yes M'am. I hate this time of year," Roberta replies. "Seen any activity lately, over there?"

"I have not seen hide nor hair of Wyatt since that day he was with Sally and that little whore. Believe you me, I keep a close eye on them," Mavis was saying. The two women sit on the ugly brown sofa in the front room.

They keep glancing over at Sally's house and my house like there is something fixing to pop out. Good grief.

"Good. His wife was so sweet when she called me up, just weeping, saying how Wyatt had been cheating on her with Sally Cavanaugh, that hussy," Roberta huffs. "His daddy Wendell would be scandalized."

"Indeed he would, God rest his soul," Mavis nodded.

"I did my Christian duty, helping her get what she deserved in that divorce," Roberta said smugly. "Imagine how she had suffered! She said Wyatt was a workaholic, and tight with a dollar. Cheating,too!"

I am rolling my eyes. Wendell knew Sharon was a cold-hearted lady. If he was alive he wouldn't begrudge Wyatt some happiness with Sally. These women are moralistic, judgmental idiots.

There's a small dog, a terrier, and he has spotted me. He looks right at me, growling low in his throat. How do dogs always know when a spirit is in the room?! I haven't figured it out. Mavis sees him looking at me.

"Hush Billybob, silly thing," she scolds.

Billybob isn't an idiot. I decide to have some fun.

I start doing a comical dance in front of Billybob, waving my hands and jumping around, sticking out my tongue. His eyes follow me as I cavort, and he barks.

The women stop their inane chatter when Billybob's tail starts to wag and he switches to glee and enthusiastically barks at me, staring right where I am dancing.

Roberta's eyes are narrowed. She knows something is going on. She may have the Sight, or at least some heightened intuition.

What the living don't know is that us dead folks can always spot the ones who are open to our presence, who believe in spirits. We just know.

Roberta believes. What a shock. She's also afraid, though. That's excellent.

I have mostly avoided the living thus far in my haunting life but now I decide to see if I can freak old Roberta out, as the kids would say. I go over to where she sits on the sofa and squat down right in front of her.

Roberta pulls back as though sensing me practically in her lap. Her face gets pale. "Lordy Mavis, it just got real cold in here. Land's sakes. Well look at the time. I better be going," Roberta says uncomfortably.

She rises quickly and steps right through me, and shivers.

Ha!

I start laughing as I rise, up and up, through the roof, up into the brilliant blue sky. Take THAT, you old busybody, I laugh.

Andrea sits on the back porch of Sally's house in the porch swing, drinking lemonade and reading Gone With the Wind. She never liked to read much before, but now she reads all the time. Without the distraction of TV, or a cell phone, Andrea is able to delve deeply into books and lose track of time.

Sally brings her books from the library.

She especially likes Scarlett, because she reminds Andrea of some girls she had known in high school, and she's not a "simpering fool."

Andrea also reads with fascination the parts of the book dealing with Sherman's Army marching through Georgia, and Scarlett's killing of the Yankee soldier.

Andrea's life has improved a lot, under Sally's guidance. She has stopped smoking weed or even cigarettes, and she only chews gum. She delights in cooking, and has added some needed weight. Beside her, Blanche stirs from her sleep and stands up on her stubby Bassett legs, tail wagging, as she looks into the corner of the room.

Andrea watches the dog, and senses she is seeing something Andrea doesn't see. She recalls reading somewhere that dogs and small children are sensitive to spirits. *Maybe it's a ghost*, she thinks.

Blanche keeps looking over to the corner of the porch, as though she is watching a play. A cloud passes in front of the sun, and a breeze blows through the screen and ruffles some papers on the table. Blanche pays no attention to those normal occurrences.

Andrea watches Blanche, and tries to see if there is a spider or other bug in the corner. Andrea doesn't see anything like that. *Blanche isn't afraid of whatever it is, more just observing*, she thinks.

I wonder if it's the ghost of Wyatt's uncle. In her heart, she feels it is him, although she cannot explain why. She puts the book down and stares at the space where Blanche is staring.

"Um, hey, Mr. Hugh, if that's you, can you help me out? Can you help me figure out what to do with my life?" Andrea says softly. She looks into the corner, wishing she could see him.

"See, this is all new to me. I come from nothing, but I want more out of my life… I've been reading a lot. Sally's been teaching me how to cook. I want to go places and learn, and be somebody. I always made good grades in school."

Andrea looks at the lazy summer air on the porch, wishing she could see Hugh. She senses he was a kind person, and obviously he liked young adults, since he was a college professor.

I stop waving at Blanche and regard the girl, who looks a lot better now that Sally is caring for her. She's wearing shorts and a tee shirt, and her hair is longer, and healthy. I sense she has a good heart. Can I communicate with her? Can I help her figure out her path?

I used to counsel students. It was always easy to spot the ones who were serious and determined, and Andrea appears to be that kind, despite her tough beginnings.

Another spirit appears in the room, a woman dressed in clothes from the 1950's. This is Andrea's grandmother Jeannie, I sense. She smiles at the girl. Andrea has her eyes.

"Can you see and hear me?" I ask. She nods.

"What should Andrea do?" I ask.

"Archaeology. She will do fine," Jeannie says softly. "She is very smart but her mother never encouraged her. I don't know how to tell her."

She smiles wistfully at Andrea, and fades away.

Maybe I can figure out how to tell Andrea.

Maybe.

Andrea sighs heavily, and mumbles "I must be crazy, talking to ghosts···"

I want so badly to communicate!

Coldness! Of course. I walk over to Andrea and place my hand on top of hers. She starts. She looks around wildly. "You ARE here! Help me Mr. Hugh!"

Blanche whines softly as I hug Andrea awkwardly. "I will try, my dear," I say, although I know she can't hear me.

Andrea shivers but looks hopeful.

CHAPTER 23

Wyatt wants nothing as much as he wants to date Sally, but until the divorce is final, he doesn't dare go back to Crossroads and risk more photos and gossip.

His days are filled with legal work and other obligations, but his evenings are boring. The guestroom at John's house is well furnished and comfortable, but at times it feels like a cell. John and his wife stay busy, so Wyatt is often on his own at their house. He takes walks in the evenings sometimes, just to relieve the boredom.

He tries hard to think of excuses to call Sally.

After procrastinating for a few days, the call is easy. It's 8 p.m. and he dials her house number. He has eaten his takeout dinner, a sandwich from a deli near John's house, and is settled in a chair by the window.

"Hey, Sally, it's Wyatt. How is everything going?"

Sally dries her hands from doing the dinner dishes and cradles the phone "Hang on. Andrea, would you mind to take Blanche out back for me? She just drank her bowl dry and I know she has to tinkle. Thanks."

"Good. How are you?" Sally says, sitting down.

"Good, good. Listen, I was thinking, since Andrea is staying with you now, why don't you get any food at my house that you want?"

Sally almost chuckles. He must have thought a good while about that excuse to call.

"Well, since I've got a key I will walk over there and see if there's anything to bring over, anything perishable."

"Great. If anything might spoil, just throw it out, okay, if you don't want it?"

"Okay. Oh, and just fyi, I am paying the neighbor down the street, Eric, to mow the lawn. He does a good job, for $10. He bags the clippings, too. "

"Hey, that's a deal. I will send you a check," Wyatt says, smiling. Small towns. No fancy lawn maintenance fees.

Sally sips from her glass of wine. "How is everything going with you? Getting your cases wrapped up?"

Wyatt thinks for a moment. "Yep. Not hard to do, actually. I have a good number of lawyer friends happy to take the cases that are ongoing, and I've settled several."

They continue talking for several more minutes.

Wyatt can tell she wants to keep talking but she is afraid to reveal too much, too fast. There is a lot of fear and anxiety behind her attraction to him.

"How is Andrea's GED test prep going?" Wyatt asks.

"Good. I got her some books from the library and she's studying."

"Good. I have a feeling she is going to do something with archaeology. She was showing me a grid map she drew of the backyard. Can you get her some books on that from the library?"

"Sure. That's a great idea. I think I can order her some textbooks, too."

Wyatt has run out of conversation.

"She staying close to home?"

"Oh yes."

Wyatt inwardly breathes a sigh of relief.

"She was going a bit stir crazy the other day, so I put her in the car and we went to Gainesville and went shopping. Most folks from Crossroads don't go that far, so I thought we'd be safe."

"Good idea. What did you do in Gainesville?"

"We got her a haircut, had lunch at a little café downtown, and went to Goodwill. She now has plenty of shorts and tops, although nothing is real fashionable," Sally says. "Oh, and she talked me into buying a small TV so she can watch movies. I have a few."

"Excellent," is all Wyatt can think to say.

"I'll look for those archaeology books tomorrow. Thanks for the suggestion," Sally says.

Andrea comes back in with Blanche. "Sally, can I watch Fried Green Tomatoes?"

Sally nods. "I need to go. Great talking to you, Wyatt."

"Yeah, you too. Take care."

Wyatt looks at his hands and realizes he was talking on his cell phone, not the landline. Ah well, they are neighbors. He can always say they talked about house issues. He wants to talk about much more, though.

Sally's birthday is June 17th, a fact he learns from Andrea. She knows Wyatt and Sally have had phone conversations and something is up. Andrea redials the landline and calls him one morning. After Wyatt gets back to John's house, as the two men sit in the kitchen eating pizza, he shares the voicemail with John, grinning.

"Um, yeah, Wyatt? This is Andrea.." Her voice sounds conspiratorial on the message. "Um, Sally's birthday is in TWO WEEKS, on June 17, so Dude, seriously, you need to get her something nice, OK? She really likes you. The address here is 699 Honeysuckle, Crossroads Georgia 30389. She likes flowers, books, candy, the normal stuff, OK? Oh, and she has an old school DVD player, and only a few movies. I found a TV at Goodwill and I've watched all those movies like 5 times each. More movies would be nice? I gotta go now. Later Dude."

Wyatt chuckles. "She was nervous. Not even my son uses the word "dude" that much."

John hands Wyatt a beer, then puts the phone back on the cradle. "She sounds like a funny kid. You sure she's not taking advantage of Sally, though?"

Wyatt shakes his head because his mouth is full of pepperoni and sausage pizza. Finally, he swallows and speaks. "I have a good feeling about her. She has a good heart. I think she's good for Sally. Sally is a natural mother."

"Sure. So what are you going to get Sally?"

"Well, I am thinking a Netflix subscription so she can get up to 4 movies at a time, and maybe send a box of Godiva chocolates?"

"Chocolates are always good," John says approvingly. "I'd send flowers, too. Seriously, Dude."

Wyatt throws a napkin at his head.

The chocolates and flowers arrive at noon on Wednesday, June 17th, and Andrea is thrilled with both, and can hardly wait to tell Sally, who works until 6.

When Sally walks in to her house, Andrea stands there grinning. The house is spotless. Every table has been polished. Every floor has been swept or vacuumed. The chandelier in the dining room has been carefully dusted. The white kitchen cabinets have been scrubbed.

Sally, an indifferent housekeeper, is amazed and touched.

"Happy Birthday Sally!" Andrea trills.

"That you Sweetie!" Sally responds, going over to give her a hug.

"I cleaned, and I made barbecued chicken, sliced tomatoes from the garden, and blueberry muffins," Andrea breathlessly explains.

"Wow! The cooking lessons are paying off!" Sally enthuses.

Sally smiles at the dining room table, which has been set with her best china and crystal. The centerpiece is the arrangement of roses.

The flowers are long stemmed yellow roses, 2 dozen. Sally is overwhelmed. Her ex never sent her roses. The card simply says "Happy Birthday! – Wyatt"

Next to them is a box from Amazon.

"Open it!" Andrea urges her.

Sally opens it. It's a box of Godiva chocolates from Wyatt.

"You must have told him it was my birthday?" she asked Andrea.

"Yes M'am. I hope you don't mind," she answers shyly.

The doorbell rings. Andrea runs to answer it. A Fed-X box is propped against the front door. Andrea brings it in.

It's from Marybeth. Sally opens the box and upends it on the table. Three DVDs tumble out – The Color Purple, You've Got Mail, and Harold and Maude. Andrea examines them with great interest. "I've never seen any of these!"

The box also contains a birthday card, two bags of microwave popcorn and two large Hershey bars.

"Well this is lovely. I don't remember ever getting so many wonderful gifts on any birthday!" Sally exclaims.

"Um, Sally? How old are you?" Andrea asks shyly.

"I am fifty, dear. Half a century. Yikes," Sally laughs.

"You don't look it," Andrea says.

"Thanks. Fat fills wrinkles!" Sally laughs.

Just as Sally and Andrea finish eating dinner, the phone rings. "I'm going to take it upstairs," Sally says, pushing her chair back and heading for the stairs at a fast trot. She throws herself on the bed and says "Hello?" breathlessly.

"Happy birthday, Beautiful," Wyatt says smoothly.

"Well aren't you a sweetie, sending me flowers and chocolate!" Sally chuckles.

"And lots of movies."

Sally is quiet, wondering what he is talking about.

Wyatt realizes his error. "You now have a Netflix subscription, so you can get DVDs in the mail, even in Crossroads," Wyatt says.

"Oh."

"You haven't checked email have you?"

"Nope, but thanks so much!" Sally enthuses. "I have thought about getting Netflix but I guess I just didn't want to incur the expense. I also didn't want to go buy another TV. However, Andrea loves movies, and since she got a TV, she's gotten me interested in them."

Andrea's voice drifts up the stairs, "Sally can I start one of the movies?"

"Yes, Hon, go right ahead!" Sally shouts in reply.

"Did you do anything special for your birthday?" Wyatt asks.

"Well, I had to work, as usual. When I came home Andrea had cleaned up the house and made dinner, so that was wonderful."

"So she's getting along okay?" Wyatt asks

Sally smiles. "More than okay. She is such a sweet girl. I love having her here."

Sally hears a noise on Wyatt's end.

"Sally, I'm getting a client call on my cell phone, so I will let you go. Anyway, happy birthday," Wyatt says quickly.

"OK, take your call. Later Dude!" Sally says.

Wyatt hangs up the phone and goes in search of John. He finds him in the family room of his house watching a baseball game, from the comfort of his recliner. John wears gym shorts and a tee shirt over his bulging belly, and drinks a beer.

Wyatt regards his friend with amusement, wondering if he should buy John some new tee shirts.

"Hey, I just got a call from some guy named Cal Milstein over at some mediation service. He said you had given him my number?" Wyatt says, trying not to sound annoyed.

John swallows his beer and nods.

"Well yeah, I thought you might like to do some mediations, even after you retire. You make decent money for just a half day or day's work."

Wyatt sits down on the sofa and looks at the huge TV screen. "Well, I'm hoping I won't have to do any work after I retire, but thanks for thinking of me."

"Sure. What did you tell him?" John asks, handing Wyatt a beer from the small cooler next to his chair.

Wyatt shrugs. "Told him I'd think about it."

"Good. Braves are winning by 2 points."

"Good. They need a win."

The two friends settle into their chairs and watch the rest of the game.

CHAPTER 24

Andrea turns 18 on July 24. Fortunately, it is a Saturday. The day before, Sally and Andrea load Blanche into the car and drive to Atlanta to spend the weekend with Marybeth.

They chat as they drive south that Friday afternoon, out of the mountainous part of North Georgia. After getting on I-85 southbound and passing through the northern suburbs, including Suwanee and Sugar Hill, they get to Atlanta proper. They only encounter light traffic, well before the Friday rush.

When they get on I-285, the multi-lane highway that encircles the city, Sally senses Andrea's discomfort. For a kid from Ringgold, interstates with 8 lanes are pretty scary. Andrea doesn't say a word, just gazes out the window, wide-eyed. Sally is glad, because she hates driving in Atlanta. She turns up the radio a little and sings along softly to calm herself, to Prince's "When Doves Cry."

Sally exits on Peachtree Dunwoody Road and they drive through a residential area of upper middle class homes. As they pull up in front of the lovely 3 story home in Dunwoody, Andrea gazes about her, feeling very uncomfortable. She has never been in a neighborhood like this. The home is a traditional model, built in the 1970's, all brick, three stories, with a lush lawn.

The yard is filled with flowering plants. The garage can hold three cars, Andrea sees when they park in the driveway.

Sally parks her old car and smiles at Andrea. "You'll love Marybeth, Sweetie."

Andrea smiles back, hoping Sally is right. She wants to go back to Crossroads.

They go to up to the front door and hear barking. Before they knock, the door opens and they are let in by Marybeth, a short plump woman wearing Capri pants and a yellow cotton top who exclaims "You're here!" and hugs Sally. Blanche happily greets Lulu, Marybeth's Shih Zu, whose backside twitches with absolute joy when Andrea and Sally walk into the light-filled foyer of the gracious home.

"Nice to meet you, Mrs. Durand," Andrea says, sticking out her hand and looking Marybeth in the eye.

As she shakes Andrea's hand, Marybeth recognizes Sally's attempt to civilize the girl, who looks far less like a waif than she had expected. Andrea is wearing a pair of Miranda's old jeans, and a light blue tee shirt, and sandals. Her brown hair is clean and cut in a long bob around her shoulders.

"Call me Marybeth. It's so nice to meet you, Honey, come on in. Make yourself at home," Marybeth says warmly. "Let's go in the kitchen. Lunch was a long time ago so I made us some banana bread."

As they walk back to the kitchen, Andrea takes in the numerous framed photos of Marybeth's children and husband, many made by a professional photographer. The neutral colors of the foyer give way to a cheery blue and yellow kitchen with a large island in the middle. A round table and chairs sit in front of a large picture window that looks out to a backyard and a pool.

"You have a swimming pool?" Andrea says, awed.

"I sure do. It's hotter than the hinges of hell right now, so I hope you brought your suit."

Sally winces. She had completely forgotten about Marybeth's pool. "I forgot. She doesn't have a suit," she says as she sits at the table.

"No big deal. My daughter leaves a suit here for when she visits and I bet it would fit Andrea. No worries," Marybeth answers, smiling.

Andrea just gazes at the clear blue water of the pool.

"Honey, come try my banana bread. It's my mama's recipe," Marybeth says to Andrea's back.

"Yes M'am," Andrea replies, her voice far away. She has been in a swimming pool only twice in her life, once when visiting a campground with her friend Megan's family, and once when her mother had taken them to Daytona when she was 7 and her mother was dating a guy named Wade, who was a really nice truck driver. Wade had taught her to swim a little, without fear.

Andrea sits down and tries a bite of the banana bread. It's warm from the oven, and tastes strongly of cinnamon. "Wow, this is really yummy!" she exclaims.

Sally chuckles. "Marybeth is famous for her banana bread. I have the recipe. Let's make it sometime."

Marybeth's cell phone rings as she pours everyone iced tea from a glass pitcher. "Hang on just a sec, I have to take this," she says, walking into the family room.

A few moments later she returns, beaming at Sally and Andrea.

Sally looks at her expectantly, knowing something is up.

"We are having a special guest for dinner tonight," Marybeth says, grinning.

"Who?!" Sally asks, eyebrow cocked.

"Never you mind, Stinky. It will be a happy surprise."

Sally frowns. Miranda and her husband are on a cruise so it couldn't be them. Surely not Wyatt? She wonders. No, Marybeth and Ed don't know him. It wouldn't be him.

"Stinky?" Andrea asks.

"Marybeth and I have been friends since third grade, so ignore the childish nicknames," Sally says.

"Oh Lawd, get past it already," Marybeth chuckles. "We are Stinky and Buttface to each other, Andrea. That's how BFFs our age roll," she says.

Andrea stifles the urge to say *Y'all are WEIRD*. Instead, she finishes her banana bread.

"Can I go swimming now?" Andrea asks, swallowing her last bit of banana bread, "Please, Sally?!"

"C'mon Sweetie, let's go see if that swimsuit my daughter left will fit you," Marybeth says, gently steering Andrea towards the stairs. "I think there's some sunscreen in the bathroom, too. Sal, why don't you take the girls outside so they can potty?" Marybeth says, nodding at Blanche and Lulu.

Sally looks at her friend and momentarily debates whether or not to make a big deal out of dinner, but decides against it.

"OK. Pooper scooper in the usual place?"

"Yep," Marybeth says cheerfully.

An hour later, Marybeth and Sally are sitting at the table in the kitchen, watching Andrea, in a bathing suit, throw a ball for the dogs, who happily jump in and out of the pool playing fetch.

"Well, she's a little rough around the edges but she seems like a sweet girl," Marybeth says, nodding at Andrea.

"She comes from nothing, and I'm still working on her, but she's intelligent and she has an innate kindness," Sally says. "I think as soon as she figures out what she wants to do she will be okay. She's interested in archaeology, so she's reading up on it."

"Sounds like she's a smart cookie," Marybeth says with a smile. "Hey, we'll have fun tomorrow. I've got a whole girls' day planned."

"Who is the mystery dinner guest?" Sally says suddenly.

Marybeth laughs. "You'll see. He's due here at 6:30."

"Are you playing matchmaker again?!" Sally says, annoyed. "I thought you had given up."

"Nope. Never say never," Marybeth says. "Now make yourself useful, Stinky. I need to get going on the potato soufflé," she says, handing Sally a bag of Yukon Gold potatoes and a vegetable scraper.

"Yes, Madame Buttface," Sally grumbles.

Ed comes in the back door at 6:28, and finds Marybeth and Sally in the kitchen, cooking and laughing. The potatoes are cooking on the stove, soon to be mashed, and broccoli is in the steamer basket. Steaks are marinating, and coming to room temp on the island counter. A cantaloupe is cut into wedges and in a bowl. A blueberry pie is in the oven.

Ed, a small, rotund man with thinning hair and wire-rimmed glasses looks like a portly vicar from an Agatha Christie novel.

"Well this is a lovely sight," he beams.

"Hey Ed, how are you?" Sally says, walking over to give him a hug.

"Just grand, Darlin,' great to see you," Ed beams.

Marybeth walks over, wiping her hands on a dishtowel. "Hello Old Thing. Where is our dinner guest? Wasn't he supposed to follow you?"

"He did just that. Then he went around the corner and over to Sycamore Road and parked in front of the Mason's house and -- he is walking up to the back door as we speak," Ed says, nodding towards the large window.

Sally turns to look, and her heart catches in her throat as she sees the tall figure of Wyatt walking up to the door. He wears blue jeans and a blue Polo shirt. She tries not to stare at him but she is hungry to see him, his long limbs moving fluidly, sunlight catching his hair.

Sally wishes she had combed her own hair and put on some lipstick.

It has been more than eight weeks since they were in the same room.

Wyatt smiles as he catches sight of Sally through the window.

"So this is the surprise?" Sally says, thinking *I wish I had worn something more flattering.*

"Yep. Ed's nephew hired him a few years back to handle a case, and he put us in touch," Marybeth says, smiling, happy to see how Sally's face lit up as soon as she saw Wyatt.

Ed walks Wyatt in the back door, which leads into the family room, and then the two men are in the kitchen.

"Hi Wyatt, nice to meet you in person," Marybeth beams.

"Great to meet you. Thanks for having me to dinner," Wyatt says, transferring a paper bag to his left hand and reaching out with his right. During that maneuver, his eyes are fixed on Sally.

"Hey there, neighbor," Sally says. "What a nice surprise." *I hope that sounded casual*, she thinks.

Wyatt beams. "When Ed called me I jumped at the chance to see you. I just snuck around and came in the back in case anyone was following me."

"Divorce drama."

Wyatt shakes his head. "Yeah. I hate it. Hate the paranoia, all the arguing. I want it done."

Neither Wyatt nor Sally notice that Ed and Marybeth have left the kitchen.

Sally wants to throw her arms around him, but she is mindful of everyone else in the house, especially Andrea, who is probably out of the shower and wanting a snack.

"I've really enjoyed our late night chats," Sally says with a grin, thinking *You have no idea how much I live for our talks, hearing your voice almost every night.*

"Me too. Those talks are keeping me sane," Wyatt says shyly. "How's Andrea?"

"She's great. She's here with me, for the weekend."

Andrea comes bouncing into the kitchen and sees Wyatt. "Hey Dude! What's up?!" She hugs him quickly.

Wyatt grins at her. "Hey there, birthday girl. Happy happy," he says, handing her a small box he has pulled from his pocket.

"Oh wow, you didn't have to, but thanks!" she exclaims, ripping open the paper and opening the box. There are gold and pearl earrings in a black velvet hinged box.

"I've never seen any earrings so, so – beautiful," Andrea says shyly.

She gives him a hug.

"The only thing I know about women is that they usually appreciate jewelry. You look beautiful, BTW. Getting a tan."

Andrea blushes. "Yeah, kinda."

She does look lovely, having changed into a yellow sundress, her hair pulled back off of her face.

"Sally, Miss Marybeth has an awesome TV in the room upstairs where I'm staying. Can I take my dinner up there and eat while I watch? Please?" she implores Sally.

"I think it will be polite for you to eat here with us, but when you finish eating you can excuse yourself and go watch TV," Sally says.

Marybeth and Ed come back in the kitchen.

"I need steak orders. We like ours pink in the middle but not super rare," Ed says jovially.

"I like mine the same," Wyatt chimes in. "Oh, here, almost forgot, brought a bottle of wine," he says as he hands Marybeth the bottle.

"Nice. Chilean cabernet. Thank you so much. Why don't we try it out?" Marybeth asks, taking down several wineglasses from an overhead rack. "Ed, meet Andrea Hawkins."

"Andrea, it's nice to meet you," Ed says warmly.

"Nice to meet you, Dr. Durand. You have a lovely home," Andrea says, shaking his hand and looking to Sally, who smiles at her.

"How do you like your steak?" Ed asks casually.

Andrea has been eyeing the steaks. "I've never had steak?" she says in a small voice.

"You're in for a treat. Ed is great with steaks," Sally says. "Try it pink in the middle. I think that's what you'll like."

After dinner, Andrea has gone to watch TV. Ed and Marybeth sit at the dining room table with Wyatt and Sally, and the talk drifts to their children, and whether or not their oldest is going to get a divorce.

Wyatt recalls a portrait of the family in the hallway outside the family room.

"Excuse me," he says, and gets up to go take the photo off the wall. He returns to the dining room very quickly.

Sally and Marybeth exchange glances, both wondering what Wyatt is doing.

Wyatt hands Marybeth the portrait.

"Which child is it? The teenager with the streak of blue in her hair?"

"Yes, that's Ann, eight years ago. Why do you ask?" Marybeth says, smiling slightly.

"Do you have a more recent photo of her?" Wyatt asks.

"I have one. It was taken last Christmas," Ed says. He pulls out his smartphone and taps the screen for a moment, then hands it to Wyatt.

Wyatt studies it. "That's her husband?" he asks, nodding at the dark-haired man beside Ann.

"Yes," Ed says.

Wyatt hands the phone back and settles back into his chair. "She won't divorce, if you talk her into seeing a good therapist. She's trying to have a baby and having issues. Her husband feels really stressed out about it. If they go to counseling together and work out the issues I think they will become parents and it will be fine."

Ed and Marybeth exchange a look of bewilderment. Ann had told them about the infertility issues but they had not told anyone else, not even Sally.

Wyatt smiles at Sally. He realized about halfway through dinner that she was feeling a bit uncomfortable about the situation, about Marybeth pushing her into a new relationship, even though she hopes it will work out. The divorce has left her fearful of relationships.

Wyatt wants Ed and Marybeth to like him. *There is nothing special about me except my Ability, though,* he thinks.

Wyatt looks at Sally and realizes she has a look of horror mixed with fear on her face, her wide blue eyes looking frightened.

"I don't usually discuss it, but I do have an ability to read people, to see what they are thinking and feeling. Comes in handy for me as a lawyer," Wyatt says quickly, realizing he has freaked out his hosts.

Sally clears her throat and tries to keep her voice from sounding angry. "You told me you had good intuition but you never mentioned you had psychic powers. What you just did, that was way more than intuition."

Wyatt clears his throat and shifts in his seat, because he realizes that he has made a stupid mistake. *Maybe revealing that was idiotic,* he thinks, *I went too far. Damn.*

Finally, Ed speaks. "Sally's right. That's pretty amazing. Can you read anyone?"

Ah, okay, that's why they are all freaked out, thinks Wyatt. *They think I can read all their thoughts.*

"The short answer is no. Some people are completely closed off and I can't read them at all. Some people are as transparent to me as water. Sometimes I think I can read someone, and I read them wrong. I took on a client once who I thought was truly injured and deserved a big settlement, and then I found out he had been lying and faking, and boy did I get duped on that one," Wyatt smiles. That was only one out of hundreds of cases over the years but it still stung.

There is a silence, as Ed and Marybeth and Sally all ponder what he has just said.

"Look, it's not foolproof and it's not constant. If I listen to music or direct my thoughts elsewhere I can shut out even the most easily readable people. You don't have to worry that I will be able to constantly read all your minds like Dr. Xavier in X Men," he says, smiling.

Nobody smiles back.

Andrea comes in the room. "Um, Miss Marybeth, can I have some more of that blueberry pie?" she asks.

"Sure, honey, help yourself," Marybeth says, as she rises. She gathers up plates and silverware to take to the kitchen. Sally stands and picks up the serving dishes.

To the astonishment of both women, Wyatt stands and starts helping clear the table.

Ed wipes his mouth with his napkin and throws it down on the table, then gets up and trots off. Wyatt knows he's headed for the bathroom. He wishes he didn't know that.

As Wyatt helps the women clear the table they are all silent. Wyatt knows Sally and Marybeth want him to leave so they can discuss his revelation. He doesn't want to leave though. He is hungry to see Sally, to touch her, to talk to her.

He is grateful when Marybeth says "You two haven't had a chance to be alone all evening. Why don't you head into the living room and I'll finish up here.

Wyatt smiles at her gratefully.

Sally shoots Marybeth a look Wyatt can't read, and she grabs her wineglass before taking his hand to show him into the living room, which is just off the foyer.

Wyatt heads over to the large gray couch hoping Sally will settle in next to him but she doesn't. She sits in the occasional chair opposite the couch.

Wyatt looks at her settling into the chair, brushing a strand of hair back, her face slightly flushed from the wine. *I want to just look at her*, he thinks. *Every day. Always.*

"Well, um, that was quite a parlor trick back there. Why did you decide to spring it on Marybeth and Ed like that?" Sally says softly. She takes a sip of wine and looks at him trying to fix her face to appear implacable.

It's worse than I feared. I really freaked her out. Shit SHIT SHIT, Wyatt thinks.

Wyatt silently counts to ten as he sits back to think. It's something he taught himself to do as a young lawyer, instead of blurting out the first words he could think of. He takes a deep breath, then stares at a point on the horizon, calming his breathing. He clears his throat. He feels like he's in a courtroom.

Don't blow this. Don't scare her off. Don't tell her you were trying too hard to impress her friends.

"These people are your friends and they love you. They want you to be happy. Marybeth thinks we have a shot at a relationship. So do I – at least, I am hopeful. I couldn't continue to know you and not tell her and Ed. They don't know me. All they know is I am a lawyer getting a divorce. I felt like I had to... demonstrate what I can do, and ease their worries about their daughter."

Sally ponders this for a moment. "Everyone around you gets this kind of demonstration?"

Wyatt inhales sharply. "No. I never even tell anyone. I mean, I have an older sister. She knows. My best friend John – I just finally told him recently. Since I am living in his house I thought he ought to know. But no, it's something I keep very private. Always have. Never wanted to appear strange or crazy. I didn't want to be lumped in with the Psychic Wacko Network."

There is a long silence.

"So you think all psychics are crazy or charlatans?" Sally looks at him expectantly, while Wyatt shifts in his seat.

"I guess so. I've never met a psychic. About all I know about psychics is…. Well, that character in Ghost played by Whoopi Goldberg. Wasn't she a psychic?"

"I believe she was a medium. She talked to dead people. Can you do that, too?"

Startled, Wyatt barks out a laugh. "No. Sorry. Jesus. No." He chuckles.

Sally frowns, trying to decide if his reaction ticks her off.

"Well, just so you know, I have believed in psychics and mediums and ghosts my entire life. My father's mother came from Ireland and she used to tell me about all sorts of things. She was a devout Catholic but she also believed in spirits and fairies, and banshees. "

Wyatt nods slowly. "Fair enough. Well, we come from different worlds, then. My father was a man of science. He was a professor of physics at Emory for thirty years. He would probably have taken me to a psychiatrist if I had told him about my intuition. I always knew that, and so I kept quiet."

There is another awkward silence as Sally digests that information.

Wyatt realizes he has never spoken those words aloud before, not to anyone. He always wanted his father's respect, and his father had no patience with anything un-scientific.

Sally sips her wine again. "I can see why you wouldn't want to share anything otherworldly with a man like that. Answer something for me, though. Can't you figure out pretty easily what your uncle was up to all those years? Why did he wall off the back yard? What's in the trunk in the basement?"

Wyatt thinks for a moment. "I know there's nothing important in that trunk. However, I have picked up a spirit energy down there, which makes me a bit uncomfortable."

"But you're not a medium?" Sally retorts, trying not to sound bitchy.

"Well, no. I can't talk to spirits. I just know when they are there, usually."

"Maybe you should try having a chat with them sometime."

Wyatt sighs deeply. *Time to change the subject.*

"You are writing a history of the town right?"

Sally sips her wine and nods. "Yes. Why?"

"Well, um, why don't you see what you can find out about my house? Grandaddy's note said there was a rumor *"and it sounded like a fairytale to me"* I believe is how he put it. I think Grandaddy heard a corrupted story, possibly based on rumor or myth, but there's usually a nugget of truth in those types of stories."

Marybeth announces her presence "Knock knock. Hate to say this, but we close up shop around here at 11 on Friday nights because Ed has an early tee time in the morning. Wyatt, Sally's going to be here in Atlanta all weekend, if you want to come back."

"That's very kind of you," he says, standing up. "I appreciate being included in tonight's dinner. It was delicious."

Ed comes in just behind his wife. "Wyatt, my friend had to cancel. Some family emergency. Want to play 18 holes in the morning? We play at Dunwoody Country Club. Tee off at 8."

Wyatt is startled. He had gotten the impression at dinner Ed was not keen on him. However, he now senses Ed wants to tell him something important, as well as get to know him better. "Uh, sure, sure. That's a nice course."

"Great!" Ed says, clapping him on the back. "Meet me at the pro shop, 7:45," he said jovially. "Good night all." Ed turns and heads upstairs. Marybeth looks meaningfully at Sally and follows her husband.

"I'll walk out with you," Sally says.

A few minutes later Wyatt and Sally are outside, looking at the stars and the bright moon overhead, having walked near the edge of the backyard.

"Wyatt, I need some time to process what you said tonight. I like you tremendously, but it's a lot to deal with, okay?" Sally says softly.

Wyatt turns to face her. "I know. I realize it sounds wacky. I never talk about it, so when I saw your face I realized tonight how big a blunder I made, but I just felt like I needed to put all my cards on the table, let you see who I really am. All my life I've hidden behind this careful façade, but I'm tired of it. I want to be understood, I guess. Does that make any sense?"

Sally sighs. "Of course. It just startled me, and Marybeth and Ed. You don't have to play golf with him, you know."

Wyatt grins. "I like him. He's genuinely kind and caring, and he adores his wife and children, and views you like a little sister, which earns him an 11 on my respect meter."

Sally chuckles. "OK, you've got him pegged right, but don't bet money on the golf match," Sally says.

"Why not?!" Wyatt asks, startled.

"He's a rascal. He's a good player but he might try to make you think he's not. If he proposes a friendly wager on the third hole just say no," Sally laughs. She reaches around Wyatt's waist and gives him a quick hug.

He hugs her back, then carefully kisses her forehead. "Good night."

"Good night. Hopefully I will see you tomorrow," Sally says, pulling away and turning to walk back to the house.

Wyatt watches her walk back up the sloping yard, past the hydrangeas, into the circle of light from the outside lights shining over the patio, and wishes he had kept his mouth shut at dinner.

CHAPTER 25

The next morning it's already 88 degrees when Wyatt gets to the country club to play golf. Summer is the only time he hates living in Georgia, because the hot sticky heat makes going outside in the middle of the day really uncomfortable. Wyatt is glad for the early tee time, and the invention of deodorant.

Wyatt realizes after he hits his ball into a sand trap on the 4th hole that Ed is watching him and trying to make up his mind about him. Wyatt debates whether to confront Ed about it or let it go. He decides to wait a bit.

After they finish 18 holes they decide to have a beer.

In the cool quiet of the bar, Wyatt gathers his thoughts. Finally, he says "Look, what I did last night, talking about your daughter's infertility, that was a dumb thing to do. I have never done anything like that before. Ever. I don't discuss my... abilities. Not with anyone. I'm sorry. I wanted to show off a bit, and it backfired – I could tell that from your faces."

Ed takes a sip of beer and nods. "You have the reputation of being a quiet, thoughtful, reserved guy, very ethical, so I think we were just kind of startled."

Wyatt sighs. "Well, here's the deal. I'm just going to be honest. I think I'm falling in love with Sally. I'm just scared Sally will think I'm a really dull guy and I am, really, but – I hate that thought. So I showed off. I shouldn't have done it."

"No harm done," Ed said. "And just so you know, you're not a dull guy. I mean, you're a trial lawyer. I've never known one of those who was dull, and I've known a lot."

"Thanks," Wyatt says.

The waitress appears and Ed signs the bill with his club number.

Wyatt waits until the waitress has walked off, then broaches a delicate subject.

"Listen, uh, this is sort of awkward, but I have to ask you a favor. I don't really reveal my "ability" to anyone, normally. Would you just keep it to yourself, and ask Marybeth to do that, too? I'd appreciate it."

"Sure. No problem. You must have a helluva winning record as a lawyer, with that gift," Ed notes, looking appraisingly at Wyatt.

Wyatt smiles. "I usually get good results for my clients, yes."

"Ever had an MRI done, of your brain?"

Wyatt looks startled for a moment. "Uh, nope. Never had need of it. Why?"

Ed shrugs. "I'm just curious as to whether your brain would show any anomalies."

"I doubt it. I mean, there are things science just can't explain, you know?!" Wyatt replies, smiling. He knows Ed firmly believes in science and doubts there is anything that can't be explained if one rigorously applies the scientific method, but he doesn't want to argue about it.

"True. Changing the subject, Marybeth thinks it would be a great idea to go out to dinner tonight, take Andrea with us, and let you and Sally eat at our house. It will give y'all some privacy. There are several places nearby that deliver food. What do you think?"

Wyatt's gloomy face brightens immediately. "That would be wonderful. Thank you. Thanks for being so understanding about my need for privacy during the divorce. I know it must have felt weird, having a total stranger in your house."

"No worries. You're not a stranger to us if you're a friend of Sally's. Why don't you come over about 6:30 tonight?"

"Sounds great. See you then," Wyatt says.

The two men stand and shake hands.

Marybeth and Andrea spend that day shopping, while Sally sits by the pool and reads a book.

At 3:30, Ed comes in, greets Sally, and heads upstairs for a shower.

Marybeth and Andrea come in at 4. Sally hears them, and goes inside and looks at the many bags on the kitchen table. After much exclaiming over their purchases - "Look Sally isn't this adorable!" - Andrea goes up to her room to put on her new bathing suit, leaving Marybeth and Sally alone in the kitchen.

Marybeth pours herself a glass of iced tea and nibbles some banana bread. Sally surveys the bags littering the kitchen.

"Stinky, you are so bad. You bought the child a new wardrobe! What were you thinking?!" Sally says, shaking her head at all the clothes.

"We bought everything from Forever 21, and I told Andrea the store owner is a friend and I got a HUGE discount," Marybeth chuckles. "It worked."

"You shouldn't have, but thanks," Sally says, chuckling.

Marybeth pours herself a glass of tea. "It was a little white lie. Listen, I miss going shopping with my daughter, since she lives in Nashville now. I am too fat to fit in cute clothes any more. So it was fun to shop with Andrea. She has a great figure and decent taste, for a kid from Ringgold Georgia."

"Well, now that she is 18 we can finally get her out of the house, so it's good she has a decent wardrobe. Will you let me pay you for half of it?" Sally asks.

"Nope. It was my pleasure. I have a surprise for you too."

"What?" Sally says, instantly alert.

"Ed and I are going to take Andrea to a movie and to dinner tonight. You and Wyatt are going to stay here and eat dinner. It will give you a chance for some privacy."

Sally looks at Marybeth, eyes wide. "Seriously?!"

Marybeth laughs. "You sound like a teenager. What an overused word. Yes. SERIOUSLY. Now let's looks at your clothes and see what sexy outfit we can put you in. You look like you've dropped a few, right?!"

It is 7 p.m. and Wyatt has just stepped out of the shower and is drying off when his phone rings. He grabs the phone. *No way am I taking that call*, he grimaces, grabbing his boxer shorts.

It keeps ringing. He keeps ignoring the phone.

A text comes through. THIS IS SHARON YOU NEED TO TAKE MY CALL ITS ABOUT THAD

Wyatt grabs the phone and answers.

"What's wrong with Thad? Is he hurt?"

Sharon's voice is icy. "No, he is physically fine."

"Then what's this about?" Wyatt asks, sitting down on the bed.

"Wyatt, I just heard that you settled the Campbell case for $245,000 and you thought you were going to keep all of that fee, didn't you?!" Sharon barked.

Wyatt sighed. "I mentioned it to Thad and he must have told you. Yes, since I did all the work on that case I expected to keep it," he said noticing John had come in to the room and was motioning for him to hand him the phone. Wyatt shakes his head impatiently, but puts the call on speaker. John sits down on the bed.

"I have Thad here for the weekend. He is very upset because I told him your lawyer is being obstinate about paying me what I deserve, and I am in a financial crisis and fixing to lose the house, and he may have to quit school."

"WHAT?! None of that's true," Wyatt shouts angrily.

"No? Well you try telling that to your son, who is crying with frustration, he's so upset."

"That's YOUR fault then —" Wyatt starts, but Sharon cuts him off.

"Now you listen here you cold motherfucker. I want it ALL. I want every penny you've got and if you don't pay me, here's what will happen. I will take the photos of you and that teenager and I will show Thad you've been screwing around on me with that little jailbait, and you're refusing to pay me what I need to live on, and he will hate you even more than he does now."

Sharon's voice has a touch of glee, of triumph, in it.

"You wouldn't," Wyatt says weakly.

"Yes, I would, and you know it."

Wyatt looks at John, who makes the hanging up motion to him.

Wyatt, puzzled, pantomimes "WHY?" and John keeps motioning. "Sharon, I will call you back on this number within the next thirty minutes," Wyatt says, and hangs up.

"What?!" he says after disconnecting the call.

John sits on the bed and sighs heavily.

"I was trying to keep this from you until after your date tonight. I'm sorry she decided to ignore advice from her lawyer and just call you. I talked to him late yesterday afternoon. Here's the deal. Henry is fixing to have to file bankruptcy. Sharon doesn't want that. So she's coming after you for every penny she can get, to pay off some of his creditors."

Wyatt stares at his friend. "So what am I supposed to do?!"

"Do you have anything on her? Do you know anything that could destroy her reputation?"

"No!" Wyatt says angrily. "You know I don't operate like that."

John sighs, then stands up and stares at Wyatt. "Sharon DOES operate like that. Look, sometimes it plays out like this. One spouse threatens to tell the child or children awful stuff, show them awful stuff – it's emotional blackmail. I've never seen someone so vicious about it as Sharon, though. You know her a lot better than I do. Do you think she would turn your son against you for money?"

Wyatt puts his head in his hands and sits for a moment. Finally, he looks up at his friend, pale and drawn.

"Yeah, I think she would. She's capable of just about anything. Just pay her what she wants. Just give her all of it. I'm tired of all this drama. I want my life back, even if I have nothing."

"Well, I hate to hear that but I know you're frustrated. How close are you to being able to close up your office?"

"Very close. All my cases are gone or settled. Once I write the checks and get the releases signed on Campbell, I can close up shop. Everyone has left except my secretary, and she starts a new job in a couple of weeks."

"Is there any more fee money? Any settlements she doesn't know about?"

Wyatt shakes his head. "Not really. I only took big cases."

John pats his friend on the back. "Well, you're welcome to stay here as long as you need to."

"Thanks buddy."

Wyatt sits and stares at the painting on the wall, a modern art Mondrian type thing with lots of orange. He doesn't really see the painting, though. He thinks about Henry, who is a spineless, nasty, petty-minded creep. However, he is also a doctor, and he runs with the beautiful people in Buckhead, a social status Sharon has always envied. He knows she will not stop until she is married to Henry, totally running his life.

Wyatt looks at his friend. "Here's what I'm going to do. I'm going to go up to Knoxville and stay with Nora and Ben until the deal is totally done, and the divorce is over. Then I'm going to move into the house in Crossroads. Wait a minute. SHIT. I almost forgot. Nora wants some things out of the house, including a set of china that was my mother's."

"So?"

"I am not supposed to show up at Nora's house without the stuff."

John rubs the back of his neck, which Wyatt knows means he is stressing. "Her attorney said she will allow you to come get the rest of your stuff any time. Sharon doesn't want it. But you know what? I think we should go get it tonight. You know what all Nora wants?"

"Tonight?! Why do you want to go tonight?!" Wyatt replies, startled. He is rarely startled.

"Wyatt, Sharon isn't stupid. It just occurred to me that she knows the stuff may be valuable and she might decide to sell it and give Henry the money."

"She can't do that, can she?!"

"She might try it. I wouldn't put it past her," John says evenly. "She might even say it was stolen."

"Shit."

John pulls out his cell phone. "I'm going to call her lawyer and tell him to tell her we will be there in an hour. No more of this ex parte communication. When we get there, I'll type up a receipt and we can just hand write in what we take, so it's all aboveboard," John says thoughtfully.

"OK. Maybe we can get in and out quickly and I can still see Sally."

John shakes his head. "Doubt it. We will need to take some newspapers and boxes so we can pack up the china carefully, and that will take a while."

"Really?"

"I'm sorry buddy," John says.

CHAPTER 26

Sally hangs up the phone and looks at Marybeth miserably. "Wyatt has to go to his wife's house and get some things tonight. He can't postpone. That woman is crazy evil," Sally says miserably.

"Damn. That's too bad," Marybeth says sympathetically.

"See, I had a chance to think this afternoon, and after last night's revelation, I really need to talk to him about his "gift" and find out if he can read every thought in my head. If I'm as transparent as water to him, I'm not sure I can deal with that, you know?"

Marybeth looks at her friend with pity. "Yeah, I completely understand why you're a bit freaked out. Totally normal reaction. If Ed knew every thought I had about him we would have gotten divorced long ago."

Sally looks thoughtful. "But here's another thing. Why didn't he tell me this sooner? I mean, he sort of told me, but not really. Intuition is not the same thing. Now I don't know how to process this."

Marybeth hugs her. "I'm sorry. Just come on out to dinner with us, Honey, have some wine. Get your mind off of it."

Sally puts her head on Marybeth's shoulder and tries not to cry. "I don't know what I would do without you and Ed, and Andrea. Y'all are my family."

"That's right. Come on, blow your nose. The Cheesecake Factory awaits."

Sally pulls back and looks at Marybeth. "Really?!"

"Yep. Andrea saw it this afternoon and asked if we could eat there tonight and I said sure. She admitted she had never eaten cheesecake."

The two friends laugh. They had once had a birthday lunch there and sampled 10 kinds of cheesecake, then gotten horrible indigestion. Now the words "cheesecake factory" evoke pained memories.

Sally wipes her eyes and grins. "I am NOT getting any cheesecake, are you?!"

"Hell to the NO!" Marybeth says cheerfully.

Sally is grateful to have Marybeth in her life.

Later that same night, Sally is propped up in bed in Marybeth's guestroom, reading a mystery novel, Blanche in bed beside her, when her cell phone rings. She has brushed her teeth and washed her face, and is settling in for the nightly reading ritual that enables her to go to sleep, so she doesn't welcome the ringing phone, but then again, she thinks, what if it's Miranda and she needs me?

A glance at the phone reveals it's Wyatt.

Sally answers it.

"Hey, wow, how are you?" she stammers.

"I am exhausted and I need to sleep, but I wanted to hear your voice," Wyatt answers evenly. "I am so sorry we didn't get our dinner date."

Wyatt is stretched out on his bed in John's guest room, having wolfed down a peanut butter and jelly sandwich.

"How did it go?" Sally asks.

"We got the things out of the house and into John's garage. Hopefully soon my sister will come pick everything up."

"It's none of my business, but what was it that needed to be retrieved so quickly?" Sally asks, trying to sound casual.

She's wondering if there is anything really valuable, like museum quality, Wyatt thinks, smiling.

"We had a set of sterling silver flatware and a set of china that belonged to my mom, plus some crystal, an Oriental rug, a small marble-topped table, some knickknacks. When Dad died it all came to my house because Nora didn't want to deal with it all. Suddenly she wants it. Or maybe she just wants her daughters to have it. I don't know."

"Nora is your sister?" Sally asks. Wyatt has only mentioned her before in passing.

"Yeah, she lives in Knoxville."

"So how is she going to get the stuff?" Sally asks, stretching out her hand to rub Blanche's belly.

"I don't know. Right now it's in John's garage. I was going to take it up to her but when I saw Thad tonight he was really upset, so I think I am going to take him to the beach for a while," Wyatt says softly, wishing he were taking Sally instead. "I have a friend who has a house down there."

"I understand," Sally replies softly. "You need time to help him process everything."

"Yep. I also need to talk to him about the divorce. All he has really heard is his mother's side of things, and I need to correct what she told him. The tricky part will be to do that without telling him about the awful stuff she has done. I don't believe in doing that to a kid, even a 21 year old."

Sally sighs. "I know. I had the same situation. Well, not exactly, but I didn't want to tell my daughter her father was a cold workaholic not all that interested in marriage or parenting. Great with cows and horses, not so much with kids -- although, strangely, most people like him. I think it had a lot to do with the fact that he was really handsome, and even though he wasn't southern he was very polite. Is polite.."

"Yeah, Sharon gets away with a lot because she is beautiful, and she can turn on the charm," Wyatt says quietly.

There is an awkward silence. Finally, Sally breaks it.

"I was going to call you tomorrow. I have a couple of questions," Sally says, trying to sound casual.

"Okay. Fire away," Wyatt replies, tensing up but also trying to sound casual.

"Well, um, I don't know how to ask this, but can you read my mind? You said your powers aren't always reliable but I really need to know," Sally says softly.

Wyatt feels his heart start to beat wildly. *Don't screw this up!* His inner voice warns. "I can't always tell, no. If we are in the same room, it's much easier. I can notice your facial expression, your posture, how much you are looking at me – all sorts of clues. Over the phone it's much harder. It's also difficult for me to read people I – uh, am close to."

"Okay. I want to try something. I am picturing something in my mind, a random object. What am I picturing?" Sally asks.

A beach ball, Wyatt thinks. Crap. Don't say it. "A mug?"

"Nope. Not even close," Sally replies, clearly pleased. "What am I picturing now?"

Wyatt closes his eyes. She is running through a series of images, quickly, like a slide show. She stops and looks at the lamp on her bedside table.

"It is a child's swingset?" he asks, trying to sound unsure.

"Nope. Well, that's a relief," Sally says.

"I told you, my gift doesn't always work, and it doesn't always work perfectly. The closer I am to someone, the harder it is to read them," Wyatt answers carefully. "It's often hard for me to read my son."

Wyatt realizes he is over-answering, but he hopes Sally will calm down.

Sally smiles happily to herself.

"So what is the china pattern of your parents' china you got back?" she asks.

"Royal Doulton Carlyle. It's supposedly valuable. Really a pain to pack. John was with me and he was like a fussy old lady, demanding we wrap each plate and cup in bubble wrap. He went to Office Depot and bought boxes and packing peanuts galore. I had never seen that fussy side of him. I guess it's because his mother owns an antique store."

They talk for another hour, until exhaustion takes over and they say goodbye.

Andrea is awake. She can't sleep.

Surprisingly, she got bored with the TV pretty quickly. She prowls around Marybeth's house, just looking at things. Sally has an old house, decorated with some nice furniture and a few antiques, but it's not elegant.

Marybeth has an innate sense of style and color, and she decorated her home with the help of a decorator. It's elegant but also warm. Andrea touches the cherry wood of the baby grand piano. She feels of the smooth leather of the couch in the family room.

She looks out the glass of the French doors, admiring the lush green landscape of the backyard, in the moonlight.

A grandfather clock in the foyer chimes softly, 12 times. Andrea goes out to look at it, before creeping back up the stairs.

She looks at the bedroom of Marybeth's daughter, decorated in shades of lavender and blue, and likes the feeling of the thick carpet under her feet.

The whole weekend has felt surreal. Her first steak. Her first "shopping spree" at the mall. Her first dinner at a nice restaurant. Swimming in a private pool.

The pool was wondrous. The feel of the water on her limbs as she floated, her hair a nimbus around her head. The lapping sounds. The peacefulness was like a dream. She resolved to learn how to swim better.

Andrea ponders whether or not an archaeologist might be able to afford an apartment with a pool one day. She has no idea.

A knock sounds at the door, softly. "Yes?" Andrea says, tensing for a moment.

Marybeth opens the door quietly. She is standing there in a bathrobe, holding a mug.

"I thought you might like some chamomile tea."

She hands the mug to Andrea and sits on the bed.

"Thank you," Andrea says, accepting the mug and sipping the tea, wondering what "chamomile" means. It sounds French, she decides. "This is good. I really had fun today."

Marybeth smiles warmly. "I am so glad you are living with Sally. She says you're studying for the GED."

"Yes M'am, it was Sally's idea."

"Sally always encourages people to improve themselves," she says, smiling. "Tell me about your mama, honey," Marybeth says softly.

Andrea frowns, and ducks her head, not speaking for a full minute. Finally, she says softly:

"When I was born my mom, Danielle, was 15. She had me and left me with my granny and took off. Those first 5 years were the best. Granny didn't have any money but she loved me and we had fun. She ran a daycare out of her house, so I always had somebody to play with. She read to me. She taught me my letters and numbers and everything.

Then my mom reappeared when I was in first grade and took me to the trailer park to live with her. I hated it and ran away, back to Granny. Danielle went to court and got something saying I had to live with her. I got to spend the first few summers with Granny, though, until she died. Danielle never wanted to pay a babysitter."

Marybeth's blue eyes are filled with sadness as she regards Andrea.

Andrea feels relief washing over her in waves, like she has handed the burden of her life to someone else, someone much stronger.

"What about your daddy?"

"Danielle said he was a boy who left her after I was born. I later found out she didn't actually know who he was. Could have been any one of several guys. I didn't care about that. My step granddaddy was a daddy to me. He died when I was small, though."

"I'm sorry. Sounds like you had a tough time."

Andrea takes a deep breath, gathering her courage.

"Miss Marybeth, do you think I could go to college? Do you think I'm smart enough? I just wondered if somebody with a GED could get a scholarship or a grant."

"I don't know. Sally could help you research that. You would probably be eligible for something. I might can help, too."

"It feels overwhelming. Nobody in family ever went to college," Andrea says, eyes downcast.

Marybeth pats her hand. "Don't stress. We'll figure it out. Listen, I need to get back to bed. I want to tell you something, though."

Marybeth leans forward and looks into Andrea's eyes. "You're a smart girl, Andrea, and a good soul. Dream big, honey. Don't give up on your dreams. Sally and I will help you. You can lean on us."

Andrea's eyes fill with tears. She hugs Marybeth.

"Thank you. Thank you for everything."

Marybeth holds her for a moment and pats her back, wishing she could slap the fire out of Andrea's worthless mother.

CHAPTER 27

A few days later it's Wednesday and Sally sits in the library where she works, scrolling through microfilm. She is looking for stories about the Jamison family. She has the names of Wyatt's grandparents and great-grandparents from old deed records, and is scanning the local newspaper for their names.

A larger town and a larger paper would be easily searchable by name.

Part of the problem is the size of Crossroads. It's never been a big town. There is a weekly paper that started publishing in 1858, the Crossroads Chronicle, but it doesn't have a lot of news that is terribly interesting – mostly farm news, and stories out of Clayton, or even Asheville. Nonetheless, she reads through everything searching for the name Jamison.

She finds a small notice about the birth of a son to Marcus and Josephine Jamison in 1866. Baby was named Jack. She keeps scrolling through the microfilm.

She is interrupted by a voice loudly calling her.

"Miss Sally! Hey there!"

Sally turns around and sees Andy Wheeler slowly making his way across the carpet to her. Andy is 90 years old but still spry.

"How you doin' Miss Sally?" he says with a grin.

"I'm just fine Mr. Wheeler. Here, let's get you into a chair," Sally says, rising smoothly and pulling one of the heavy oak library chairs over near her.

"Thank you darling," says Mr. Wheeler.

"How is Emmaline?" Sally asks louder than her usual voice. Mr. Wheeler is hard of hearing and forgets to wear his hearing aid most of the time.

"She takes real good care of me," Mr. Wheeler says. Emmaline is his daughter, herself 64 years old. "Say, what you lookin' at here?" he demands, seeing the microfilm reels.

"Oh, I was just trying to do some research," Sally says. She sits down opposite him and looks at him thoughtfully. "You remember the Jamison family? Lived in the house next to mine?"

Wheeler closes his filmy blue eyes. For a moment, Sally wonders if he has had an attack of some sort. Then he opens his eyes and smiles.

"Yep, good folks. Never did bother nobody. Kept to themselves."

She has a lot of things she wants to ask Andy Wheeler but courtesy dictates she can't just blurt out questions.

"I've got some extra squash and tomatoes this year from my garden. Would y'all like to have some?" Sally asked.

"Homegrown tomatoes?" Wheeler asks. "Lord yes. Emmaline didn't plant any this year, said her arthritis was botherin' her too much. We would love some."

Sally smiled. "Well all right then. I'll bring some over after work tonight. Would that be okay?"

"Absolutely. Thank you kindly, dear. Say, how's that brother of yours?"

"Luke? He's just fine. He and Linda have three boys, all grown now. They live in Clayton. Do you need some plumbing work done?"

"No, no. Just wondered. I remember when he was the star quarterback at the high school. He was a good boy."

"Yes, thanks," Sally answered, wondering if the old man would ask about her younger brother Sam, who lived in California and built websites.

She takes a deep breath and decides to go ahead and ask her question, before the old man tires and has to go home.

"Mr. Wheeler, have you ever heard a rumor about a treasure being buried somewhere in Crossroads? Something like looted Confederate gold or things the Yankees stole during the war and hid?"

Mr. Wheeler's ancient face lights up, and he grins wide, showing shiny dentures, then cackles delightedly. "Lordy lordy, yes. Those tall tales were all over when I was a boy. Nobody will ever find that treasure, if it exists. You think old Hugh Jamison was lookin' for it, huh?!"

Sally smiles. Andy Wheeler is nobody's fool. He was a mechanical engineer for 40 years. "Well, I think old Mr. Hugh might have been hunting for it, yes. His nephew found a letter indicating there might be some truth to that old tall tale. I've been thinking on it, wondering if it could be true.. If it was true, I wonder why Hugh didn't find the treasure, you know?"

Wheeler cleared his throat, and his smile dims somewhat. "Hugh was a good man. Too intellectual, though. Not a practical bone in his body."

Wheeler falls silent, then coughs softly.

"You want some water?" Sally asks anxiously. It's a very hot day.

"No darling," Wheeler says. He leans closer to Sally after he looks around, but there is nobody else in the library to hear. "You know about the Jamison family, right?"

"Well, uh.. Know what about them?"

"Well, Wendell and Hugh come from a long line of mountain folk, average people, farmers and such. That's only half of it, though. Their mama was who encouraged them to get more schooling than most. She come up from Charleston, on a trip on the train to Asheville, and liked Crossroads and decided to stay a day or two. She was Elizabeth Fellows. Beautiful lady. Tall and blonde.

Educated. Never did know why she decided to marry a farmer and stay in this little town."

"Ah, okay. So she was Hugh's mother."

He nods. "Yep. An unusual marriage. She raised two sons to be university professors. That's something, for those days."

"Yep. Sure is," Sally replies, knowing how unusual it is for mountain folk to marry outsiders.

From outside, a car horn honks. Sally looks towards the front door. There's a red Cadillac out in front. "Your caddy sure likes nice."

Wheeler stands slowly. "That's Emmaline. Wish I could still drive it. Now I've had my walk, had my rest, and we're goin' over to Bob's Place, get some lunch."

"Well all right then," Sally says, walking with him to the front door and opening the door. "Tell Emmaline I'll run over around 7."

"That's when Jeopardy's on," Wheeler says.

"I won't stay. I'll just leave the produce on the porch," Sally says, grinning. She knows all old folks love Jeopardy.

Come to think of it, she used to love Jeopardy.

CHAPTER 28

Wyatt sits at the island in John's kitchen eating a club sandwich from Firehouse Subs for dinner and pondering the events of the last several weeks and months. He has just signed the final agreement and the divorce is officially over. He knows John is not pleased about it.

John belches and rubs his belly. He has just finished a foot long meatball sub.

"How was the beach?" John asks. Wyatt has been back for a month but John had been busy and forgotten to ask him. Wyatt had also gone to a seminar in Wisconsin for a week, a welcome respite from Atlanta's August heat.

Wyatt regrets that he wasn't able to get up to see his sister. He had to do damage control with his son, so they had spent two weeks at St. Simon's Island.

"It was good. We had a place right on the beach. Notice the tan?" Wyatt chuckles.

"Did you get some fishing done?" John asks.

"Yeah, did some fishing from the beach, and one day we chartered a fishing boat and went out, but nothing interesting took the bait," Wyatt replies, wiping his mouth. "Thad was nauseated the whole time, too, so he didn't enjoy it."

John grunts sympathetically. "That's too bad. Those kind of boats make me queasy, too. Listen, I still think you should have let me fight for you some more, my friend," John says. He has finished his potato chips and is rapidly drinking a beer.

"John, how many divorces do you only work for four months? We set a record?!" Wyatt grins.

John sighs. "Wyatt, I didn't want to get it done that quickly. I wanted to fight."

Wyatt shakes his head. "I know you didn't want to give her what she wanted, but here's the thing: as long as we were arguing back and forth and I was scared to see Sally, I was miserable. I hated my life. HATED IT. Now I feel free. Almost happy, even."

John stares at his friend, wondering about the new Wyatt. "You're poor, but you feel free and light-hearted? I don't hear that too often."

Wyatt throws his sandwich wrapper in the trash and looks at his friend.

"John, I have my freedom, and a nice house in the mountains, and some money, and my life has turned a corner. Yeah, I feel great. My dad used to say never look back, something might be gaining on you. I think he was quoting someone famous."

The two men chuckle.

John belches again. "I thought you were going to go see Nora up in Knoxville?"

Wyatt shrugs. "I'll see her soon, sure, but no hurry. Tomorrow, I'm going to rent a U-Haul and attach it to my car, load up all my stuff and head up to the mountains."

John's eyebrows shoot up. He looks at Wyatt's grinning face.

"And do what? And what are you going to live on? That ex of yours got everything," John grouses, shaking his head and throwing his sandwich wrapper away.

Wyatt chuckles. "Not everything. When Dad died I gave my sister Nora the entire inheritance. I didn't want it. She invested it. Now she's giving back half to me. I have a fantastic sister. So now, I have enough of my inheritance from my father to pay the bills and buy groceries for a while, and by then I will have a clear path ahead. I may practice a little law up there."

John looks puzzled. "Why didn't you tell me this?"

Wyatt drinks a long swallow of beer. "I am not entirely ignorant of divorce law. If Nora had given it back to me already I would have had to declare it. Sharon would have figured out a way to get it. This way, the divorce is over and what Nora gives to me is entirely mine. Sharon won't get the satisfaction of seeing me destitute."

John stares at his friend. "How did Sharon not know about this?"

"She did know. When Dad died, I told her Nora was on the verge of bankruptcy and I needed to give her the entire inheritance. It wasn't true; Nora was financially fine. Sharon liked Nora and felt sorry for her, though. She didn't argue about it. Plus, I had just settled a big case so we had plenty of money. It worked out."

"That was just a few years ago. Did you know then you were getting divorced?" John asks, remembering Wyatt's ability.

Wyatt is thoughtful for a moment. "No, well... Who knows? I just knew I didn't need the money right then, and I trust Nora."

"How much is it?" John asks, almost afraid to hear the answer.

Wyatt looks thoughtful for a moment. "I don't know, exactly. But listen, I'll be in the mountains. My car is paid for. The house is paid for. I don't use credit cards because I hate debt. My expenses will be minimal. It will be fine."

The two men watch a baseball game for a couple of hours and then head to their rooms.

After he strips down to his underwear in preparation for bed, Wyatt emails his sister and asks her how much is in the IRA. She answers quickly. It's not what he had hoped. His half is a bit less than $75K. Wyatt grimaces at the number. After he pays for his son's final year of college there won't be a lot left after he pays penalties for cashing it in early.

Wyatt sighs and calls his sister. She answers on the first ring.

"Hey, it's me."

"Yep, I knew it was you, little brother. What's up? You divorced yet? Is it final?" Nora is watching a Braves baseball game with the sound off, her husband beside her, asleep.

"Yeah, we are officially over, thank God."

"Good. I never liked her," Nora said, vehemently stage whispering.

"Really? You were always nice to her," Wyatt answers, startled.

"She was your girlfriend and then your wife. I didn't want to alienate you, so I was nice to her. She was always too cold and efficient, though. Too perfect. Yikes."

Wyatt thinks about Nora, who loves teaching art to first graders. Nora's old, messy house is warm and comfortable. Her husband Ben, a physical therapist, is a huge bear of a man greatly loved by his patients. Their house is not professionally decorated and kept pristine as Wyatt and Sharon's house was, but it is filled with love and warmth.

"How are Ben? The girls?"

Nora's two daughters are grown and living on their own, one a flight attendant in Charlotte and one a stay at home mom in Nashville.

"Everybody's good. Thanks. What's up? You don't usually call this late," Nora asks, glancing at the old clock radio on the bedside table.

"Well, you know I told you to deposit the money from Dad's estate in my bank account?" Wyatt asks.

"Yeah, I did it this afternoon. Good thing we have the same bank," Nora answers. "I'm sorry you weren't able to come see us but I know it was important to spend time with Thad before school."

"Yeah, we had fun at the beach. I got some fishing done. Listen, I don't mean this as a criticism, in any way, but I am puzzled as to why there wasn't more money?" Wyatt asks cautiously.

Nora takes a deep breath. "Well, you recall that when Dad died you were involved in that big case? The three week trial in federal court?"

"Well, yeah. What does that have to do with anything?" Wyatt asks, trying not to sound annoyed.

"Well, brother, when you are in trial mode it's pretty tough to talk to you. I know I told you that the estate taxes were godawful, and when we sold the house we found out there were three mortgages and we lost money."

Wyatt is silent for a moment. He vaguely recalls Nora telling him exactly that, in an email, but he was in "trial mode" as she said, and it hadn't really registered.

"Yeah, right, now I remember. Okay. Sorry to bother you."

"Hey, don't hang up. We haven't talked in a bit, not about YOU. How is your girlfriend, Sally? Okay to call her that now?"

Wyatt smiles. "She's fine. We talk almost every day. I'm going to see her tomorrow. I'm excited to make the big move."

"Awesome. How long has it been since you've seen her?"

"I was able to have dinner with her a couple of months ago, at a friend's house here in Atlanta."

"Wow, she must be a keeper," Nora says thoughtfully.

"Yeah. I told her about my... ability."

There is a silence of a full minute while Nora digests that revelation.

"Wow. I thought you were never going to tell anyone?" Nora asks, cautiously.

"Yeah, well, I wanted to come clean with her. It might have been a mistake. Now she thinks I'm weird."

Nora swings her legs off the bed and stands up. "Well of course. Can you read her?" Nora asks, going out to the living room to talk, since Ben's snores are getting louder.

"Yeah. That used to freak me out, when I was in college and trying to date, remember? That's why Sharon was so intriguing. I couldn't read her at all."

Nora sighs heavily. "Yeah, well, I have a theory about that."

"What?"

"You won't like it."

"Why not?" Wyatt often cannot "read" Nora.

"Look, over the years, whenever you've told me about the rare occasion when you couldn't read someone – other than family -- I have learned that it's often because they are... well, evil."

"Evil? What do you mean, evil?!" Wyatt's legal brain is highly skeptical of that word, which seems almost cartoonish to him.

"Okay, don't jump down my throat," Nora snaps, sitting at the kitchen table and pouring a tot of Sherry into a small glass. "Remember that fraternity brother of yours who was convicted of rape? The psychopath?"

Wyatt remembers very well. Leonard Price had been a cold-blooded guy, and Wyatt had never been able to read him. He had been shocked by the allegations against Price.

"Yeah, he was evil. Sharon is a bitch but I wouldn't call her evil, though," Wyatt says, thinking about her as the mother of his child.

"She took all the money you earned and left you with nothing – or so she thought. If that's not evil, what is?!"

"True."

"Look, you should have gone into criminal law, except you wouldn't have wanted to represent anyone you couldn't read," Nora says softly, sipping her Sherry.

"I wouldn't have made a good criminal lawyer."

"True. If they were guilty I don't think you could have handled it."

There is a pause.

Wyatt thinks about the fact that Nora has always known him better than anyone, and loved him anyway. He sometimes keenly misses having his father available to talk to, however.

"Listen, as soon as I get settled into my mountain house, Uncle Hugh's house, I want you and Ben to come down for a weekend. It's beautiful there. Really lovely. You remember it at all? The way the mountains surround the town? Tell Ben there's a good fishing hole."

Nora laughs. "You and your fishing holes. All right. Yeah, I vaguely remember it. We would love to come. The fall is a great time to be in the mountains," Nora replies, staring at the calendar. It's September.

"Well, thanks for the talk. I know you need to get up early," Wyatt says.

"You call me whenever you need to talk, Little Brother. I love you."

Wyatt feels tears burning in his eyes. "Love you too, Sis."

I like to visit Sally's house, and watch her comings and goings. I love to see her lovingly plant and tend her garden – such a variety of wonderful vegetables and melons.

I love to see Blanche's flip over and joyously root around in the grass.

I wish in my life I had been a better neighbor. I wish I had gotten to know this lovely woman who lived just steps away from me.

Andrea's delight in the garden, and in books, and in Sally's love – that's the beauty of being alive, I realize. A mother has found another child, a child has found a mother, and both are caring for each other like family.

I am fascinated to see how Sally teaches Andrea. She is a natural teacher, and Andrea is eager to learn.

All summer long she has shown the girl how to grow vegetables and melons in the garden soil, rich from composted veggies and organic matter like coffee grounds and eggshells.

Together they plant and prune and fertilize the rich soil. Andrea acts like a child on Christmas morning when she discovers each bloom on the tomato plant, each squash nestled under the leaves.

"Oooh look Sally!" she squealed, the first time she saw a tiny green tomato on the vine. I loved the look of sheer joy on Andrea's face.

One sunny day they pulled out the old baby pool and Blanche got a bath and a nail trim. Blanche loved the attention.

Another day, they went to Home Depot and got a bunch of materials and built a fire pit. That night, they roasted marshmallows and made s'mores.

Sally laughs more now. She clearly loves having someone to share her life with again.

Andrea soaks it up like a sponge, finally able to relax and be a kid.

I watch it all, and then the days grow cooler and the leaves start to change. It's quite something, drifting above the treetops, watching the leaves turn to flaming reds and oranges. One day I realize there is a hot air balloon close by, as lovely as a huge butterfly.

Then one cool September day Sally does something strange. She makes a coffee cake and puts it in my house. She and Andrea go over and air out the place, dust the whole house, throw out

the old food, put new food in the fridge –
strawberries from the garden, some brie cheese,
a six pack of beer.

Finally, while Andrea sweeps the front
porch, Sally goes into the biggest bedroom, the
one that was mine, and strips the bed and puts
fresh white sheets on there, vacuums, and puts a
jar of zinnias on the bedside table. She takes out
boxes of clothes and puts them in the carriage
house.

She looks around and smiles a bit to
herself, as though the carriage house holds a
treasure.

I can remember when it held horses.

Sally is wearing old gym shorts, a tank top,
and flip flops, without a speck of makeup, her
hair in a messy topknot on her head. Despite her
age, she has never looked more beautiful.

Wyatt needs to hold onto this one.

CHAPTER 29

Sally checks the mirror one final time and wipes off a smear of eyeliner. She rarely wears makeup on a day when she isn't working, but today Wyatt is moving in next door and so her excitement level is off the charts.

Despite her unease about his mind-reading powers, Sally has decided to see what happens romantically with Wyatt, hoping something real will work out. She is afraid to say (even to herself) that she loves him, but deep down, she knows that she does.

The many late-night phone calls have established a level of emotional intimacy she never shared with her ex-husband. Sally and Wyatt have talked about everything from his cases to Sally's difficult library clients, to small town life, to their first cars. One day they laugh through a whole conversation about what they taught their kids to say when needing to use the bathroom.

Sally has never shared so much with anyone, even Marybeth.

Wyatt, always reserved and quiet, has never shared so much of himself with anyone either -- certainly not with his wife. He thinks about that as he drives north in the early autumn sunshine.

The day of Wyatt's arrival in Crossroads is normal and yet different.

Andrea is on the computer, as always when not at work. She has already determined the courses she needs to take at the junior college in Gainesville so she can get her Freshman and Sophomore year general courses out of the way.

Andrea has been waitressing at Bob's Place for over a month, working the dinner shift and cleaning up on tips. Leaf season in the North Georgia mountains always means an influx of tourists.

Andrea confided in Marybeth and Sally that she wants to go to college and be an archaeologist.

Sally checks the clock – 1:25. He's a little late. Must have gotten into the Saturday leaf traffic. She glances out the front window for the 54th time and sees Wyatt pulling into her driveway, towing a U-Haul trailer behind his car. She had told him to do that because his little house doesn't have a driveway. Her Nissan Pathfinder is parked in front of the house.

Sally casually walks outside to greet him.

Wyatt unfolds himself from the car and stretches his legs. When he sees Sally his heart lightens. She is wearing red Capri pants and a white cotton top. It's unseasonably warm for September. Her tanned arms and lack of jewelry impress him. He is ready for open and simple.

"Good to see you, Stranger," Sally says, walking over for a hug. There are crinkles around her blue eyes from smiling.

"You too, Beautiful," Wyatt says with a grin.

He hugs her and smells of her hair, which smells like flowers.

"How was the drive? Any traffic?" Sally asks, pulling away, mindful of neighbors.

"Yep, it was heavy, but not until I got off 85 did it get really slow."

"Leaf traffic. Well, at last you're here!" Sally replies, "And going slow lets you see the leaves, although they haven't peaked yet."

"I never really noticed how beautiful the leaves were, until today," Wyatt answers thoughtfully.

Blanche wakes up from napping in the sun and runs over and stands on her hind legs for Wyatt to hug her. "Well hello beautiful canine girl," he says, reaching down to hug her wriggling body.

Wyatt looks up and notices the carriage house door is open.

"I cleaned out the carriage house and hauled a bunch of crap to Goodwill, so the space is yours," Sally says. Sally told Wyatt on the phone he could to put anything needing to be stored into the carriage house, since he has no garage or storage in the tiny Jamison house.

"Awesome. It will just be for a short time. I will probably buy one of those garden sheds or build on a carport or something," Wyatt says as he opens the Uhaul's door.

Andrea bounds out of the house and runs over to hug Wyatt. "Dude! You're here!"

"I am here."

Andrea wears cotton shorts and a tank top, and smells like soap and toothpaste.

"And you're finally FREE! Yay!" Andrea says. "We have so much to show you. Me and Sally, we grew cantaloupes and strawberries and squash and tomatoes – they are SO good! --and I am going to get my driver's license. Sally is teaching me. Hey, look at all this stuff! Want me to start unloading?"

Wyatt grins at Sally. "Sounds like y'all have been busy."

"We have had a busy summer," Sally replies, smiling.

Andrea opens the U-haul. Wyatt: "You can unload the sports stuff but don't try to lift the boxes of books. They're too heavy," Wyatt says, striding over.

"After you get settled in, holler at me and let's figure out dinner," Sally says.

"Will do," Wyatt says.

Wyatt opens the car door and grabs his suitcases and heads towards the front porch. After he puts them down he turns back to the car and spends ten minutes with Andrea. Working together, they get Wyatt's golf equipment, fishing gear, and several boxes of books and papers stacked neatly against the wall of the carriage house.

He finally tells Andrea he will see her in a little while and heads inside to grab a shower.

Immediately after stepping into the house, he knows he is not alone, but he senses the presence is confused, not evil, so he decides to pretend he doesn't know it's there.

Five hours later, they are once again sitting on Sally's screened porch, finishing up a delicious early dinner.

Sally had fixed barbecue, potato salad, broccoli salad, and peach cobbler, and served sliced tomatoes from the garden. Wyatt had never had homemade barbeque sauce, and complimented Sally on it.

"Well that's from growing up here, in a small town," Sally chuckles. "One time, Mama started to fix barbecued chicken one Sunday and realized she had no sauce, and all the grocery stores were closed, so she figured out her own recipe. It's basically ketchup, vinegar, honey, Tabasco, and some seasonings."

"Well I've never had anything that good. Thanks," Wyatt says appreciatively, trying not to burp.

Andrea had eaten and left for work an hour before, after first getting Wyatt to promise they would go back down to the cellar in the morning.

"Did you pick up on anything when you got back in the house today?" Sally asks, trying to sound casual. She has deliberately waited to ask.

Wyatt clears his throat and pushes his chair back from the table. *How much should I tell her?* He wonders.

He reaches down to scratch Blanche's velvety ears while he ponders his response.

"Well, there's still a spirit there but it didn't bother me. I focused on the biggest task, which was just finding room to store my stuff. I really appreciate you and Andrea going over there and dusting and airing out the house, and getting Hugh's personal stuff boxed up."

"It was no trouble. Oh – that reminds me. Hang on a second," Sally says, getting up to go inside the house. She returns a moment later with a small plastic bag and hands it to Wyatt. "We found these. The clothes are all in three boxes in the carriage house. Didn't think anyone would bother them. I thought you might like to have the jewelry, though," Sally says.

The bag contains a college ring from the University of Georgia, and a small circle of what looks like gold. Wyatt squints at it. It's obviously a woman's ring.

"Well this is clearly Hugh's college ring but this looks like a woman's wedding band. Wonder why he had this?" Wyatt muses. He pulls the ring out of the bag and instantly an image forms in his mind, of a woman in pain, pulling the ring off and flinging it into the back yard, screaming something.

"Are you okay?" Sally asks, noting Wyatt's face, which has paled.

"Yeah. I just picked up on some negative energy around this ring. Wow."

"So you can pick up images from objects?" Sally asks.

"Sometimes." Wyatt decides not to tell her that it's very rare but when it happens it's always something negative.

Sally takes the plates into the kitchen and Wyatt helps her clear the table.

After stacking plates in the sink Sally turns to Wyatt. "Well, I have to go in to work tomorrow, even though it's Sunday and we are closed. The library board is meeting at 1:00 to go over next year's budget. I have to get ready for the fun event."

"Sounds like a party. I need to run to the grocery store and then turn in early, too. Thanks for putting the food in the house, and a wonderful early supper," Wyatt says, getting up.

Sally walks with him to the front door, wondering if he will kiss her.

He does, but it's not a long passionate kiss. He simply reaches down and kisses her lightly on the lips, after a brief embrace.

"Good night," he says, pulling away from her.

"Good night," Sally replies.

Wyatt walks back to his house and looks up at the sky, which is now pink and purple. A small breeze ruffles his hair. He looks at his little house and has a profound realization. *My family has lived here for over a hundred and fifty years, and I am reclaiming this place, for us all. There is such peace here, a peace that I won't find anywhere else.* He can hear his father's voice, in his head, GOOD JOB BOY! Wendell used to roar. *Thanks, Dad.*

CHAPTER 30

Wyatt's trip to the grocery store is a new and unique experience for him. He has not been to a grocery store in years to buy real groceries, because Sharon always bought all the food.

During the months he stayed with John he ate out most of the time, or made himself sandwiches or cereal, which he bought in quick dashes into Publix. John's wife only cooked about twice a week, and he didn't want to impose, on those nights. While they were at the beach Thad went to the store.

Wyatt hums the song playing overhead, "Brandy," as he strolls down the aisles of the Kroger on the outskirts of town marveling at the huge variety of products available.

Wyatt doesn't cook at all, so he decides to stock up on sandwich makings, frozen Stouffer's meals, a few snack items, and beer.

He heads over to the bakery section. He marvels at the selection of cakes, muffins, and cookies. Lemon cake. Wow. He puts it in the buggy. He buys a caramel cake, too.

Croissants! They nest in their plastic box looking fantastic. He says the name to himself, "Kwah-sahn," as he puts them in the buggy. He has never forgotten his high school French.

A pimply faced girl in jeans, with a drooling baby on her hip, grabs another box of croissants. "I just love these things! Man them frenchies sure do know how to do bread, right? I'll be done with these croissants in three days," she says, smiling and snapping her gum. She pronounces the word "croy-saints."

Wyatt smiles and nods at her. She's pregnant again, something he wishes he didn't know. She also grows marijuana in her basement, he realizes. Yikes. He turns his buggy in the opposite direction.

After perusing the cookie aisle for a few minutes, Wyatt picks up three packages of Oreos, and a half gallon of milk, and buys some frozen shrimp. *They shouldn't be too hard to fix*, he thinks, *just microwave them for about ten minutes*. He loves shrimp.

As he is standing in front of the produce feeling vaguely guilty, knowing he should buy some fresh vegetables, a familiar voice assails him.

"Wyatt, that you, son?" the older voice calls out.

Wyatt turns around and sees Ben Walters, the elderly attorney, holding a basket containing deodorant, fresh strawberries, a loaf of bread and a 6 pack of beer. Walters is wearing jeans and a casual sport shirt.

"How you doing, Mr. Walters?" Ben asks politely.

"Just fine, just fine. Looks like you're buying enough food for a few weeks," Walters says with a grin, motioning to Wyatt's buggy.

"Well, yes. This store sure does have a lot of stuff."

"You here for the weekend, then?" Walters asks.

Wyatt smiles. "Nope. I just got divorced. I closed my practice in Atlanta and decided to take early retirement, although I might hang out a shingle at some point and practice a little law, when the fish aren't biting," Wyatt responds jovially.

"Well good for you. You got a nice house there, a historic place. I'm glad to see somebody young living there. You gonna fix it up?"

Wyatt ponders this. "I probably will start a few projects, but take it slow. Eventually I'd like to add a garage or something, but there's no hurry," Wyatt answers, throwing some bananas in the buggy.

Walters adds several limes to his basket. Wyatt knows he's thinking about having a vodka tonic as soon as he gets home.

"Funny running into you here. I've been meaning to call you. Don't know if you know this, but I'm a fourth generation practicing lawyer here in Bell County. I was going through some old files my great granddaddy had, in an old storage unit, and I found a file involving some of your family. Thought you might like to see it, so I saved it."

Wyatt is instantly alert. Walters thinks the old legal file might have clues as to the secret of the house, but he's not going to say anything about it in the grocery store.

"I would love to see that file. Could I come by your office next week and take a look?" Wyatt asks.

"Sure, sure, that would be great. I'm in depositions Wednesday but otherwise I'm pretty open. Just give my gal a call Monday morning and get a time. I'll look forward to seeing you," Walters says.

"I'll do that. Good to see you again," Wyatt responds, shaking the old man's hand. *I wonder how many secretaries are referred to as "my gal" in small towns?* he chuckles inwardly.

Later that night, after eating half a package of Oreos, and reading for a couple of hours, Wyatt decides it's time to sleep. He strips off his clothes and is wearing only boxer shorts as he lies on the bed, making a list of things to do the next day, an old habit.

The house is locked up, curtains drawn, and yet even after he stops making his list and puts his phone on the charger and turns out the lights, sleep won't come, because the air seems charged. There is an energy in the air that is nearly visible to Wyatt, but he can't say why.

Wyatt dozes off for a little while, but then he opens his eyes, sensing he isn't alone in the room. It's 11:11, he sees, as he glances at the glowing red numerals on the digital clock by the bed. The plastic bag with the two rings is atop the dresser. He senses it has attracted the presence.

A shadowy figure of a middle-aged woman stands in front of the rolltop desk, wearing a long flowing dress. She is thin and pale, and her brown hair is drawn back severely. She looks at him with great sadness.

"Who are you?" he says softly. He is aware that his heart is pounding and his breathing is coming in shallow, quick breaths. He has never seen a spirit before, only sensed them. He tries to decide if he feels fear, and decides not. He is simply in awe of the fact he is seeing someone no longer human.

The spirit stares at him with sadness, then she looks at a stack of books on the rolltop desk.

"Are you trying to give me a message?" Wyatt asks, sitting up slowly, and swinging his legs over the edge of the bed.

The spirit says nothing, but points at a book on the bottom of the stack. Wyatt stands up, blinks, and she disappears.

He sits for a moment, pondering the ghost. He knows instinctively that she appeared before him because she is related to him. They share the same blood. He gets up and starts taking the heavy old books off the stack. At the bottom is a heavy New Testament, with thick vellum pages. He looks at the publication date: 1855. In the flyleaf, in elaborate cursive, *Josephine Adams* is written, and in a different hand someone has added Jamison.

I need to learn more about this lady, Wyatt thinks. *She has something to do with the trunk.*

He grabs his laptop off the desk and sits on the bed and opens it, hitting the ON button. Nothing happens. He hits the button again. Nothing. *It was fully charged three hours ago and now it's dead, wow.*

She must have somehow zapped the energy from it, Wyatt thinks. *Why do I know that?* he wonders. He's glad he thought to have Sally arrange for an internet hookup in his absence.

He picks up the phone and calls his sister. She's usually up late on Saturday nights. She doesn't pick up. He leaves her a voicemail. He ponders calling Sally but decides it's too late and she might be asleep.

Finally he decides to try talking to the ghost. "Okay, great grandmother Josephine. I don't know anything about you, but I am guessing you know something about that trunk in the cellar of this house. This was your house originally, wasn't it? I will make you a deal. I will try to find out what I can about what happened, what secret Uncle Hugh was trying to uncover. Whatever the "treasure" is, if it's still around, I will do the right thing if I find it, okay? You need to move on. Go on to heaven, or the afterlife, whatever that may be. I will be just fine."

He senses that what he has said has gotten a good reception. As he heads into the bathroom to brush his teeth he hears a faint rustling sound, like the heavy skirts of a lady rustling as she walks down the hall.

I watched great grandmother appear and I am amazed at Wyatt's response. He didn't seem fearful at all.

She is a restless spirit, not at peace, but I cannot help her.

I watch Wyatt get into bed and think,
you're finally where you are supposed to be, boy.

I rise up and up, into the beautiful night
sky, and look down at the sleeping town. Wyatt is
going to be fine here, I sense. I want to know
what he figures out about the trunk, though, and
the treasure. I spent years on it and got nowhere.
I have a feeling a lot of secrets will soon come to
light.

CHAPTER 31

Mavis peers through the telephoto lens of the camera in front of her window and watches Wyatt's house intently. She is on the phone with Roberta.

"Well?!" Roberta demands shrilly.

"I don't see anything Bertie. He went in there with groceries. He stayed in there. The lights went off about 10:30. That's all I seen," Mavis grouses, sipping a bourbon and coke.

"Wylene down at the Kroger said he bought enough food to last for weeks. Plus a lot of beer, frozen shrimp, Oreos, croissants and two cakes. Now why would a man buy all that?" She pronounces the word "croshunts."

"Maybe he likes sweets?" Mavis grumbles, settling down in her lounge chair in the family room, after setting down her drink on the end table. "What difference does it make?"

"I'll tell you what difference it makes. He eats all that crap. He gets hog fat. He won't want to have sex. He won't marry Sally and move into her house. I need him to leave that house again."

"Oh good godalmighty –" Mavis starts but she is interrupted.

"Mavis, don't you take the name of the Lord in vain!" Roberta hisses, mindful of her sleeping husband next to her. "Ask Jesus to forgive you!"

"Bertie, Jesus and I are best buds, Hon, so leave it alone."

"You coming to church tomorrow?"

Mavis rolls her eyes and sips her drink. "I don't know. What if I don't? Nobody's gonna take roll."

"Everybody needs to talk to the Lord on Sunday," Roberta huffs.

"Well girlfriend, you're trying to hoodwink a man out of his house, so maybe you need to ask forgiveness," Mavis says mildly.

"You know I got claim to that place."

"I don't think your claim is all that strong, but whatever. I need to let you go. They're selling those crystal drawer pulls on QVC and I need to concentrate. Bye."

Mavis hangs up and wonder for the hundredth time if Roberta is crazy like a fox, or just crazy.

Wearing just a tee shirt and panties, her freshly washed hair smelling of shampoo, Andrea empties her tips onto the bed and starts counting them out. The grand total is $77.38 – not too bad for a Saturday night.

Sally knocks on the door.

"You decent?" she calls out.

"Yes M'am, come on in," Andrea responds.

Sally enters, wearing a bathrobe. Blanche follows behind her and jumps up on the bed, wallowing and grunting in the pile of change and dollar bills.

"How did you do?" Sally asks. She hands Andrea two blueberry muffins.

"Almost eighty bucks. Not bad. Hey, where's Wyatt?" Andrea asks, rubbing Blanche's head.

"Well, he's at his house, of course."

"He didn't stay here?" Andrea asks.

Sally chuckles. "He's not going to be spending the night over here any time soon. We are just friends, at this point."

"Yeah, I guess. But listen, if you want to be more than friends, I'm cool with that. I like Wyatt," Andrea says, biting into her muffin.

"Andrea, I've been divorced for years. Wyatt's newly divorced. The first year or two afterwards, you feel shell-shocked, trust me. He's got to get used to being single again. He was married for a long time."

"Yeah. You think his wife cleaned him out?" Andrea says, rolling Blanche over on her belly and rubbing her.

"Yep, she sure did. Of course, he got divorced in only 4 months. That's pretty unusual, especially for people with a lot of assets. I think he was just ready to change his life, simplify. That's what he told me," Sally replies, reaching under Blanche to collect some of the coins. She takes the shoebox off the dresser and drops the coins on the pile.

"You need to roll these up and take them to the bank," Sally reminds Andrea.

"Yeah, I know. I'm not working tomorrow, so I'll get it done," Andrea replies.

"Did I get anything in the mail today?" she asks Sally, finishing up the muffin.

Sally smiles. "We didn't get the letter from the college, sorry. My cousin works over there. I'll give her a call Monday and see if she can find out what's up with your application, okay?"

Andrea smiles happily. "Okay. Thank you Sally."

"You're welcome Sugar," Sally replies, standing up. "I need to get some sleep. Fun day of working tomorrow, for me."

"That sucks. You'll be home for lunch, right?" Andrea asks hopefully.

"Early lunch, yes. Get some sleep."

"Okay," Andrea responds, scooping up the rest of the coins and putting them in the box. She gives Blanche a bite of the second muffin, then heads down the hall and into the bathroom to brush her teeth.

When Andrea looks in the mirror, she sees, just for a moment, a young blonde woman's face in the mirror. Startled, she drops her toothbrush and gasps.

The woman looks like Sally, but she is young, and in pain.

She disappears as fast as a blink.

Blanche barks at the space behind Andrea.

Could it have been Miranda? Andrea wonders. But no – Miranda is in Atlanta with her husband in her fancy condo in Buckhead. Andrea has seen the photos.

She debates whether or not she should say anything to Sally, but decides not to. Maybe it wasn't Miranda. Maybe Andrea is just tired.

Nonetheless, it takes her a long time to get to sleep, and she is glad to hear Blanche's breathing in the quiet room.

CHAPTER 32

Sally awakens to the ringing phone on Sunday morning. She grabs the phone by her bed, startled to see that it's already 8:10 and Blanche hasn't awakened her. Blanche usually likes to be let out at 8, to tinkle.

Sally mumbles "Hello?"

Marybeth's voice is deadly calm, and pitched low. "Sally? Sorry to wake you so early."

Sally knows by Marybeth's tone that there is something wrong. She sits up quickly, and drinks a sip of water from the glass by her bed.

Sally's stomach clenches. Marybeth always calls her Stinky or Buttface, on the phone. Using her Christian name is a very bad sign.

"What's up?" Sally replies.

"Is Andrea at home?" Marybeth asks.

"Yes, she's asleep. She had to work until 10 last night. Why?"

"Did Wyatt get moved in?"

"Yes. He's at his house."

"Good."

"Marybeth WHAT IS GOING ON?!" Sally nearly yells, frustrated.

"I'm glad you're not alone. Look, I have awful news. Nick called me this morning. Miranda... well, she lapsed back into using drugs. He's been trying to get her to go to rehab, but she wouldn't discuss it."

Nick is Miranda's husband.

"Drugs? What kind of drugs?" Sally asked, horrified.

"Not sure. Nick said she went out clubbing last night with friends. She wasn't home by 4 this morning, and wasn't answering her phone."

Marybeth pauses. Sally can hear the heaviness in her friend's voice.

"Just tell me."

"She overdosed, Sally. Cocaine, ecstasy, not sure what else. She was dumped at the hospital. She's at Piedmont. Nick called me half an hour ago, crying. They couldn't save her."

Sally sits silently for a moment. *There has to be a mistake.*

"Say that again."

Marybeth's voice is heavy. "She's gone, Hon. The doctors couldn't save her. They tried. I'm so sorry –"

"I have to pee. I'll call you back," Sally mutters, and hangs up the phone.

Sally stands up and walks into the bathroom to pee, her brain still trying to process what Marybeth just said. As she flushes, she goes to wash her hands. On the wall of the bathroom is a square Sally had made when Miranda was a baby, a print of her baby footprint, with the date of Miranda's birth. Sally gasps, and runs out the door, not wanting to see it.

Sally pulls on sweatpants and a tee shirt and stumbles downstairs into the family room saying over and over to herself *it has to be a mistake has to be a mistake no no no not my baby no...* and sees a photo of Miranda made on her wedding day four years before, looking young and gorgeous, smiling next to her husband Nick.

It's not a mistake. Nick must have called Marybeth for her to tell me. She's my best friend.

As she stares at the 8x10 in a silver frame, Sally sinks to the floor, her hand over her mouth. A primal wail erupts from deep in her. *My baby can't be gone! She CANNOT BE GONE!* Sally hugs herself and starts rocking, as she sobs.

Andrea's door flies open and she runs down the stairs, worry furrowing her brow. "Sally! What's wrong?!" Andrea says.

Sally just sobs and rocks, shaking her head slightly. Andrea tries to hug her, but Sally doesn't respond. Andrea decides to get Wyatt.

Three minutes later, Wyatt and Andrea come back in. Sally is still sitting on the floor of the family room, sobbing. Wyatt looks at her and knows Miranda is dead.

"Her daughter has died. Do you have Marybeth's number? Call her," Wyatt says quietly.

Wyatt sits on the floor and pulls Sally into his arms. She shakes with sobs, but quiets a bit when she feels Wyatt's arms around her. Wyatt can feel her terrible sadness and despair, her sense of failure.

Sally shivers uncontrollably. Wyatt picks her up and carries her to the sofa, where he can cradle her in his arms, transmitting his heat and warmth to her.

"It's not your fault. Addicts relapse. They just do."

Before Andrea can get Sally's address book off the shelf in the kitchen, the kitchen phone starts ringing again. She grabs it. It's Marybeth. Andrea speaks, then pulls the long phone cord into the family room and hands it to Wyatt.

For Wyatt, the hours at Sally's house that day are like a slow-mo nightmare, the only worse day he can remember being the day his father died.

He has never seen a person grieve so hard as Sally. He tries to imagine how he would feel if his son Thad died, but it's too painful to contemplate.

Sally's brother Luke arrives an hour after Marybeth's call, driving up in his silver minivan, his wife Marion beside him. Wyatt, who has been sitting on the sofa holding Sally while she sobbed, has never met Luke and Marion. All he knows is that Luke is a plumber and Marion a housewife and they have grown sons.

After hugging Sally and being introduced to Wyatt and Andrea, Marion bustles around, cleaning up the kitchen and family room and living room, dusting and straightening. Wyatt watches the petite, chubby lady, and marvels at her energy.

Luke is tall and heavyset, with thinning brown hair and Sally's same bright blue eyes. Wyatt gets the impression Luke hates being disturbed by all this and isn't particularly surprised his niece has died.

Luke is gruff and businesslike, wanting Sally to make decisions about the funeral, the body, the service. He sets up a conference call with Miranda's distraught husband Nick. Sally just sits ashen-faced, hardly saying a word.

Luke tells Nick to let them know when the coroner releases the body so it can be brought back to the Riverton Funeral Home in Crossroads. Nick, swimming in his own grief and guilt, agrees.

Wyatt can hear the despair in Nick's voice, and feels sorry for him.

"Somebody needs to call Steve," Sally finally says quietly. "He needs to know."

"That's her ex-husband," Luke says to Wyatt.

"I know," Wyatt responds. "Sally and I are friends," he adds lamely. He can see that Luke is wary of him, wanting the whole business of the funeral and its aftermath to be over.

"You know, that's a call I need to make," Sally says. "I'll go in the kitchen."

As soon as the words are out of her mouth, Marybeth's car pulls up. Andrea walks outside to hug her. Marybeth gives her a quick hug, then barrels into the house.

As soon as Sally sees Marybeth, she hangs up the phone and starts sobbing anew. The two friends hold each other close for several minutes. Luke, who has been standing there holding Sally's small leather address book, hands the book to Wyatt and walks outside with Blanche.

Wyatt knows since he and Andrea aren't family they should probably decamp to his house, but he cannot bring himself to do it, as the house fills up with family, friends and neighbors. Finally, at 4:10, Blanche squats and pees on the kitchen floor, eliciting a storm of protest from Sally's elderly aunt Patsy, who grabs a broom to swat Blanche. Wyatt quietly takes the broom from her hands and looks at Andrea. "Take Blanche to my house, okay?"

Andrea nods, glaring at Patsy.

"I'll come over in a minute," Wyatt adds. He wipes up the pee.

After telling Sally goodbye and reassuring her Blanche will be well cared-for at his house, Wyatt grabs the bag of Blanche's food, her leash, and her water bowl, and leaves. Marybeth calls out after him as he reaches his porch.

"Wyatt! Please wait a minute," Marybeth huffs, trying to match his long strides with her short legs.

"Okay," Wyatt says, turning to look at her.

"I wanted to talk to you a minute," Marybeth says breathlessly.

"Come on in and let's talk inside," Wyatt responds, opening the door.

A few minutes later, Wyatt and Marybeth are at his kitchen table eating coffee cake and drinking Sherry, the only liquor in the house besides beer.

Marybeth swallows a last mouthful and sighs as she wipes her mouth with a napkin.

"I need to tell you how this is all going to go down. Sally is going to be beset with relatives, most of whom she rarely sees, except at weddings and funerals. Sam, her gay brother who lives in California, will be here tomorrow. He and Luke don't get along. Steve will likely be here tomorrow or the next day. Decent guy, gets along okay with Sally, won't make trouble. Luke likes him, wishes Sally had never divorced him. Sam will tolerate him as long as he isn't mean to Sally. Luke..."

She pauses, her brow furrowed. Wyatt marvels at this tiny dynamo who loves Sally like a sister.

"Luke thinks because Sally is single and he's the big brother he should run the show, right?"

Marybeth nods, a look of disgust on her face. "Yep. You got it. Luke runs his own successful plumbing business.

He's used to being in charge, bossing everybody around. Marion is like his faithful lieutenant. Sally loves Luke and Marion, but they drive her crazy."

"What about Sam? I think Sally has said Sam is her biggest supporter."

"Sam is a gay website designer. He and Sally are close, but not as close as they once were. Sam has had a great boyfriend in his life for a few years now and they travel a lot. Sam will be Sally's ally against Luke, though, which is important."

"Why? What are you talking about?" Wyatt asks.

"There might be a big hullaballoo over the funeral service. Sally's family will want a regular Catholic mass. Steve probably will too, since he is a Catholic, at least nominally. Sally won't want that. She quit going to church years ago. I don't know if she will be strong enough to buck most of her family though and just do a quiet non-denominational service at the funeral home, and cremate the body."

The two sit in silence for a moment. Finally, Wyatt speaks.

"Sally never told me Miranda had a drug problem."

"She doesn't like to talk about it. After Miranda moved to Atlanta about 6 years ago Miranda was running with a wild crowd. Sally went to see her and was appalled, and got her into an expensive rehab place. She and Steve thought the problem was solved."

"Sally did tell me she hadn't seen Miranda in months, which was unusual," Wyatt mused, scratching Blanche's back.

Marybeth shakes her head, looking sad.

"They once were so close. Then Sally's mother started getting sick, taking up a lot of Sally's time and energy, and Miranda resented that. Only child, you know. They never really fully repaired that rift, much to Sally's sadness. I think that's why Andrea has been so good for Sally. Here's a new daughter figure in her life, one who clearly loves and respects her."

Wyatt is aware that Andrea is just out of sight in the other room, eavesdropping.

"Do you think Andrea should continue to stay with Sally during this time, I mean with all the family in and out, and everything? Couldn't that be a bit controversial?"

Marybeth frowns, thinking it over. Finally, she speaks. "I think I need to stay with Sally. I can sleep in the guest room," Marybeth says, getting up.

Andrea appears looking stricken. "I don't want Sally more stressed out. I can stay here with Wyatt, in the guest room, right?" she says, looking at Wyatt. He nods.

Wyatt knows she is upset and worried about Sally.

Marybeth and Wyatt exchange a look. Wyatt says. "You can have your old room, kiddo," he says, forcing a smile.

"Thanks Wyatt," Andrea says softly.

'I guess we need to go pick up something for dinner here," Wyatt says quietly, thinking about all the sandwich makings and frozen food he has, and not wanting any of it.

"Nonsense. Didn't you notice all those folks already bringing food? This is a small town. Sally already has enough food to feed everyone for a week. We may need to put some of it in your house. Andrea, come on with me."

Ten minutes later, Andrea and Marybeth return to Wyatt's house carrying numerous grocery bags and set them down on Wyatt's table.

"Overflow," Marybeth explains. "Good godalmighty, I've never seen so much food."

Andrea is beaming as she pulls out the casserole dishes from the bags.

As she unpacks the dishes Marybeth directs her remarks to Wyatt. "I'm going back and about 8 o'clock I will shoo everyone out so Sally can have some peace. I'll spend the night."

Marybeth turns to Andrea and points out that Blanche is eying the food greedily. "Until further notice, Blanche is your responsibility, ok? Make sure she can't reach the food. She can pull things off the counter if you put them close enough to the edge."

Andrea smiles and nods, her mouth full of corn muffin. "I know. Sally told me a while back."

"What about –" Wyatt starts to say then chuckles, startled, as he sees Marybeth pull a casserole dish from one of the bags and hold it away from her as though it contains nuclear waste, frowning.

Andrea, too, swallows her bite of muffin and looks at Marybeth. "What is it?"

"I thought old Mrs. Calvert was dead, but I have proof she is not," Marybeth says quietly. "This is a chicken surprise casserole made by Rebecca Calvert. Do NOT EAT IT. Do NOT even give it to Blanche. It will make her sick. It contains chicken, turnips, olives, crushed potato chips, and God knows what else. Rebecca Calvert is a TERRIBLE cook, but nobody has the guts to tell her that," Marybeth says, shaking her head as she pours the casserole dish's contents in the garbage and puts the dish in the sink, squirting the dish with lots of Dawn dishwashing liquid.

Wyatt looks at Andrea and they both laugh.

I have spent the day hovering above Sally's house, watching the parade of people going in and out.

Death of a child, untimely death, always brings out the best and the worst in people.

I am aware of the spirit of Sally's daughter hovering nearby, but I sense an inability to communicate with her, or perhaps it's just that she doesn't want me to communicate. She must have been a very beautiful young woman, with long flowing blonde hair and Sally's bright blue eyes.

A new SUV pulls up and a tall man steps out. This must be the child's father. Instead of heading into the house, he walks into the carriage house and pulls a kite down from the wall, and starts crying.

Spirit Miranda sees him sobbing and her face mirrors his sadness.

So much sadness.

CHAPTER 33

The next day is Monday. Wyatt awakens early, as is his habit, at 6:30 on the dot. He rolls over and stumbles out of bed. After he has showered, and shaved, he makes himself a cup of coffee and hustles Blanche into the backyard.

Blanche squats obligingly. As he surveys the small yard, Wyatt senses a presence, but it's not Josephine.

Wyatt wonders how Miranda's death will affect his burgeoning romance with Sally. Will she be able to commit to him? How should he handle everything?

He has no answers.

He finds himself mentally saying a small, tentative prayer. *God, if you're up there, or wherever, please help Sally to handle this. Help me to support her. Help us to love each other. Amen.*

He feels some sense of peace after that prayer. A breeze blows through, making the leaves rustle. A bright red cardinal lands on the grass and looks at him. He knows instinctively this is a sign of a spirit presence, and he nods his head slightly at the bird, grateful, suddenly, to be in Crossroads, surrounded by the calming presence of the mountains.

Fifteen minutes later, over a breakfast of Frosted Flakes, Andrea broaches a subject she has long wanted to ask Wyatt about.

"Um, you know I'm trying to get into the college in Gainesville, right? The junior college?"

"Yep, Sally had mentioned that. That's great," Wyatt says, wondering where she is going with this, because he can't tell her thoughts at the moment. She's dressed up, a bit, he notes. She has on khaki pants, a white button down shirt, and a blue cardigan. Except for the white Converse high tops, she looks quite preppy. Her hair is pulled back in barrettes.

Andrea scratches Blanche's ears and puts her cereal bowl down so Blanche can drink the remaining milk.

"Okay, well, here's my issue. They require a transcript from my high school, and I called the school and they said I can come pick it up. They won't mail it, because I never formally withdrew from school and they want me to do that before they release the transcript. I also need to get a copy of my birth certificate so I can get a driver's license and buy a car. I'm tired of riding my bike and it's fixing to get cold. If my mother doesn't have my birth certificate, I guess I'll need to go to the courthouse and get it? Not sure on that. I need my social security card, too, and I'm not sure if my mom has that. I also want to get a few things from my mom's place, and I don't want to see her boyfriend, Jimmy," Andrea finishes, looking down at her bowl, which is now licked clean. She picks it up and puts it in the sink.

Wyatt knows that speech had been rehearsed, and his heart goes out to Andrea.

"So you want me to drive you to Ringgold and help you collect this stuff?" Wyatt asks, putting his own bowl on the floor for Blanche.

Andrea nods, then looks up at him with tears in her eyes. "I'm scared to go by myself, and I'd have to take the bus, because Sally can't take me now. She was supposed to take me this week, but now..."

Wyatt nods. "I totally understand. Look, why don't we go today? You aren't working, right?"

Andrea shakes her head. "Nope. I'm off. Shouldn't take more than two or three hours to get there, depending on the route."

Wyatt looks at his watch. It is 9:08. "Tell you what, let me walk next door and check on Sally, and tell Marybeth what's up. In the meantime, why don't you walk Blanche, for a few minutes?"

"Okay. Thanks," Andrea says, her voice much lighter. She grabs Blanche's leash.

The drive to Ringgold takes them through the Nantahala National Forest, a beautiful and scenic drive. Wyatt realizes after a few minutes that although he generally finds driving relaxing, he needs to pay attention to his driving on the narrow, hilly road.

His visit to Sally had been heart-wrenching. Marybeth was already there, and when Wyatt asked what she thought about the plan of taking Andrea to Ringgold, Marybeth nodded.

"Best thing you can do. Get Andrea away from here. Get yourself away. The house will be flooded with visitors and family members. I can handle things."

Sally had come drifting out, looking pale and exhausted, and hugged him. He held her and kissed the top of her head, wishing he could take the pain from her. "You okay here while I take Andrea?" he asked gently.

"Yes. Best thing to do, get her stuff she needs. I know she is worried about seeing her mother again," Sally said softly.

Wyatt frowns at the memory as he drives.

To get his mind off the memory of Sally's ravaged face and tear swollen eyes, Wyatt decides to get Andrea talking.

"So you making decent tips at Bob's?"

"Yep, I know a lot of the folks who come in, now. It's okay. Plus, I get a 50 percent discount on everything and they let me take home any pie that doesn't sell, most nights."

"Well that's a hell of a deal. Do they sell chocolate pie?" Wyatt asks.

"Oh yeah. It's really good, too," Andrea grins. "We usually sell out of it, though."

Wyatt and Andrea talk some more about her job, school, Sally, and then she talks about her early life, and how much she misses her grandparents.

"Did you have a good relationship with your grandparents?" Andrea asks.

Wyatt thinks for a moment. "I did, but we didn't see them all that often. Grandaddy didn't like to leave Crossroads, and Dad didn't like to leave Atlanta, so there wasn't a lot of visiting back and forth. I was fond of my grandmother, though. She would usually come to Atlanta a couple of times a year."

"What was she like?" Andrea asks.

"Tall, blonde, lovely. Loved to read. Always talking to me and my sister about the importance of education. Very smart lady. Dad adored her but he was kind of scared of her, too."

"Scared? Why?" Andrea asks.

"Well, she didn't finish college, but she was incredibly intellectual. She would do things like read the Encyclopedia for fun," Wyatt chuckled. "She was very smart. She always knew who would win any election."

There is a silence in the car. The thought occurs to Wyatt that maybe he got his ability from his grandmother. Something to ponder.

When they reach the outskirts of Ringgold, Wyatt spots a Kentucky Fried Chicken. "Say, let's grab some lunch here before we head over to the school, okay?"

"Sure. I like KFC," Andrea responds.

Wyatt ponders the fact that there is a Kentucky Fried Chicken in every small town in Georgia, even if there is no other place to eat.

After they get their food and sit down, Wyatt realizes one of the girls behind the counter is staring at Andrea.

"You know that young lady?" Wyatt asks, nodding at the girl.

"Yeah. Knew her in high school. She's looking at me wondering if it's actually me, Andrea Hawkins. I looked a lot different in school," Andrea says thoughtfully.

"You're looking a lot more healthy looking than the first time I met you," Wyatt says quietly, before biting into a chicken leg.

"I've gained about 15 pounds, and I don't wear all that dark makeup. I took out my piercings. Also I'm eating a lot better. Sally fixes vegetables every night, and we talk about stuff while she cooks. I drink a lot more water now, you know, and it's helping my skin. My hair looks nice now," Andrea says, sipping her tea. "Sally said if you don't eat right it shows in your skin and hair and nails. She's really smart. I like her as a person, you know?"

"Well, I know Sally likes having you around. She told me so. She and her daughter weren't all that close," Wyatt says.

"Why not? I mean, Sally's so nice," Andrea asks, taking a bite of biscuit.

"I don't know how to answer that, even though we're good friends. Marybeth told me Miranda was a really girly-girl, liked makeup and parties and all, and Sally is more of an intellectual earth-mother type. They just were very different. Miranda resented Sally divorcing her dad, then having to take care of her mom, too. Sally loved her very much, though."

After their meal, they head over to the high school.

As they turn into to school parking lot and look for a Visitor's space, Wyatt can feel Andrea tensing. She's afraid of stares and questions.

"Want me to go in with you?" he asks.

"No thanks. I can handle this."

Wyatt sits in the car and reads a book while Andrea goes in. She reappears ten minutes later.

"Well, that was easy," he remarks, as Andrea opens the passenger side door and slides in.

"Yep. No big deal. Um, can you look at the transcript and see if you think they will let me in college?" Andrea asks quietly.

Wyatt knows somebody in the school has said something hurtful to her, but he doesn't press. Andrea hands him the papers.

Except for B's in Spanish her Freshman year, there are all A's, until she left just after Christmas, nearly eight months before.

"This is a very impressive transcript, Andrea," Wyatt says quietly. "You also passed the GED with honors. I have no doubt you can get the Hope scholarship, and do just fine at junior college. Then maybe you can go to UGA."

Andrea is silent for a moment.

"I was real proud that I could get good grades, despite Danielle's not ever helping me with anything."

"Danielle?" Wyatt asks.

"That's my mom. Never did like calling her mom. She wasn't much into it, either. Used to tell people we were sisters," Andrea says softly.

Wyatt just nods, knowing there is a lot of pain behind that remark.

"I never wanted people to think I was like her," Andrea says softly.

He clears his throat. "All of life is a series of choices. You can choose to be whatever you want to be," Wyatt says quietly.

"Yeah, I know. Sally says that, too. I guess we better go on to the trailer, get it over with," Andrea says, sighing and looking resigned.

Wyatt can hear the dread in her voice.

Following Andrea's directions, they arrive at the trailer park less than ten minutes later. There's a beat up Ford Escort parked beside the old white single-wide trailer, and rusted metal garbage cans with garbage overflowing sit next to the trailer door. "Hang on just a second," Wyatt says, grabbing his phone off the charger. He steps out of the car and makes a quick call, and hangs up.

Andrea keeps looking around fearfully.

"I'll go in with you," Wyatt says.

"Good," Andrea replies, her voice heavy with relief.

They knock on the door but when there's no answer, Andrea pushes it open. Wyatt steps into a dirty, dimly-lit room reeking of cigarettes, pot, and body odor. The only furniture is a stained plaid couch, a cheap wood laminate coffee table, a card table, and two metal folding chairs. Fast food garbage covers the old card table in the dining area.

Andrea heads down a narrow hallway and pushes open a door. She has brought a plastic garbage sack and she proceeds to fill it with some clothes and a few old toys, and comes back out.

"I'm going to put this in the car, then come back for the photo albums," she says.

Wyatt nods. He looks at the trailer wondering how anyone can live like this.

Andrea reappears a minute later. She returns to her room and takes three photo albums and puts them on the floor by the front door. "Those were my granny's albums. I want to keep those," she explains.

"I understand. What about your mom? Where is she?" Wyatt asks.

"Danielle's sleeping. I can hear her snoring in her room, from my room. I'm going to knock on the door," Andrea says quietly.

Andrea knocks on the door at the end of the hall. A rough, raspy voice calls out "What you want?! I ain't got nothin' Wayne!"

"It's me," Andrea says. Rustling noises are heard, and a moment later Danielle opens the door.

Wyatt has never seen someone look so beaten and unhealthy. Danielle is only 33 but looks ten years older. She is small and skinny, with smudged makeup and hair a fake blonde, tangled. She wears only panties and an old ragged tee shirt. She looks like she hasn't eaten in weeks. Wyatt knows she uses meth.

"Well look who's here," Danielle says, looking at Andrea. "Come back to get your stuff? Who's he?"

"He's a friend."

"Friend? Right."

"He is my FRIEND, Danielle. I need my birth certificate and my social security card," Andrea says as Danielle pushes past her and walks into the main room to grab her pack of Marlboros.

"What makes you think I have 'em?" Danielle snarls, lighting her cigarette.

"Granny gave them to you, remember?" Andrea says, trying not to panic.

"I put that box of stuff under your bed, years ago," Andrea replies. "Why you want that stuff?"

"I'm applying to colleges," Andrea says, before turning to go back into her room.

Danielle looks startled, then sad. "You payin' for that?" she asks Wyatt.

"No, she's eligible for scholarships, but I will help her any way I can. Don't you want to know where she's been all these months?" Wyatt asks. He is having trouble reading her, perhaps because her brain is so crowded with drugs.

"Heard she ran off to Atlanta. Didn't worry none. She's a smart cookie," Danielle says, inhaling deeply.

Andrea reappears carrying a small cardboard box and sits on the sofa to look through it.

The door flies open and a tall man with long greasy hair, wearing a stained orange tank top and dirty jeans riding low on his hips comes in the trailer, crowding it. "What the fuck is going on?" he asks, glaring at Wyatt.

Wyatt is taller and weighs more, but he knows this is the abusive boyfriend, Jimmy.

"Found 'em. Let's go," Andrea says. Wyatt can feel her fear, and also her anger.

"Wait just a damn minute. You took something of mine when you left, Andy. You OWE me," Jimmy snarls.

Andrea glares at him. "Yeah I did. I took your box cutter. You can go buy another one at Walmart, asshole – "

"Took more than that, you little bitch –" Jimmy steps towards Andrea, his fist drawn back. Wyatt immediately steps in front of Andrea.

"You don't want to do that."

"Who the fuck are YOU?!" Jimmy snarls.

"Just a friend."

"I want back what she took," Jimmy repeats.

Wyatt pulls himself up to his full height and looks down at Steve, using his quiet menacing voice usually reserved for tense courtroom questioning.

"You took something from her much more precious, didn't you Jimmy Turner? You took her virginity. You took her innocence. She was underage. That's statutory rape, and it carries a sentence of up to 10 years. You've also got a business going on selling meth, right out of this trailer. Unless you want me and Andrea to talk to the police, you need to back off," Wyatt says quietly.

"What the FUCK?!" Danielle screams, glaring at Jimmy. "You messed with my DAUGHTER?!"

"He's lyin' I ain't done nothin' — "Jimmy starts, but his eyes grow big when he looks out the trailer window and spots a sheriff's patrol car.

A knock sounds at the door. Wyatt strides over and opens it. "Hi Deputy, can you give us just a moment? Then we'll be right out. Thanks," Wyatt says smoothly. He turns around and looks steadily at Jimmy, noting how Andrea sticks the box under her arm and scrambles to stand beside Wyatt.

Suddenly, Wyatt understands everything.

"So Andrea told me how you and Danielle took four thousand dollars her grandmother left her, and spent it on drugs. That's money she needs for college."

"What? That ain't true!" Jimmy says in a loud stage whisper.

Wyatt steps close to him, close enough to smell the combined odors of cigarettes and old sweat. "You got just about that same amount hidden over there under the sink. You go get that cash right now and hand it to me, and I won't blow the whistle on you. Don't do it, and I will step outside and tell that sheriff everything you've been up to lately – the Oxy, the illegal gambling, the dogfighting, all of it."

Jimmy draws back, startled, fear in his eyes.

"You can't prove any of that shit."

Wyatt gives him the laser stare, the one he uses on recalcitrant witnesses in court.

"Really? I'm a lawyer. I can prove anything. I know things. Like I know about that pistol in the dresser drawer. I know about how Danielle's thinking she's fixing to kick your sorry ass out in about two minutes. I know how you got that scar on your shoulder? Yeah, that one. When you were in prison and you got shanked. I know all about that. Maybe we should tell Danielle you were in prison for molesting another little girl."

Danielle stares in horror at Jimmy. "Motherfucker!"

Jimmy goes over to the kitchen and yanks open the cabinet door under the sink and reaches back and grabs an envelope. He strides over and hands it to Wyatt.

"Everything okay in there?" the sheriff's deputy calls through the door.

"Yes, Officer Williams. We'll be right out," Wyatt calls.

Andrea has grabbed her mother's cell phone and written down the number on the lid of the cardboard box, with a pencil.

"Bye Mom. I'll call you sometime," she says. Danielle is sobbing, ugly wrenching sobs. She grabs Andrea and hugs her. "I'm so sorry, baby. So sorry I didn't believe you. Stay in touch, you hear?"

Andrea hugs back. "Yes m'am. Let's go," she says to Wyatt.

As they step out of the trailer, Wyatt inhales deeply, grateful for relatively clean air, despite the smell coming off the garbage cans.

"Thank you for meeting us here, Officer Williams. I was afraid there might be trouble, but we didn't have any," Wyatt says.

"We know these two real well. Jimmy's been selling Oxy, weed, lord knows what else. We just haven't been able to catch him."

"Well, I'm going to make a suggestion, but I'd like you to say it was an anonymous tip. That's his truck right there. I was just thinking what a good place it would be to hide pills, inside the gas cap. You might want to check that."

The deputy is young and still has pimples, but he isn't stupid. "I might just have to do that. I'll have probable cause anyway, seein' how those two are screamin' up in there," he grins.

Indeed, Danielle is heard screaming at Steve, and from the crashing sounds, she's throwing things, too.

Wyatt hands the deputy his card. "We need to be getting home. Good luck to you," he says, smiling.

Andrea is already in the car. She directs him back to the road that leads to Crossroads, but doesn't say anything for a while. Finally, she turns to him. "You have ESP don't you? That's how you knew that stuff about Jimmy? What he did to me? Where he had the stuff hidden?"

Wyatt sighs. "I guess it's ESP. I have never known what to call it. I usually refer to it as my ability. I know when things are hidden. I can often read people, know what they think but don't say. It's not perfect, though, my ability. Sometimes I'm wrong. I try not to flaunt it or exploit it."

"But you knew he had... messed with me?!" Andrea said quietly. "Sally told you?"

Startled, Wyatt almost misses a yellow light, but brakes in time.

"No, absolutely not. The first time I met you I just knew. Sally has never shared anything like that with me. I promise you."

There is a long silence.

Wyatt notes that every few miles there is either a Baptist or Methodist church.

"I told Sally."

Wyatt is not surprised. "That's good. Talking is better than holding it all in, right?"

"Yeah. I know that now."

"Well, I'm glad we were able to do what we needed to do."

"Me, too. What about the money?"

"The money is to pay for a car or for school, right? I mean, you should use it to your benefit," Wyatt says. "It will pay for things the scholarship doesn't cover, like a dorm room. I'll help you count it out, and we'll go to the bank tomorrow, open up an account."

"Sally already helped me with that, but thanks. I've got almost two thousand saved."

"Good. Let's get back to Crossroads," Wyatt says, turning onto the main road that leads over the mountains and home.

"Thank you for taking me, Wyatt. I was scared."

"I know Sweetheart. It's okay."

In two minutes, Andrea is asleep.

CHAPTER 34

I am drifting above the old homeplace again, looking at the Honeysuckle Road house where I grew up with my brother Wendell, wishing it was surrounded by acres of farmland again. Just down the way I can hear the traffic noises from the main road, and almost smell the exhaust from all the cars. It was such a peaceful way to grow up, here on the farm, surrounded by the mountains. I wonder why I didn't appreciate it more.

I wish my father hadn't sold the land in 1968, after his heart attack had forced him to stop farming. All the acreage went towards building new houses and roads. At least we kept the house.

Suddenly, the air shimmers, and the house disappears, dissolves like it was never there!

Another flashback. The grassy meadow and lack of scrub pines tells me this is the way the land looked long before there was a farm.

A Native American rides up on a gray stallion. He gets off his horse and looks around for a minute. He looks like a mixture of white and Indian, I believe, and wears white man clothing and a brimmed hat, but there's a feather stuck in the hatband and his face shows clearly the mixture of races. There is something familiar about his face but I don't know why.

A short time later, another rider on horseback appears.

He is an older, portly white man with graying hair. The Native American man stares at the older white man.

The white man speaks.

"Littlefeather, I am Matthew Adams, agent of the United States government. I am here to explain to you how President Jackson made a treaty with your people. You and your family have to leave this land and move, to the west of the great Mississippi River."

The Native American just stares at him, contempt and anger burning in his face.

"You speak English? Your people know it?" Adams asks.

Littlefeather is a soft-spoken man, but he speaks with great contempt. "My people? My mother is Cherokee but my father was a white man. I have as much right to stay on this land as any other man. These lands have been Cherokee since long before any white man appeared in these mountains."

Adams shakes his head."It's 1838. The treaty will be enforced. The time has run out. If you and your family will go peacefully to Fort Buffington there will be no trouble. If you refuse, the government has authorized whatever means are necessary to facilitate the removal of all Cherokee from this area."

The two men look at each other, the white man calm and self-assured, Littlefeather radiating anger and disgust.

Littlefeather almost spits out his words. "I heard what happened over in the settlement last week. I heard how the Cherokee were rounded up and marched out like slaves to that fort. We all know what happens at Fort Buffington. It's an evil place. The land out west isn't good land, either. This MY LAND, in my Cherokee family for generations, and I will not abandon it," he says, staring at the white man.

Adams scowls. "I thought you might act like this, so I brought some insurance." He whistles, loudly.

A rider appears over the brow of the hill. In front of his horse, a young part Cherokee woman walks, a toddler in her arms, who stares at the men with wide green eyes. The rider is holding a rifle.

Littlefeather looks horrified, and shouts something in Cherokee. The young woman answers in the same language, her voice filled with anguish.

"Are you going to go peacefully?" Adams says harshly to Littlefeather.

"You have no right –" Littlefeather begins, but he is interrupted by the soldier pointing the rifle at the young woman.

"No!" Littlefeather shouts. He dismounts and starts running towards the woman, who starts running towards him. The mounted soldier fires, killing the young woman with a bullet to the head. Littlefeather reaches to his waistband. The mounted soldier immediately turns the gun towards Littlefeather and another shot rings out.

The baby screams as his father falls to the ground.

"James, that was a damn stupid thing to do!" Adams grumbles. "This could've been handled better. Damn you."

The soldier who fired the shots has dismounted and pulled the screaming baby from the dead woman's grasp and is trying to comfort him. "You said shoot 'em if they resisted. Looky here, this baby don't even look savage. Both the mama and daddy was half breeds. Look at them big green eyes on this little feller," he says.

Adams shakes his head in disgust. "What a mess. What a damn mess!"

"They was half breeds. Don't matter nohow," she soldier whines.

"Ride back to the settlement and tell the chief about the bodies so they can be buried. See if anybody will take the baby. If not, take it to the orphan asylum in Clayton," he says to the soldier dismissively, mounting his horse in disgust.

"So this land is yours now, right?" the soldier says. You can claim it down at the courthouse?"

"Yes, yes, here's your payment for this business," the older man grumbles, tossing a small leather bag to the soldier.

The soldier smiles, oblivious to the baby's continuing screams.

The shimmer happens again, the sunlight wavering, as the terrible scene fades. So Matthew Adams, who was the father of William Adams and grandfather of Josephine, took the land unfairly.

I wonder what happened to that baby?

CHAPTER 35

When he is almost back to Crossroads and the lengthening shadows fall across the two lane road, Wyatt's cell phone rings. He pulls it out of his pocket and answers.

"Wyatt? Hey it's Marybeth. How did it go?"

"Oh, it was fine. I'll tell you about it when I see you," he says, thinking of Andrea asleep.

"Good. Well, I need a favor," she says.

Wyatt knows she is beyond tired and stressed out. "Sure. What's up? How is Sally?"

"She has slept a lot today, and eaten almost nothing. House is full of delicious food, and she keeps saying she can't swallow. I am trying to be patient but it always worries me when people don't eat."

"Okay, but what else?"

"You have another spare bedroom, right? With a double bed?"

"Yep, sure do."

"Sam is driving up from the Atlanta airport right now, and there's no place here to put him. The hotels are full because of leaf season. I'm staying in Andrea's room so I can keep an eye on Sally. The guest bedroom is more of an office now, and there's not even a couch in there. I don't want Sam spending the night here, even on the sofa downstairs, because I'm not sure it will be good for Sally –

Sam and Luke tend to argue a lot, as I mentioned. Sally always hates seeing her brothers argue."

Wyatt passes a gas station and realizes he needs to stop at the next one and pee. "Sure, sure, that's fine. No worries. Whatever will cause the least stress for Sally."

"Right. It's a shame, but Luke is too macho to handle his gay brother very well. Look, Sam will be here soon and I have to push Sally in the shower and try to get her to act semi-normal so I need to go. Andrea okay?"

Wyatt glances at her sleeping form. "Yep. I don't blame her for leaving there, though. Listen, we should be there in about 45 minutes. We'll walk over when we get there. Hey, did you think to walk over and check on Blanche?"

"No, but Sally went over and spent some time playing with her, and took her out. She's fine."

"Good. Animals can be a great comfort."

They disconnect.

Wyatt wonders if the other bed, which would be Sam's bed, has clean sheets. He decides to check as soon as they get home.

"Home" strikes him as odd. The little house doesn't feel like home, yet. The big house in Atlanta he shared with Sharon isn't home any more, though. He realized that the night he went over there to get his family heirlooms. It was completely Sharon's house, and it contained no traces of him. No photos of him hung on the walls. None of his books were on the shelves. The garage was completely empty of sports equipment or grilling implements. *I need to make the new house mine*, he decides, *as soon as things calm down*.

In their late-night talks Sally had mentioned that Sam lives in California and designs websites, but that's all Wyatt knows about him. He recalls the Sam from all those years ago, a bratty little towhead taunting Sally about throwing the baton.

I wonder if he remembers that? Wyatt thinks, smiling.

Andrea awakens when they turn onto Honeysuckle.

Thank God there are no cars there now, Wyatt thinks.

"There's no hell on earth more horrible than watching your child screw up their life with drugs and being helpless to do anything about it," Sally says quietly.

It is 7 p.m. that night, and Marybeth, Sally, and Wyatt are sitting on Sally's back porch, wearing sweaters due to the chill. Everyone else has left. Sally has clearly lost weight in just two days, her cheeks looking hollow and dark circles under her haunted eyes.

Andrea ate dinner and went to the movies with a friend. Wyatt and Marybeth ate a lot of "funeral food" for dinner – fried chicken, ham, squash casserole, pecan pie.

Sally picked at a plate of food but ended up giving most of it to Blanche.

Wyatt and Marybeth exchange looks. Marybeth's thoughts flash clear as day to Wyatt – let her talk about this. At least she isn't crying right now.

"You don't know the story Wyatt. I mean, you know the part about her going to Atlanta, but you don't know the whole story," Sally says quietly.

"So tell me, baby," Wyatt says quietly.

Sally sits quietly for a moment, her eyes far away. Finally, she speaks, her voice heavy with grief.

"I raised this beautiful little blonde angel, this intelligent, headstrong child. She was always fearless – jumping off the playground equipment, jumping into every creek or lake or pool we'd let her go in. She laughed all the time, like everything was funny. Her father and I adored her... maybe too much. She was a bit spoiled, I'll admit. When she became a teenager, she was just wild. Staying out all the time. Neglecting schoolwork. Always popular. But she was sweet, too, and she helped me a lot, with her grandmother, with whatever I asked her to do. When Miranda was 18, she was arrested for possession of pot. I couldn't bail her out the night she was arrested because Mother wasn't doing well, so she spent the night in jail. I thought that would cure her, but it didn't. For months she had been running around with some kids I didn't know, coming in really late, being really mouthy and disrespectful to me. Mom's Alzheimers was pretty bad by then. It was extremely stressful for me."

"A night in jail didn't cure her?" Wyatt asked quietly.

"Well, it scared her, and for a few days she stayed home. She told me it was too depressing seeing her grandmother in such bad shape. She and Mother had been very close."

Marybeth looks thoughtful. "That's right. I was thinking she didn't start with the drugs until after she got to Atlanta."

Sally shakes her head. "No, she started here."

Wyatt and Marybeth exchange looks. Finally, Sally continues the story.

"I did everything I could to help her. My insurance didn't cover any sort of drug rehab. She wouldn't go to meetings on her own. I took her to a therapist but she refused to talk, and I couldn't really afford it anyway. It was a nightmare."

"Tell him about the rehab," Marybeth says quietly.

"I called Steve and he agreed to pay for Miranda to go to a rehab place in California. It took a lot of doing but we finally got her to go. She was there for a month."

The three friends sit in silence. Sally has a look of utter anguish on her face.

"Listen, it's getting chilly out here, let's go inside, OK hon?" Marybeth says finally.

Sally nods mutely. Wyatt and Marybeth pick up their plates, and clear the table.

When they are settled in the family room, Sally hands Wyatt a photo of her daughter. Wyatt looks at it and sees a very pretty blonde girl, but also an unhappy teenager trying to cover it up with a lot of makeup and hair products and a smile pasted on her face.

"She was a beautiful girl," he says quietly.

Sally nods. "She had just come back from California when that was made. When she went to Atlanta she was going to Narcotics Anonymous meetings and checking in with her sponsor, and calling me every few days. Then she became a hairdresser, and the partying started again. She met Nick, and he helped her get back to sobriety again, and they had a big fabulous wedding in Hawaii, and everything looked great."

"Do you have any recent photos of her?" Wyatt asks.

Sally is silent. She finally shakes her head. "Oh, wait – Marybeth?"

"Ed and I saw Miranda at Phipps a couple of weeks ago. I asked Ed to take a photo of us," Marybeth says quietly. She pulls out her phone and scrolls through the photos, then hands the phone to Wyatt.

He studies the photo. Marybeth looks relaxed and normal. Miranda is smiling and most would be unable to see what Wyatt sees.

"Do you want to know what I see?" he asks Sally.

Sally looks terrified for a moment, but then nods.

"She was scared of something. I don't know what, but she was scared of -- failure, maybe? I think she was scared of trying to find a job. Fear drove her back to drugs."

Wyatt hands the phone back to Marybeth.

Sally's face is stricken. "That son of a bitch. I suspected he was having money problems. He sold his BMW and bought a cheaper car a few months ago, and Miranda told me they were looking for a new home."

Wyatt and Marybeth exchange a look.

Marybeth tries to be calm. "Sally, blaming Nick for Miranda's death doesn't accomplish anything. He loved her. He didn't want her to die."

A knock sounds at the door and a voice calls out "Sally? It's Sam. I'm coming in."

The door opens and Sam barrels in. Sally looks surprised for a moment, then quickly gets up and walks over to him. Blanche barks and runs over, tail wagging. Sam hugs Sally tightly. The siblings stand there for a minute, Sally holding onto her brother.

Sam is about 5'9, Wyatt guesses, and has carefully colored blonde hair, receding a bit. He has the same blue eyes as Sally and looks a lot like her. He's dressed in jeans and a purple Polo shirt.

Finally Sally pulls away and tries to smile. "You look wonderful, Sam."

"The traffic in Atlanta was a nightmare darlin' sorry it took so long," Sam says. "Yes, I see you Miss DuBois, yes I do," he says leaning over to hug Blanche and rub her head.

"Hey, Blanche gets a hug before I do? Well I never," Marybeth groused. Sam hugs her.

"How are you Mrs. Stinky Buttface?" Sam chortles. Marybeth chuckles.

Wyatt has stood up and is watching this with amusement.

"Wyatt Jamison," he says, sticking his hand out. "Just moved in next door."

Sam shakes his hand. "Nice to meet you. Sally says y'all are already friends. That's great."

Wyatt maintains his composure but he feels somewhat uncomfortable because Sam is checking him out thoroughly, from head to toe.

"Have you eaten? We have TONS of funeral food," Marybeth says. "Come on in the kitchen."

An hour later, Sam has eaten some squash casserole and a piece of fried chicken without the breading, which he gave to Blanche.

"I am trying NOT to gain the middle-aged spread most men over 40 gain, the horrible spare tire," he said.

"Good luck with that," Marybeth chuckles.

"What funeral arrangements are in place?" he asks.

Sally gets up and walks off, headed to the downstairs bathroom.

Marybeth looks at Sally's back, sadly. "They are supposed to release the body tomorrow. There had to be an autopsy. Death by overdose was the verdict. I talked to Nick. He's just barely functional."

Sam nods thoughtfully. "Where will the funeral mass be held? Clayton?"

Marybeth looks uncomfortable. "Well... Nick and Miranda didn't go to church or anything so he's not pushing for a church service in Atlanta, which is good. He's leaving the funeral stuff entirely up to Sally. I told Sally, let's just let the funeral home here do the cremation, and have a short service at the funeral home. She agrees."

Sam frowns. "What does Luke say about that?"

Marybeth leans in to speak softly. "When Luke came in today and saw Sally, I knew he wouldn't fuss at her about anything. He hugged her and I saw tears in his eyes."

Sam sighs heavily. "Well thank God for that."

Marybeth nods. "I think yesterday he was on autopilot but today he was shattered. I've never seen him cry. Unfortunately, all the aunts and older relatives want Sally to give Miranda a full Catholic funeral mass at the church in Clayton, but Sally is saying no, she doesn't want that, and thankfully, Luke is backing her up."

Sam nods. "Miracles happen."

Sally comes out of the bathroom and says "I'm sorry. I just need to go to bed," and goes upstairs, not looking anyone in the eye.

Wyatt clears his throat. "Sam, Marybeth and I think it might be good if you just stay with me while you're here. I have a spare bedroom. Marybeth's staying in the spare room here. We thought you'd be more comfortable on a bed than on the couch here."

Sam looks surprised but covers it well. "I would. Thank you Wyatt. Appreciate it."

"Well, I've had a long day, lots of driving, so I am going to head home. Tell Sally I will see her tomorrow?" Wyatt says to Marybeth.

"Of course. Oh, and Wyatt, I went over and put some clean sheets on that guestroom bed, and freshened up the room. Hope that was okay," Marybeth adds.

"That was really nice of you. Thanks," Wyatt says quietly.

Everyone is quiet for a moment, but they can all hear Sally sobbing in her room.

"I'll head on over now," Sam says quietly. "Oh, when are they going to do the funeral?"

"Wednesday at 4 p.m.," Marybeth says quietly.

When they have gone Marybeth turns off the lights and locks the doors downstairs, and prays for Sally. The house feels so solemn and wrong that Marybeth almost cries as she plods slowly up the stairs.

CHAPTER 36

At Wyatt's house, Sam and Wyatt sit in the den drinking beer. They have been chatting for over an hour. Wyatt likes Sam, despite being very different from him.

Sam fills him in on what it was like growing up in Crossroads – a small town, where Catholics and gays were viewed with great suspicion, which explains why Sam left at 18 and never moved back.

There is a lull in conversation. Wyatt senses that they are not alone in the room, although he's not sure who the spirit is that's observing them.

"I should tell you something, Sam," Wyatt says. "The other night I saw a ghost in my bedroom. I've heard her other times, too. She's not malevolent. Just wanted to warn you."

Sam's face registers shock. "A ghost? Seriously?"

"Yep."

"Um, not to be rude or anything, but had you been drinking?" Sam asks.

Wyatt chuckles. "No. Not really. I'm just sensitive to things."

Wyatt can almost see Sam's struggle to be open-minded. Sam has a very analytical, scientific mind, and thinks most people who see ghosts are delusional.

The door opens and Andrea walks in. Wyatt introduces her to Sam.

"Andrea, I forgot to tell you about the ghost I saw the other night —" Wyatt begins, but she interrupts him.

"I think I heard her in the cellar last night," Andrea says. "So cool. I wish I could see her, like you did."

Sam is startled again. Andrea looks like a sensible, intelligent girl. *She's clearly enthralled by Wyatt*, he thinks.

"Wyatt, did you tell Sam about the trunk in the cellar?"

"Um, nope, it didn't come up," Wyatt replies, sighing.

"What trunk?" Sam asks.

"Apparently one of my forebears who owned the house around the time of the Civil War put a huge old-fashioned trunk in the cellar, but it's locked and we can't find the key, so we have no way of knowing what's in there. My uncle tried for years to figure it out."

"An antique? I would love to see it," Sam says enthusiastically. "Can we go down there right now?"

Wyatt sighs. "There's no power down there, and no air. Let's wait and go tomorrow."

"Okay," Sam says, clearly disappointed. He thinks for a moment. "I have a friend who sells antiques. I bet he can help us identify it, and maybe he will have some ideas about how to get it open," Sam says enthusiastically.

The next morning, Wyatt and Sam eat cereal for breakfast and Sam walks Blanche, then they head down to the cellar.

Andrea is awake and enthusiastically goes down the stairs first, carrying the lantern.

Sam follows, and whistles when he sees the room. "Creepy. Looks like an old root cellar, where they used to store stuff to stay cool in the summertime."

"That's a thought," Wyatt says.

Andrea looks mystified.

"A long time ago, before electricity or refrigerators, people would dig root cellars in the ground, store things like potatoes, melons, anything they wanted kept cool. Notice how much cooler it is in here?"

"Yep. Never thought about that, though. Interesting," Andrea replies, looking at the room more closely.

Sam examines the old trunk with delight. "Wow! This is a real find. Mind if I fire off a few shots?" he says, pulling out a small digital camera from his pocket.

"Go right ahead," Wyatt answers. "I don't know if there's enough light, though."

Sam adjusts something, then takes shots from all different angles, and reviews them. "I wish the light were better but these might do."

Wyatt and Andrea exchange looks. "Do for what?" Andrea asks.

"My friend Barry has an antiques shop and I bet he could tell us more about the trunk, including maybe how to open it," Sam says enthusiastically. "I'll email him the shots."

"Let's go back up," Wyatt says. I don't want to burn out the lights, and I hear Blanche whining."

They all ascend the stairs and go back to the kitchen and sit around the table. Sam has his laptop out and is typing away.

"OK, Barry has the photos, but it's earlier out there so we may have to wait for a response."

"No problem," Wyatt says amiably. "Andrea, are you working today?"

"Yep, but not until tonight."

"I think we can figure out how to get the trunk open – maybe we can just take the entire lid off," Sam says excitedly.

"OK, but I don't think there's anything interesting in that trunk," Wyatt says quietly.

"What? How would you know that?" Sam asks, skeptical. "You said you've not gotten it open."

"I just know. Call it ESP," Wyatt replies evenly.

Andrea is nodding. "He just knows stuff, Sam. It's amazing."

Sam nods, but looks mystified and uncomfortable. Wyatt knows he is processing it alongside the ghost comment and trying to figure out if Wyatt is crazy.

Finally, Sam speaks again. "Was this the so-called treasure your uncle was looking for, all those years?"

Wyatt sighs. "I think he thought there was some underground tunnel or something, with some lost treasure. I highly doubt such a thing exists. I think he was just delusional or getting senile or something. Sally said there have always been rumors about some lost treasure from the Civil War being somewhere around here, but there's no proof of anything."

Sam nods thoughtfully. "Bummer. Anyway, maybe we can get the trunk open and find out for sure?"

"Yeah, I'd be interested to hear what your friend thinks. Thanks for asking him."

Wyatt looks at Andrea. "I have an appointment downtown. Would you tell Marybeth I'll be over later?"

"Sure," she nods. "I didn't hear her crying last night, did you?"

"Nope, and I hope that's a good sign," Wyatt replies quietly.

Sam looks puzzled.

"Sally sleeps with her window open and Sunday night I could hear her crying, pretty much all night," Andrea says quietly. "I hate that she's so torn up. I love

Sally. She's been so good to me," Andrea says, a sob catching in her throat.

Wyatt walks over and kisses the top of her head. "When the funeral is over and everyone leaves, we will be here for Sally, Sweetheart."

Andrea nods, even as a tear slides down her cheek. Wyatt pats her back.

Sam has observed this. "Hey, I'm going to walk next door for a few minutes but I won't stay, because there are too many people there already. After that, why don't we take Blanche to a place I know, take a little mountain hike?" he says to Andrea. "Have you hiked up to the top of Warrior Mountain? The view from up there is spectacular."

Her face brightens, "I'd love that," she says quietly.

CHAPTER 37

Attorney Ben Walters' office is just as Wyatt remembers it, all expensive but outdated furniture, heavy back issues of Southern Living and Town and Country, and little else. Behind a desk there's an elderly receptionist with a 1971 bouffant hairstyle and a purple dress. Wyatt sits in the small reception area leafing through a magazine from 1992, and then tries not to laugh when Ben hollers from inside "Send the boy in, Sara!"

Wyatt likes being called a "boy" at 52. He carefully puts down the old magazine, then heads into the small office.

Walters' office was decorated in 1985, with maroon carpet and pale green grasscloth walls. His diplomas hang on the walls, but the only other decorations are photos of Walters playing golf in Augusta and on another course Wyatt doesn't recognize.

"Sit down, Wyatt. Can I get you a cup of coffee or anything?"

"No thanks, I'm fine," Wyatt says, wondering if he should ask Walters where he plays golf locally.

"Settled in now? House okay?"

Wyatt nods. "Pretty much. House is old but fine, thanks. Thanks for helping me with the will and everything. Very well handled, and at a reasonable cost."

"Glad to do it."

There is an awkward pause.

Finally, Walters sips his coffee and says quietly "Heard about the Cavanaugh girl dying. Such a shame. She was a pretty gal. I think she dated my youngest son a time or two. How's her mama?"

"Oh, you know, torn up. Awful thing, losing a child," Wyatt says. He realizes, startled, that Ben Walters is thinking how lucky it is that his son didn't date Miranda for long, because she had a reputation as a "wild child."

Wyatt clears his throat. "So, uh, what was that legal matter you were talking about?"

"Oh yes, got it right here," Walters says. "My girl made a copy of it because the letter is so old it's delicate. Anyway, here it is."

Wyatt tries not to chuckle at the elderly lady being referred to as "My girl." He accepts the proffered letter and reads it with great interest.

It's dated December 8, 1911 and it's to Jack Jamison, Wyatt's great-grandfather. The paper was obviously heavy and watermarked, which surprises Wyatt.

Dear Mr. Jamison,

I want to bring to your attention the fact that the land located along Honeysuckle Road, in the northwest part of Bell County and more fully described as The Adams Farm, was obtained by illegal means and therefore the title is not valid.

The land was lawfully owned by my great grandfather, Hiram Littlefeather, until he was murdered by Matthew Adams in 1838. My grandfather, an infant at the time, grew up in an orphanage and was unaware of his parentage until recently.

Hiram Littlefeather, my great grandfather, was half Cherokee and half white. He married my great grandmother Sara and they had my grandfather Ned in 1837. Ned worked in the sawmill all his life and never knew what had happened to his parents. I did the research and learned of the murders, and the taking of our land. It rightfully belongs to me, not any descendant of Tom Adams. I will be commencing a suit against the Jamison family forthwith, unless the land is returned to us.

Samuel Burke

Wyatt finishes the letter, then re-reads it. "Wow. Never knew this. Is there more in the file?" he asks quietly.

"No, I didn't find anything. I imagine what happened is my grandfather spoke to Burke and told him he had no case."

Wyatt rubs his face thoughtfully. "My grandparents sold the farmland in the late 1960's, just keeping the parcel where the house is located. I assume the title was clear?"

Ben Walters looks thoughtful. "Oh yes. My dad handled that. Burke was long dead by then."

"So do you think there is any truth to this crazy story?" Wyatt asks.

Walters clears his throat. "I did a little digging in the history books, out of curiosity. In 1835 the Treaty of New Echota was signed, giving the government Cherokee lands in exchange for compensation. The Cherokee that wouldn't voluntarily leave North Georgia by 1838 were rounded up and sent to a holding fort, Fort Buffington, in Cherokee County, before they went to Oklahoma on the Trail of Tears. If there was any resistance, they were often shot. Nobody did anything about it. They were considered savages by the white folks."

"Wow. I don't remember studying that. So that must have been why the land never went back to the Cherokee families?"

"Probably. The treaty was never revoked."

"Hmm…. Do we know if this Samuel Burke has any descendants in Crossroads today?"

"Yes, I believe Roberta Kingston is his daughter. Her maiden name is Burke."

Wyatt's eyebrows shoot up. That explains the hostility. *Surely Roberta couldn't be blaming me for something my ancestor did more than 150 years ago?* he thought.

Ben Walters is watching Wyatt's face thoughtfully, and Wyatt sees clearly what Walters is thinking.

He is warning me to be careful of Roberta, in his very roundabout way, Wyatt realizes. Maybe Roberta was behind the photos that were sent to Sharon. *But why would she want me to get divorced?* he wonders. *Maybe she assumed I wouldn't want the house and we would have to sell it as part of the divorce settlement?*

"Say, do you have the title records on my house, in your file?" Wyatt asks Walters.

"The oldest land titles in Bell County are at the county archives room, and that's in the main library," Walters explains. "You will need to make an appointment to go over there and look at them."

Wyatt frowns. "Make an appointment with Sally Cavanaugh?"

"Yes. Of course, we don't know when she will go back to work."

"No, no we don't."

"I can assure you there is no legitimate lien on the land. The title is legally clear."

Mavis knocks on the door of Sally's house carefully, while also holding a small plastic platter of pigs & blankets. Ostensibly she is there as a neighbor being neighborly, but she is really there at the behest of Roberta.

Sally's aunt Jessie opens the door and peers at Mavis. "Yes?"

"I am Mavis Burke Johnson and I live across the street. I just wanted to say how sorry I am. I brought some food."

"Well thank you. Would you like to come in?" Jessie inquires.

"No, thanks. I can see there's a crowd. I was just wondering when is the funeral?"

"Tomorrow afternoon at 4, at the funeral home," Jessie says.

"I used to be a professional photographer. Would Sally like photos of her daughter perhaps, in the casket, to remember her?" Mavis asks.

Jessie pulls herself up to her full 5'2 and stares at the strange woman, shocked she would suggest such a creepy thing.

"Sally's daughter has been cremated, so no, uh, thanks."

Mavis stands there, shocked that anyone wouldn't have a proper Christian burial. "Okay," she mumbles, and turns to head back across the street.

CHAPTER 38

The day of the funeral dawns cloudy and overcast. Sally wakes up at 7 and looks out the window of her bedroom dreading the day like she has never dreaded anything in her life. The beautiful vista of her yard is tinged with gray shadows and even the familiar mountains look like giant tombstones in the distance, to Sally.

Thirty minutes later, Sally sits in her favorite old chair in her room, having taken a shower and put on her black funeral dress, a dress bought three days ago. It's a plain cotton shirtwaist dress with no adornment.

After donning her own black skirt and knit top, Marybeth brought in a cup of coffee and helped Sally pull her hair back into a chignon.

Sally has resolved not to cry. The funeral will start in two hours.

Luke is downstairs with all the relatives, trying to pacify the ones who are furious about the non-Catholic funeral.

Sally doesn't care about their anger, or about anything. All she can feel is a terrible black void where her daughter used to be alive.

Sally looks at Marybeth, sitting there on the bed, new worry lines around her eyes and mouth, her dear friend who has been by her side throughout the ordeal, and realizes she has to unburden herself of the terrible guilt she has carried for years, or she might as well die.

"There's something I never told you," Sally begins. "It's about why Miranda left here at 19 and went to Atlanta."

Marybeth frowns. "You told me when it happened. You said she wanted to be a hairdresser and get out of Crossroads."

"No. Well – yes. She wanted those things, both of them. More importantly, she wanted to get away from ME. She wanted to not be around me. Frankly, I didn't want to be around her, either."

Sally looks at the small table beside her chair and picks up her rosary, needing the comfort of feeling it in her hands.

"When you are the mother of a child who is a drug addict, you get to a place, finally, a terrible place, where you cannot enable them. You cannot stand on edge all the time, teetering, waiting to fall into the pit of despair that yawns wide open when they start using again. You get tired of it all. Tired of the late nights waiting for them to come home, wondering if they will call you from jail. Tired of finding the pills or the joints in their rooms. Tired of the zombie that used to be your child. Tired of trying to help them, to encourage them, tired of trying.

I had reached that point. I had reached the point where I simply couldn't be her enabler any more, and she knew it.

I used my savings to get her to Atlanta, get her into an apartment, get her into that beauty school. I had to get her out of my house, or I was going to lose my mind.

Even though what I did was ultimately for her benefit, I didn't do it with pure motives. I just had to cut her loose, let her go. Regain some peace. I also knew there was a chance she would kill herself with drugs."

"But she had been to California and gotten clean, I thought?" Marybeth asks, confused.

"She came home and went right back to smoking pot, which she said didn't count," Sally says heavily. "Of course, that led to other things. I could hear in her voice when she was using. I always knew, just from her phone calls."

Marybeth stares at Sally with furrowed brow, knowing Sally's heart was filled with love for her child, and is still filled with it, but trying to understand how a mother could watch her child stumble and not try to catch them. Then again, Marybeth had to admit she had never tried to mother a child who was addicted to drugs.

"She could have stayed here in the area. Luke offered to let her work in the office of the plumbing company. He needed help. She could have lived in Clayton. She didn't want that," Sally says heavily.

"She always wanted to go to beauty school. She did, and completed it successfully. So why do you feel guilty?" Marybeth asks, gently.

"Her father wanted her to come out to live with him. What if I had encouraged that? Everything might have been different. I dissuaded her from going," Sally says miserably. "I wanted her in Atlanta, far enough away so I wouldn't see her often, but close enough to drive home if she wanted to come..."

Sally put her face in her hands in anguish.

Marybeth sits there quietly for a few moments. She thinks of the issues she has had with her own daughters over the years, but they pale in comparison. Finally she sits up straighter and squares her shoulders, regarding her friend with as much authority as she can muster on this terrible morning.

"Sally, going back and playing "what if" accomplishes nothing," she begins. Sally doesn't react.

Marybeth waits but Sally says nothing. Marybeth finally stands up and goes over to the chair and kneels in front of Sally, happy she isn't wearing pantyhose. She gently pulls Sally's hands away from her ravaged face and holds them.

"Sally, my dear sister of the heart, please listen to me. You LOVED your daughter. You did the very best you could. You gave her everything you thought she needed. You tried your best."

Sally casts her eyes down, unable to look at Marybeth.

"I could have done more. I failed her."

"You couldn't control her after she was grown, Sally."

"I should have tried harder!" Sally says through gritted teeth. "You don't understand."

Marybeth sits back, thinking hard.

"Didn't your dad drink a lot? Seems to me I remember that from when we were kids."

Sally looks up, perplexed. "Yes, Daddy liked to have a few drinks in the evening. It never interfered with his work, though."

"You mom liked her cocktails, too."

"Yes. So?" Sally says, agitated.

Marybeth looks at her friend. "Oh Sally, don't you see it? Your parents kept Miranda when she was small, and you were working in Steve's office, remember? The first four years of her life. She spent the night over here a lot too, remember? Not every night, but once a week or so, right? She was around alcohol abuse. She saw it."

"Her grandparents adored her!" Sally says, now irate.

"I'm not saying they didn't adore her, Sally. I'm saying she saw that behavior, that drinking to have fun type of behavior. Drinking to celebrate. Drinking to relax. The experts say by the time a child is three years old, their personality is pretty much set."

Sally stands up and goes to the window to look out, both angry at Marybeth and wondering if she is right. It feels like she could be right.

"I will have to do some research on that," she says quietly.

Marybeth rises off the floor awkwardly, feeling her age. "Well the whole point is, do NOT blame yourself. Don't blame anybody. It accomplishes nothing, Hon."

"You are saying she was genetically predisposed to addiction?"

"No, not necessarily. Maybe? I don't know. I just know blaming anyone is a waste of time and energy. Your parents were a product of their generation, and when they were young everyone drank and smoked. Blame is useless. It accomplishes nothing. What's done is done. Try to let it go."

For a few moments the two friends are quiet, both pondering drug addiction.

Sally finally looks at her friend. "Should I try to put on some makeup?"

Marybeth shrugs. "I think it would be a waste of time, to be honest. Nobody expects you to look anything but devastated."

"I keep seeing her in this house, like a ghost."

Marybeth hugs Sally's shoulders. "Let's go to Mike's place at Hilton Head tomorrow, and be beach bums for a while. It would do you good."

Sally nods. "I would love that. I haven't been on a vacation in years."

A knock sounds at the door. Marybeth goes over and opens it. Wyatt stands there. "I was thinking Sally should ride with me."

"Good idea," Marybeth says. "What about Andrea?"

Wyatt frowns. "She, ah, she is having a female situation, not feeling good. I told her she could stay at my house and skip the funeral."

Sally almost smiles at the phrase "a female situation," but then doesn't.

Marybeth grabs Sally's purse. "C'mon Stinky. Let's get this over with."

Wyatt is happy to get Sally in the car and get out of the house. As he drives, he decides not to make polite conversation. He reviews his time at Sally's house the day before.

There were too many people in there. Too much information popping out at him that he doesn't want to know – like the fact that Luke drinks too much beer, Aunt Jessie's false teeth are loose, and Sam wants to get back to California and do a three day "cleanse."

Wyatt had gone over to Sally's at noon, to see if help was needed, and ended up staying until 3:30, alternately repulsed and fascinated by all the friends and relatives in the house.

Without being able to listen to music or distract himself from all the input, Wyatt decided to zero in on certain key folks he doesn't really know, see what makes them tick.

Luke took a pile of Honeybaked Ham and made a huge sandwich that Wyatt envied. Blanche watched him carefully. Wyatt makes a mental note to leave Blanche in his house during the funeral, so the food won't be in danger.

Luke wondered if Nick deliberately killed Miranda for insurance money. That guy watches too many TV shows, Wyatt thought as he chewed a brownie.

Wyatt studied Nick, just to see if Luke's suspicions were founded, and decides they weren't.

Nick is a tall, handsome young man with brown hair and brown eyes, in an Armani suit. Although he drives a Lexus, he was in a near panic, wondering how he is going to make a living since his business is going under and his wife has died. He loved Miranda but the marriage was faltering before the drug use started back. Wyatt felt sorry for him as he watched Nick throw back a glass of bourbon.

Sam spent a lot of time fussing around the house, out of nervousness. He dusted the mantel in the family room, loaded the dishwasher, and changed his tie twice. Wyatt was amused to hear Sam's thoughts about every guy in the house, and whether they were handsome or not.

Less amusing were Sam's unspoken suspicions that Wyatt may be unstable. He doesn't like the talk of ESP and ghosts, as he is a totally rational, practical guy.

Wyatt ate a large piece of pecan pie and a small piece of pound cake, pondering what to say to Sam to convince him he's not crazy, but made no decision.

Steve, Sally's ex, spent most of his time sitting on the back porch looking at his phone, horrified at the lack of usability of it. Tired of the smell of hair spray and Luke's obnoxious cologne, Wyatt walked out to the porch and chatted with Steve for a moment. Steve regarded him with curiosity but no malice.

"I'm really glad you're next door," he says to Wyatt. "I also understand a young friend has been staying with Sally, which is great. I think it's better she's not alone now."

"Yes, it is. I like Sally a lot. We're good friends. I know she is devastated but I will help her get through this in any way possible," Wyatt said sincerely.

Steve nodded.

Wyatt saw a balding, slightly underweight man who was once a self-involved jerk but is now seeing how important family is, the death of his only daughter hitting him hard. He felt he has failed as a father.

Wyatt pitied him.

The funeral is mercifully brief. Sally wanted no music or eulogies. Luke's oldest son Patrick, a young priest not yet assigned to a parish, conducts the service, although he is very nervous to do so outside of a church.

The small, plain room at the funeral home has nothing religious in it – no crucifix, no icons, nothing.

After the final prayer, Sally has tears sliding down her face, but she looks relieved, not upset. Wyatt puts his arm around her shoulder and leans over to kiss the top of her head.

I hover in the parking lot, glad it's not raining, and look at the small crowd of Sally's friends and family members. I wonder if Miranda is still on earth, or has gone on to whatever else there is.

I don't sense her anywhere, so I figure she is probably in heaven.

I watch the mourners get in the cars to head back to Sally's house. I know Sally just wants this whole thing to be over with. I feel sorry for her.

I wonder if I can help her in any way.

The man from the funeral home has cornered Sally and is asking her about settling the bill, and what to do with the ashes.

Sally's face is stricken.

To my shock, Luke appears, grabs the guy's arm, and hustles him away. I can hear him saying he will take care of the bill, and someone from the family will be by for the ashes in a day or two.

Poor Sally. She has no idea what to do with the ashes, not that it matters.

At the same time, back at Wyatt's house, Blanche is barking so loud that Andrea cannot sleep, or even read. She gets off the twin bed and walks out to the front room, and to her astonishment she sees through the window a heavyset older woman holding a plastic grocery bag walking around the front porch of Wyatt's house.

"Helloo?" the woman calls. Blanche woofs enthusiastically.

Andrea studies her and realizes she has seen the woman before, eating at Bob's Place. She's usually really bossy and talks to Bob like he's her servant, which amuses Andrea.

Andrea senses the woman knows good and well that Wyatt isn't home. She looks around carefully and tries the handle of the front door.

Andrea realizes with shock that the door isn't locked. She also decides, in that split second, to hide and watch what the woman does. Crouched behind the living room chair, Andrea observes.

The woman carefully eases the door open, and Blanche runs over, barking. The woman pulls a pork chop out of her plastic grocery bag, and throws it out in the yard. Blanche bounds after it, settles down with the pork chop, and gnaws it happily.

What IS her name? Andrea thinks, trying to remember. *Roberta! That's it.*

Roberta marches back into the house and looks around like she owns it.

Andrea watches with fascination as Roberta heads down the hallway to the bedrooms.

Andrea slips out the front door and goes out in the yard to grab Blanche's collar so she can't run off and get hit by a car or lost.

Blanche ignores Andrea, she is so intent on polishing off her pork chop.

When Andrea comes back in the house with Blanche and shuts the front door, she loudly says "Blanche, you bad girl! What were you doing out there?" so Roberta can hear her.

A moment later Roberta comes out of the largest bedroom and walks down the short hallway to the living room.

"Hello, Dear. How are you?" she says in a falsely cheerful voice.

"I'm fine. Aren't you Reverend Kingston's wife?" Andrea asks.

Roberta looks stunned for a moment, then realizes this girl is a waitress at Bob's.

"Well, yes, I was trying to find someone to leave this food with, for the Odalshalski child."

"Everyone is at the funeral but you can leave it with me and I will make sure Sally gets it," Andrea says evenly.

Roberta smiles and hands the bag to Andrea, who accepts it and then opens the front door pointedly. Roberta walks out without a word.

Andrea steps over to the window and watches Roberta get into her car and drive off, then peeks into the plastic grocery bag. It holds two more cooked pork chops in it, just loose, not on a plate. Funeral food, or a pacifier for Blanche? Andrea suspects Roberta intended all three chops to go to Blanche. The fact she knew about Blanche being here in Wyatt's house concerns Andrea.

Andrea shakes her head and drops the bag into the garbage, unmoved by Blanche's whining.

CHAPTER 39

After 45 minutes of post-funeral socializing, Sally has had enough. Her heels are off and she walks into the kitchen and finds Marybeth.

"Look, I can't deal with this anymore. Can you handle these people and let me go lie down?" Sally asks.

"Sure. You go and rest. You've had a terrible day," Marybeth replies.

Wyatt walks over to Luke. "Can we get these people out of here? I think we've socialized enough and I know Sally is exhausted."

Luke looks at him in annoyance, wondering how Wyatt would know what Sally feels, but after a moment he nods. "I'll encourage everyone to head out," he says curtly.

Wyatt walks into the back yard and sighs, staring up at the sky, wishing it were dark already. He hears a strange sound and looks over to a stand of trees. *There's someone back there crying*, he realizes, wondering who it is and what he should do, if anything. He takes a few steps in that direction.

Sam steps out of the shadows wiping his eyes.

Wyatt looks at him. "You okay?" he asks softly.

Sam nods. "Yeah. I saw a photo of Miranda I've had in my wallet for years, and I just lost it. I always felt like she was mine, as much as anyone's, because Sally and I are close. I don't really know Luke's kids that well."

Wyatt just nods.

Sam blows his nose loudly and looks at Wyatt. Wyatt knows he is trying to decide what to say. Wyatt waits patiently.

"My friend looked at the photos of the trunk and said you might be able to get a couple hundred bucks for it, if you can get the lock open, but he didn't have any advice on that, unfortunately."

"Thanks for letting me know. I'm not really interested in selling it."

"I understand. Look, I am glad you and Sally are together," Sam says.

"Well, we are and we aren't. Right now we are just good friends. I'm hoping when everyone is gone we can become more than that."

Sam sighs and runs his hands through his hair, but finally nods. "I see your point, but I think Marybeth is planning to spirit her away for a while."

Wyatt is puzzled. This is the first he has heard of it. "I was not aware of that."

"Well, she said something about the beach. I need to get back inside," Sam says.

The two men walk back inside. Mercifully, only a few family members are still in the house. Wyatt finds Marybeth in the kitchen.

"Sam said you're planning to take Sally away?" he asks, hoping it's not true.

Marybeth looks up from loading the dishwasher and nods. "I should have told you but we just discussed it today, right before the funeral. My brother has a house on Hilton Head, right on the beach, and he said we can use it for a week or two. It may be too cold to swim but we can walk on the beach, shop, read – just relax, away from all the reminders of Miranda," she finishes, nodding at photos of Miranda on the fridge and the wall.

"I understand. It would be good for her, I think," Wyatt acknowledges.

"Can you keep Blanche?" Marybeth asks.

"Absolutely."

Wyatt knows the beach trip is as much for Marybeth as it is for Sally but that's okay.

Sally has slipped off her funeral clothes and sits in her chair by the window in her room. She is wearing sweatpants and an old tee shirt, rosary beads in hand, gazing off, into the past. She is thinking about the last phone conversation she had with Miranda, a month before she died.

She remembers it in painful detail, and wishes she didn't.

"Hey Mom, how's it going?" Miranda said.

"Okay, and how are you Sweetie?" Sally asked, setting her grocery bags on the table. Andrea was at work and Sally had just returned from the store.

"I'm good. When is that guy moving back?"

"Wyatt? He has to finish his divorce stuff and take care of some things in Atlanta before he can move up here. He's never lived here, so it's not moving back, actually."

"Whatever."

Sally can tell by Miranda's voice she finds the subject of Wyatt boring, but she was making a small effort to be polite.

"How is Nick?" Sally asks.

"Oh, you know. Always busy. I rarely see him. His business isn't doing too good, though."

"Doing too well."

"Jesus Mom can we have a conversation without you correcting me?!" Miranda barks.

"Fine," Sally says, looking at the ice cream melting on the counter.

"Look, um, this is weird to admit but... I wonder if you could loan me some money?"

Sally's eyebrows shoot up. "Money? Why?"

"I just need it."

"Miranda, you're married to a stockbroker and you live in Buckhead. I work part time at a library in a small *town. I just don't have much money. I have a little bit in savings, and I might be able to part with some of it, but not unless you tell me why."*

There is a long pause. Sally puts the phone down for a moment and grabs the ice cream and sticks it in the freezer.

When she grabs the phone again she hears Miranda's voice. "...it's just a minor procedure, no big deal, and it's only a few weeks along."

"Wait a minute. What's a few weeks along? Are you pregnant?" Sally asks, hoping against hope she is wrong.

"Jesus don't you LISTEN? Yes. Not much though. Termination is no big deal at this point."

"Why would you do that?" Sally asks, unable to disguise the revulsion in her voice.

"Nick is having a lot of trouble financially. He thinks he's going to lose his job. He wants me to go back to work. I don't want to cut hair and be pregnant. Besides, as I've always said, I don't want to be a mother. Not now, probably not ever."

Sally sighs.

"It's only a thousand bucks Mom."

"I'm sorry. I'm not going to loan you the money to abort my grandchild. There are always alternatives. Lots of couples would love to adopt a healthy baby. Or I will raise her."

"Shit. NO MOM! I'm not going to get all fat and gross. Eeeuw. Just forget it. Forget I asked. I knew you wouldn't understand."

"Miranda —" Sally starts, but Miranda has hung up.

Miranda's calls, always sporadic, dropped to none over the next few weeks. Sally thought about sending her the money, but it was a lot for Sally to part with, and despite herself she just couldn't get past the idea that her money would end the life of her grandchild.

Sally sits with head bowed and tears slide down her cheeks. She had meant to call Miranda back, but Miranda wouldn't answer her phone.

A knock sounds at the door. Miranda's husband Nick enters and sits near her, on the corner of the bed, looking tired and uncomfortable. His suit coat is downstairs with the tie, and his blue dress shirt is rumpled and has a stain on it.

"How are you holding up, Nick?" Sally asks softly.

"I will be okay," he mumbles, head down. He doesn't look her in the eyes. Sally suddenly realizes he knew about the pregnancy and the abortion. She thinks about slapping him but realizes it wouldn't do any good now.

"This will take some time to process," Sally says.

"Yeah. Uh, I am selling the house. I need to get rid of Miranda's stuff. What do you want me to do with it all?" Nick asks.

Sally frowns, thinking how cold and businesslike the phrase "get rid of Miranda's stuff" sounds. "I guess I can come to Atlanta and get it sometime."

Nick stands up suddenly and paces, running his hands through his hair. "Well, uh, I'd like it gone really soon. I might have an offer on the house."

Sally stares at Nick, wondering where the shy young man she liked so much has gone, disliking this man in front of her who is pacing around like a caged dog, looking agitated.

"When are you going back to Atlanta?" she asks.

"Tonight."

Sally nods, thoughtfully, then speaks. "Marybeth was going to go back tomorrow anyway, and get some clothes and things for our trip. I will go with her and we can run by the house. Can you be there tomorrow at lunchtime? Noon?"

"Yeah, sure, I can be there to let you all in."

"Thanks," Sally says drily.

"Not the furniture, though, just her personal items, ok?"

Sally thinks for a moment. "Miranda bought all new furniture. She didn't want anything from the family. So I have no attachment to any of the furniture." *But why did you have to sound so cold, Nick?* She wonders.

Nick suddenly stops his restless pacing and drops into a squat in front of Sally's chair. "Sally – I – I am so sorry about Miranda. I didn't know what was going on. I swear. She had gotten really distant from me these last few weeks and I... I should have paid more attention. I was just sunk in my own misery. I am *so sorry*," he says, a sob catching in his throat. "I loved her. I can't bear the thought of my life without her!"

Sally shakes her head, trying not to cry. She knows, deep down, that despite his immaturity Nick loved her daughter.

"Would you go downstairs and ask Wyatt to come see me, please?" she asks gently.

Nick nods, and stands up, wiping his eyes.

Wyatt appears a moment later. "What's up?"

"I need to go to Atlanta tomorrow and get Miranda's personal items from Nick. I'm going to put everything in Marybeth's garage and then we will head to the beach. I was thinking, I don't know if Andrea will feel comfortable staying in this house alone. Can you talk to her about it?"

"Sure."

"If necessary, could she stay with you? And Blanche?"

"No problem," Wyatt responds. "Can you leave me a number where you can be reached while you're gone?" Wyatt asks.

"Yes, of course. My cell should actually work, too."

"Yes, outside the mountains they are much more reliable."

There seems to be nothing else to say. Wyatt can almost feel the roiling thoughts in Sally's mind – the terrible grief but also a bit of hope.

Wyatt clears his throat. "Look, Sally, I need to say something to you, and I'm not good at talking about emotions. So I'll just blunder through this as best I can, okay?"

She sees his fear. Without thinking, she walks over and puts her arms around his waist, burrowing in, to rest her head on his chest.

"Wyatt, this is the most terrible thing I've ever had to endure. Just knowing that you are next door, that you are there, it – it gives me hope, that my life, well... that the rest of it won't be so terrible."

Wyatt holds her and rubs her back lightly. "Sally, I hate that this tragedy has happened. I am here for you, though, in any capacity you need me. Whether you want only friendship or – something else – it's your call."

Sally pulls back a little bit and looks at him, then without realizing the unconscious need, she stands on tiptoe to kiss him.

Wyatt leans down and kisses her carefully at first, then with great tenderness, and finally an intensity he almost can't control. The feel of her soft curves pressed against him awakens him powerfully.

Sally responds to him with an intensity of her own, unable to process anything but the awakening passion that has been dormant for years. She feels as though she is melting in his arms, and time has stopped.

WHAT THE HELL ARE YOU DOING! Sally hears her mother's outraged voice in her head.

Suddenly she pulls back, almost violently, pushing Wyatt away.

"NO! I can't do this!" she exclaims, the anguish evident in her voice.

Wyatt stares at her, almost seeing the roiling emotions in her. Sally sinks to the ground shaking.

"Honey −" he says tenderly.

"NO! I am not that woman! I mean not − not a SLUT! Only a crazy woman, only a slut, would fornicate with a man and her child barely cold! NO!"

She shakes her head violently.

"Sally −" he starts to say, before she interrupts him.

"I just can't do this now, Wyatt. I'm so sorry," Sally says, starting to sob. She curls into a ball on the floor.

"I'll send in Marybeth −"

"NO! I want to be by myself!"

He sighs heavily, and leaves the room.

Andrea knocks softly on Wyatt's door twenty minutes later. "Come in Andrea," he calls.

Andrea comes in smiling, wearing pajamas, Blanche trotting at her heels. "Hey. Haven't had a chance to talk to you all day Wyatt. How is Sally?" she asks, before sitting down on the bed cross legged.

Wyatt pulls off his reading glasses and puts down his book. He's sitting in an easy chair in the corner of his room, a beer next to the chair. He wears sweatpants and a clean but wrinkled tee shirt.

"She's... coping. I am sure she is going to be okay. How are you feeling?" he asks.

Andrea blushes. "Lots better, thanks. Hey, but listen, there was this weird woman that came to the house this afternoon during the funeral, and I thought I should tell you about it."

Wyatt looks at Andrea seeing her recollection of Roberta's visit.

"Was it Roberta Kingston?" he asks.

"Yes! I recognized her from work. She was trying to pretend to be a mourner but she came HERE, not to Sally's house, and she was snooping in the house. She brought pork chops to distract Blanche!"

Wyatt chuckles.

"Well, she has some silly notion that we have a treasure here, and she thinks she has claim to it."

Andrea frowns. "How do you know?"

"Well, apparently her second great grandfather was part Cherokee and was killed when he wouldn't voluntarily give up his land to my third great grandfather, Tom Adams. Roberta's grandfather wrote a letter in 1911 and tried to argue that this land was his, but the law was on the side of my family. The Cherokee removal was a tragic thing, but it was all over by 1838 when my ancestor got this land."

"How could that happen?"

"President Jackson made a treaty with the Cherokee, paying them for the land. Not all Cherokee agreed with it, though."

"Wow, that's a trip," was Andrea's response.

"Yep."

"I'm going to research that removal thing. I don't know much about it," she said, scratching Blanche's tummy.

"Well, none of us are responsible for our family members," Wyatt says softly.

"Thank God," is Andrea's response. "Say, what about getting the trunk opened?"

Wyatt stands up and stretches. "Well, I will figure it out one of these days. Time for me to get to bed. I suggest you do the same."

Andrea unfolds herself. "Gotcha. Night."

CHAPTER 40

Sam sits on the back porch of Sally's house and looks at the stars. It's a clear night and the sight of the stars calms his anxiety. He wishes he had a shot of vodka. He wishes he still smoked. He wishes he could somehow bring back his niece, and un-break his sister's heart. He curses the people who sold Miranda the drugs that killed her.

He ponders what happened earlier in the evening.

About 10:15 Sam had noticed there were few people left in Sally's house, and he saw Wyatt quietly go out the back door, his face solemn. Sam started the dishwasher and finished wiping down the kitchen counter.

He headed into the family room and told Luke to go home, that he would finish cleaning up and lock up.

Luke sat in a wingback chair, looking at a photo album. He closed it and stood up slowly, then looked down at his younger brother. "Thanks. Got an early day tomorrow. Need to get some sleep. You leaving tomorrow?"

"No, not until Friday. I need to get back to California, take care of some business," Sam said carefully.

Luke nodded. "Gotcha. Have a safe trip back."

Sam realized Luke was trying to be nice. Luke stuck out his hand. "I'm glad you came, little brother. She needed you here."

The two men shook hands solemnly.

Sam looked at his older brother and saw a man with gray hair and new wrinkles around his eyes, and an added 15 lbs., worried about his sister. "You know, I am really grateful you stayed close to home," Sam said.

Luke nods gruffly. "Never wanted to live anywhere else, but…. I hate this whole thing. Hate seeing Sally suffer."

"Me too," Sam agreed.

"Have a safe trip back," Luke said solemnly.

Now, sitting under the stars, Sam inhales deeply and looks at the quiet backyard, shrouded in shadows. His older brother had often hit him and teased him when they were kids. *I actually was able to get along with Luke, for once*, he marvels. *I should come home more often, mend fences a bit more. I should stick closer to Sally, let her know I'm here for her.*

Sam stands up and stretches, then turns to head back in the house. For just a moment, he thinks he smells Estee, the perfume his mother used to wear. *I'm trying, Mom*, he thinks. Then his rational mind kicks in and he scowls, and thinks, *you're losing it! She's long dead*.

Sam hates mess or disorder and he decides to clean a bit more. After throwing some paper cups in the trash, and sweeping the kitchen floor, Sam cuts off the downstairs lights and walks upstairs to Sally's room.

He stands in front of her door for a moment. From down the hall, Marybeth's door opens and she hisses at him.

"Get away from there!"

Sam turns and looks at her, surprised by the vehemence in her voice. Marybeth has on no makeup and her hair is in disarray. She wears an old bathrobe over a big tee shirt.

"I wanted to see –" he begins, but Marybeth glares at him and motions him to come over. After he walks over she pulls him into her room and shuts the door, but still speaks softly.

"Thanks for cleaning up. I was just wiped out. In case you're wondering yes, Wyatt is in there with Sally. I doubt he will sleep in his own bed tonight."

Sam looks puzzled. "I don't think so. Wyatt left a while ago."

Marybeth looks puzzled. "Oh Damn. I thought they were in there making out."

"Nope. I can hear her saying the rosary. She always does that when she's stressed out."

Marybeth looks puzzled. She is Methodist. "But Sally doesn't go to mass any more. Hasn't gone in years."

Sam shrugs. "Once a Catholic..."

Marybeth shakes her head softly, and reaches for a glass of wine and takes a sip.

"Well, Wyatt is good for her. I hate that she is pushing him away because of Miranda's death."

"I didn't realize it was that serious."

Marybeth sighs and drops onto the bed. "Well, yes. Sally wouldn't be anything but his friend until his divorce was finalized, but that relationship is a great thing for her. I will be so relieved when she goes ahead and sleeps with him, because in her mind only then will they be a couple, but Wyatt is in love with her – has been for months."

"Wow. Well that's great. I like Wyatt," Sam says thoughtfully.

"Oh yes, Ed and I like him too, and Ed isn't easily impressed, you know."

"You don't think the ESP and the ghost stuff is a bit weird, though?" Sam exclaims, pacing in the small room.

Marybeth rolls her eyes. "Lord, Sam, you live in California and you can't deal with that?! Let it go. Wyatt is extraordinary. Not crazy."

"C'mon Marybeth. He said he sees ghosts!"

Marybeth fixes him with a steely glare. "I don't care if he sees giant unicorns having sex in the back yard every damn day. He loves Sally and he's good for her."

Sam stops and frowns. There's an uncomfortable silence. Finally Sam clears his throat.

"Are you all still going to the beach tomorrow?"

Marybeth shrugs. "I really hope she will go, but I will let Sally decide."

Sam looks around at the girlish pink room that was Miranda's and remembers when it was Sally's room. It saddens him to think of the little girls that are gone. He finally gazes down at Marybeth.

"You remember when we were all kids? I was so annoying to you and Sally?"

Marybeth smiles. "You were obnoxious at times, but also adorable, and smart as a whip. I knew you would go far in life."

"I never told you this, but that time you caught me drooling over a photo of Rob Lowe in Sally's teen magazine, and you talked to me about being gay, it meant a lot to me. It made me feel I wasn't abnormal. I had literally never told a soul how I felt because I thought I was such a freak. You told me it was no big deal who I was attracted to, and that there were other boys like me out there. From that day forward, life got easier. I've never thanked you for that."

Marybeth looks at the handsome man with a $100 haircut, smelling of expensive cologne, and smiles, seeing the little boy. "I always knew you were gay, Sam. I'm proud of you for leaving here and going where you could be a success, and be accepted fully. I am your biggest fan."

Sam hugs her, then pulls away. "I'm so thankful for everything you've done for Sally. She is very lucky to have such a wonderful friend."

Marybeth's eyes well up. "I love her like a sister. I just don't know if we can all love her enough to get her past this heartbreak. Nothing could be worse than losing a child."

"We have to try!" is Sam's heartfelt reply.

CHAPTER 41

The next morning, the watery sunlight illuminates the newly planted roses and pansies Andrea planted in the back yard, and Sam finishes up his coffee on Wyatt's back patio. After lying awake worrying for hours, Sam finally decided to let go and trust that Marybeth, Andrea and Wyatt can get Sally through her terrible grief.

Wyatt's insistence on having ESP and seeing ghosts is troubling, but Sam tries not to think about it.

What could be in that old trunk? he wonders.

He looks at a squirrel busily trying to lift the top of the bird feeder, and suddenly has an idea.

Excited, Sam puts down his coffee mug and goes back in Wyatt's house.

Andrea is asleep in her room. Sam quietly opens the closet door and props it open, staring down into the darkness.

Holding his flashlight high so he can see each step, Sam ascends slowly. He grabs a Coleman lantern and lights it as soon as he is down the stairs.

In the dimness, the old trunk looks massive, squatting there.

Sam carefully shines a light behind the trunk, illuminating the small space behind it. Squatting down, Sam pushes the trunk. It feels as though it is filled with lead. He cannot move it at all.

Suddenly, light fills the corners, as another Coleman lantern is lit.

Andrea squats down beside him, wearing pajamas. "You think there's something under the trunk, huh?!" she asks.

"I think maybe the trunk is actually in front of a hole, but it's just a theory," Sam says softly. "Let's try it together, okay?"

"Okay," Andrea agrees, and puts her shoulder into it and pushes.

"No, together, that's the way to do it," Sam admonishes. "On the count of three. One, two, three –"

They both lean forward and push, but the old trunk doesn't budge. They try it again. The trunk still doesn't budge. They both sit back, panting from the exertion.

Wyatt appears at the top of the stairs.

"What's going on?" he says, yawning.

Sam stands up and turns around. "I think if we can push the trunk back into the niche, maybe there is something underneath. Worth a look, right? Except we need help. This thing is so heavy.."

Wyatt walks downstairs and frowns at the trunk. "Looks like over the years it has settled into the floor a bit. Maybe we could tip it forward, push it aside that way?"

Wyatt and Sam try that, but to no avail.

Andrea stands there frowning. "I think it's filled with bricks or something. I really do. Can't you see into it?" she asks Wyatt.

"Nope. However, I saw the ghost of my great great grandmother the other night. I have a feeling she is connected to this trunk somehow."

Sam looks very uncomfortable but he says brightly "Well, my plan is to go over to Sally's and get some breakfast."

Andrea nods, smiling at Sam. "Good plan."

Fifteen minutes later they are seated in the kitchen of Sally's house, eating eggs, bacon, and biscuits. Wyatt has finished his eggs and bacon and is eating the remainder of a cherry pie someone had brought in the day before.

Sam sips another cup of coffee.

Sally comes into the kitchen wearing jeans and a tee shirt. "Morning all."

"There's plenty of food, dear. Help yourself," Sam says.

Sally looks at Wyatt and looks away, embarrassed, then helps herself to some scrambled eggs and bacon.

"Did you sleep well," Marybeth asks.

"Eventually," Sally replies, sipping her coffee.

The phone on the wall rings shrilly. Nobody answers it. Andrea looks at the adults, eyebrows raised. Everyone chews quietly.

Finally, after the fourth ring, Marybeth answers it, says "Hello?" listens a moment, and hands the receiver to Sally.

Sally is grateful for the long cord on the old phone, and grateful to be sitting down. Her brother Luke's voice is resigned but firm.

"Aunt Catherine is going to be there this morning at 10 a.m. and she specifically said she wants to speak to you, so please just be there and talk to her," he says. "I got a big job over in the next county, replacing all the toilets in the old Granger school building they're making into a museum."

Sally's face registers shock and her hand clutches her throat.

"But Luke, you can't make me face her alone," Sally says desperately.

Marybeth looks at Sally, puzzled. Sally mouths "Aunt Catherine," and Marybeth starts as though she has seen a ghost.

"Uh huh," Sally says, and goes to hang up the phone.

Sam looks at his sister, puzzled by her pale face and her vanished good mood. "Aunt Catherine is coming this morning. She was in Asheville visiting her daughter and couldn't make it to the funeral, but she is coming this morning to talk to me," she says quietly.

"Oh dear God. I need a Xanax," Sam says, his voice almost cracking from stress. Wyatt takes one look at Sam's face and knows he regrets quitting smoking.

Marybeth has gone pale. Wyatt knows she wants a Bloody Mary.

Sally is twisting a lock of her hair and looks like she wants to scream.

Wyatt can feel a pall of tension that has dropped over everyone. "Who is this and why is everyone freaking out?"

Silence ensues.

Finally, Sally takes a deep breath. "Catherine Donnelly," my mother's sister. She is 88 years old. She runs the family. She's like the godfather, only not as warm and kind."

Wyatt grins. "Oh come on, how bad can a little old lady be?"

Sally looks annoyed. "She told me once that a divorce is a one-way ticket to hell and as far as she is concerned I am still married."

"Good grief," Wyatt says.

Sally looks at him, and looks as though she is about to cry. "She is going to take me to task for not having a full funeral mass," Sally says quietly. "She is a hard shell Catholic."

Wyatt frowns. "But Miranda was your daughter."

Marybeth's hands are trembling as she clears dishes from the table. "She told me when I was 24 and pregnant with my first baby, that I looked like a pig and if I didn't fix myself up, Ed would leave me. She will say anything to anyone, and she doesn't care if their feelings are hurt."

Sam frowns. "She once told me if I'd find a nice girl and settle down and get married I'd stop wanting to mess with boys."

"When I named my daughter Miranda she said it wasn't a Christian name and she would grow up to join the circus," Sally says.

Wyatt 's face has a quizzical look. "I still don't —"

Marybeth interrupts Wyatt. "She is pure-T meanness and I'm not kidding. My family lived here until I was seventeen. She once told me I spent so much time over here that I was a yard child, and ever since then she has referred to me as The Yard Child. She didn't mean it as a compliment."

Wyatt stifles the urge to chuckle.

"I remember her telling Mother once that only a heathen would let guests use paper napkins," Sam chimes in, trying not to grin.

Marybeth says "Oh my God, that was her favorite word. I overheard her once telling your mother that I was a Heathen Yard Child that wouldn't know the difference between a salad fork and a dessert fork if they both hit me in the rear end."

Sam starts chuckling. Andrea's face is red from trying not to giggle.

Sally's face has finally relaxed and she says: "She said last time she was here that Blanche was a wonderful name and I wasted it on the dog."

Sam guffaws.

"I told her she was named after Blanche DuBois from A Streetcar Named Desire, because she relied on the kindness of strangers," Sally adds, grinning.

"I'm amazed she didn't chastise you for naming the dog after a heathen playwright's crazy lady character," Sam adds, then laughs out loud.

Andrea finally cannot control herself and she giggles.

"She sounds delightful," Wyatt observes drily. He is laughing now.

"Wyatt tell her as soon as you see her that you are NOT gay and you know the difference between a salad fork and a dessert fork!" Marybeth laughs, almost unable to get the words out.

Full scale laughter breaks out, finally, all around.

After a few minutes, Sally wipes her eyes, stands and speaks clearly. "Enough levity, heathens. It's 9:15. Sam, thanks for straightening up last night. Please clean up the breakfast dishes and sweep off the front porch. Wyatt, please stay with me for moral support and make sure the driveway is clear. I'm going to jump in the shower. Marybeth, just do whatever you think needs doing, Yard Child."

"I'll go ahead and walk Blanche, and keep her at Wyatt's house," Andrea says, looking cautiously at Sally. Nobody says a word. Andrea gets up and grabs Blanche and snaps her leash on her.

The next 45 minutes are a frenzy of activity.

CHAPTER 41

Catherine Donnelly arrives at exactly 9:59 and parks in the driveway of Sally's house. Wyatt is on the front porch. He is startled to see the gleaming white Cadillac has only one occupant.

The morning sun bounces off the car, which looks as if it just rolled off the showroom floor.

Wyatt wears a white button down shirt and gray slacks. Sam had wanted him to wear a tie but he had vetoed that idea.

Sam's rented Accord is parked two doors down, which Wyatt thinks is silly, but funny.

Wyatt walks down the front steps and strides over to the Cadillac, idly wondering if he will be able to read the old lady.

The Cadillac's door opens and Wyatt has an impression of red leather interior and the faint smell of lavender.

He turns his attention to the woman who slowly and carefully exits the car and stands there looking at him.

Mary Catherine Donnelly wears a black skirt and white button down blouse with a gray cashmere sweater. Her back is ramrod straight and there is very little fat on her 5'2 frame. Her thick white hair is clipped close to her head, not styled in an old lady bouffant, which surprises Wyatt.

She wears no makeup except a light pink lipstick.

"Mrs. Donnelly, I'm Wyatt Jamison. I just moved in next door and I'm a friend of Sally's. I thought you might like a hand getting into the house," Wyatt says, slightly louder than usual.

"Young man, I am not deaf. My hearing is augmented by a device, allowing me to hear everything with crystal clarity, which is sometimes unfortunate. I will not need your assistance in getting in the house. I am not infirm. However, I will take your arm as I mount the steps, since it looks like nobody has swept them in a while and I don't want to trip on the debris. Come along then."

Wyatt stares in astonishment as the old lady marches over to the front steps and waits on him. He hurries over and sticks out his right elbow, which she grasps lightly.

They are soon standing on the porch.

Wyatt has two impressions: one, she thinks he is handsome but he needs to lose the spare tire around his middle, and two, somehow she knows he is Sally's boyfriend.

Before going into the house, Catherine squares her shoulders and takes a deep breath. She is nervous, Wyatt realizes, with surprise.

Wyatt reaches around her to open the door for her, realizing she was expecting him to do that.

They step inside the foyer, and Sally greets Catherine. "Aunt Catherine. So nice to see you," Sally says smoothly.

Wyatt looks at Sally and realizes she is trembling slightly. She wears the same plain black dress she wore to the funeral, and a plain gold cross, small but beautiful. Her hair is pulled back severely into a bun and she wears no makeup.

Catherine looks at her niece, and moves to embrace her. "Sally, come here dear, and give me a hug."

Sally complies, and what her aunt cannot see is her eyebrows, raised in surprise. Wyatt wonders if he should leave or stay.

"Thanks for coming to check on me, Aunt Catherine," Sally says.

Catherine hugs Sally in a full embrace. Sally inhales the scents of lavender and hairspray, and recalls hugging her mother. She sighs deeply. Catherine, feeling the sigh, rubs Sally's back.

Then she pulls back and looks at Sally searchingly.

"I am so sorry I didn't get to the funeral yesterday. I should have been here. I am here now, though. Let's go sit down in the kitchen and talk, shall we? I could use a cup of tea."

The women walk to the back of the house, Catherine's arm in Sally's. They are almost the same height.

Wyatt watches them go and decides to not follow, but to stay outside the kitchen in the family room, where hopefully he can hear everything.

The kitchen is spotless. After the tea is poured, Sally pours milk into hers, and adds sugar, then joins Catherine at the kitchen table

Catherine stirs her tea, then sips.

"I'm sorry I couldn't make it to the funeral," Catherine says.

"It's all right. I was just on autopilot, trying to get through it," Sally says quietly. "I had to keep it short and simple or I wouldn't have been able to deal with it," Sally says carefully.

"I understand dear," Catherine says.

"Thanks."

"You know, I remember when your parents bought this house. I thought it was too small, but your mother said it was fine. She was a strong woman, my sister."

"Yes, she was. I still miss her," Sally says.

The two women sit in silence for a minute.

Catherine takes a sip of tea and then looks Sally in the eye. "I am going to tell you something I never talk about. Never. I don't know if anyone in the family ever told you."

"Ah – okay?" Sally says tentatively, not knowing what to say.

Catherine closes her eyes for a moment, then sits up straighter and takes a deep breath. "I know what it feels like to lose a child."

Sally is astonished. "What? Mom never told me that. What happened?" she asks gently.

Catherine puts her teacup down and looks down at the oak table, lost in thought for a few moments.

"Albert and I had only been married a few years. We had Liam and then the twins, only two years apart. Then I got pregnant again."

She pauses, as though gathering her courage.

Sally wonders about this child named Liam she has never heard of before.

"We went on vacation to Myrtle Beach. I was 5 months pregnant and already huge. Allison and Annie were 2. Liam was 3. I took the children to the beach one day, and sent Albert back to the room because I forgot to put the thermos in the swim bag with everything else. The girls were building a sand castle, of sorts. It was early in the morning, before the sun got so hot. There weren't many people on the beach."

Catherine pauses, and drinks a sip of tea. Wyatt, listening in the other room, can see the images in her mind, and he knows what is coming.

Catherine clears her throat and speaks carefully, as though she has rehearsed a speech. "The girls started fighting. One hit the other. Both started crying. Toddler drama. I didn't see Liam wander over to the water. He was a good swimmer, and I thought he had on one of those blowup swim ring things. This was 1959, before all the things they have now. Albert got down there and helped me get the girls settled down, then asked where Liam was, but we couldn't find him. We searched and searched. There was a bad undertow that day."

Catherine stares at the table, her face a mask of anguish.

"Aunt Catherine...?" Sally says softly.

"He drowned, less than 20 yards from where I was on the beach."

Catherine pauses. Sally's eyes are full of tears, and she reaches for a box of tissues and hands them to Catherine.

"Not a day goes by that I don't think of my son. Not a single day, in all these years. I would give anything to be able to go back in time and pull him out of that water. Anything. But I cannot."

The two women sit in silence for a minute, each lost in grief.

"I would give anything if I had been a better mother," Sally says softly.

Catherine shakes her head slightly. "You are lucky, Sally. You had your daughter for many years. She grew up, married, lived her life. You did the best you could do. She made her own decisions. You didn't cause her death."

The last word is said with a sob. Catherine buries her face in her hands and cries, great wracking sobs. Sally gets up and moves to embrace her aunt.

"I never knew. I am so sorry. So sorry."

Catherine's sobs subside and after a few minutes she blows her nose and looks at Sally. Sally moves back to her own chair, and wipes her own eyes.

Catherine looks down at her hands and fiddles with the large diamond wedding ring. Finally, she turns to Sally.

"I let that experience warp me, Sally," Catherine says with intensity. "I let it make me bitter. I went on to have 5 more children and they grew up with a mother who was hard and bitter and judgmental. God forgive me."

Sally's face is filled with compassion. "You did nothing wrong. Mothers cannot be everywhere at once. Accidents like that happen all the time, unfortunately."

"Yes, those are truisms, and I've heard them a million times, but they do not negate the horror of knowing I brought a child into the world and then he died because of me," Catherine says, her voice shaky.

The two women sit in silence again. Sally wonders why her mother never told her about the cousin she never knew.

Finally, Catherine sips her tea, clears her throat, and sits up straighter in the chair.

"I didn't mean for this to be a confessional, Sally. I wanted to tell you I am free from that mental prison I locked myself in all those years ago. I never thought I'd be free, but I am. I truly am."

Sally is startled by the change in the older woman. She stares at her aunt.

"You know my youngest, Linda, lives in Asheville?"

Sally vaguely recalls hearing that. "Um, the one married to the real estate guy, right?" she says hesitantly.

"Well, yes, but Linda owns a bookstore specializing in all the New Agey stuff, the candles and crystals and all that." She pulls a business card out of her purse and hands it to Sally. "Linda introduced me to this woman recently. It changed me."

"Ah, okay," Sally says tentatively, looking at the card.

"Call Marie. She will put your mind at ease about your daughter."

Sally looks at Catherine, then looks back at the card, which simply has a name and phone number on it, in dark purple ink. "Thank you."

Wyatt sighs, softly, and gets up and goes outside to the back porch of Sally's house, where Sam is carefully hiding.

"Tell me what you heard," Sam says softly.

Wyatt drops into a chair and rubs a hand across his bears, then looks into Sam's eyes. "Sounded like Catherine was being very kind to Sally, telling her about her own loss of a child."

Sam looks puzzled. "What? I've never heard that."

"Apparently it happened long before you were born, and it made her bitter."

"Wow. What an understatement. Bitter is mild. The term I would use is more... verbal savage."

"I've never seen a grown man so fearful of an old lady," Wyatt says, then chuckles.

Sam glowers at him. "She is the ANTICHRIST."

"Not any more," Wyatt replies. "Let me give you the details." He tells Sam of the conversation between Catherine and Sally. Sam's face registers astonishment.

They both start when they hear Sally calling.

Wyatt and Sam scramble up from chairs and run into the kitchen. Catherine tosses her car keys to Wyatt. "There are several boxes of produce in the trunk. Please bring them in."

Turning to Sam, she smiles. "Hello Samuel. Come give me a kiss."

Sam smiles weakly as he moves to kiss her papery cheek. "Lovely to see you, dear."

Catherine laughs. "You're such a bad liar. Go help Wyatt."

A few minute later Catherine is staring at the boxes of apples, corn, tomatoes, green beans and squash, on the counter.

"You know how to put these up?" she asks Sally.

Sally shakes her head. "No M'am. My mother didn't do that."

"Oh that's right. I had forgotten. You have someplace around here where you can buy canning jars?" Catherine asks, annoyed.

"I – I think there's a hardware store in Clayton that sells them," Sally says. "But, uh, I was headed to the beach."

Catherine frowns. "No m'am, no beach. You need to put up this food. Keep your hands busy. That's how you're going to deal with this nightmare. Not walking along a beach."

Wyatt knows Catherine hates the beach. He and Sam exchange a look.

"Aunt Catherine, we'll help with this project. It was so kind of you to visit," Sam says.

"Oh no, I'm not leaving today. I'm going to get Sally started on this. I booked a room at that B&B downtown. Today, we get this food squared away."

Marybeth comes in then, and sees the bounty. "Well hello, Aunt Catherine, so nice to see you," she says carefully.

Catherine straightens up and assesses Marybeth. "Hello. I'm glad you're here. You know how to put up food?"

Marybeth's eyes widen and she steps back. "Uh, no M'am, I sure don't," Marybeth says with a nervous laugh. "My mama taught me how to buy good farmer's market vegetables and put them in the deep freeze!"

"Well, these skills need to be passed on before they die out. I'll teach you, and you teach the next generation. Sally needs to stay busy."

Sally and Marybeth exchange a look. Sally's look says "What can I do?!"

"Uh, Aunt Catherine, I need to speak to Wyatt for a moment."

Sally pulls Wyatt into the family room. "I was supposed to go to Atlanta today, to clean out Miranda's personal items from her house. Now I can't just leave and hurt Catherine's feelings. Could you possibly go?"

Wyatt nods. "Sure, but how will I know what to get?"

"You have that ESP thing going on. You should have no trouble!" Sally says brightly.

Sam walks in. "I have been told to drive to Clayton and buy 5 dozen canning jars. Wish me luck," he says, stooping to kiss Sally's cheek.

"You remember how to get to McAllister's store?" Sally asks.

"Sure."

Sally pulls out her cell phone and shows Wyatt the phone number for Nick, and he puts it into his phone. "Call him when you get where you can get reception. The townhouse is in Buckhead. He can give you directions."

She stands on tiptoe and kisses his cheek.

"Yes M'am, on my way."

CHAPTER 42

Two hours later, Wyatt finds the large and elegant townhouse with no trouble, and Nick lets him in. Nick wears black sweatpants and a stained blue tee shirt and his face is pale and unshaven.

"Hey man, thanks for coming. Sorry Sally didn't come. I wanted to see her one last time. It's this way," he says, turning and walking to the master bedroom.

Wyatt notes the neutral colors of the enormous place, with its leather sofas and glass tables, looking more like a rental condo than a home.

The master bedroom, done in shades of teal and peach, shows a jumble of clothes on the bed, and half a dozen brown cardboard boxes on the floor. Wyatt knows Nick is nervous and wants Miranda's things gone, for reasons he hasn't told Sally.

"It shouldn't take long to get the clothes in the boxes but I was trying to think of things that might not be in this room, that were hers. What about books? Sports equipment? Coats and jackets? Kitchen items?"

Nick frowns. "I will look around."

Wyatt looks at the clothes thrown carelessly on the bed and decides on the rolling method. He rolls up all the shirts and places them in one box. Then he rolls up all the pants and puts them in another box, then puts dresses on top of those. He notices a jewelry box and picks it up carefully. There is a photo of Miranda and her father, but there are no photos of Sally.

He empties the dresser drawers of the socks, bras, and panties, and just puts them in a box. Almost done.

He walks into the walk-in closet and puts shoes and purses in another box. As he lifts a small black beaded evening purse, a pack of matches falls out. It says Cheetah on it.

The Cheetah is a well-known strip club in midtown. Wyatt shakes his head, but suddenly an image pops into his head, of Miranda as a stripper.

Wyatt suddenly realizes that she has been a stripper this whole time. That's why she didn't want a pregnancy. She didn't want Sally to know her secret. He spots a shoebox on the shelf and pulls it down and opens it. It contains pasties, g-strings, and a package of condoms.

Wyatt is standing there holding it when Nick walks in and sees Wyatt. "Oh hey, man, what the hell?!" he sputters.

"Thought these were her shoes," Wyatt says quietly.

Wyatt suddenly knows everything. The drugs. The partying. All of it. He puts the box back and looks at Nick, who quickly looks away and swallows hard. Wyatt decides to avoid a confrontation.

It would do no good now.

"Looks like I've got most of it. Give me a hand, okay? I think we can cram these in the back of my SUV. If there's anything you find that's Miranda's and you want to get it back to Sally, call Marybeth and she will pick it up," Wyatt said quietly.

Nick looks confused for a moment, then nods.

Wyatt gets back in the car and decides to drive by his old house, see what it looks like. He turns the car south on Peachtree and then takes North Druid Hills Road to Briarcliff. As always, he appreciates the fact that Atlanta is filled with trees, even in the city.

He turns down his street and drives past his neighbors, finally coming in sight of his home of 22 years. He is startled to see a For Sale sign in the yard. He stops the car and looks at the sign, frowning. *Housing values are down*, he thinks. *She won't get a good price.*

In his mind, he sees the house the way it looked the first time he saw it, newly finished and looking awkward, with mud in the front yard. He blinks. He sees Thad as a toddler, taking unsteady steps across the grass of the front yard. He sees him on his bicycle, wobbling as it goes down the driveway, Wyatt running behind. "Look Daddy!" Thad yelled.

So many memories.

His last memory is bitter — Sharon standing on the driveway, screaming at him as he drove away with John after they had packed up the last of his things. Sharon had been drunk. Wyatt had never loathed someone as much as he had loathed her. The fierceness of his antagonism had scared him.

He stares at the house for a moment, then shakes his head and drives away, happy to be headed back to the mountains, and Sally.

Sometimes it's best to just let go of the past to make room for the future, Wyatt decides, his eyes fixed on the horizon, waiting for a glimpse of the mountains.

CHAPTER 43

As soon as Wyatt gets on the interstate headed north out of Atlanta he calls the house and tells Sally he is on the way back but has to make a stop. He pulls into the parking lot of the First Lutheran Church a few minutes after 3, and locks the car before heading to the church office.

Roberta sees him coming in and meets him in the outer office. There is no-one else there. Roberta wears her standard outfit of black stretchy pants plus a black turtleneck. Her eyebrows are drawn inexpertly, which Wyatt tries to not stare at. *She has no business drawing them on without wearing her glasses,* he thinks. *They look like they belong on a Halloween pumpkin...*

"Well, uh, hello, Wyatt, how are you?" Roberta barks awkwardly.

"I'm just fine Roberta, and yourself?" Wyatt inquires with a disarming smile, the one usually reserved for charming clients or juries.

"Fine, thank you," Roberta replies. "George is not here. He had to do a funeral over in Toccoa."

"Oh that's okay. I just need some information, and I think you can help me."

Roberta looks wary. "I will try. Have a seat," she says, pointing to a couple of upholstered chairs in front of a secretarial desk.

They sit in the modest office.

"I am trying to do some research. Do you have records of everyone buried in the church cemetery?" Wyatt asks, smiling pleasantly.

"Well, sure. Most everything is on the computer, except for the really old ones," Roberta says carefully, wishing she had worn lipstick.

"Well, here's the situation. Josephine Adams Jamison was my great great grandmother and I believe she died young, sometime between 1865 and 1867. The family bible says she gave birth to a son named Jack, and then there's nothing else in the book, except the birth of Jack's son, who was my grandfather."

Wyatt looks at Roberta and knows her mind is roiling and she is fighting to stay calm. She goes to a closet and opens it, then motions Wyatt over. He sees there are shelves in the closet, heavy wooden ones. Roberta points out an enormous antique ledger on a high shelf.

"This has all the post civil war deaths," she says quietly. "Can you lift it for me?"

"Of course," Wyatt says, gently taking the old book from the shelf. It is a huge book, bigger than any Wyatt has ever seen outside a courthouse, and is covered in cracked leather.

"Let's put it right here," Roberta says, pointing to a sturdy wooden refectory table under the window. Wyatt sets it down.

Roberta grabs some white cotton gloves from a desk drawer and hands a pair to Wyatt, who pulls them on gingerly, because of his large hands and long fingers.

Roberta puts on her reading glasses and opens the book, and laboriously flips pages for a minute. "Here are the J's," she says softly. She starts running a finger down the page and muttering.

"Jackson, Johnson, Jamison. Here she is," she finishes, stepping back to show Wyatt. He puts on his own glasses and peers at the spidery brown writing.

"It says there was a funeral service for her, but that her body wasn't recovered. Recovered from what?" he asks, straightening up and looking at Roberta.

She clears her throat nervously. "Well, uh, I actually have an old old letter that says she disappeared around 1866, not long after she gave birth. Just disappeared."

Wyatt looks at Roberta. The letter speculates about the lost treasure in his house, too, Wyatt realizes. That's why Roberta wants his house, so she can dig up the yard and find the treasure.

"Well thank you so much for taking the time to show me this," Wyatt says politely. "Let me help you put it back."

Wyatt lifts the book and carries it over to the closet, replacing it on the shelf.

"So how long are you in town for this time?" Roberta asks.

"Oh I've left Atlanta and moved up here permanently. I love the mountains," Wyatt says with a smile.

Roberta smiles weakly at him. He can see inwardly she is seething. "Well good luck with everything. I know you'll want to renovate. Hope there aren't any termites," Roberta says.

"Oh I don't think there are any. It's a solid old place," Wyatt replies grinning. "Take care."

CHAPTER 44

Wyatt walks into Sally's house ten minutes later, smelling the fragrance of tomatoes cooking. Sam, Andrea, and Marybeth are all in the kitchen wearing aprons and looking tired.

Sally spots him and smiles. "Oh good, you're back. Thank you so much for taking care of that for me," Sally says.

"You're more than welcome. Where's Catherine?"

Marybeth and Sam exchange a look. "We took her out for a late lunch and then she went back to the B&B for a nap and we haven't seen her since."

"Can I do anything to help here?" Wyatt asks, nodding at all the mason jars filling the kitchen table.

"Well, we aren't sure where we are going to put all of these. Could you put some in your house?" Sally asked.

"Sure, no problem," Wyatt said. Blanche runs up to him and stands on her hind legs for a pat. "Why don't I take Blanche for a walk right now?"

"Great idea. I will join you," Sally says, whipping off her apron.

Marybeth and Sam stare at her. "You sure you have the energy to walk, Hon?" Marybeth asks.

"Yes. I need to walk," Sally says carefully.

A few minutes later Sally and Wyatt are strolling down the street, Blanche in front of them on her leash.

"Good day?" Wyatt asks, already knowing the answer.

Sally sighs. "Well I actually started off thinking it might be fun, but OH MY GOD, the work."

"More than you're used to, huh?" Wyatt chuckled.

"Well, first of all Catherine was astonished I don't have a pressure cooker. So everything had to be done in a water bath. All the jars had to be sterilized. Fruit had to be peeled and cut up. We put up so many quarts of apples! I thought it would never end. I don't mind peeling one or two potatoes or apples but you saw how much she brought! Fortunately, Marybeth asked if she could take home some of the veggies and thank God. I have no room for all that stuff."

"I know it seems odd, but Catherine was really trying to be helpful," Wyatt notes. "She feels like staying busy is the best remedy for grief."

"Well, I certainly wasn't thinking about Miranda all day," Sally says with a rueful smile.

"What did you think about her revelation about losing her son?"

"I had never heard that story. Never – and my mom and I used to talk family a lot. I thought I knew it all. How terrible, for your child to drown when you're close by. You could tell it was really hard for her to discuss, even all these years later. I can almost forgive her for all the mean things she said over the years," Sally says, smiling slightly.

"Almost, but not quite, huh?!" Wyatt responds, nodding and smiling at an older man clipping a rose bush in a yard they passed.

"Well, old legends are hard to kill," Sally replies, smiling and waving at an older couple pushing a stroller with a dog in it. "That's a mighty cute girl y'all have there!" she calls. Sotto voce, to Wyatt: "Those people have had that Schnauzer for twenty years and they treat her just like a baby."

Wyatt chuckles. They stroll in companionable silence for a moment.

"Uh, how about I put the boxes from Miranda's house in the carriage house? Even though I have stuff in there, there's still plenty of room," Wyatt asks, casually.

"Sounds great. Let Sam and Andrea help you. Was it awful?" Sally says softly.

"Well no, but then I never met her. It would have been worse if you had done it," Wyatt says, glad she didn't see the shoebox with the Cheetah items in it.

Sally stops walking and turns to face Wyatt. "True. Look, Wyatt, I need to apologize for last night. I was just feeling a massive wave of grief and guilt. I care about you very much and I want to have a relationship with you. I just need to take things really slow for a while."

Wyatt looks down at her and nods carefully. "I know you're grieving. You have a lot of processing to do. I will be close by, in any capacity you need me to be."

Sally hugs him, tears in her eyes. "That means so much to me."

I look at my nephew and Sally and smile, because I know they are going to be in love for the rest of their lives.

Wyatt has such a good heart, and such rare gifts. I wish I could see all of his future, but I have no idea what will happen.

I do know Roberta is still scheming and wants to get in the house, badly. I haven't been able to scare her away from it. She does have a claim. Her ancestor was murdered because he wouldn't leave his land. So much tragedy. I wonder if any whites realize the incredibly high price paid for the land?

If Roberta succeeds in getting the land back, she won't find what she wants to find. She won't find peace. She has nursed her hatred for a long time and it's part of her now.

Blanche looks right at me and wags her tail.

Wyatt, who has been embracing Sally, looks at Blanche and knows she is seeing me.

Time to go.

CHAPTER 45

Wyatt and Sam sit at Wyatt's kitchen table, talking.

"So you're really retired? No more working?" Sam asks.

Wyatt sighs and sips his beer. "Well, yes, I am retired, but my ex pretty much cleaned me out. I am going to do some mediations, though, in Atlanta. I have one in a few days. It's good money for just a day's work. That should tide me over pretty nicely, two or three of those a month."

"Well, uh, have you thought about what you will do if you actually find a treasure here?" Sam asks.

Wyatt chuckles. "There is no treasure. There's a mystery. My great great grandmother died mysteriously. I don't know exactly what happened, though. I am going to do some research, try to figure it out."

"I was talking to a friend of mine and he said there is a way to pop out the hinges on those old trunks and just lift the lid. He described it to me. I think I could do it, or Luke could."

Wyatt looks at Sam. "When is your flight back?"

"I changed it to day after tomorrow."

"Why?" Wyatt asks, already knowing the answer.

Sam takes a deep breath. "Now don't get mad, but I asked my brother Luke to come over and bring tools and try to help us get that lid off the trunk on Saturday, when he's not working."

"Why would I get mad?" Wyatt asks, smiling.

"Well, I didn't check with you first. It's your house. It also means I will be your houseguest a few more days."

"You're more than welcome to stay as long as you like," Wyatt says. "Marybeth had to get back to Atlanta unexpectedly as her daughter is in the hospital, so I am glad you're here. Sally needs you around, for support."

Sam nods. "Well, I will always be supportive of her. Look, I have enjoyed talking to you but I'm going to turn in. Good night."

"Night." Wyatt says. He puts the glasses in the sink and turns off the kitchen light.

Andrea has gone back to Sally's and reclaimed her room, which is good. Wyatt walks past the door and looks at the neatly made bed in the small room, and misses her. He looks at the bedroom closet and decides to see the trunk again. He walks down the cellar stairs, and stares at the old trunk. *What mystery is there in that old thing* he wonders. Then he notices that the trunk seems to squat in front of the slight niche like an old toad.

Wyatt squats down and feels behind the trunk. The cellar has wooden walls except for this area. It appears as though the slight depression behind the trunk was hollowed out of dirt. Wyatt stands up again and closes his eyes and concentrates his abilities, tuning in to the energy in the space.

Suddenly the temperature plummets and Wyatt's eyes fly open as the lantern flame wavers. He knows Josephine's spirit is in there with him. "I wish you could tell me what happened here?" he says softly. He hears a sound like a woman's sob. He waits a few minutes but hears nothing more, and he finally trudges wearily back up the steps.

On Saturday, Luke arrives at 9 a.m., just as Sam and Wyatt are finishing breakfast. Luke's huge black Ford 250 pickup seems to fill the little driveway between Wyatt's house and Sally's house. Luke steps out and sucks in his gut, seeing two ladies jogging by the house. He wears blue jeans and a long-sleeved blue shirt, and his favorite Adidas running shoes.

Sam observes Luke from Wyatt's front porch and chuckles. "Luke's here," he calls into the opened living room window. Wyatt comes out a minute later. "Good morning," he calls to Luke.

"Hey."

"Need any help?" Sam calls.

"Nope."

Luke pulls tools out of the back of the truck and walks over.

"Sally in on this little party?" he asks.

Sam shakes his head. "She went to Clayton for the day, shopping with Aunt Catherine. Good for her to get out, do something fun."

Luke looks puzzled. "Shopping with Catherine?"

Sam chuckles. "Catherine has mellowed. I'll tell you about it later."

After all three men finish their coffee, and Luke fixes a slow toilet, they head down to the cellar. Andrea follows.

Luke looks at the small room with rough walls, and wonders what the walls could say if they could talk.

"Let me try something simple here for a minute," Luke says. "Talked to a friend of mine at the hardware store about this."

After a few minutes of working with a crowbar and a hasp, Luke manages to pull the lid off the old trunk. It comes loose with a painful screek of metal. Luke sets it aside and peers into the trunk.

The three men and Andrea crowd around it, staring.

The trunk is filled with bricks. The bricks are bound together by mortar.

"Damnation," Luke says softly. "Why the hell would anyone do that?"

"No wonder we couldn't move it," Sam says.

Wyatt looks at Andrea. "You said a while back you thought it was filled with bricks. I think you have really good instincts, Sweetheart."

Andrea beams.

Luke stands back and looks carefully at the trunk, studying the situation. "I think whoever put this trunk here did it to stop someone from getting into that hollowed depression in the wall. I think there's another room or a cave back there. Think about it – it's like the boulder that was rolled in front of Jesus' tomb, to keep anyone from going in."

Sam's face registers abject surprise. "I think you're right Bro."

Wyatt nods. "Makes sense. Hugh walled off the back yard because he was convinced there was a tunnel. Didn't you find where he had dug holes, Andrea?"

She nods. "Yeah, well I found places where it looked like he had done some digging and then filled in the holes. I think he thought there was a tunnel. Do you think there is one?"

Wyatt shakes his head. "No, I really don't."

"Yeah, but why would there need to even BE another room, or a cave?" Sam asks.

Wyatt looks thoughtful. "Maybe the rumors are true. Maybe some of the Confederate treasure was stored back in there."

Andrea looks at the area behind the trunk and notices now that the lid is off that there's definitely an opening behind the trunk. "Why couldn't we open it up more, go in from the side?" She looks at Wyatt.

Wyatt looks at Luke. "You think that would work?"

Luke rakes his fingers through his hair. "Well, let's think a minute. What would be easier – getting the bricks out of the trunk so it could be moved, or going in the side like that? I don't know."

Wyatt finally says, "Let's see how hard it might be to pull the boards off that wall, try it Andrea's way, first. I have a feeling that's the way to go." As Wyatt is talking he realizes that he feels certain Luke is right, that the trunk is hiding a room.

He steps over to the wall and squats down. The wooden boards nailed up around the trunk are surprisingly easy to pull off, since they were obviously nailed up quickly. After a minute, everyone is staring at the earthen wall. Sam attacks it with a shovel and pulls out the dirt, mounding it up in the corner. Soon there is a hollowed out space beside the trunk.

Andrea squats down and works for a while with a small spade, then shines the flashlight. "I can see it! I see a hollowed out space!" she yells.

Wyatt and Luke exchange a look.

"How long do you think –" Wyatt starts to say, but Andrea is pulling the dirt away with her hands, and the men can clearly see the opening starting to get wider.

"Andrea, I think I can do it faster, Hon –" Sam says.

Andrea sits back. "OK, I'm taking a little break," she says. Her hands, face, and shirt are streaked with dirt.

Sam hands her a bottle of water and she drinks thirstily, after moving aside.

Sam attacks the opening with a shovel and soon it's much wider. He gets on his hands and knees and asks Wyatt to hand him the flashlight.

They all hear a muffled "Wow" as Sam's head disappears into the opening. A moment later he pops out.

"There's a small hollowed out space behind the trunk."

"What's in it?!" Wyatt asks.

"I didn't see anything. It's a small space and really dark, with spider webs and roots and things hanging down," Sam says. "Andrea, do you want to see what you can see?"

Andrea doesn't answer but takes the flashlight from Sam, and gets down on all fours and crawls through the opening. "It's not a big space, but I see a book, and a box, and OH MY GOD!!" she shrieks, then comes scrambling out of there.

"What?!" Wyatt demands, seeing her pale face. "Skeleton!" she says, shaking. "Oh my God!" she sobs. Sam puts his arms around her to comfort her.

Wyatt and Luke pull off more boards and then Wyatt grabs the shovel and quickly makes the opening wide enough so he can wriggle through. He crawls through and finds that he cannot entirely stand up in the tiny space but he shines the flashlight around and sees the skeleton Andrea saw. It appears to be slumped over a small trunk, bits of cloth clinging to the bones. On the floor near it is a small book.

This is a grave, Wyatt thinks sadly. What a terrible way to die, boxed in here, unable to escape. A wavery light fills the opening and Wyatt sees the same spirit he has seen before, Josephine. She looks at the book on the ground and points to it, then her image fades.

Wyatt is careful to touch nothing, and wriggles out of the cave again.

He gets back to the others and wipes his hands on his pants. "It's definitely a human skeleton, and we need to call the sheriff and report it, even if she's been there since 1866."

Andrea looks at him, embarrassed. "Here I am, wanting to be an archeologist, and I freak out. Sorry Wyatt."

"No worries, Sweetheart. We're all good."

They all climb the stairs and head for the kitchen.

Sally is in the kitchen putting food in the fridge. Wyatt looks at her, surprised. "Hey beautiful. What's up? You weren't gone long."

"I hate shopping. I told Catherine I had a headache and she brought me back." Sally chuckles. You are all covered with dirt and sweat and you look like you just saw a ghost!" she says. "I brought over some more funeral food for you."

"I need a drink," Luke says quietly.

"Me too," Sam echoes.

Andrea's white face alarms Sally and she pulls the girl into her arms. "You found something bad?" Sally asks.

Wyatt nods.

"It was awful, Sally," Andrea says with a sob, burying her face in Sally's shoulder. Sally pats her back and looks at Wyatt questioningly.

"A human skeleton was in a hidden space behind the trunk. It's okay. Give me a moment."

Wyatt pulls down a bottle of brandy and gets glasses out. Sam and Luke sit at the kitchen table. While he is pouring shots, Sam fills Sally in. "We found a hollowed out space

behind the old trunk, Sally. There skeleton appears to be a woman and I'm betting it was Wyatt's ancestor."

Sally looks at Wyatt. He nods as he pours himself a tot of brandy. "Did you see her again?" Sally asks Wyatt.

"Oh yeah, the ghost appeared to me for a moment. Pretty sure that skeleton is her. Looks like the remains of a dress there."

Luke frowns. "You seeing ghosts, Wyatt?"

"I've seen her several times, yes. I never saw any spirit before I moved in this house. Sensed them sometimes, yes, but never saw them."

Sam looks very uncomfortable. Andrea, who has detached from Sally and poured herself a glass of orange juice, sits down at the table.

"Wyatt has the Sight," Andrea says. "My granny used to say some folks have it, and she had it. I might have a little bit of it."

Luke looks at Sally, who nods almost imperceptibly at him.

Sam shakes his head. "Ah the old Irish superstition. I don't believe any of it," he says with disgust.

At that moment, a bottle of ketchup on the kitchen counter falls off and breaks. Sam jumps to his feet, his face pale. Nobody was near the ketchup before it fell.

"Who - who did that?!" he stammers.

Sally grabs a roll of paper towels. "Now don't be thinkin' it's all nonsense, boyo. Wyatt's granny's ghost knocked that bottle over to show you what's what," Sally says in a thick Irish brogue. Luke and Sally and Wyatt all chuckle. Andrea grins.

"Very funny," Sam grouses. "Don't we need to get the sheriff in here?"

CHAPTER 46

Sam stays another few days, and observes the goings on with great interest. The Sheriff, Mark Wisham, makes a trip out to the house and he calls in the GBI [Georgia Bureau of Investigation] who conclude the skeleton is over a hundred and fifty years old.

Wyatt has no doubt the bones belong to Josephine Adams Jamison. After much discussion, it's agreed that there's no need to run a full-scale criminal investigation or call in an anthropologist.

The small trunk found under the skeleton is empty except for a rotted old piece of brown ribbon.

Sam takes an early flight home to California right after the GBI finishes.

A few days later, Wyatt drives over to the First Lutheran church and parks beside the office and goes in. Reverend Kingston greets him at the door. He is a small man, completely bald, wearing a black shirt and pants, and a white collar.

"Wyatt, I knew your daddy a long time ago and I did Hugh's funeral, so just call me George," he says warmly. He had presided at Hugh's funeral but had to leave right afterwards so Wyatt had not met him formally.

"Great, thanks George," Wyatt responds, hoping Roberta isn't around.

The two men sit down in George's small office.

"Would you like some coffee?" George asks.

"No, thanks. I'm fine," Wyatt responds. "As I said on the phone I want to discuss a couple of things, starting with finding my great great grandmother's skeleton."

Wyatt knows the gossip mills in Crossroads have been in overdrive since the GBI van pulled up to his house.

"Has the GBI finished their investigation?" George asks.

"Yes, all except for writing a formal report. They agreed with me, there's nothing to be gained from continuing. There was a book found near the bones, and it's got the name Josephine Adams in it, and she disappeared right around the date in the book, so it's pretty clear someone killed her and put the body down there, or killed her there and left the body. That crime happened a long time ago."

"Who do you think killed her?" George asks gently.

Wyatt sighs and runs his fingers through his hair. "Honestly, I think her husband killed her. It's rather creepy, knowing I am the descendant of a murderer."

George nods. "You are also a descendant of many other people though, good people, moral people. Many of them are buried out there," he says, indicating the cemetery behind the church. "I always tell folks in your situation, we choose who we want to be."

Wyatt looks at the man with the kindly brown eyes and small hands and realizes he is in the presence of someone filled with compassion and kindness, a truly holy man.

"Can we just bury her next to her son, Jack, and his wife Sarah?" Wyatt asks.

"Of course," George says. "Do you want a service?"

"No. I think not," Wyatt says. "That would just cause more gossip."

"True. I will call the GBI office and tell them to send the bones up here. I know the guy to talk to about it."

"Thanks," Wyatt says, relieved. "How is Roberta?" Wyatt asks.

George sighs and looks at the window for a moment. "She found out that there was no treasure in your house and had a fit. I don't want to make you feel bad, but she cried and carried on to such an extent I had to raise my voice to her."

Wyatt's eyebrow shoots up. George continues "I had never raised my voice to my wife in more than 53 years of marriage."

The two men sit in silence for a moment.

"Why does she care so much? Is it because she thinks the house should rightfully belong to her?" Wyatt says evenly.

George nods.

Wyatt pulls a copy of the Burke letter out of his pocket and unfolds it, and puts it on George's desk. "I was recently given this."

George picks up the letter and reads it, his brow furrowed. Finally he sighs and puts it down.

"So it seems my grandma Josephine was the daughter of a not so nice man," Wyatt says.

George frowns. "Wyatt, most of the land around here was owned by the Cherokee before the removal. If we started trying to give it all back to the original owners it would be quite a mess. I had to tell Roberta that, very sternly, to get her to see reason."

"Did she? See reason, I mean?" Wyatt asks.

"Well, yes and no. Our daughter Emily and her family live in Asheville, and the grandchildren are in college. None of them want to come back here to live. Roberta wants to get the property back to pass down to them, but they don't want it. So I think I've gotten her to calm down about it."

Wyatt nods.

"Now there's something I have to tell you that makes me really uncomfortable," George says, straightening up in his chair and clearing his throat. He gazes at the large crucifix on a table behind Wyatt and says a silent prayer that Wyatt hears perfectly.

"My wife's cousin Mavis Johnson lives across the street from you, and she used to be a photographer for the schools and such. She talked to your wife Sharon the day she heard the rat. Sharon eventually spoke to Roberta. Roberta got Mavis to take some photos of you and Sally and sent them to your wife. I knew nothing about it until Mavis came to me and told me about it yesterday. She said Roberta came to her last week and wanted her to sneak into your house and go down into the cellar. Mavis thinks Roberta is getting a touch… senile. I told her she needs to make a full confession and ask the Lord, and you, for forgiveness."

Wyatt stares at George aware of how embarrassed he is by this revelation.

There is an awkward silence.

"Well thanks for telling me. I'm glad that was cleared up."

George looks at him shrewdly. "Roberta stuck her nose into your business, where it didn't belong, and the gossip around town is that you came out of that divorce financially wiped out. Is that about right?"

Wyatt nods. "Yeah, Sharon got everything. I was not having an affair, just so you know."

"I never thought you were. Sally Cavanaugh is a fine woman. I know her character."

"She is simply a good friend," Wyatt says quietly. "Andrea Hawkins is a kid who needed a friend, and Sally took her under her wing."

George looks thoughtful. Suddenly his eyes narrow and his face goes pink. "Roberta!" he says loudly.

Wyatt flinches, startled.

"I know you're there. Come in here immediately," George says.

Roberta appears in the partially opened doorway, looking like she has eaten a lemon. "I was just passing —" she starts but George interrupts her.

"You were loitering out there and listening. You think after 53 years of marriage I don't know your antics?" George says sternly.

"I was not, George. You need to get your hearing checked," Roberta grouses.

"You owe Wyatt an apology."

Roberta pulls herself up to her full 5'1 and glares at her husband. "I do not."

"Mavis told me everything."

Roberta glares at Wyatt. "That land and that house should rightfully be mine."

Before Wyatt can think how to respond, George interjects. "Well they aren't yours and they never will be, Roberta. So get past it. You still owe Wyatt an apology."

Roberta purses her lips. "I'm sorry," she mumbles.

"Louder," her husband commands sternly.

"I am sorry about the photos. I'm sorry Sharon got everything in the divorce. But your ancestor KILLED my ancestor!" she shouts suddenly. "Your family took our land!"

"Roberta!" George says through gritted teeth. "We need to talk!"

Wyatt stands up. "It's okay George."

Wyatt can see Roberta seething. "Well, I'd say that you got your revenge on my family. My wife was cheating on me, not the other way around, but I got wiped out in the divorce. I have very little money. There is no treasure on the land, or buried out back. I just have a car, some bones, and an old house that needs a lot of work."

There is an uncomfortable silence for a full minute, then Roberta pulls herself up to her full height and smiles frostily. "Yes, I'd say we're about even."

CHAPTER 47

A week after the skeleton is found, Wyatt, Sally and Andrea sit at his kitchen table wearing white gloves, and they examine the fragile old book found with the skeleton. The little homemade book has Josephine's name in it. Because of dampness and age, the writing is very difficult to read.

The cover says Devotional. The first few pages are bible verses, but the rest of it is a diary.

"I have a feeling we're missing something about this diary, and I want to try and determine what it is," Wyatt announces.

Sally and Andrea exchange a look. Andrea goes to her backpack and pulls out a camera and a laptop. "I think I can help you Wyatt," she says.

The camera is a nice one, a Canon.

"What are you doing?" Wyatt asks, startled.

"Andrea's been researching ways to read old documents and this looks like a good method. She's going to take photos of the pages and then download the photos to the laptop so she can adjust the images, make them more readable," Sally says.

Wyatt looks skeptical.

"Just let her give it a try," Sally says.

Wyatt can tell Andrea is itching to try this so he nods.

After two hours of painstakingly photographing each page and getting it in the computer program, they all crowd around the laptop.

"I think Josephine put the word Devotional on the cover to stop her husband from being interested in looking at it," Wyatt says. "The word diary would have caused him to snoop."

Sally looks at Wyatt. "Remember when you held that little wedding band and got the feeling she had torn it off and thrown it on the ground?"

Wyatt nods thoughtfully. "Yep. I saw that clearly. It must have not been a happy marriage. I get the feeling she married him just because there was nobody else."

Andrea frowns. "Like Danielle always hooks up with losers just to say she isn't single?"

"Something like that," Wyatt says quietly.

"Andrea, in that time, women couldn't own property in their own name. They couldn't vote. They were viewed as truly inferior to men, intellectually, emotionally – in every way. A woman without a husband or father looking out for her was vulnerable," Sally explains.

"Yep, a bad time," Wyatt notes. "Let's see what we can see here," he says nodding at the laptop.

After the entire 17 pages of text have been scanned in, and the images sharpened, Wyatt reads quickly. The first entry of interest is from January 25, 1866, a few months before baby Jack was born. Wyatt reads it aloud:

"I was outside hanging laundry and heard Cooter barking, and I walked over to some high grass by the road, thinking it was a dead bird or snake. When I saw what he was barking at, my heart nearly broke. A young negro woman, Susan, was lying beside the road clutching a baby, both nearly dead. I got them in the house and fed them, gave them some water, and tended to the baby. I was thankful Marcus wasn't home. We went down to the root cellar and I made her and the child comfortable. I had not been in there in a long time, and I was amazed to find a great quantity of valuables – jewelry, money, silver – in the old trunk. I slipped some earbobs and a gold thimble into Susan's hand before she took off two days later, knowing she could sell them and use the money to buy food. I dared not try to keep her around because Marcus hates negroes and would be cruel to her and the child, I felt sure."

Wyatt sits back and runs his hands through his hair.

"Now it all makes sense. Marcus was with Sherman's Army and he obviously looted farms and deserted. He must have stored everything in the cellar. Josephine found it and used it to help freed slaves, after the war."

Sally nods. "A lot of freed slaves were in a terrible fix when the war ended, free but with nothing, and ill-equipped to get work anywhere. It was a terrible time."

Andrea listens and looks at Wyatt. "Do you think Marcus killed Josephine?"

"I think it's possible," he says quietly. "Would you go grab the ring off of my dresser?"

Andrea returns a moment later and hands Wyatt the ring. As soon as it touches his hand, he feels the negativity, the anguish. He closes his eyes and hears the soft voice of a woman – *He didn't love me. He killed me.*

Wyatt opens his eyes. Sally and Andrea are staring at him. "Did you hear her?" Wyatt asks, already knowing the answer as soon as the words are spoken.

They both shake their heads.

Blanche, who has been sleeping, wakes up and her ears perk up. She lifts her head and looks at the air between the fridge and the wall, following something with her eyes.

"She sees a spirit," Andrea says softly.

Blanche watches for a full minute, then sighs and puts her head back down.

Sally and Wyatt look at each other. "Does this strike you as funny?" Sally asks. "All three of us just spent a full minute watching the dog looking at nothing."

Wyatt chuckles. "Well, she's got the gift."

Sally sighs and stands up to stretch. "Well, I've got to be up early for work tomorrow, so I will see you both tomorrow."

"I'll walk you out," Wyatt says, rising.

"I'm going to finish photographing all the pages and reading, okay?" Andrea says pleadingly. "I don't have to work tomorrow."

"Sure. I'll be back in a minute," Wyatt notes. He whistles for Blanche and she stands up.

Outside, a moment later, Sally shivers in the October cold as they walk the short distance to her house.

"How do you feel about what we found?" Sally asks.

Wyatt shrugs. "I was hoping for a treasure but then again I would feel guilty to have found a bunch of stuff looted from people's homes. I'm glad Josephine used it to help people who truly needed help. Just seems odd there would be many ex slaves coming to this area."

"Well, maybe she figured out some other way to help. Anyway, the mystery of your house is solved. So what's next for you?" Sally asks.

"I don't know. Hopefully some more mediation work will come my way," Wyatt answers truthfully. "I'll be fine."

Sally puts her arms around his waist and hugs him. Wyatt kisses the top of her head and hugs her briefly.

Wyatt knows she wants to reassure him that she will come around soon, but she isn't really sure when. He sighs, realizing there will be more of a wait, but he is resigned to it.

CHAPTER 48

Andrea knocks on Wyatt's door later that evening.
She is still dressed and her hair is pulled off her face with a
headband. The excited look on her face is what Wyatt
notices immediately as he opens the door.

He rubs his eyes and opens it, wearing only pajama
bottoms and an old tee shirt. "You don't have to knock,
Honey," he says.

"Well,, I'm sorry to bother you so late, but I read
something in the book that you should hear," Andrea says,
guarded excitement in her voice.

"Okay, come on in," Wyatt says sleepily. "Let's go
in the kitchen. I've got Oreos."

Andrea grins. "You know me too well. First I need
to run down to the cellar for a minute, okay?"

"Okay, but take a flashlight," Wyatt says.

A few minutes later they are munching Oreos and
drinking milk. Andrea swallows a bite of cookie and shows
Wyatt a page of the book that appears to be just a drawing
of a tree.

"Look, I know this looks like a tree, and that's all,
but it's more. There are tiny words in the leaves. I couldn't
read them until I scanned it and enlarged the image. The
words are instructions, to find a letter. Inside the top of
the trunk there was a cloth lining, and inside the lining I

found the letter," Andrea says excitedly. She slides a letter sealed with wax over to Wyatt.

He looks at the small, spidery handwriting faded to gray and frowns. Andrea hands him his reading glasses, which she has fetched from his room.

"Thanks," Wyatt says. "You know me too well."

He notes the broken sealing wax. Wyatt tries to scan the pages quickly but gives up.

He senses Josephine is there in the room with them. "Okay Grandma, I know you want me to read this, but help me out here. Your handwriting is kind of illegible to a 21st century guy."

Andrea's eyes get wide. "She's here with us?! In the kitchen?"

"Yes, but there's no need to be afraid," Wyatt replies, smiling. "Let me give the letter another look."

He studies it for a few minutes, then closes his eyes for a moment and calls upon his abilities to help him, and the handwriting becomes clearer. He reads aloud.

"My Dear Mrs. Jamison, I wish to tell you of the wonderful way in which your generous gift has been used. You took such a risk getting the treasure to us, and I will be eternally grateful to you for your help. On the next page is an accounting of each item and the price we got for it."

Wyatt stops reading and looks at the next page. "It's a list of the treasure. Wow. Take a look," he finishes, sliding the paper over to Andrea. She looks at it with great interest.

"Wow, lots of stuff," Andrea says quietly.

Wyatt looks to the corner where he thinks Josephine is hovering. "Sorry about the remark about your handwriting. Obviously you didn't write the letter."

He resumes reading.

"I know you took a great risk in spiriting away the treasure the way it happened, but that was the only way to be sure Elijah and Andrew wouldn't be caught. After the wagon left Crossroads, the journey to Charleston was long and perilous. All the treasures arrived safely, though, thanks to my servant Joe's quick thinking. Nobody wanted to look inside the hearse or the caskets! We were able to sell the entire lot to several different stores, and one trader from Boston, and everything fetched good prices."

Wyatt puts down the letter and thinks for a moment. "I wonder....?"

"What?" Andrea asks.

"My mother's people were from Charleston. Anyway, let's finish the letter."

He resumes reading. *"With the funds from the sale we were able to help a great many freed slaves to learn to read and write, and to establish themselves in small businesses, to support their families. Reverend Cain of the Emanuel African Methodist Episcopal Church used the money wisely. Some of it has also helped in the rebuilding of the church, which had been burned down by an angry mob just after the war. God bless you for your kind heart. Many lives have been saved and many hungry children fed because of your kindness. Cordially, Susanna Johnson."*

Andrea was listening with wide eyes. "Wow, so most of the treasure was sent to Charleston and ultimately ended up rebuilding lives. That's awesome! Josephine was a hero!"

"Well, she certainly took a huge risk, but yes, she was. I'm glad you stuck with this. I bet Josephine's husband found this letter and became enraged, and that's what caused him to kill her."

Wyatt hears what sounds like a heavy sigh, and the rustling of skirts, and he realizes he has guessed correctly.

"So sad, the way she died. I mean, she was such a sweet lady."

"Yes, apparently she had a hard life and a terrible end. I hope she can find some peace now," Wyatt responds.

The two sit in silence for a moment. Finally Andrea pushes her chair back from the table and stands.

Andrea carefully puts the letter back into the antique book and puts the milk back in the fridge.

"I have to work tomorrow, so I will go on back to Sally's. Thanks for the cookies, Dude," Andrea says, kissing him on the cheek. "Can I keep the letter for a bit?"

"Sure. Let me walk out with you."

Wyatt walks her to the front door, and watches from the porch until Andrea is safely back inside Sally's house.

He goes inside and locks up, then brushes his teeth and heads to bed.

As he falls asleep, he wonders if he should go visit that church next time he is in Charleston. He feels a personal connection, now.

I watch Wyatt sleeping and I am glad he can rest, and now the secret of the house is revealed, at last.

I drift out the window and float over the back yard.

Everything is peaceful, then suddenly it's not. Clouds scud across the moon. The wind picks up. It's looking like rain. The air shimmers. I realize I am once again in a time warp, only this time at night, which is creepy, even for a ghost.

I look down. The houses around my house have disappeared and the land is back to farmland. I see a faint glow and I fly closer, searching for the glow. It comes from an oil lamp.

Josephine is holding it up while two men load a wagon in front of the house. The wagon doesn't appear to have treasure – it's painted black and the word O'Connor Funeral Home is stenciled on the side in gold lettering, I see. Everything is in caskets. Clever.

One of the men puts a small bundle into one of the caskets and presses the lid down.

"Please be careful," Josephine says quietly. "I think our ruse will work but we must still take precautions. "I forged a letter from a doctor saying the bodies died from Typhoid, so hopefully if someone wants to open those caskets they will be spooked."

"Thank you M'am," the older man says. He is an older white man with a slightly Irish lilt to his voice. Josephine hands him the letter and a sack. "I packed some cornbread and cold chicken, for the journey."

"Much obliged, M'am," the older man says, taking the sack and climbing into the wagon.

"Be safe. Please write when the load has gotten to its destination," Josephine says anxiously."

"Will do."

The wail of a baby is heard through an open window. Josephine watches the wagon as the driver pulls it onto the road, then hurries into the house to see about the baby.

There's a sudden clap, like thunder, and for a moment I see nothing.

Then it's another night, I can tell, because the sky suddenly is clear and there's a fat full moon high in the sky. I hear voices in the house, yelling.

I swoop lower, and look in the window. Josephine and Marcus are fighting. Josephine stands defiantly, hands on hips, looking tired but unbeaten.

"Yes, it's gone, and I'm glad of it. I couldn't rest, knowing you profited from the misery of my people," Josephine says quietly. She pulls off her wedding ring and hurls it out the open window.

For a moment, I just survey the scene with horror. Marcus wears only a dirty union suit. His hair is wild, his face unshaven, and he has been drinking. Josephine is in a long white nightgown, her hair loose and flowing down her back.

"You took what was mine!" Marcus screams.

"It was NOT yours! You stole it from families all over north Georgia. I'm glad it's gone!" Josephine retorts.

Marcus snarls, moving quickly as a cat, and punches Josephine in the face, hard. I hear the sickening sound of bone crunching, knowing he broke her nose. She slumps to the ground. He kicks her in the ribs. She groans, blood streaming down her face. He grabs her by the hair and pulls her into the other room, opening the door leading down to the root cellar and pushing her down the stairs.

I hear a series of thuds, and I know she has fallen down the stairs. I hate the ugly scene that's unfolding but I fly down the stairs wondering if I can intervene somehow. Can I do anything at all? I have to try.

The root cellar is in chaos, with things overturned and out of place. The trunk has been pulled away from the wall and the space behind it – where the treasure was once stored, obviously – is empty.

Josephine is crumpled on the floor. Marcus has run down the steps and now he lights the oil lamp and puts it down on a shelf. He then stands over her, sneering. She raises her bloodied face to look him in the eye and sneers, "You've LOST. You lost, you scoundrel! I already got word the treasure is safely at its destination and being used for GOOD!"

Marcus, still enraged, roars "NOBODY steals from ME and LIVES!"

He steps forward and starts choking his wife. She tries to fight back but she is no match for his fury.

I pull myself together and try to appear before him, concentrating as much as possible to utilize my energy and stop this terrible scene. "Aaaargh!" I shriek.

Marcus is still choking Josephine and he ignores me or cannot hear me – I don't know which.

I fly toward his loathsome form and lock my spectral arms around him, trying to pull him away. He grunts. He seems to feel the cold but he's ignoring it.

I squeeze as hard as I can. Nothing. Marcus is still choking Josephine. She claws at him desperately. I pick up a small book lying next to Josephine – her journal, I realize. She must have had it in her hands when she fell down the steps. I throw it against the wall. Marcus sees it fly across the small room. His piggy eyes narrow. He's scared, but he doesn't stop choking Josephine.

An otherworldly being appears before me. This is no spirit. This is a demon – a black face with glowing red eyes. He growls, low and guttural.

I feel the most heart-stopping terror I have ever felt. It obliterates all conscious thought. This demon lives in this house, in this terrible time. Dear God, I do not want to be here. I sense the demon will harm me, and suddenly I am terrified, all my spirit peace gone.

I want to fly up and away but I am paralyzed.

Josephine stops struggling and goes limp.

Marcus laughs. The demon laughs, an evil, grating sound.

I realize that Marcus is infused with evil.

I don't want to see any more of this. I finally recover my courage and will myself to soar upward, out the window, into the night sky.

I fly and fly, feeling the cold wind embrace me and the night sky cover me like a quilt. I finally calm myself. What a terrible man he was. How cruel. She was only trying to help people, trying to erase the crime committed by her husband. He was like so many of Sherman's raiders who stole everything from hungry people.

If I were still in my body I would be sobbing, knowing my grandfather grew up feeling like an orphan, like his mother had abandoned him.

I pause atop a pine tree and stare at the moon for a few minutes, trying to clear my head and not think about the terrible scene below, in the cellar.

Grandmother Josephine's spirit appears beside me. She smiles.

"I am so sorry about what happened to you! I wish I could have intervened."

"You could not. You could not alter the past," she says. "Thank you for trying. My fate was set long before you were born."

"Can you go on now?" I say to her. "Can you find peace?"

She nods.

In the corner of the night sky, a glowing ball appears, a ball as big as a garden shed. It descends a bit, getting bigger and brighter, and then Josephine shoots up into it.

I blink, and it's gone.

I wonder if it's time for me to go too? I drift awhile, thinking. I decide not.

Wyatt still needs me, I feel sure.

CHAPTER 49

Two weeks later, after doing a lot of reading and fishing, Wyatt decides to tackle some of the renovations on his house. He found where Blanche had pulled up a section of his bedroom carpet and chewed it very thoroughly. He also discovered a short in the wiring to the stove, which rendered it useless. Andrea had been showing him how to cook scrambled eggs and other simple dishes but then they had to abandon that until an electrician could come out.

The more time Wyatt spent in the house, the more he realized it was badly in need of renovating.

He called Luke, hoping for good suggestions about how to go about the project. Luke put him in touch with his son Brian, an affable young man starting his own renovation business after three years of working for someone else.

With Brian and Andrea's help, Wyatt strips the old carpet off all the floors in his house and discovers pine floors. They refinish the floors over the course of a week's time, except for Wyatt's bedroom.

In his bedroom, Wyatt replaces the dated carpet with new carpet, and buys a mattress, new sheets and a bedspread for the bed. He lets Andrea choose the colors and she does a great job. The blues and greens are tranquil.

Wyatt also gets Andrea and Sally to help him pull down the curtains and take them to Goodwill, and he replaces them with blinds. They paint the walls neutral colors, and slipcover the sofa and easy chairs, which is the cheapest option for covering up the 1970's furniture. They also paint the paneling a shade called "antique white" which lightens up the living area a great deal.

Wyatt talks to Brian about stripping the wallpaper out of the kitchen but decides to postpone that job. They discuss reconfiguring the kitchen to make the living room and kitchen one big room, but Wyatt cannot take on that major renovation until he has money, and that's in short supply.

On Thanksgiving Day, Wyatt drives to Atlanta and spends the day with John and his family, with Thad visiting in the evening. Sharon had insisted that Thad go out to an expensive buffet with her in the middle of the day, and then monopolized his time most of the afternoon.

The day after Thanksgiving, Wyatt has a mediation in an ugly divorce case that lasts 7 hours, but they finally iron out the details. Wyatt drives back to Crossroads and gets in at 6:30, tired and relieved to be home.

As he gets out of his car he hears a huge WOOF and Blanche runs over to him, Andrea following behind, and Sally. He embraces Sally and Andrea and scratches Blanche's furry head.

"How did it go?" Sally asks, as Wyatt takes his overnight bag out of the car.

Wyatt shrugs. "Okay, I guess. I wish Thad and I had had more time together, but so be it."

"Come eat with us, Wyatt. We have great leftovers!" Andrea says with a grin.

"Great plan. Let me change clothes and then I'll walk over."

Fifteen minutes later, Wyatt is looking at a plate filled with turkey, dressing, green bean casserole, mashed potatoes, and cranberry sauce. A piece of pecan pie is at his side. He was already tired of turkey but he didn't say a word to Sally about that.

Sally and Andrea are also eating turkey and side dishes. Blanche sits right next to the table watching every forkful go into each mouth.

Sally swallows a bit of turkey and looks at Wyatt. "I have some news for you that you might find interesting."

Wyatt nods because his mouth is full.

"I have been doing some more research, specifically into your family's farm. Hiram Littlefeather and his wife were not killed by Matthew Adams, but by a militiaman named James Hopkins. There was an investigation into the incident, but Hopkins wasn't punished. Adams said Littlefeather and his wife were resisting. Very tragic, but not uncommon in those days."

"So they could just kill the owners and take the land, just because the owners were part Cherokee?" Andrea asks with horror.

Wyatt nods. "It happened. What most folks don't realize is that most of Georgia was settled by whites because the native people were driven out. Besides the Cherokee there were the Chickasaw, Creek, Apalachicola, and more. When I was a kid the history books just glossed over it, if they mentioned it at all. Nowadays I think they do a better job."

Sally swallows a bite of turkey and dressing. "I've been doing a lot more work on my history of Crossroads, because it helps me if I stay busy. Much of the land for the town was taken from Cherokee families. I'm not going to shy away from that."

Andrea gives Blanche a bite of turkey, then another question occurs to her. "Wyatt, I've been thinking since your family has been on the land more than a hundred years, there may be some artifacts other places on the property. Would you mind if I bought a metal detector and looked in the back yard?"

Wyatt knows she is keen to do this. "It's fine with me, and it's fine if you dig around. I'm not going to do anything else to the yard until next spring."

"Thanks. I was talking to a UGA archaeology professor who came in the restaurant the other day, and he gave me his card. If I find anything interesting I said I'd call him."

"Go for it," Wyatt responded with a smile. "I think you're going to make a first rate archaeologist one of these days, Andrea. You've got the intelligence and the tenacity, and Sally and I will help you all the way."

Andrea feels big tears fill her eyes. She stands up and moves around the table to hug Wyatt from behind, then kiss his cheek. She does the same with Sally.

"I wouldn't be anything without y'all. This is the happiest Thanksgiving I've had since I was a little bitty girl. I love y'all."

"We love you, Sweetheart," Sally says softly.

An hour later Wyatt has finished doing dishes and he realizes Sally is upstairs. He wipes off his hands and walks over to the foot of the stairs and calls towards Sally's room "You okay?"

"Yes, I'm going to turn in. Glad you could come over," Sally calls.

"Okay, I'll see you tomorrow," Wyatt says. He sighs, then tells Andrea goodbye and heads home. Andrea is watching a movie in the family room. He knows Sally is crying, but decides to let her grieve.

Sally sits on her bed holding a photo of Miranda. It's her first Thanksgiving without her. Sally cradles the photo and tries not to cry loudly and alarm Andrea. She thinks of all the Thanksgivings and Christmases ahead,

without her daughter, and wants to just hibernate from
the world and nurse her pain.

I watch Sally crying and wish I could do
something to help. Grief is a process, though.

I fly into the back yard of Sally's house and
sit on a pine branch, looking at the houses all
around, with lights in their windows. In the house
behind Sally's a father sits next to a fire pit with
his little 10 year old son, roasting marshmallows.

Andrea can be seen through the window of
her room watching a movie.

Andrea has a bright future ahead of her,
but she cannot help Wyatt or Sally with their
biggest concerns.

I have learned that there is an elderly lady
in Savannah who is my aunt, and she is not long
for the earthly world.

I rise, up and up, and head for Knoxville to
see Nora and Ben. My winged journey through
the night sky is brief.

I swoop down to peer in the window when I
get to my niece's house.

Nora sits in her living room at her
computer typing away, frowning. Behind her, on

the wall, is a photo of her and Wyatt with my mother. I bump the wall and it falls to the carpet below.

Startled, Nora looks around and sees the framed photo on the carpet, and reaches down to pick it up. She wipes the dust off it with the sleeve of her bathrobe and stares at Mother. Nora has her high forehead and lovely green eyes.

She sits thoughtfully for a moment, then turns and does a Google search using mother's full name.

Thank goodness.

CHAPTER 50

Wyatt's cell phone rings as he stands at the pond, fishing. It's a beautiful day in early December, with temperatures in the upper 60's, and a clear, clean blue sky. Wyatt looks at the mountains surrounding the pond and feels gratitude that he gets to live in such a beautiful place. He wonders how he ever got along in the city, where every day was a push for money, for clients, for bigger and better everything.

The sounds of birds and the smells of earth calm him.

He rarely hums any more, or whistles. He used to do it all the time, to get away from all the information flooding into his head. Here in the mountains, he welcomes the peaceful sounds. He loves knowing that the bluebirds are making their music in the tall pine trees, and a rabbit's nest is about 25 feet behind him in a copse of trees. He doesn't mind hearing cicadas, or the chittering of squirrels.

Living in the mountains is idyllic except for one thing: money.

It's almost Christmas and Wyatt ponders the fact that he has no money. Mediations dropped off after the busy fall, a fall in which he had to pay taxes on his house and replace the roof, and pay for repairs to his car's transmission. The renovations weren't costly but they were done in the hopes that more mediation work would come along. Now there is no work and he has a very limited budget for buying presents for anyone.

As much as he hates the thought, he is seriously thinking about hanging out a shingle and going back to work as a lawyer. What sort of cases will he get in a small place like Crossroads, though?

He stares at the cell phone. Nora is calling. He waits for her number to come up as the call connects, then answers, after putting down his fishing pole. This is going to be an interesting call, he knows.

"Hey there, how are you?" he says, trying to jovial. "Only twenty shopping days until Christmas."

"Yep, but I already have most of my presents and my house is decorated!" Nora laughs. "I bet you haven't bought a thing."

"You know me too well, Sis. What's up?" Wyatt says.

"Well, I am super excited Brother. I mean, SUPER excited!" Nora practically shouts.

Wyatt sits down on a fallen log, instantly alert. Nora never gets that excited about anything. "Why?"

"Okay, you remember I told you I was going to start doing some genealogy stuff, some research?" Nora says breathlessly.

"Yeah, sorta. What did you discover? Are we related to the queen of England or something?"

"Probably, but no, that's not why I'm excited. Our grandmother's name was Elizabeth Olivia Fellows. She came from an old family in Charleston, a really old MONIED family. They cut her off when she married our grandfather. She gave up a really wealthy, easy life, to marry him and live in the mountains."

"Well, we always knew that was the family lore but I have no memory of her ever talking about her early life, do you? I mean, she acted like she had no life before she married Grandaddy."

"True, but I have come to find out the true story is far more interesting than we even thought."

Wyatt can tell Nora is fascinated by the romanticism of the story. "OK, but why is this interesting now?"

"Wyatt, I was only researching for a short time before I talked to a lady in Charleston named Louisa Fellows last week. She is our great aunt. She is 104 years old!"

"Well, good for her, I guess? Hopefully we got some of those longevity genes."

"Wyatt, she never married and has no children. She was granny's only sibling. She thought she was the last of the line! She cried when we were talking, because she was so excited to reconnect with her sister's descendants. I tried to call you but you know how your cell phone doesn't work half the time in Crossroads?"

"Well, yeah, but I am getting a landline soon. Why didn't you just email me?"

"My computer was screwed up. Got hit by lightning. I ended up having to get a new CPU. Long story. Anyway, I got a call today from Louisa's attorney and she died yesterday, and left everything to US!"

Now Wyatt understands Nora's excitement. His logical Spock-like lawyer brain kicks into gear immediately. "Everything? Define that."

"Okay, Mr. Lawyer. She owned one of those gorgeous old homes in Charleston, filled with antiques, and the lawyer said she has an investment portfolio worth millions, which we will inherit and split! He said the income just from the investments runs into about fifteen thousand dollars a MONTH."

Wyatt stands there thinking for a moment. "Email me the lawyer's name and phone number. I'll see if we can expedite getting the inheritance. You're right. This is big news!"

He hears Nora's pealing laugh. Ben says something.

"What did Ben say, Nora?!" Wyatt asks, thinking of the delight in his brother-in-law's voice.

"He said we need to come see you. You busy this weekend?" Nora asks. "We've been wanting to see you anyway but now we really need to talk."

"Yeah of course. Today is Thursday. You want to drive down tomorrow?"

"Let me talk to Ben and call you back."

Wyatt disconnects the call and grins as he packs up his fishing gear and walks back to his car.

CHAPTER 51

As Wyatt drives home, he ponders this change in circumstances. He tries to envision what could complicate the situation, but then decides not to over think it.

Pulling up to park on the street in front of his small house, Wyatt glances over at Sally's house, which is dark. Sally has been working a lot of extra hours, staying at the library long past closing to do research. Wyatt knows she dreads going home, where there are so many reminders of her daughter.

Andrea will start college in January, and live in Gainesville, and Wyatt worries how Sally will manage without Andrea there. She has become a substitute daughter.

Wyatt goes in the house and sits down at his kitchen table and powers up the laptop. A few minutes later he is on the phone to the attorney in Charleston.

Louisa had changed her will three days before her death. The attorney didn't think probate would be delayed or that anyone would contest it.

Wyatt hangs up the phone and Googles the law firm. Old firm, in business over a hundred years. Very conservative.

The problem is, the lawyer said getting everything worked out and money in hand was unlikely to happen until after Christmas. He walks out to a high point in the back yard where cell phone reception is a bit better and calls Nora back.

"OK, but this is still exciting, Brother!" Nora enthuses. "When are we going to Charleston?"

"I don't know. When are y'all coming down here?"

"We'll see you in the morning, okay?"

"Okay."

There had been an email from Sam, too, and Wyatt calls him next. After the usual pleasantries he gets to the point.

"Hey, you coming to visit for Christmas?" Wyatt asks.

"Yep, and I am bringing Jake with me, and we should get there on the 23rd."

"Awesome. I look forward to meeting him."

"Hey how is Sally? I've tried to call her several times and she hasn't called me back," Sam asks. Wyatt knows he is fearful for his sister.

Wyatt sighs heavily. "I don't see much of her. She works a lot, or she and Andrea are off shopping or doing school things or girly things."

There is a silence while Sam assesses that. "Okay, well, not to be too nosy but what about your relationship with Sally? I want that to go forward. You're good for her," Sam says quietly.

Wyatt sighs and looks at his small, homely kitchen. He looks forward to renovating it.

"She told me just the other day after we had dinner together that she can't even think about a relationship until she has grieved for her daughter and it's still too painful," Wyatt says quietly.

"Can you get her out of Crossroads, maybe take a little trip somewhere romantic?" Sam asks.

Wyatt smiles. "I don't know but that's a good thought. I just inherited a house in Charleston and I will see about going down there soon."

"Awesome. That's so exciting! Take care!" Sam enthuses.

Wyatt walks outside to get his mail a few minutes later and sees Sally's car pull into the driveway. He waves at her. She waves back but she looks distracted.

Just a moment later, another car pulls up, a blue Prius. Wyatt watches, fascinated, as a 60ish woman with long gray hair steps out of the car and shuts the door. She wears blue jeans, a white tee shirt and a long purple cotton sweater. She holds a drawstring backpack in one hand, and the sun glints off of her wire-rimmed glasses.

She looks around, sees Wyatt and looks at him with frank assessment.

"Well hi there, how are you?" she says, walking towards him.

"I'm just fine," Wyatt answers politely. "I'm Wyatt Jamison."

"Marie Barrows. Nice to meet you," she says, sticking out her hand.

Wyatt shakes her hand. As he does that, Sally walks over with Blanche. Wyatt sees that out of the corner of his vision but it only registers for a moment. He is hyper aware of the feeling of Marie's large hand in his own, warm and solid. She regards him with her head slightly cocked to the side, through jade green eyes.

"You have the sight," Marie says quietly.

Wyatt chuckles nervously. He cannot read this woman at all, which makes him nervous. "Well, uh, I have some ESP kind of abilities, yes."

"He's being modest, Marie. Wyatt has incredible powers of perception," Sally says. She gives Wyatt a quick hug.

"May we talk for a few minutes, inside your house, Wyatt?" Marie asks.

"Uh, sure. That's fine," Wyatt responds, looking at Sally. She is stressed out. She's scared, but she is determined, too, he realizes.

"Marie just drove down from Asheville. She's going to try and help me connect to the spirit of my daughter," Sally says. As they walk into Wyatt's house, he is aware of Marie looking around carefully, as though seeking out something hidden.

Inside the living room, Marie stops and closes her eyes for a moment, then opens them, smiling slightly. "This house was built in 1849. It looked far different then. The fireplace is original, though," she says, looking at the small fireplace.

"Yes, my grandparents renovated the whole house sometime around 1970," Wyatt says. "Since it's mine now, I am renovating again."

"You're doing a great job," Marie says softly.

"Would you like something to drink?"

"Thanks, but not at the moment," Marie replies. "May I look around?"

"Sure."

She walks down the hallway and peers into each bedroom, then peers into the kitchen and back yard before returning to the living room.

"What did you pick up on?" Sally asks. Blanche is on her back on Wyatt's living room couch, happily snoring away. Sally sits next to her. Wyatt stands at the window, rubbing his chin, deep in thought.

"There's a lot of residual negative energy here, but also a very strong spirit presence counteracting that. Did someone die here not long ago?" Marie asks Wyatt.

"My uncle was found dead out in the yard about 7 months ago," Wyatt replies, clearing his throat.

Marie nods. "Small man, balding, with blue eyes. He is smiling and happy. He says you solved the mystery?" she says questioningly, looking at Wyatt.

"There was an old trunk guarding a secret room off the cellar, and we found a skeleton in there a few weeks ago," Wyatt responds. "Uncle Hugh thought there might be treasure here, and spent years looking for it."

Marie nods. "There was a treasure here, stolen items."

Wyatt and Sally exchange a look. Marie's skills are impressive.

"What —" Wyatt starts to ask, but Marie interrupts him.

"Do you have a lighter or a match?" she says, looking troubled. "There's an evil presence here. I want to burn sage and see if I can get that presence to move on."

"Evil?!" Wyatt says, uneasy, thinking of Marcus Jamison. Wyatt's mind reels, trying to figure out if he has felt evil in the house. He has never felt that. Then again, Marcus was his ancestor, so maybe he's not evil towards his descendants. Wyatt ponders that for a moment.

Marie regards Wyatt steadily. "You never know when evil will reach for the living. Best not to let the presence linger."

Wyatt finally nods reluctantly.

Sally stands up quickly. "I know where there are matches in the kitchen."

Marie sets down her backpack and pulls out a small twist of plant matter. She places it on a small ceramic dish and Sally returns with matches. "Here you go."

"Thanks," Marie says. "This is sage. I'm going to sage your house. This energy is from a spirit that is quite angry, a man who died about a hundred years ago."

Marie walks into the next room.

Wyatt looks at Sally. "How do you know this lady?"

"Oh, this is the lady Aunt Catherine told me about, from Asheville. I called her to see if I could meet with her and she said she would come to me, which I thought was great," Sally replied.

They watch for a moment as Marie walks from room to room in the house, waving the burning sage around.

When Marie comes back to the living room, Wyatt says "I'm getting ready to renovate the house some more, hopefully soon, so will I need you to re-sage the house after that?"

Marie looks at him, eyebrow cocked. "You have the sight, yet you don't fully believe in my abilities?"

"Well, I – okay, I sorta do and sorta don't. I mean, I've experienced spirit energies all my life, but only since I moved in here have I actually seen spirits," Wyatt says. "I'm sorry. I tend to believe my own eyes, but I must admit I'm very skeptical of others' abilities."

Sally looks at him with horror, a look Wyatt hasn't seen in her blue eyes. Wyatt almost laughs at her, but doesn't, because he sees there's still so much un-processed grief.

Marie smiles. "You've never encountered a psychic medium, or even another psychic, so of course you're freaked out. I get it. Can we chat for a moment?"

"Sure. There's no dining room but come on in the kitchen," Wyatt responds with false bonhomie.

A minute later they are all seated at the old formica table, and Wyatt has offered Marie every beverage in the house. She decides on water. Wyatt drinks a cold beer and Sally drinks nothing, but sits in her chair with her arms wrapped tightly around her, glad to be wearing a heavy sweater. Nervousness always makes her cold.

"Wyatt, I charge most people a good bit of money for my services, but I'm not going to charge you because I see you as a colleague," Marie says. "Truthfully, the moment I saw you I knew you were a powerful empath and I could actually learn from you. I also looked at your house and saw faces staring back at me from the windows. So many spirits here. I was drawn here."

Wyatt looks at her, still intrigued by a woman he cannot read at all, who certainly seems legit. He decides to just be as calm as possible and see if she gets anything utterly wrong.

"Are you picking up on anything now?" Sally asks anxiously.

Marie gets a far off look in her eyes, then Wyatt sees a shadow of pain fall across her face.

"Right now I see a woman in a long dress, looks like from the mid nineteenth century. She is Josephine. She is your blood, Wyatt. She had a hard life. She wants to thank you for finding her, and laying to rest all the rumors about a treasure here."

Wyatt nods, unsure what to say.

"I also see a tall man, a handsome man -- and who looks like you. Your father? He says you used to play golf together, and he taught you to fish in Lake Lanier."

Wyatt smiles. "Yep, that's Dad. Hey there Dad," Wyatt says, surprised to find tears in his eyes. He has missed his father terribly, something he hasn't wanted to acknowledge.

"Wow, this is interesting. I see a tall blonde lady who is your grandmother Elizabeth. She says Louisa is with her, and her parents. She realizes she was wrong to turn her back on her Charleston family and now she is happy that you and Nora will know something of them."

Sally frowns, looking puzzled. "Wyatt?" she says.

Wyatt smiles at Sally. "I just got off the phone with Nora a little while ago. My grandmother came up to the mountains as a college girl, fell in love with Grandaddy, and her rich family in Charleston didn't approve so she turned her back on them. Now her sister has died, though, and Nora and I inherited, as the only descendants. Pretty interesting development."

Marie has listened to that but now takes Wyatt's hand in her own. "The contact helps me, Wyatt, and your grandmother wants you to know that even though the money will make your life easier, she doesn't want you to stop using your abilities. Oh – and another message. Don't sell the house. She wants you to promise that you won't."

"The house in Charleston?" Wyatt asks.

"Yes yes. The one that's been in her family for two hundred years."

"She says let Nora's daughter Page live there."

Wyatt stares at Marie. "Can she predict the future?"

Marie smiles and takes a sip of water. "They have a good sense of what is a good possibility, yes, but there's always free will."

Marie pulls her hand away from Wyatt's and looks at Sally. "Sally, there's a very insistent spirit that wants to speak to you, Miranda."

Sally makes a sound halfway between a cry and a cough, and clutches the sweater around herself even tighter.

"Sally it's okay," Wyatt says gently. He stands up and moves behind Sally to place his hands on her shoulders.

Sally responds by un-tensing a bit, and placing her hands over Wyatt's.

"No need to be afraid, Sally. Miranda is quite insistent. She desperately wants you to know how sorry she is," Marie says. "She was so unhappy, and so lost. She had too much anger and anxiety inside her, and she thought the drugs helped her deal with everything. She thought she could handle the drugs. She wishes she hadn't used that last time. However, she is happy now. She is with Barbara and Tom, her grandparents, and she is at peace."

Tears run down Sally's face. "Tell her I love her SO MUCH!"

Marie smiles at Sally. "She knows. She sees you crying and she hates it. She wants you to be happy. She says stop pushing Wyatt away. Let yourself be happy. You deserve it."

Sally swiftly stands up and turns to Wyatt, going into his arms and burying her face in his chest. "I am so sorry. I love you," she sobs.

"I love you, darling," Wyatt responds, kissing the top of her head and rubbing her back.

"Wait, there's a bit more. Miranda also says that Andrea is your other daughter, the child of your heart, and to give her your mother love and she will return it. It's a beautiful thing. Miranda is happy that Andrea is in your life."

Sally sobs harder. Wyatt rubs her back and holds her. Marie leaves the kitchen for a moment and returns with a box of Kleenex.

After a minute, Sally pulls away from Wyatt and smiles.

"Feel better?" he asks gently.

Sally nods. "I'm going to blow my nose," she says, and heads off towards the hall bathroom.

Marie sits back and sighs heavily. "Wow, that was a lot of powerful energy."

Wyatt looks at Marie, and suddenly he sees her, clearly. "You're able to surround yourself with barriers around someone like me," he says quietly, his voice wondrous. "Now I see, though, and you have a beautiful soul. Very tender-hearted, which informs everything you do."

Marie smiles. "Takes one to know one, my friend."

Wyatt chuckles, and realizes he hasn't even sipped his beer once since he opened it.

"Wyatt, I don't know if I will ever see you again, so I want to say a couple of things to you. Please don't get mad," Marie says.

"You're putting on weight, and you need to start taking better care of yourself, and your heart. Eat better. More vegetables and fruits. Cut back on the beer drinking. Get out and walk, bike, hit the treadmill – just move more, and eat better and drink more water, okay?"

Wyatt frowns, realizing nobody has spoken to him like that in a long time. He starts to get angry but then sighs heavily. "You sound like my sister, Nora."

"Well, Nora loves you and feels responsible for you, so listen to me, and to her," Marie says with a smile.

Sally reappears. "I can't tell you how much I appreciate what you said. It really helps me. I feel like this huge burden is off my heart."

Marie stands and hugs Sally. "When you called yesterday, I had the strongest feeling I should drive down here and see you. I rarely leave Asheville, but I just had to come here. I'm so glad I did."

Marie stops and looks into the empty air by the fridge. "I thought I was done but nope. Hugh is here," she says softly. "Wyatt, he says his work here is done. Josephine is at peace. He's going on. He is glad to see you with Sally."

Wyatt stares at the air, seeing nothing. "Tell him I will take good care of the house."

Marie smiles. "He knows."

Sally looks at Wyatt, then at Marie. "Marie, are you staying tonight? Can we take you to dinner?"

Marie shakes her head. "I want to get home, so I will take my leave."

"You're welcome to spend the night," Sally said.

"Thanks, but I need to get home and see about my furbaby," Marie says with a smile.

"Okay, drive safe," Sally replies.

Later that evening the new landline phone in Wyatt's house rings and he answers it. Sally is at her house preparing dinner. Wyatt is reading. He gets up from the living room sofa and answers the phone on his kitchen wall. Like Sally's phone, it has a very long cord and he can sit in the family room and chat. He settles back on the sofa.

John's voice is jovial. "So your landline really works!" he says with a chuckle.

"Yep, old school technology but so what?!" Wyatt answers. "What's up?"

"Well, I have news of your ex."

"OK. I saw months ago where she had the house up for sale."

"Well, not any more."

"No?"

"Nope. She and Henry have broken up."

"Really? Why, I wonder" Wyatt muses.

"Word on the street is that Henry has found him a new sugar mama, a 30 year old doctor with plenty of money. Dumped Sharon. So she took the house off the market and quit his practice."

"She quit?!" This is odd, Wyatt thinks. "Sharon worked there for over ten years."

"Yep. She is now managing the office of a podiatrist, and not making much."

"Wonder how much of my money wound up in Henry's pocket?" Wyatt mused.

"Apparently, not too much. Sharon put away at least half of it to pay for Thad's graduate school. He announced he is going for a Ph.D. When have you spoken to him?"

Wyatt thought. "About two weeks ago, I guess. He came up for the weekend. He mentioned he was thinking about it and had applied a couple of places. Wow. Good for Sharon, I guess. I hated seeing her with Henry."

"Well, I just thought you'd like to know the deal," John finished. "I gotta go. Emily and I are headed out to dinner."

"Okay, take care. Oh wait – big news on my end. My great aunt died and Nora and I inherited her entire estate, which is substantial. I'll tell you about it later in detail."

"Awesome! Glad to hear it, Buddy."

Andrea bounds in the house, Blanche close on her heels. "Hey Dude! Sally says come on to dinner!" Her smiling face mirrors Blanche's smiling dog face and wagging tail.

Wyatt chuckles and stands up.

"Good! I'm starved."

Wyatt leaves his house and walks over to Sally's but before he goes inside he turns around and looks back at the old house, sitting there in the moonlight, solid, warm and almost matronly. Then he looks at Sally's house, lights shining through the windows like a face filled with love.

It's a good night to be home, he decides, surrounded by those who love him, safely in the embrace of the mountains.

THE END

Afterword

Leaf Season started out as a short story and evolved into a novel of love and mystery that took shape over many months. I was intrigued with the idea of someone in my age bracket [mid fifties] wanting to retire early and simplify their life. I also liked that Wyatt and Sally would have a chance to fall in love.

Few books have main characters in my age bracket. Some folks in their fifties still have children at home, and some of us are grandparents. Some of us are nearing retirement and some of us are into second careers. I used to think of age fifty as OLD, until I celebrated my own 50th birthday. It's weird being in your fifties because you aren't young, you're a bit past the middle of life, and yet you're not elderly either.

Because the book deals with some fairly tragic occurrences [messy divorce, the death of a child] I felt like it needed some levity and mischief, and Hugh's ghost provides that. I also liked writing the character of Andrea, because older child adoption is near to my heart [my children were adopted at ages 13 and 10] and Wyatt and Sally emotionally adopt her. Plus, her abiding curiosity about the trunk forces Wyatt to try to solve that mystery.

After I finished writing this book [originally known as Wyatt's House, the working title] friends generously read the manuscript and gave me terrific feedback. My childhood BFF and lifelong sister/friend Joanne Cheng always reads and makes great suggestions. Jack Wheeler, a retired attorney, read the manuscript to make sure my attorney characterization was in line, which I greatly appreciate. Jack also encouraged me, and I greatly appreciate his fatherly advice and counsel. As always, my mother [Elva Hasty Thompson] read the manuscript and pointed out the typos and where I needed to improve. She reads 2-4 books a week so her feedback is always spot-on.

Few people outside of the south really know the beauty of the North Georgia mountains, and yet it's one of the most scenic and lovely areas of the world. Every fall, tourists flock to the area to see the gorgeous autumn leaves, a time known as "leaf season." On a symbolic level, Wyatt and Sally are no longer young but they aren't ancient either; they are in the autumn/leaf season of their lives. Yet autumn is a season of spectacular beauty.

The Blue Ridge Mountains are old mountains, and my family has always loved vacationing in their embrace. My maternal grandmother, "Memaw" Hasty, used to always say she had to get up to the mountains so she could breathe. (She had a pretty stressful life.) My grandfather was always happy to take her to the mountains because he loved them too.

The mountains are healing, in so many ways, and they are a part of me because many of my maternal ancestors lived in the North Georgia mountains. I also loved to ride up to the mountains of East Tennessee during the many years I lived in Knoxville, and I grew accustomed to being able to get in the car and drive just a short while before hitting the scenic Blue Ridge Parkway. I miss the Tennessee mountains, and I miss the many friends that still live there.

My cousin Linda Harris took the gorgeous cover shot, and I am very thankful for her help.

My first book, **Ghosts in the Garden City**, was set in Augusta and Atlanta Georgia, but I wanted **Leaf Season** to be set in the mountains.

I hope you enjoyed the book.

Dee Thompson

September 2019

Dee Thompson is a freelance writer and paralegal, and currently writes books, articles, blogs, essays, and the occasional poem. She earned a BA in Drama from the University of Georgia and an MA in Creative Writing from the University of Tennessee. She is a published author of three books, Adopting Alesia: My Crusade for My Russian Daughter, Jack's New Family, and the novel Ghosts in the Garden City. In recent years she also contributed essays to the bestseller The Divinity of Dogs: True Stories of Miracles Inspired by Man's Best Friend and the acclaimed anthology *Call Me Okaasan: Adventures in Multicultural Mothering*. For more than 15 years, Dee has blogged at The Crab Chronicles. Dee lives with her mother and son in Atlanta and enjoys walking her basset, Lola, cooking, reading, and movies.

CPSIA information can be obtained
at www.ICGtesting.com
Printed in the USA
LVHW031125141019
634125LV00001B/43/P

9 781696 285223